"A CLASSIC INTERNATIONAL THRILLER"

—*The Milwaukee Journal*

Stalin, accompanied by bodyguard Rusakov, was striding toward his apartment in a furious temper. Seeing Cabeza coming out, he stopped abruptly, his every instinct leaping to self-preservation.

Rusakov's hand blurred to his gun . . . an ex-fighter pilot, he had been selected for his reflexes and intuition.

But Cabeza's assessment was faster. His dismay became awestruck apology in the blink of an eye. He spread his free hand well clear of his body, his eyes not on Stalin but on the bodyguard.

He read Rusakov's changed response, saw the striking snake of his hand freeze. But it remained on the gun, poised for instant reappraisal.

"Who are you?" Stalin shouted, his eyes squeezed tight, body braced. "What were you doing in my apartment? Who sent you?"

Cabeza slipped his hand in his pocket, felt the handle of the knife. He pressed the button with his thumb, felt the blade come open against the lining . . .

RED OMEGA

John Kruse

PUBLISHED BY POCKET BOOKS NEW YORK

POCKET BOOKS, a Simon & Schuster division of
GULF & WESTERN CORPORATION
1230 Avenue of the Americas, New York, N.Y. 10020

Published by arrangement with Random House, Inc.
Library of Congress Catalog Card Number: 81-40230

ISBN: 0-671-44670-3

First Pocket Books printing March, 1983

10 9 8 7 6 5 4 3 2 1

POCKET and colophon are registered trademarks
of Simon & Schuster.

Printed in the U.S.A.

Book
ONE

1

THE DARKNESS was absolute—black sky, black sea. Only their boiling wake and thundering engines told what speed they were making. It was like rushing blindfold through limbo.

Joaquín Cabeza stood beside the American skipper in the control cabin of the old M.T.B., his square, powerful body braced against the thrust, his eyes fixed on the radar screen. But it was a poor substitute for vision. He was a man who needed vision, needed always to relate to his environment, solid objects. He progressed through life by a kind of earthy triangulation, rock to rock. The sea was not his element.

In his thirty-nine years he had made only two sea trips. Both of them turning points in his life. Both disastrous. This third could turn out to be no exception. But there were questions that had to be answered. Passionate questions, which had gnawed their way into his sleep these fourteen years. At long last he had picked up the dice and shaken them. They were rolling. When they hit the cushion there would be no more doubt to plague him.

The lanky skipper thrust a pack of Lucky Strikes lazily toward him as he spun the wheel northward. Cabeza shook his head. Everything had to be lazy with the Americans. As though to appear to be trying somehow lessened their manhood. The blond-bearded bosun lounged in the companion-way, idly scanning the North African shoreline astern through night glasses. His crewman toyed yawningly with a can of beer as he monitored the Spanish Coast Guard traffic through his headphones. Cabeza could find no common ground with Americans. Their casual approach to life baffled him.

Yet it had been to an American nightclub that he had gone immediately after landing in Tangier from Mexico City—not to his contacts in the Spanish quarter. He had even avoided taking a Spanish-driven cab from the airport. His fellow countrymen had long memories. Rumor of his presence here could cross the Straits in one telephonic flash. Then the Guardia de Asalto would be waiting for him. And wherever he landed in Spain, they or their spies would be waiting.

In his dark, baggy suit he had stood out somberly in the flashy nightclub, which was filled with American expatriates. Like the bars of Madrid back in '36. Cabeza remembered the atmosphere in those bars—a strange electricity, as if something awesome were about to happen. The same feeling was here again. In '36 it had been the imminence of civil war. Now, in '53, it was just money.

Money was happening to Tangier. It was a free port, internationally governed, permanently neutral and no taxes—the capitalists' dream. The New Town was growing, spreading its white sugar loaves around the bay. Hucksters and oppor-tunists, traffickers were flocking in off every plane. They were all around him now, in their gabardines, Levis . . .

Cabeza limped to the bar and ordered a drink. He leaned close to the barman and spoke his requirements. The man said nothing, just swilled the liquor around on the rocks, pushed it toward him and took his money. But presently a lanky American appeared beside him. He spoke in a slow drawl. Phony, of course; he was from New York. Nothing was real here.

"What's the problem, friend, no passport?" Slightly mock-ing.

Cabeza turned slowly. The man's eyes widened as they took in his face—the scarred cheeks and jaw, the once-aquiline nose flattened above spread lips, the face of a *real* man who had lived a *real* life, endured *real* suffering—and survived intact; the eyes indomitable still, compelling, animal.

Cabeza shook his head and said in his rasping English, "I have a passport."

The American's tone lost some of its mockery. "Then what's wrong with the ferry, *amigo?*"

Cabeza paused. He must make no mistakes. He had brought only a limited stake. "You are a *contrabandista, de veras?* When next you carry a consignment, I wish to go with it. And when you carry the next, I come back. *Claro?*"

"Now hold on—"

"I pay you for one trip and a half. Return fare, *entiende?*" The spread lips stretched a little. It was a smile.

The American scowled. "You telling or asking?" He beckoned to a second American, who left a group of girls and came over. This one had a blond beard and wore a single gold earring. "Hank, tell this guy our rule. He's angling for a two-way hitch."

The bearded one took the cue. He sucked in his breath and shook his head. "Our rule's no people, mister. The administration won't wear it."

"Any other cargo, okay," endorsed the other. "Free port. Export what you like. But people . . ."

"No dice. Colonel Le Grand's shit-hot on it, and he's the boss in this town."

"So we don't crap on our doorstep, see."

"We're Mr. Clean America Class of '53 here so far."

"We aim to keep it that way."

They broke off and waited for him to say something.

Cabeza's eyes moved slowly from one to the other. Cowboys. He leaned forward a little and inspected his shoes. As he did so a small gold ingot on a chain swung from under his shirt. Just a flash. Then he straightened and put down his glass. *"Adiós."* He made for the door.

The Americans stared after him. They exchanged glances.

"Hey now, hold it." The tall one moved after him.

Cabeza paused with apparent impatience.

"Maybe . . . maybe you're a special case, I dunno. Do some talking. Convince us."

"To break your rule? Shit on your doorstep? No, *amigos.* That would cost me more money than I have to pay."

The tall one made a tough chin. "We're trying to shake you down, that what you're saying?" To his friend: "That's all the thanks we get for trying to help out. Go to hell, mister." He turned away.

"Prove me wrong," Cabeza said.

The American froze. He turned back slowly. "Okay," he said softly. "Name your own price."

"Two hundred dollars."

The Americans burst out laughing.

"Oh boy," Hank said.

"It is all I have. Ten times the cost of the ferry. Enough for so little work."

"Guy's a nut," Hank said. "C'mon, Jimbo, the gals are waiting."

"Hold on," Jim said. His eyes hovered around Cabeza's wishbone. "That thing around your neck. What's it worth?"

Cabeza scowled. "To you—nothing."

"Mind if I take a look?" He picked the ingot out from the black hair of Cabeza's chest, weighed it in his fingers. Hank took it and weighed it in *his* fingers. Five ounces, maybe more. They turned it over to check the hallmark. Cabeza watched them calculate. Watched them quicken, try to conceal it.

"Tell you what," the tall one drawled at length. "It's worth around seven fifty, right? Our price is one grand. Gimme this, we'll call it quits."

"I said two hundred."

"For that you get the full treatment. Both ways. Clean. No additional expenditure."

Cabeza hesitated.

"Come on, man. Opportunity only knocks once in a nightgown. We're sticking our necks out for you. What more d'you want?"

"Car to meet him, maybe," Hank said.

Cabeza chuckled. The Americans joined in. The first stuck out his hand. "Deal?"

Cabeza gave it another few moments. He sighed. "Deal."

They shook hands. "Pier Two, four P.M. Thursday." The tall one held out his hand again. "Payment in advance."

"Payment when I'm aboard," Cabeza said. *"Hasta luego."*

He limped along the Boulevard de France toward his

pension, grimly satisfied. He hadn't starved for the first twelve years of his life without learning the value of money. The smallest coin represented so many sweated minutes of work, so many grains of corn to make bread, the sleeve of a shirt, rope sole of a shoe. Money was a token of man's toil and, as such, not to be bandied about lightly or gambled with, as these Americans were doing. What toil was there in risk? He had offered them two hundred dollars. The gold of the ingot was worth exactly that. The filling inside was lead.

As Cabeza stepped out on deck twenty-eight knots of cold December air flattened the baggy suit against him, penetrating the cheap Mexican fiber. But his body was immune to cold. His three years in the Siberian labor camp had seen to that. He was searching for the horizon. Land should soon be visible. His land. The land he had given his blood for. But he could see nothing. Then he could. A solitary light.

Voices sounded from the control room. Jim, the skipper, had seen it too, pointing forward, the phony ingot glinting around his neck.

The light resolved itself into three gas lamps hung close above the water from the stern of a sardine boat. The crew of four were fishing, hauling in their nets. They paused to peer anxiously, then wave, as the bosun, Hank, flashed the signal.

At last! Cabeza stamped the cramp out of his bad leg and moved to hang on the fenders. A rope was tossed him as they came alongside. He smelled fish, kerosene. The afterdeck of the fishing boat was piled high with sardine boxes, some of them filled. Behind him Hank was unbattening the after hatch. A crop-haired old Spanish skipper stood waiting for the bucking to lessen. He came aboard clumsily, smelling of *anisado*.

"*Hola!*"

"*Hola,* Lucito—we have eighty cartons," Jim told him. "*Ochenta.*"

"*Ochenta,*" the Spaniard said to the youth who had come aboard behind him.

"*Ochenta,*" whispered the youth to his mates as he moved aft. Cabeza heard them all start to count quietly as they chained the cartons across into the fishing boat, careful not to thump the sides. Sound carried at sea. They were sitting ducks out here for any patrolling gunboat. Nick, the wearer of headphones, watched the radar screen closely. Jim and the skipper pushed in beside him, Cabeza following. Jim thrust a bundle of notes into the Spaniard's hand. "You have a passenger." He indicated Cabeza.

"Passenger?"

"*Pasajero.*"

The skipper looked from the notes to Cabeza. It took a moment to sink in. "*Pasajero? No, no!*" He thrust the money back as if it were hot.

Jim pushed it back.

"*No! No podemos!*"

"Sure you can. So we have a rule. So we break it once in a—"

"No!"

"Take it, you damned old goat! It's a bonus."

"We have a blip!" Nick cut in suddenly, pointing to the screen.

Jim moved to his side without hurry. "Coast Guard?"

"Could be. Five miles. Close inshore."

"Okay. No sweat. First . . ." He made to stuff the money down the front of Lucito's shirt. But the skipper backed away from him.

"*Guardacostas?*" The old man bolted from the control cabin like a frightened rabbit. The American reached out and dragged him back.

"Now, cut it out!" Jim snapped.

Cabeza moved forward. "Enough," he said. "I will do it." He disengaged the skipper from the American's grasp and put an arm around his shoulder. The man's eyes were jumping.

"*Cálmate, compañero,*" he said gently. He took the money from the American. "How much?"

"Five thousand pesetas."

"Five *thousand*? You frighten him with so much money." To Lucito: "How much you make from a good night's fishing, *compañero*—five hundred pesetas?" The skipper nodded dumbly. "*Bueno.*" Cabeza peeled off one note and placed it in his hand. He passed the rest back to the American. "Now you have had a good night with the fish, *suficiente?*" His arm still held the man close. Lucito blinked into the darkly compelling eyes, puzzled by the reassurance they generated. He found himself nodding. "You are a patriot?" Cabeza inquired gently. Lucito nodded again, vigorously this time. "Then we are brothers," Cabeza said. "Kindly take me to shore."

The skipper's resistance crumbled. He turned and meekly led the way out of the control cabin.

Cabeza paused to glance back at the surprised Americans. *"Hasta luego, hombres."*

Lucito steered the fishing boat for shore, jumpy as a cat, his ears cocked to detect the all too familiar throb of the gunboat's motors. The penalty for smuggling blond tobacco was fierce, but nothing to the sentence he and his *muchachos* would get if they were caught running human cargo. Yet not even that could wholly account for the chill that was spreading in his gut. His instincts were trying to tell him something.

His eyes kept going to the passenger seated quietly in the bows. His face, just visible in the light from the fishing lamps, was averted shoreward, but there was something about that square blue jaw . . . The high cheekbone, hunched shoulders and, above all, the feeling of animal power that came from him just sitting there, all seemed disturbingly familiar. A scene from the past fumbled its way into Lucito's mind.

A downhill road . . . He was chucking stones . . . Goats! That's right, he was driving the *dueña* Elena's goats back to her *finca* in a hurry. He was scared. It was nearing dusk and people had stuck close to their homes all day, because the Civil War was over, the Republican army had collapsed and the Falangists were driving toward the town, mopping up as they went, and no one was sure what they would do when they got there. The first fascist truckload had arrived in the afternoon and set fire to a house. But the bulk of the column was still in the mountains. He wanted to be indoors, bolted in with his family, when they finally reached the town.

He was still a kilometer out of Marrazón when he heard vehicles on the road above him, coming down fast through the bends. His goats were filling the road. He wasn't sure whether to try to clear them off or run. He yelled and threw some rocks at the leading goat, then tumbled into the ditch, as two big old open touring cars came rushing around the bend. They slithered to a stop halfway into the flock, in a cloud of dust.

For a moment everything was fog and confusion, goats bleating, horns blowing. Then he could see there were five men in the first car and more in the second. They had guns and they were in a big hurry, and Lucito knew immediately they were Republican survivors fleeing from the fascists.

The cars paused only for an instant, then pushed on, gathering speed as the flock scattered. But in that instant, as the dust was clearing, Lucito had glimpsed a face—an unforgettable face—calm amid the hooting and shouting, bearded, battle-weary, but unmistakable. He had seen the aquiline nose, the compelling eyes many, many times on newsletters posted in the town. Perhaps the best-known face in all of Spain.

Peering now at his passenger, Lucito felt his knees weaken. He reached behind him for the near-empty bottle of *anisado* and took a hard pull. Wiping his lips on his sleeve, he crossed himself and put on speed.

Though beardless now, his features scarred and broken by heaven knew what misfortune, the man in the bows was without doubt the present regime's most deadly enemy—the Communist peasant General El Duro!

2

CABEZA LIMPED toward the coast road, his eyes probing the stunted pines above for signs of any human shape. The Guardia patrolled these lonely stretches at night, he knew, riding silently on their bicycles, sometimes standing for hours in shadowy observation. Glancing back, he could barely distinguish the fishing boat moored in the small bay below, or the van without lights that had driven down to meet it.

The road, leading east to Almuñecar, west toward Málaga, seemed quite deserted. He stood listening for a moment, then got down and put his ear to the surface. Though he remained there for a full half minute, he could hear nothing save the faint stirring of thistle heads in the verge grass, the brush of thorn against rock. The sounds of his country.

Even in this barren spot he could feel it around him—the strange something that was peculiarly Spain, that he had fought to hold in his mind through all the nights of torture in the Lubianka, that had sustained him beyond all natural endurance.

He got up quickly and looked for a way up into the hills. To tramp the three kilometers into Almuñecar by road would be to invite an encounter with the Guardia Civil. Though he was carrying forged papers, the fewer people who saw him the better.

Unburdened by so much as a haversack, he climbed steadily. The old fisherman had recognized him, Cabeza knew. But would he talk? He'd expose his own very profitable sideline if he did. But old soaks did crazy things. Digging their own graves with their tongues was one of them.

He had been wise to underpay Lucito, he decided. That way, he had put the donkey in *his* stable, made the trip to shore a gift from the old man to him. A gift was something he could be proud of. It left a better, a more honorable taste. Cabeza understood well the subtleties of the peasant character. It was as fine as the hands were rough. Perhaps *because* they were rough.

His own were callused by the age of nine. By twelve he was head of the family, working the tiny plot behind the *cabaña* till his fingers bled, scraping up the manure of passing horses to goad the red dust into making vegetables, keeping it moist through the parched summers with water stolen from the radiators of the trucks serving the mine. That wasn't all he stole.

With his father dead and no wages coming from the mine, he began creeping out at night when his mother and younger brothers and sisters were asleep, raiding the backyards of the village, taking anything—junk mostly, for the district was poor—that would sell for a few *céntimos* in the market. He told his mother the money came from doing odd jobs. He thought she believed him, till the day a fine young horseman rode up to the cottage.

Joaquín was out in back, hoeing the patch, his two younger brothers helping, his sisters playing with the goat. His mother was busy with the washing in front. Along the dirt road came the horseman, riding very straight, his black hat tilted forward against the afternoon sun. His clothes were immaculate and his saddle chased in silver. He rode with his hand on his hip, as the gentry did in those days.

The peasants of Estremadura were rugged and individualistic people. They hated the authorities that taxed and suppressed them and gave nothing in return, not even piped water for their parched lands. They hated the monarchy, and the army and police that upheld it. And the gentry were an extension of the monarchy, they hated them too. None more than Joaquín.

Scowling, he dropped his hoe and came around to the front to watch the *hidalgo* pass.

But he didn't. He turned his horse in toward the cottage and walked it up to their mother, dipping his hat to his raised finger.

Their mother squinted at him, once, between the clothes on the line, then carried on as if he weren't there. She wore black, in mourning for her husband. With her strong brown arms, black hair scraped back from high cheekbones, she looked like a Gypsy. She had been a fine-looking woman.

"*La viuda* Cabeza?" inquired the *hidalgo*. "I am Don Miguel Sebastián de las Casas."

Their mother dropped her basket of pegs. Joaquín gasped. Rage choked him. This was the son of the mine owner who had caused the tragedy in which his father died! Without hesitation he flew at the man and tried to claw him off his horse.

The horse sidestepped. Don Miguel spurred him forward easily. "*Basta, basta.*" He tried to fend Joaquín off with the butt of his whip as he sprang at him again. "Steady, *muchacho,* steady." He spurred the horse on further, trotting it in a circle around Joaquín. The horse sidestepped neatly each time the boy charged, in a graceful way that was quite unlike the movement of any other horse. But Joaquín was too enraged to notice.

"Come down! Come off there! I'll kill you!"

"Control yourself, *muchacho.* Another killing would solve nothing. Both our fathers are dead. It was a bad and terrible thing, but it is over."

"It's not over," Joaquín snarled. "It can never be over!" He made another rush at the horse. It sidestepped again, spurted forward, then went into a kind of dance with its forelegs. The trick infuriated Joaquín still more, but he realized he could never beat the horse.

His mother had watched without moving. But the fire in her eyes showed her feelings were the same as her son's. Now she moved to him, crossed her arms over Joaquín's chest from behind and demanded of the man, "What do you want? Tell us, then go."

"I have come to make amends," said Don Miguel, his proud, sharp young features serious and sympathetic. "My father's ways are not mine. I loved him, but he was of the old school. I understand why your husband did what he did, and how hard things must be for you now. If you're short of food . . . If there is anything you need . . . I would like to help."

"We don't need your help," Joaquín cried, starting forward again. But his mother held him. For a small woman she was incredibly strong.

"We need nothing from the likes of you," she said. "Now go quickly, before—"

"Go!" screamed Joaquín, fighting free from her. "Or I'll—"

The horse danced away from him a few paces, then stopped. Don Miguel turned in the saddle. His face was sad. "So be it," he said. "I had thought perhaps the *muchacho* could use a job. But . . ." He left the sentence unfinished and wheeled his horse.

He had gone only a few paces when Joaquín's mother cried, "Wait!" Her manner changed, she moved after him swiftly. "What—what would you have him do?"

"I don't want a job," Joaquín shouted.

Don Miguel shrugged. "Sweep out the stables, fodder the horses . . ."

"He could do that," his mother said quickly.

Don Miguel eyed the boy doubtfully. "I think perhaps he is a little too wild."

"He's overwrought. He'll settle down. You have my word."

"But do I have *his* word? That he wouldn't try to kill me?"

"No!" cried Joaquín.

Don Miguel eyed him grimly. At length a faint smile twitched the corner of his mouth. "Then I'll just have to take my chances, won't I? Report to my foreman tomorrow." He spurred his mount away.

"He'll be there."

"I won't!" Joaquín cried, turning on his mother angrily.

"You will."

"I'd rather—"

14

"Go to jail?"

Joaquín stared at her.

His mother put her arms around him and held him, rocking him as she had when he was little. No words were needed. She understood why he did what he did. But it had to stop.

"All the same, I'm not going to work for him," Joaquín muttered at length, pulling away.

His mother said nothing. Just took down his good shirt and pants from the line.

Don Miguel's estate was vast, with a fine *hacienda* and many stables. Joaquín discovered that besides owning the mine Don Miguel bred *rejoneador* horses for the bullring. *Rejoneadores* were the *matadores* who killed from horseback, and because they needed both hands to fight the bull, their mounts had to be trained to respond to pressure from the knees only. They had to be agile and disciplined and were also expected to perform elegant tricks for the crowd. But of all the fine horses in the *remuda*, none was the equal of the one Don Miguel rode himself.

The work was hard and the pay low, but Joaquín stuck it out for his mother's sake, taking his wages home to her every week, keeping only a fraction for himself. And though it went against every instinct, he gradually grew to trust Don Miguel. Even not to hate him quite so much for being rich. He learned to ride and was presently entrusted with exercising the precious animals. The one horse he was never allowed to ride was Don Miguel's own. It was worth, he was told by the *vaqueros*, more money than any of them could earn in six lifetimes. Then they weren't paid enough, Joaquín said hotly. No animal was worth more than a man. But he felt a thrill of curiosity as he looked at the horse. What must it be like to ride such a noble beast?

One day Don Miguel had to go to Madrid. His mount remained in its stable, unexercised for several days. Joaquín told himself that this was not right, the animal would lose its sharpness.

Payday came around. He took his money and seemed about to set out for the *cabaña* on foot, as was his habit. Instead he doubled back to the stables and saddled up the horse—with

Don Miguel's fine saddle (what else was good enough for such a beast?)—and led the animal to a safe distance, then mounted him.

It was like riding the air! The creature seemed to have no legs, it flowed. It could, moreover, read his mind and was soon carrying him along the road to the *cabaña*. Joaquín pictured his mother's face when he rode up to the cottage on the very animal that had made a fool of him not many months ago.

He had not gone far when two mounted police stopped him, staring first at his mount, then at his ragged appearance.

"Why, it's the Cabeza brat," said one. "What're you doing on such a horse, peasant?"

"And with such a saddle," the other added.

Joaquín started to explain, but they wouldn't listen. They called him a thief. "Like father, like son—born scum, agitators, bandits—you're under arrest!"

Joaquín went white with rage. He almost attacked them with his bare hands. One made to seize his bridle, but Joaquín pressed with one knee and the horse danced aside. Then the other tried. The horse danced the other way.

"Monarchist pigs!" Joaquín spat. He spurred the animal neatly between them and galloped away, confident that they could never catch him on Don Miguel's marvelous horse. Nor could they. Finally one of the police reined in his gasping animal and unsheathed his carbine. He took careful aim and shot the horse from beneath its rider.

The beautiful animal plunged forward with a cry and slid on its neck for many meters before coming to rest in a cloud of dust, Joaquín flung far from its saddle. It raised its head and pawed the ground trying to get up. Then collapsed, dead.

Joaquín was dragged off to jail, where he protested his innocence in vain—because when they demanded evidence he was too ashamed to name Don Miguel as the horse's owner. How could he face his benefactor or ask for his help when he had caused the death of the thing he prized most? So he kept silent.

As a peasant brat he didn't merit a trial. He was transferred to the state prison and locked up among hardened criminals for an unspecified time. When finally, through a guard's carelessness, he escaped, he did not dare head for home, only partly because that was where they would look for him; mainly because he could not face his mother. He took to the hills and became one of the most ruthless bandits in the region. He was fifteen.

Cabeza dwelt on these things moodily as he limped over the rough terrain toward Almuñecar. He wondered what had happened to Don Miguel. He still felt bad about the horse. But since those days he had seen too many good people die. Animals had to take their luck with the rest. It was a brutal world. Both his brothers had been executed by Franco's troops—simply because they were his brothers. And two of his sisters also. Of the third, Lucía, he had heard nothing in all these years. Nor of his mother. It was these two that he had come to find.

3

THE SUN had been up an hour when he came in sight of the town. He stood on a hill above the rubbish dump and looked down across the big sprawl of buildings that thickened into a mound about the church, and smelled the thin sweetness of charcoal smoke on the January wind.

He had been here once, a long time ago, and had thought it a poor place. Now it looked to him like paradise. The very epitome of Spain.

Behind and around the town was a sea of fruit trees irrigated by a river winding down from the *sierra*. It was up one of the *barrancas* feeding this river that the *cortijo* Valdez lay. He could remember the view from it across the valley, and the almond trees, and the beating of them in late summer to bring down the nuts. But looking now, he couldn't remember which valley.

The Valdezes were his sister Lucía's husband's family. He had written to them several times from Mexico, asking for news of Lucía and his mother, but had never received any reply.

Qué va, he thought. I will have to ask the way. He started down toward the perimeter road—not without a qualm, for he had just noticed a sardine boat being winched up onto the town beach. It looked like Lucito's. With his pockets so full, the old soak would almost certainly make straight for the nearest *bodega*. After a couple of drinks, if he was going to talk, that was where and when he would do it.

Cabeza limped along the road, head down. A car or two passed him, but it was early yet. The cottages, with their vines trimmed hard back against the winter and their closed shutters, seemed lifeless. He came to a small wineshop. It was almost the last house of the town, and it was open.

He paused for a moment, then shuffled in, eyes averted, so as to give the owner no cause to remember him. He surveyed the shelves of flasks in their rough baskets, feeling the eyes of the *patrón* on him. He was about to ask him the whereabouts of the *cortijo* Valdez when he was startled by a great cry: "Joaquín!"

The next moment he was clasped by wiry old arms and hugged and danced—"Carla, Carla, see who is here!"—then held at arm's length and studied by sun-wizened eyes in a leathery face, the jaw of which protruded like a drawer full of old crocks. The *patrón* was Pío Valdez himself—a miracle!

He was hauled into the kitchen, where the wife sat huddled against the charcoal range, staring up at him. Cabeza could barely recognize her. She wore the peasant black and held a small rush mat for fanning the embers. His memory of her had been one of rounded limbs and erectness and energy. He and the Valdez family had never been close, but he had admired the cheerful competence with which she had managed her family of five. But that robustness had shriveled into parchment. She was a cripple.

"How can it be?" she demanded in almost masculine tones, her deep-set eyes showing incredulity. But they were dead eyes, extending no warmth to him. Pío pushed a chair against his legs.

"Sit down, sit down!"

"But how can it be?" Carla repeated. "We heard you were dead."

"Oh, we heard many things," cried Pío, laughing, pulling a chair under himself, patting Cabeza's shoulder. "First you were dead, then you weren't, then that you had gone to Russia."

Cabeza nodded. "I went to Russia. But you two—what are you doing here behind a counter? The *cortijo* . . . ?"

"Oh, we sold up," Pío said, too casually. "Bought this *cantina* with the money."

"So you're members of the bourgeoisie now. Well, well!" Cabeza cocked a wry eyebrow, but he was puzzled.

"It offends his politics," the woman said, unsmiling. "How could we work the land? Look at us, Communist—what we have become."

"She has a problem with her leg," Pío explained, embarrassed by her tone. "We're both getting old. But you, *hombre*—you look well. He looks well, Carla."

"His face . . ."

"Tell us your news. How *was* it in Russia? Was it the workers' paradise you wished us to believe?"

Cabeza shrugged. Then thought, No, that was too easy. He shook his head. "There was no trust. No equality. No justice. The people suffered."

"*Madre.*"

"And were you as outspoken about that as you were of the regime here?" The deep-set eyes challenged him.

"Of course."

"Did it do any good?"

"They stripped me of my rank. Threw me in jail."

The woman nodded. He detected a tiny glint of satisfaction.

"So—so it was no better there than here under the monarchy?" Pío asked.

"Worse, my friend." He could have told him how much worse, that the Soviets were ruled by a madman, but he felt the cauldron of terrible hate begin to simmer inside him. His hands shook. He clenched them. When he spoke, it sounded as though someone were standing on his stomach. "It is over. Let's forget it."

"You walked out."

"Escaped."

"Where are you living now?"

"Mexico. You never had my letters?"

They shook their heads.

"No matter. Here I am. This—this selling of your land . . .

That was a big step, Pío." He let his doubts as to the wisdom of it be felt.

The old peasant laughed. "Yes—it took some getting used to, I can tell you. The figures." He mimed dizziness. "But we solved it in the end. I keep a tally of what we sell, what we buy in. Enrique, the son of our neighbor, he puts it in writing for us, works out the sums—"

"But the children—" Cabeza interjected.

"The *vino* is all local," Pío went on quickly. "From the hills." He gestured around. "Good stuff, *hombre*. You must try a little."

"But what good is a *cantina* to leave your children? They need land. A little age, a bad leg—what are children for but to work the soil for you when these things happen?"

Pío laughed oddly. "Times have changed. And Carla couldn't manage the slope down to the *barranca*. It was better we move. Better this way. I—I'll get some glasses. We must celebrate." He hurried out into the shop.

There was a silence.

Cabeza looked steadily at Carla. She sat, face averted, fanning the charcoal to redness.

"Out with it, woman."

"They are dead," she said flatly.

Cabeza's eyes narrowed. "All of them? What—?"

"All of them," she cut him off.

"You mean . . . Juan . . . ?"

"Juan and your sister Lucía—all."

The shock emptied him. He sat there in stricken silence. For a moment the child danced before him, the young woman smiled, tossing back her dark hair, her voice called to him, echoless, across the red-dust plain. The fleeting images died.

"When?"

"At the end of . . . your war."

"How?"

"On a bayonet."

Cabeza's lips whitened into a line.

"Your brothers, too," she added.

"I heard about them. But Lucía . . ."

"All, all," the woman suddenly wailed, throwing her head back. "The fascists killed them because they were your kin.

And our children because our families were connected. Everyone connected with you was hunted down and murdered. You destroyed us all!"

"Carla, he wasn't to blame!" Pío was back. "Blame the generals—blame Franco!"

"Shh!" the woman hissed. "Keep your voice down."

Pío put the glasses and a *porrón* of golden wine on the table. "Forgive her, Joaquín—women don't understand these things. Joaquín didn't make the revolution, Carla—the generals made it. He fought to stop them." Then: "Did you tell him his mother is still alive? Or was."

Cabeza looked at him quickly, "Where, Pío? Tell me."

"Let me see . . . Carla?"

"She was hidden by friends," Carla muttered to the stove.

"That's right. Then . . ." Pío closed his eyes, thinking back. "She worked for a time in Granada. For a family called—"

"Don't tell him," snapped the woman, turning. "Would you bring death to her, too?"

Cabeza made an angry movement. Pío said quickly, "She's his *mother*, Carla. Anyway, they wouldn't kill her now. If they did, I should think she'd die gladly for just a sight of him. Their name was . . . Caldes. Adolfo Caldes." He handed Cabeza a brimming glass, then one to his wife. She waved it away. He raised his own. "Your health, Joaquín."

Cabeza shook his head and got up. "No, I have awakened bad memories. It is better I go. It's been good to see you, Pío . . ."

"Oh now, come on!" Pío laughed and prodded him with a cupped hand. "She doesn't mean it, *hombre*. Please. Taste the wine. Vino Pío! Taste it. Tell me what you think. *Por favor?*"

Cabeza hesitated. For the old man's sake he took a sip, nodded, drank some more, then put down the glass and smacked his lips. "Good soil. *Bueno! Adiós.*" He looked at the woman, but she didn't turn.

Pío followed him out. "Wait! You go now to Granada?"

Cabeza ignored the question, moving out into the pallid winter sunlight.

"What time is it?" Pío demanded.

"Almost eleven."

"Bueno. Listen—there is a truck—the fish truck. The driver is a friend. He is due past here any moment. If I ask him he will give you a lift."

Cabeza walked on a few paces, then slowed. Pío looked embarrassed for the question he was about to ask. "You—you are allowed here in Spain now?"

"I will take the truck," Cabeza said.

"Bueno. I ask because . . . there was a death sentence . . . Or was it canceled?" He searched Cabeza's face anxiously.

Cabeza put out a hand and touched the bony shoulder. "The less you know, old friend, the better you'll sleep."

The fish truck braked to a halt. Pío spoke to the driver earnestly for a moment, then stood back. *"Vaya con Dios,"* he said, gripping Cabeza's hand.

Cabeza swung up into the cab. Pío stood for a moment and watched the truck diminish along the road that wound up toward the blue *sierra*. Then he turned and went back into the shop.

No sooner had Carla heard him return than she called out in her man's voice, "Get Enrique!"

Pío went in to her inquiringly. "Why?" He was startled to see that his wife was quite beside herself.

"Why do you think? Get him. Send him for the Guardia!"

Pío stood shocked. "You—you can't be serious?"

"Do it!" she screamed. Her clawed hands were twitching and clutching in frenzy. "Do you think someone won't recognize him? Then what happens? They trace him back to us!"

"But no one saw him here."

"Idiot! The truck driver saw him here."

"But he won't—"

"That old bitch across the road—what has she ever missed? I tell you we'll be ruined. He murdered our children—now us!"

Pío stared at the spittle flecking her lips, the flare of her eyes. He moved to her in alarm and took hold of her shoulders. *"Cálmate, cálmate,"* he said. "It was the meeting —the suddenness. You're overexcited. It will pass, and then . . ." He ran out of words. He stayed holding her, trying to soothe her. But his expression was uneasy.

23

"Listen," Carla said, more quietly but no less intensely. "He's an enemy of the regime. You know what that means. They'll take away our license. We'll be out on the street, homeless, penniless, you with no work and me a cripple!"

The picture frightened him. "But he's our cousin by marriage."

"'Cousin'! If he were my brother I'd do the same. Pío, this has nothing to do with how we are related or the past—it has to do only with our survival. It's—him—or—us, understand? Now hurry and fetch Enrique—or they'll wonder why we took so long."

"Carla . . ." Pío stood agonized. "I—I can't."

"Blessed Mother," she screeched. "Do I have to fetch him myself?" She struggled up, grasping at the mantel. Pío caught her as she tottered. He pulled her back into the chair.

"All right, all right—uh—I'll see if he's in." Anything to give himself time to think. The boy was seldom in at this hour, but he would pretend to look for him. It would give her time to cool off. He had never seen her in such a state.

But as he went through and out of the shop, who in the name of Fate should he run into but Enrique, bringing back the latest batch of invoices and receipts.

"*Hola!*" The youth grinned cheerfully, pushing past him into the shop.

Pío grabbed at him and missed. "Wait!" he whispered, going in quickly after him.

But too late. Carla had already heard his voice.

4

ALMUÑECAR HAD receded. The hills drew their curtains behind the truck, leaving only a distant view of the sea in the rearview mirror, then only of terraced hillsides that swung and spun as the road began to writhe up into the true mountains.

The driver was young. Cabeza was thankful for that. Less chance of recognition. And he was preoccupied, driving for the most part in silence, his tongue, to judge by the swelling, on a bad tooth, which could not have been improved by the wind that grew colder as they climbed, cutting into the cab through the ill-fitting windows. Cabeza was thankful for this, too. It gave him time to "feel" his situation.

"Feeling" had become an important element in his running battle for survival. It was the act of harkening to one's instincts and not interrupting their flow with questions. Harkening to them now, he felt a sense of danger, a steady warning signal deep inside him. He didn't challenge it, just waited for its cause to define itself. It did so quickly. Carla.

Carla and the expression in her eyes when he told her of his imprisonment by the Russians. The glint of vindictive pleasure.

And who could blame her? he thought sadly. Her beautiful children, brought up so well on so little . . .

Millions had rallied to defend the republic in '36. His crime was that he had captured the public imagination in the process. The Communist bandit who had thrown in his lot with the great peasant leader Valentín González provided good copy for the international press. And when, between them, with twenty-eight men, one machine gun and a few rifles, he and González had halted General Mola's advance on Madrid—well, they were heroes from then on. Heroes of the republic. But to the fascist junta they became public enemies numbers one and two—to be shot on sight. Their families and friends included. And the junta had won the war. That was his other crime: to have been on the losing side.

He wondered how Carla would have reacted if he had told her the whole story of his incarceration in Russia—how they had stripped him naked and flung him into a cell not much larger than his body, kept him there a week, then transferred him to a larger cell with seven other inmates, four of whom died before his eyes during a year of absolute silence, deprivation, near starvation and torture. Would it have blunted her vindictiveness?

The object in the Lubianka was the calculated destruction of the individual spirit. Many of its inmates, he found out to his disgust later, were staunch Communists, thrown in there without trial, sometimes by mistake, or simply because they had been denounced by someone, a madman even, it didn't matter. The vast projects in the Arctic Circle had to be fed with slave labor, and here was their source of supply. Prisoners were systematically humiliated, isolated by not being allowed to speak, weakened by the diet of black bread and cabbage soup and lack of sleep, harassed by nightlong interrogations, until in utter despair they signed a full confession.

Why the NKVD bothered to extract such a confession before pronouncing sentence was a quirk of Russian nature that was beyond him. But there were many things about the Russians that were beyond him. Their submissiveness, for one. How they could exist under Stalin's despotism without rising up and tearing the Kremlin apart with their bare hands baffled his own fierce imagination.

Well, *he* hadn't submitted. Nor would he ever, to any injustice, in any shape, Fascist *or* Communist.

For four thousand and fifteen hours—he had clocked up every one of them as a means of keeping sane—he had sat on his bunk with a book, open on his lap, which he was not allowed to read, his eyes fixed on the peephole in the door. That was the order—Watch the peephole, do not move! Eight human beings, with thoughts and emotions and memories of families and children to agonize them, sitting there closely confined, in total silence, watching that peephole for hour upon hour upon hour. He didn't even know their names, where they came from, what they were accused of having done, for not one word ever passed among them. Statues. If their eyes strayed for one instant, the guards came in and clubbed them. They were even forced to sleep with their eyes visible from the peephole. One position. Forbidden ever to turn.

And the interrogations. Always at night. The clatter of bolts. Two guards would seize him by the arms, drag him out, march him, march him through the interminable corridors. Up, down, around, through the vast building. At last a door opening. The sharp glare of lights. The smell of cigarette smoke. The bland faces of his NKVD interrogators. Questions. Accusations. The pen. He would not sign. Though he was skin and bone, almost too weak to stand, hallucinating, he endured one thousand four hundred and sixty hours of interrogation, and would not sign.

How had he managed to resist? The answer, he guessed, lay in one word—hate. Not against communism. Incredibly, he believed in it still. But against the regime that could so distort its ideals. Against Beria, whose secret police enforced its dictates with such ruthless brutality. Against Colonel Grechukha, his chief interrogator. Above all, against the power source, the instigator himself—Josef Stalin. One day, he had vowed, his eyes fixed on the peephole, one day . . . *somehow* . . .

"Stop the truck."

The driver, assuming he needed to relieve himself, pulled in to the side.

Cabeza had spotted a track leading away around the contours of the mountain slope. It offered a convenient excuse. He jerked a thumb. "Just remembered. Some friends live around there. I will pay them a surprise visit."

The driver looked from the track to him blankly. "I can't wait, *amigo*."

"No, I'll stay the night, catch another lift tomorrow." He swung down onto the road. "I should get that tooth fixed when you reach the city."

"When they remove a tooth, they also remove your shirt," grumbled the driver. He flipped a dour hand and let in the clutch.

Cabeza watched the truck grind away up toward the pass. He moved toward the track, just to satisfy any backward glance, and then, when the truck had gone, turned to the road's edge and looked back the way they had come. He traced the zigzags down and away carefully to the point where they vanished, a mere cottontail in the V of the hills, allowing time for any vehicle hidden by the fall of the land to appear.

One did. A car. It was a long way back. He stared at it till his eyes watered, but could make out no details, save that it was blue.

He gauged the rocky slopes above with a practiced eye. It was going to take every ounce of his energy and skill to cross the rest of the Sierra Nevada without using the road. But it was from the road that danger would come. A lot of sweat for just a hunch. But it was only because he had trusted his hunches that he was still alive.

He climbed through the rest of the morning and most of the afternoon. He had not eaten since the sandwiches and beer the Americans had shared with him as they passed Gibraltar. But in a strange way it was good not to be eating again. Life in Mexico had become too regular. Too many tortillas at the appointed hour, Margarita ringing the big old bell on the porch of the *hacienda* to summon them in from the corral or from the range. The bell could be heard far across the pastures where the fighting bulls grazed, and she expected him and the *vaqueros* to return when they heard it. Needless to say, he came in his own time. But not too much so, because he ran the ranch as a collective. Each had his task to do, and each task was of equal merit. Margarita's was the cooking. She took great pride in it and was good at it. Though not as good as she was in bed. She didn't share *that* with the collective, however. She was *his* woman. She had bought in like the rest of them and had had her pick of the several handsome and young men. She had chosen him, the leader.

Cabeza was fond of Margarita and respected her. Sometimes he even felt he loved her. She had beauty and charm and came from a good family. But he could never forget that his true wife lived in Russia.

Yes, it was good to feel the pangs back in his belly, the stickiness of thirst in his mouth, the cold biting through his clothing to be instantly repelled by the body heat produced by climbing. That was what Mexico had lacked. Uncertainty. And a goal other than profit. He wondered for a moment whether he hadn't concocted this whole trip in order to escape from the bourgeois predictability of his postwar life.

The blue car had come and gone. Other vehicles passed, most of them open trucks. He could see what they carried from this height. All normal merchandise. No hidden contingents of police.

Perhaps he had been wrong about Carla. Or perhaps Pío had talked her out of taking vengeful action. He hoped so, because it was becoming clear that his only way through the pass would be via the road. The slopes on either side were almost vertical, and above there was snow. He was not equipped to climb through snow. His leg was beginning to give him trouble.

Maintaining a level course—the first rule of mountaineering: Never lose height—he picked his way along the mountainside and let the road come up to him.

He paused and looked back down the ribbon of it. It showed at intervals, curving in and out of view, then again, far below, weaving between the scrubby pines, then straightening as it crossed a bridge over a narrow gorge with, at the bottom, a glint of quicksilver. Crossing the bridge was a car.

The car had a long climb ahead of it before it reached the pass. Cabeza estimated that he could be through the pass and up among the rocks again before it arrived. He jumped down onto the road, his leg buckling a little, then squared his shoulders to the icy wind that came rushing through from the north, and started to walk.

He had not gone far when he saw that the deep cutting continued unrelieved for further than he had estimated.

There was no way off the road. The car must be getting close. He put on speed.

Five minutes later, head bent against the increasing wind, he was half hobbling, half running through the shadowy darkness cast by overhanging rocks, the sweat freezing on his body. Behind him he imagined he could already hear the car. Why the sudden feeling of desperation? It was probably just a tourist vehicle. But the feeling persisted. The darkness, the cold . . .

He was back in the Polar Night. The work party had drawn ahead of him, trudging through the snow. He must catch up with them before the gates of the compound closed. Once the guards closed the gates there was no reopening. Whoever was left outside had to stay out there in the snow. By morning he would be just a mound. No one would dig him out. The NKVD would march the work party out past his frozen corpse without a backward glance. He hobbled on, his leg shooting agony through the whole of his body.

The one terrible fear in Vorkuta was of sickness or injury. You were fed just sufficient calories daily to sustain a twelve-hour shift in the mine. Get injured or sick and the calories were halved. Your ability to recover was impaired. You weakened. You died. Men and women died every day. No one cared. More were on their way to replace them. Tens of thousands more.

Cabeza, despite not having signed a confession, was drafted to Vorkuta on a ten-year sentence. Clad in little more than rags in temperatures around forty below, he worked like a demon for his calories. Food was his sole aim. He stole it, fought for it, on one occasion killed for it. Only if he could maintain what was left of his health and strength, he knew, could he survive long enough to get away. No one had ever escaped from the Arctic camps, surrounded as they were by thousands of kilometers of frozen wilderness. But he was determined, somehow, to be the first.

He nursed himself diligently for a year, never missing a day's work or a calorie. Then in the winter of 1944 the demand for coal was stepped up to support the war effort. They were forced to work longer shifts. Precautions were abandoned. Timber deliveries fell short. They had to work on through the naked coal without roof supports. There were frequent cave-ins. Men and women were buried in their scores. No one dug them out. The next shift simply worked around the bodies and on into the seam. It seemed inevitable that he, too, would become a victim. The inevitable happened.

The fall buried him completely but, fortunately, not too deeply. Choking, he managed to dig his way out with his hands. His right leg was crushed. He lay there, gasping in agony as his comrades moved to help him. The guard told them to work on, then went off to call for a stretcher team. Cabeza knew that the moment he reached sick bay his calories would be cut. The leg would not heal. He would die there.

"Motherfuckers!" He bellowed it again and again till the galleries rang with the sound of his frustration and hate. The shift peered uneasily back to where he writhed on the ground.

"Hush, comrade—or we will all be punished."

"Motherfuckers!" The furious pounding of his blood was releasing what reserves of energy and defiance were left in him. He suddenly sat up and beckoned two of the men to him. They were scared to comply, but he was the shift leader. He ordered them. They came slowly.

"Splint it!" He was damned if he was going to die there, betrayed in his beliefs by a Georgian pig. "Splint it—hurry!"

He forced them to align the broken bones roughly and lash the broken leg to a pick helve. It was a race against time. He groaned with the agony. When it was done, he got to his feet, half fainting, and staggered to the coal face. His comrades watched disbelievingly. Someone handed him a pick. With all his weight on his good leg, he swung it, buried the blade in the seam and hooked out a tumble of coal. The shift let out a cheer.

When the stretcher bearers arrived, he was working steadily. And he continued to work—in a continual fog of pain, but never missing a shift or a calorie until the day of his escape in August of that year.

But the four-kilometer tramp through heavy snow from the camp to the pit and back again at night was the memory he would carry to his grave—the hobbling struggle not to be left behind, the splint cutting off his circulation, exposing him to the ever-present danger of frostbite, the bones grating, grating . . .

He was still half running when the car caught up with him. It sailed by with a blast of its horn. It had a GB touring plate. Two children waved to him out of the back window.

Cabeza eased his way out from under the pile of corn husks and sat for a full minute scratching every part of his body. The mites that infested all such stacks had given him a hard night. Pale early-morning sunlight showed through the shrunken timbers of the hut door.

Brushing the fibers from his crumpled clothing, he got up and went outside, the breath white before his face, and looked first at the road where it passed two hundred meters below him, noting its emptiness with satisfaction. He followed its undulations northward between the winter-bare fields and scattered villages toward the distant city of Granada.

It lay like a mirage on the high plain, its buildings rising from the mist. Above them the battlements of the Alhambra reared with the sharpness of cast gold against the blue mountains beyond. What with this vision and, here and there, a prick of silver from the river Genil and, in the tail of his right eye, the snows of the Sierra Nevada, hurtingly white . . .! His heart swelled. If Almuñecar had seemed the epitome of Spain, what was this but its essence?

The hut stood exposed and lonely on a smooth hillside, and he moved away from it quickly, following the contours of the stony gray fields till he found a *barranca*. He drank from the stream, the coldness of the water aching inside him, then rinsed his face, scrubbing at the stubble on his jaw to soften it. He shaved painfully with the safety razor that was his sole luggage. It was important to remain clean-shaven—the lack of a beard was his only disguise. Then, keeping the road sufficiently to his left to avoid the *pueblos* that straddled it, he trudged across the rolling *vega* toward the city.

Three hours later he had penetrated the dusty outskirts as far as the river. There he squatted in the shade of a building and watched the flow of traffic and pedestrians across the bridge. If news of his destination had been flashed ahead of him, this, surely, was where they would seek to intercept him.

But though he watched for a full thirty minutes, he could see nothing to suggest that entrances to the city were being monitored in any way. Relieved, but still wary, he crossed over into the town and found a small back-street café—empty. He tucked himself away in a corner and ordered breakfast. The pleasant-faced young proprietress met his eye with not a flicker. She passed the order through a hatch, then moved about casually, sweeping a little, wiping a little, while admonishing a small crop-headed boy who was wandering from table to table, pushing at the chairs with his stomach. "Do you hear me, dreamy-boots? Finish eating and get off to school—now hurry!"

The child ignored her, toying absently with the few squares of black chocolate and crust of bread that was his breakfast. The Spanish breakfast—Cabeza had almost forgotten. And the woman was wearing the Spanish national costume—a maternity smock! He stifled a grin. He was beginning to feel at home.

"Yes, he is five," the woman said later as she served his meal, the child having gone at last. "He goes to the school. They call it a school. He learns nothing. He can read, but they do not teach him. Not even to count. Yes, it is a religious school. But there is no system. None at all. He is like a savage. He goes at nine—or half past nine—or ten—it is equal. The doors are always open. Bah!"

Cabeza chuckled. "Señora, do you know the Calle Daralhorra?"

"Of course." She directed him with her pencil, drawing on the tabletop, as a man would.

"Thank you. That is very clear."

"*De nada. Buen Provecho.*" She moved away flat-footed, her stomach thrust before her.

Cabeza ate the baconlike ham, the eggs, the cheese, the beautiful bread and unsalted butter and finished two small jars of apricot jam and the pot of black coffee. He paid and went out into the cool winter's sunlight and followed her tabletop map through the bustling city to a northern suburb. No one looked at him twice.

The Calle Daralhorra was in a prosperous residential suburb. The houses varied, some built in the Moorish pattern, closely adjacent, with high walls screening verdant courtyards where pomegranate and bougainvillea grew in profusion. Others, of more recent design, stood in their own gardens behind screens of cypress. The Caldes villa was one of these.

Cabeza walked past it casually, concealing his limp, his eyes taking in everything. A young servant was shaking out a mat on the veranda of the villa opposite. She glanced down at him almost coquettishly before carrying the mat back indoors.

No undercurrents there, Cabeza thought. If there had been police activity anywhere in the locality, she would know about it and the look she gave would have been a different look.

Through a gap in the Caldes hedge he could see part of a small, almost unnaturally green lawn, which an old man was sweeping very carefully with a twig broom. Outside the wrought-iron gate a smart German coupé was parked. The upper windows of the house were shuttered. He could just hear a radio barking intermittent speech and music somewhere on the premises. Then he was past.

He walked on to the end of the road, wondering what his mother could have been doing in such a house. Domestic work, he supposed.

The road petered out in an olive grove, as though the habitations were gradually being extended into the *vega*. He walked on into the grove and sat down on the hard red earth with his back to a tree. From here he had a view back along most of the *calle*.

He sat there for an hour, listening to the distant bustle of the city, watching the unhurried movements of the few residents who showed themselves outside their homes.

Then he got up and walked back along the road. But for some reason he still could not bring himself to approach the house. He returned to the city center, found a post office, looked up Adolfo Caldes in the directory and telephoned the number. A girl's voice answered, and he could tell by its harshness and pitch that she was a servant.

"The Señor? No, no—he is not here—who is speaking?"

"Who, then, is there?" Cabeza asked.

"The Señora is here. She— You wish to speak with her? Who shall I say?"

"I will speak with her."

The girl seemed to hesitate. Then she put down the phone and went away, and he could hear her calling through the house.

Presently the instrument was lifted and a rather breathless, impatient voice demanded, "*Sí?* Who is this?"

"I am a relative of María Cabeza," Cabeza said. "I am trying to find her. I was given your name."

There was a moment's silence at the other end. "Cabeza?" The voice sounded brittle. "I know no one called Cabeza. You must have the wrong house."

"I have the right house. But you may know her by another name. She is dark, perhaps a little gray now. Not tall. Aged fifty-nine. From Estremadura. Her position with you possibly was domestic."

"I know no one of that description," the woman said tartly. "You have a wrong number—"

"Don't hang up," Cabeza cut in quickly. "I am a true relative. You have nothing at all to fear. María has come into some money. It is to her advantage that she be found."

"Money?" The woman sounded surprised. She seemed to hesitate. When she spoke again it was in another tone. "I would rather not discuss such matters over the telephone. Perhaps if you came to the house . . ."

Cabeza still, for some reason, did not want to go to the house. "No. We should meet outside somewhere. In the town would be best."

"No," the woman said. "I'm extremely busy and I'm under no obligation even to speak to you. If you want my help, you'll have to come here."

"In the town," Cabeza repeated. "Name a place, señora. Convenient to you."

The woman was silent. Cabeza half expected her to hang up. But at length she huffed a sigh and said, "Do you know the Café Central?"

"Not a café, señora. Somewhere . . . more open."

"Very well." Terse now. "There is a place by the river . . ."

"And not the river." A river halved one's line of retreat. He was thinking like a soldier. "A public garden would be best." He added, "And not the Generalife." It lent itself too easily to ambush.

The woman laughed shortly. "I don't know why I have to take orders from you, but—all right—do you know the old *paseo?*" She gave him directions.

"I will find it."

She hesitated. "How will I know you?"

"I will present myself. Just say how you'll be dressed."

"Uh—in gray. A gray dress with a red bandanna. So . . ." She drew in her breath. "I have some things to do now. After that is *siesta*. I will be on the *paseo* at five o'clock."

"Not five." Cabeza tried to make his tone respectful but firm. "In twenty minutes." He checked with the post-office clock. "At twelve-fifteen. Until then." He hung up quickly before she could refuse.

He made his way to the rendezvous and reconnoitered the lie of the land. Busy shopping streets ran on either side of the central reservation, which was bordered by trees, ornamental shrubs. He strolled for part of its length, noting the incidence of side streets, alert for any signs of police. Seven minutes to go. But if she came, she would be late, he knew. Women of her type did not like to be pushed around. Lateness would be her gesture of protest.

He crossed through the traffic to a snack bar and ordered a coffee and sat down in the window facing onto the streetcars, the shoppers, the maternity smocks pushing along already overflowing prams. Where will they all go when Spain is full? he wondered. He thought of Siberia and the Soviet solution. He had been surprised by the freedom and affluence he had witnessed since his return. It seemed almost as if life even under the butcher of Badajoz, Franco, was preferable to that under Soviet Communism. But it was an illusion. It had to be. Somewhere, well hidden, were the labor camps, the . . . He elbowed the thought to the back of his mind for later contemplation. Right now he had to be very alert. Carla had known whom he would contact here. So, then, might the Guardia.

He scanned the scene outside repeatedly, "feeling" for anomalies, the slightest change in the logical pattern of movement. It was twenty-past now.

Ten minutes later there was still no sign of the woman. Twenty . . . Now it was beginning to look as if she had indeed taken offense at his manner.

A tall, slim woman of about forty entered his line of vision. She had dark hair that contrasted tastefully with the red bandanna fastened at her throat by a coiled gold ring. Gray dress . . . She was strolling slowly, rather stiffly, along the *paseo* opposite.

As he watched she came to a stop and looked slowly around her, one high heel dug in the path, toe tilted.

Cabeza laid a five-peseta piece in the saucer beside his coffee, but did not otherwise move. He watched along the street as far as he could see, first one way, then the other, then studied the people strolling in her vicinity.

Seeing nothing suspicious, he got up and went to the doorway. The woman had moved on, though only saunteringly. He looked again up and down the street, waited for the traffic to clear, then started across the road.

Somewhere a car hit peak revs. He glanced around quickly and saw it rushing toward him. Simultaneously he heard another car coming the opposite way. He leaped backward. A bell clanged in his ear—the steeling of brakes! The streetcar fender actually gave the back of his knee a glancing blow before he could check himself. The car squealed to a halt across his path. He had a flash image of Assault Police, bristling guns, before he dodged around the back of the streetcar, his knee almost collapsing, gripping it with one hand, reaching with the other for the rear-door handle as the tram moved away from him, picking up speed. He just managed to catch hold of it.

The passengers stared at him, some blankly, some fearfully, as he dragged himself aboard. Police were disgorging from the second car, coming after the streetcar on foot, the first car giving chase, blasting its horn.

The streetcar driver seemed unaware of what was happening at first, but the passengers now were beginning to shout at him, and the first car was trying to edge past to head him off, but the oncoming traffic forced it back. A van burped to a halt in its path. A truck banged into the back of it. A snarl built up quickly, boxing the police car in. Its occupants sprang out and continued their pursuit on foot. And still the streetcar was moving away.

Then suddenly it wasn't. It was braking. The nearest police were forty meters back, but now beginning to gain.

Cabeza had no alternative. He swung down to the road, ran, hobbling into a side street. A young man was getting out of a car. Cabeza thrust him aside and started to get in. But the man grabbed him, pulling at him, shouting loudly. Cabeza shook himself free and ran on. But ahead now were more police, pelting toward him, holster flaps open, guns in hand. He was the meat in a sandwich. He turned quickly into a shop, slammed the door shut behind him, fumbled the catch down. He turned to see the startled faces of the staff, racks of belts, handbags, a cluttered counter, a rear door. He ran through, hauled it shut after him, felt for the key. There wasn't one. He was in a small annex with another door leading into an open courtyard. He hurried out, hearing the police burst into the shop behind him. The yard was L-shaped. He ran around the corner, stumbled over some ashcans and fetched up against a wall. The yard was enclosed! Other doors gave access to it from other shops. He tried one—locked. Tried another. The police poured out into the yard behind him, their guns aimed straight at him. More and more police—more and more guns.

Cabeza froze. He turned slowly, his barrel chest heaving, his hands well away from his body. He looked at the array of twitching guns and from them up toward the pale blue heavens—and wished that he could fly.

5

GAIL LESSING quickened as she saw the tall man coming through customs. In his mid-thirties, slightly tanned despite the winter, handsome in a Cary Grantish kind of way—she did not need to observe his prearranged hand signal to know that this was "Mr. Wiz" himself, David Kelland.

She scarcely had time to smooth back her corn-colored hair and assume the servile neatness of an embassy driver before the blue eyes found her. They had met only once before, very briefly, back in the "pickle factory." Yet he moved toward her directly, brows only slightly raised. She gave the counter-sign and turned with him. She had to hurry to keep pace as he strode out along the main hall of London airport.

He paused once to glance back toward the crowds still issuing from the channel.

"Car out front?"

"Yes, sir."

In a moment they were outside and the chill January wind hit them, spattering them with rain. "Lead the way, Miss Lessing."

Had he really remembered her from that short meeting? They said he never forgot a face, but even so, it seemed unlikely. Maybe Washington had cabled him her description:

39

Female Caucasian, age 29, height 5'6", eyes green, hair honey-blond, features molded, regular, complexion medium, freckled.

She trotted ahead of him across the lanes of arriving and departing traffic. The Ford limousine stood over by the far curb, where parking was restricted. His plane had been late, but, fortunately, the police hadn't picked up on the car yet, probably because of its CD plates.

Kelland dumped his hand luggage on the back seat. He glanced around again before he slid in beside her. She drove out and around the traffic system. Sandalwood aftershave. He adjusted the rearview mirror and peered back through it for a moment, then straightened it again without explanation. It was not until they were on the dual highway heading toward town that he said, "I'm being followed."

Gail lifted her eyes to the mirror.

"Two cars back. Mercedes 240. Guy beside the driver with a black moustache. He's been with me since Ankara."

It was too far to see the man, but she made out the registration number of the car, reversed it in her mind, memorized it.

"What do you want me to do?"

"You have a cutoff point somewhere, I presume?"

"In London. Chelsea."

"Fair enough." He reached for his briefcase, opened it on his lap and took out some papers. He settled back.

Gail drove on in silence, aware of the car behind them and the fact that he had shelved it calmly in favor of what looked like a typed report, that the report was somehow of vital importance. Gleaned, she assumed, from their Ankara station. In which case, why had he stopped off in London with it instead of flying direct to Washington? She could feel the vibes of concern coming from him as he reread it, item by item, marking certain passages with a gold Sheaffer. Everything gold, Longines wristwatch, signet ring on little finger. Brown hands perfectly manicured above the knifelike creases of the worsted trousers. Scotch tweed topcoat . . . all with the tabs removed or false ones sewn in, you could bet your boots.

Kelland was not his name, she knew that much. But as far

as the world was concerned, it would check out as deeply as any human agency could probe, right down to the personal details in the file in the Treasury Department, where he was listed as an investigator in the Bureau of Narcotics. She supposed the cover had been designed to enable him to travel freely in Turkey, North Africa and Asia without attracting suspicion.

Something big was happening, she could smell it. After the routine work of the last six months it was a breath of fresh air to have even fleeting contact with a GSL6 in the Overseas Arm of the Clandestine Service.

"Any news from this end?" he asked suddenly of the papers in his lap.

"Uh—in what context?"

"Moscow."

She thought carefully. "No. But I'd probably be the last to know. They seem to have marooned me on a little island here." She added, "For some reason," wondering if he knew she was in the doghouse.

"Mm?" He was frowning at a paragraph. He underscored it heavily.

"Not that I'm complaining," she added quickly. "I guess everyone needs an ease-up of pressure once in a while. It's just . . . Well, I didn't enroll to play cleaning lady."

Kelland finished the bit he was reading. "Well, don't throw in the tow— the dishcloth yet, Miss Lessing. I have some work right here for you."

She waited, but he didn't elaborate. His mind had jumped to another track.

"Who've you got there?" he asked.

"Where?"

"In the safe house." A touch of impatience.

"Benson left yesterday."

"That isn't what—"

"Holz. He's my fixture."

Kelland looked at her, surprised. "They gave you Holz?"

She nodded.

He was silent for a moment. He seemed impressed. "You got a scrambler there?"

"Every mod con."

"All right. Save time. I'll move in with you."

It was Gail's turn to look surprised. "They've booked you in at the Cumberland."

"You can cancel."

"You want me to take you straight to the house?"

He nodded and returned his attention to the papers.

The Mercedes stayed with them, almost imperceptibly, vanishing completely sometimes but always managing to be with them through the traffic lights. It looked easy, but she knew it took years of experience to tail a car so deftly. Well, let's see how you make it through the chicanes, she thought.

King's Road looked old and kind of cozy, with the lights coming on in the boutiques, glowing through the steamy windows of the coffeehouses. This was to be coronation year, and here and there pictures of the young Queen were incorporated in the window displays.

As they approached Sloane Square, Gail swung sharp left into a side street, spurted, took another left, then a right turn. She drove into a small cobbled mews lined with rented garages topped by little brightly painted maisonettes. She stopped, facing a pair of blue doors, and got out.

Kelland shuffled his papers away, alert now, as she unpadlocked the doors and opened them, revealing a small, empty garage, at one side of which a flight of colorfully carpeted stairs led up to the bijou dwelling above.

As she got back in the car, she spotted the Mercedes out of the corner of her eye—just crawling past the entrance of the mews. All right, you're good, she thought. But now watch the birdie.

She drove into the garage, cut the motor, turned on the sidelights, and got out and pulled the doors shut, bolting them. The panes in the door had been painted over. Standing on tiptoe, she peeked out through a small peephole scratched in the paint.

The Mercedes had vanished, but it would be parked just out of sight. A pair of eyes would be watching around the corner, she was certain, though she was unable to detect them.

Kelland got out of the car questioningly. "Now what?"

In answer, Gail moved to the rear wall of the garage. It seemed to be of whitewashed brick but she lifted it easily. It swung up on its counterbalance to reveal another, similar garage, facing out onto another mews in back.

"Help me, please."

She let off the hand brake, and together they pushed the car through into the other garage. Only when the connecting wall was safely shut behind them did she remove the magnetic CD plates. She got in and restarted the motor. Kelland opened the outer doors for her.

Within moments they were driving through a maze of narrow streets toward Cromwell Road.

Well, say something, she thought.

But Kelland remained silent, watching out of the back window. When he was quite sure the Mercedes was no longer with them, he said, "Who thought that one up?"

"Verner." She could see he was wondering how driving to such an address would fit in with his cover.

She gave a reassuring smile. "Your man will think we went up into the flat above. When he checks, he'll think that's where they've fixed for you to stay. He'll watch the place for hours, maybe days."

Only then did Kelland permit himself a smile. His teeth were pearly white. They would be.

The house was one of a terrace of Georgian residences overlooking a strip of tired-looking grass and trees behind Cromwell Road. Gail led the way in. She showed Kelland quickly around the ground floor, just to give him the layout. The rooms were rather dark, furnished with overblown antiques, a bit like a film set. She took him up the winding stairway.

"This is the suite, right? Bathroom through there. Dressing room, telephone . . ."

Kelland dumped his hand luggage on the bed and moved straight to the window. He looked out and around the square carefully.

"Where are you?"

"There are two more rooms above this. I'm above them, way up top."

"And Holz?"

"He lives in the basement. I hardly see him."

Kelland returned to the bed. He opened up his briefcase.

"Well, tell him about our tail. I want him to keep a sharp lookout."

"Right. I have the number of the car. Shall I pass it on to COS at the embassy?"

"No." Kelland had pulled out some fresh papers. "I know who they are. And this is what they're after." He handed her the papers. "The work I promised. For translation."

They were photostats, typed in Russian. Gail just had time to read the first-page heading: "Strategic Dispositions Warsaw Pact Armor."

"Give me a rough how-long?"

Gail counted the pages. "Six hours."

"Fine. Now, don't rush it. There are a lot of figures in there—I want them accurate." He added, "So long as it's ready to cable to Washington sometime tomorrow. Now what do you do about food here?"

"We have a well-stocked kitchen."

"Who cooks?"

She tapped her chest, a shade ruefully.

"Well, you'll be busy. So I'll just grab something when I feel like it. Okay?"

The blue eyes rested on hers. It was a genuine question. Cooking was the women's department—the only subdivision where she was asked instead of told. She nodded and moved to the door. She paused.

"Can I ask how long you'll be staying?"

Kelland thought about that. "You may as well know now." He reached back in the briefcase and brought out a photograph. "Just long enough to square this away. No longer."

He came to her and stood close, holding the picture for her. It looked like a blown-up holiday snap, a bit blurry, and showed a man standing in the sea, his back to the camera, wearing swim trunks and a straw hat. Not a well-muscled physique, but fairly trim. Aged anything between thirty and forty. Another male bather stooped, laughing, to splash water, half in and half out of frame. Beyond them, an incidental figure to judge by the focus, stood a third man, youngish, bearded.

"Little bonus from our Ankara station," Kelland murmured.

Gail waited, peering at the picture, aware of his nearness. Her flesh tingled strangely, as though close to a power source.

"That's the Black Sea, by the way. Near Odessa. And that's an Englishman." Then as an afterthought: "You don't recognize him, by any chance?"

"Oh, sure." She laughed. "I know so many people from their naked back view." Then she saw that he was serious. Not a glint of humor. She ended lamely, "No, hardly."

"It's not impossible," Kelland said. "But I guess you're right—you'd have to know him pretty well. See?—that's a scar."

"So I noticed." It ran in a white loop below the man's left shoulder blade. She looked up at Kelland curiously. "Who is he?"

Kelland shrugged. "I don't know—yet." He added, "The man on the right is Leonid Sokovsky."

"The Russian agent?"

The blue eyes surveyed her with just the smallest hint of surprise. "You've heard of him?"

Gail nodded. "So we have an Englishman with a Russian agent on the shores of the Black Sea. For that to be a bonus, he has to be a member of British Intelligence—right?"

"Right, Miss Lessing. And according to my informant, he's been spilling a whole can of really deadly beans. Some of which he seems to have stolen from Uncle Sam's icebox."

6

WHEN SHE took in his morning coffee, Kelland's bed was empty. She heard the whine of his shaver coming from the bathroom. She had not got to bed herself until two, but she had been aware of him long after that, moving about, making phone calls, the wet-finger-rubbed-on-a-windowpane sound of his voice filtering up to her through the silent house. Yet he had already been down for the daily papers. They lay scattered about the place, as though he'd been riffling through them in search of some particular item of news.

She put the coffee down on the night table. The ashtray beside the phone was full of butts. The room smelled of stale smoke and sandalwood. She moved to the window and lowered the sash a little, glancing out automatically for any signs of surveillance. A night smoker. He hadn't touched one cigarette during all the time she had been with him yesterday. The square outside looked dismally normal. A fine rain shone on the limbs of the plane tree opposite, like sweat on a boxer's body. No sign of the Mercedes.

Kelland appeared behind her, patting away the tired lines under his eyes with astringent. He wore just pajama bottoms, and his body looked supple, even muscular. A gold ankh gleamed about his neck on a little chain. Everything gold.

"Good morning." She smiled. "Black coffee, one spoon of sugar, okay?"

He nodded. "I heard you tapping away. How's it coming?"

"It's come. Finished."

A surprised tilt of the head said, Good girl. He moved past her and took a taste of the coffee. He turned as he drank, to look her over, his eyes examining every detail of her appearance, as if for the first time. His whole manner seemed different this morning.

He put down the cup and sauntered back to stand close, very close, looking down at her speculatively, almost intimately. A hand toyed with her lapel for a moment, as if he were debating something. A finger flipped open the top button of her shirt, then the next. Gail stood quite still as he drew out the Saint Christopher medallion she wore and studied it . . . tucked it back, his hand under her blouse now, lightly encompassing her breast. As his thumb found her nipple under her bra, she gasped and stepped back quickly—into the barrier of his other hand. It was like iron! She was held powerless by the nape of the neck while the caress continued, light as thistledown. Pain and pleasure clashed at her nerve centers, her blood pounding against his grip, striving in vain to reach her brain. Senses swimming, she felt a distant body—could it be her own?—go into limp, delicious submission.

Then, just as suddenly, the hands were gone. Gail reeled. Her circulation came rushing back, and there stood Kelland, watching her coolly, as if gauging her reaction.

"Care for a walk?"

"A . . . ?" She stared at him, dazed, angry.

"In the park."

Something warned her against an emotional response, that how she handled this was in some way important.

"Isn't—isn't Washington waiting for the translation?" she managed.

"Washington, Miss Lessing, is still asleep. And will be for several hours yet. Go put on that sharp trench coat. I'll join you downstairs."

The eyes never left her, following her as she went out. Head still spinning, she fetched her raincoat. So he groped you, she told herself. What's new? You're a woman of the world. But the memory of the sudden terrifying power he had exerted haunted her—like the mere wink of a door behind which lay something . . . molten.

Now, don't go working up a thing against him, she warned herself. Your career is all at this point. Take it in your stride.

The door to the basement was open. She poked her head through. "Holz?"

She descended a few steps. "Holz, we're going out."

Getting no reply, she went all the way down into what had been the kitchen quarters of the house. The rooms were deserted. Holz's drawings and sketches lay around, his paints open on the table. It was an odd hobby for a man of his profession, she had always thought. But they were odd paintings. Surreal. A lot of eyes and flowers and creepy-looking animals. The eyes were somehow flowers, and the flowers eyes.

The back door opened behind her, and Holz poked his heavy yet elfin face in. He had evidently been standing out on the area steps, his eyes level with the sidewalk, watching the square. The thick lips beneath the button nose wore their meaningless yet somehow endearing permanent grin. His hair, bushy at the sides and thin on top, glistened with rain.

"Holz, did you hear? We're going—" she began.

"I heard." His soft Wisconsin accent carried the sound of his smile. "How long'll you be?"

"We're going for a walk. Your guess is as good as mine."

"A walk. Ah yes. Kelland always has his walk." He came in, still smiling, and picked up a painting and held it up for her to see. It showed a sort of sinister giraffe reaching up to pick blossoms from a tree. The blossoms were eyes and they were all looking at the giraffe.

Holz smiled and waited for her opinion.

Gail was never sure what to say when he did this. "Tell me about it."

"You don't recognize yourself?"

He stretched his neck, reaching up with his mouth like the giraffe. Standing on tiptoe, with his thick body looking even thicker in the heavy-knit sweater, the muscles of his powerful throat corded, he looked extraordinary. Despite her mood, she burst out laughing.

He chuckled with soft resonance, like the starting up of a

Rolls-Royce engine. He watched her for a moment to see if she had read the meaning in his picture. Then touched her arm. "Have you made it with him yet?"

She pretended shock. "Holz, you have a dirty mind."

"Sure, I have. So have you. We all have. But I'm just waiting to hear from someone who has—made it, I mean. Just curiosity. He's a strange one."

"Listen who's talking." But her eyes grew ruminative.

"At least I sleep nights. In he comes at sparrow fart this morning—"

"At what?"

"'Oh, sorry,' he says. 'I didn't mean to wake you, Holz.' 'Wake me,' I says. 'You nearly got your brains blowed out!' 'Good,' he says. 'Nice to know you're on the ball. What's through there?' 'The scullery,' I says, 'where the maid used to wash the dishes.' Then he wants to know what's outside." Holz jerked a thumb toward the area steps. "'Just a john and a coal cellar,' I says. And bust my britches if he don't want to see inside 'em. At six in the morning—me in my skivvies!"

Gail stared out at the cellar door, just visible through the window. "Holz, you're making this up."

"Scout's honor." Holz crossed his heart. "I takes him out and he has a good look-see. 'Interesting, Holz,' he says, 'stuck out there under the sidewalk like that. Crazy, these old English places.' Then he asks me what time the newspapers are delivered, and when I tell him, off he goes back to bed."

Gail searched the grinning face, waiting to be let in on the joke. Holz met her gaze without a flicker. She said, "You must have been dreaming."

Holz shrugged and chuckled. Suddenly Kelland's voice cut in on them, calling to her from upstairs.

Holz winked. "There you go. If you don't believe me, ask him. Enjoy your walk." And he moved back outside to resume his watch.

Kelland strode with hunched intensity, hands buried deep in his topcoat pockets. Gail kept pace with difficulty—along past the Natural History Museum, then left and up into Hyde Park. Inside the gates he turned right. Oh Lord, she thought. He's going to drag me around the whole perimeter!

The path ran parallel to Rotten Row, where a few hardy

riders were making the same circuit, heads bowed against the rain. She needed a horse to keep up with him, she thought miserably. The rain had become a steady downpour. She shrank as deep into her trench coat as she could and gritted her teeth.

"Now, tell me about yourself," Kelland said, as though nothing whatever had happened between them.

So it was going to be one of *those* walks. "Well, the first thing I think you should know," she said coolly, "is I've got shorter legs than you."

"Sorry." He cut his pace. "That better?"

"*Much* better. Thank you."

He gave it a moment, then: "And the second thing about you?"

"The second thing"—she groped a shade uneasily—"is that you've read it all in my file."

"I want the part that's *not* in your file."

She forced a laugh. "Just like that? Hopes, fears, loves, hates, all neatly packaged?"

"Have a stab at it." He waited—in vain. "I thought women liked to talk about themselves."

"But I'm not a woman, am I," she said. "Not in the accepted sense. I've been trained to keep my mouth shut." She added, "And you can't get much more unfeminine than *that.*"

Kelland gave her a sidelong look. "Don't undersell yourself, Gail. You're a woman, all right. And a real treat for the eyes—and don't kid me you don't know it."

How about the hands? she thought dimly. But he seemed hell-bent on putting things right between them. After all, a little grope, a little rain, were a small price to pay for the company of one of the Agency's star turns. So why wasn't she responding? She knew why. The bonhomie was an act. He was trying to refurbish her ego for a purpose.

"All right, I'm a knockout. Fine. Yes. Now what?"

"No need to sound so defensive."

"I can't help it. I'm— There's something on your mind. Can we come to the point?" The rain was getting into her lashes, blurring her vision.

The smile on Kelland's face died. "Okay, so you read me. But I'll get there in my own time. Don't rush me."

"Well, can you hurry, please. I'm getting terribly wet. My hair—"

"So you *are* a woman." He twisted a smile. But the bonhomie was gone. His voice was hard. "There's a cold war on. A hot one in Korea. The Russian veto. Our boys getting brainwashed and we can't find out how. And on top of that, something big liable to blow in Moscow at any moment— thanks to our English friend in the straw hat. We don't know what shape it'll take, but at worst it could expose our sources of intelligence there. And that could tip the whole balance toward world communism—so don't talk to me about your hair, Miss Lessing! Just let me get around to what I'm about to say in my own way."

"I—" Gail's insides had gone suddenly cold.

Kelland continued severely, "You could have a part to play. I have to know if you're up to it. I'm checking you out. Files are full of crap. They don't tell you what a person's made of. That's—"

"Look," she interrupted. "I'm sorry—I had no idea—"

"Too long playing cleaning lady in a safe house? I understand." He smiled grimly. His tone modified a little. "All right. I'll tell you what I do know. Your father was Commander Jonas Lessing of Naval Intelligence. My guess is that's where your career ambitions began."

"His ambitions," Gail corrected.

"You didn't opt for this work?"

"I was sold into slavery." She smiled.

"Via Georgetown's Institute of Languages?"

She nodded. "If he'd had a son, I guess all I'd have rated would have been the local High."

"Well, it's just as well he didn't. Eight languages!"

"I love the work now that I'm in it. I can't imagine any other way of life."

"You did a distinguished refugee-interrogation stint for AI in Korea last year. Transfer to Chile. Not so good there. A personal involvement of some sort. Lost us a man."

Gail's step faltered. Explanations surged. But all she said was, "I . . . learned my lesson."

He studied her for a moment, then nodded. "Okay, so you're smart enough to be smart. But what I need to know, Miss Lessing, is—are you smart enough to be dumb?"

She looked at him blankly.

"Maybe I should say, to *play* dumb? Can you play a role—act—con somebody? Could you sell me a goldbrick?"

"You?" She laughed nervously. "I very much doubt it."

"How are you in bed?"

"What?"

"In *bed,* Miss Lessing. Could you sleep with . . . let's say, Holz—and make him feel like the greatest lover since Clark Gable?"

She thought about it. "I might," she ventured.

"It wouldn't bother you."

"It'd bother me, yes. But—"

"Morally?"

"Not morally. But if there was a good reason—yes, I—I'd do it."

"You hesitated."

"No, I didn't."

"You were wondering what it would do to you careerwise if you were to allow the Agency to use you on a physical as opposed to intellectual level."

"It did cross my mind."

"Just *cross* it?"

"Yes."

"You realized the fear was groundless?"

"Yes." She added, "Unless, of course, they started making a habit of it."

He was silent. She guessed he was evaluating her replies. He looked doubtful.

"Yes, I can play a role," she said suddenly, with more conviction. "I've been playing one ever since I joined. I saw the kind of person the Agency needed and became that person. Or kidded myself that I had. And if I can kid myself, I can kid other people, wouldn't you say?"

Kelland smiled. "At last," he said. "An honest statement. So tell me . . . what kind of person are you really?"

"More imaginative, less secure."

"Go on."

She knew she was getting into deep water. Somehow he had managed to get her to paint herself into a corner. She was within an ace of opening up to him completely, to a man she hardly knew, didn't know if she could trust. She could talk herself out of a career that way.

He read her hesitation and sighed. "It went, didn't it. There was a window, but it went." Unexpectedly he slipped his arm through hers and said quietly, "Okay, don't let it bother you. You pass. Frankly, I don't have much choice. You're our only female operator in London at this time, and what has to be done has to be done fast. Providing you're willing." He stopped, swinging her around to face him.

They had reached Hyde Park Corner. The statue of the Gladiator loomed above them. He looked even wetter than she felt, but at least he had a bronze shield to ward off the rain.

"This is about the Englishman with the straw hat, isn't it."

Kelland nodded. "I did some checking last night. Came up with two possibles, one probable."

"You want me to sleep with the probable. See if he has the scar . . ."

"You're pushing again. Let me do the talking. He's an MI6 agent, recently in Washington, where he had access to some of our classified information—God knows what the DCI was doing letting him, but maybe Records goofed and he saw more than was intended. He's cool, full of the usual 'old boy' sort of crap, but beneath it, sharp as a fox. You'll have to watch yourself. He was on a mission in the Mideast at the same time that photo was taken. His name is Michael Anderson."

"Can I ask something? Why are we handling this? Shouldn't we pass his name to British Intelligence, let them—?"

Kelland looked almost fierce. "I don't work that way. I deal in proven facts, not suspicions. When we're sure, we'll hand them their guy on a plate. Until that moment—show your hand in this business and you wind up with a fistful of nothing. The Intelligence world is a whispering gallery, Gail. Trust is a lump of meat on a wolf's nose. Security—forget it. I'm where I am because I'm my own man. I move first and report to the DDP after. That's why I'm still around, still dealing. Now, you with me?"

"You mean Washington doesn't even know . . . ?"

"If you're worried about clearance to use you, I've got it. But I gave them no"—his gaze fixed beyond her—"details." His voice trailed off.

He took her arm casually and started walking.

"Jeezus," he muttered to himself. "How dumb can you get."

"What is it?" She started to look around, but his fingers bit into her arm.

"No, don't look. Just keep walking. Nice and casual." After a moment: "Our moustached buddy—he's back with us."

She almost stopped in astonishment. "But . . . how?"

"Someone has my name in his file. Under 'Habits' it must say, 'Morning walk.' Brackets: 'Nearest park.'"

He was steering her toward the curb. He signaled a cab. It was full. So was the next. She ventured a cautious look around.

The man was about thirty yards from them, face averted, sauntering. Beyond him, stopped because they had stopped, was the black Mercedes. She guessed it had been crawling along behind them for some little time.

A cab pulled in to a halt alongside them. Kelland pushed her in and plumped in beside her. When they were moving, he slid the driver's window aside and stuck his head through.

"Buddy, listen. You've seen it done in the movies, now let's see if you can do it. See that Mercedes back there?"

The cabby took a look. He grinned around incredulously. "You want me to lose him?"

"There's a couple of extra pounds in it if you can. I'm warning you, though—he's good. You're going to have to stand this thing on its ear. Think you can do it?"

The cabby uttered a happy chuckle. "Watch me! Hang on!"

So saying, he swung clean across five lanes of traffic, and out through the Dorchester exit, before the Mercedes had even got under way.

7

"ARE YOU paying attention?" Kelland barked in her ear.

"Yes! Uh—what did you say?" She was hanging on to the strap, buffeted from side to side as the cab swung from one Mayfair side street into another—down tiny lanes she had never dreamed existed.

"I said Anderson rents an apartment in a block called the Ivory Tower."

"I know it."

"Great. Because you've got a date there this afternoon." He added, "Not to sleep with him necessarily. How you play it is entirely up to you. Maybe you can get what we want without that. Jeezus!" The cab was turning right around in its tracks in the midst of heavy traffic. He glanced out of the back.

The Mercedes was trying to duplicate the move but couldn't begin to make it. They just had time to see it try to use the pavement—and fail—a snarl start to build up around it, before their cabby, with a great guffaw of mirth, swung away down a side street no wider than his fenders.

Kelland dragged his mind back with difficulty. "In the building there's a pool and squash courts. Anderson plays squash there every afternoon between four and five. A slave

55

to habit, like me. Nearly always with the same partner—another MI6 man, name of Tim Grierson. Now, Grierson—"

"Two quid you owe me, guv!" the cabby called back through the window. "Now where do you want me to go?"

"Do a few more tricks, just to cinch it, then drop us at the Natural History Museum," Kelland told him. "Nice work!" He turned back to Gail. "Grierson doesn't live at the Tower. He's married, has a house up by Regent's Park. So now what I've fixed is this . . ."

Gail tied the laces of her sneakers and stood up. She tucked her Airtex shirt into the top of her white shorts, pulling it down taut before she buttoned the waistband. She inflated her lungs with the rubbery air they seemed to mint specially for locker rooms and looked at herself sideways in one of the mirrors, running her hands down her flat tummy to her crotch as she listened absently to the echoing thwacks coming from the nearby squash court. Michael Anderson was in there, she had already ascertained, warming up, waiting for his partner to arrive. Well, he had a surprise coming.

A nice surprise, she hoped, shaking loose her hair. She felt curiously light-headed. Maybe it was in anticipation of a possible sexual interlude. Maybe it was just the undressed feeling one always got wearing sports gear. The problem was, it was a long time since she had played squash. Anderson would think it a bit strange if it turned out she couldn't even hit the ball.

A final touch of lipstick, a thrust of her face toward the mirror as she rubbed her lips together, inspected her smile. None on her teeth. She picked up her racket.

Anderson was speeding around the court, punishing the ball, when she opened the door behind him.

"Oh, I'm sorry," she said. "I—I thought it might be my partner in here."

Anderson looked around. He did a very slight "take," which was flattering. He was taller than she had deduced from the photo, with a good head of dark hair streaked slightly with gray, disheveled now. Perspiration glistened on the long, rather intellectual face with its dark, well-defined, sensitive mouth and alert eyes.

"It's all right, I'm only knocking up. Waiting for my

partner too, actually." He spoke in a lazy public-school drawl, but his eyes snapped her up in a flash.

Gail made to back out again, feigning exasperation. "I can't *think* what's happened to her! Getting anyone to take exercise in this city is like coaxing blood from a stone, don't you find? Perhaps you don't—maybe you have a sporting circle of friends. But for a stranger . . . believe me! I mean, this place is empty. In the States they'd be lining up. But I'm sorry—I'm interrupting your game . . ."

"No no," Anderson said. "You're from the States? Where-abouts?"

"Boston. But I mustn't keep you. I'll go bang a ball around next door till she comes." She went out, almost closed the door, then poked her head back in. "Do you have the right time by any chance?"

"Uh—four-thirty-one. Look—hold on." He sauntered across to her, bouncing the ball on his racket. "My chap looks as if he isn't going to show now. If you feel like a game . . ."

Gail grimaced. "That's very kind, but . . ."

"Until your friend turns up."

"It'd be a bore for you. I'm not very good. I've only been playing a few months."

"No matter. Seems silly us knocking up in two different courts."

Gail appeared to hesitate. "Well . . . If you promise not to get mad at me." She came in and shut the door. "Promise, now."

He smiled. "My name's Michael Anderson."

"Gail Davenport."

He shook her hand solemnly. "Start with a warm-up?" He hit the ball gently against the back wall.

Somehow she managed to hit it back. And there it was— Phase One accomplished, no sweat, no dropping of handkerchiefs, no collisions trying to grab the same taxi.

Anderson stoked up the pace gradually, testing her out, but careful not to overtax her. She missed completely a couple of times, but he neither laughed nor showed impatience. That adds up to a gentleman, she thought. Whatever else he was.

He interspersed the odd question between flurries. Had she been over here long? Was she a tenant in the building? She told him she was a buyer for Logan-Schrieber Fashions, here on business. She was staying with her aunt in Bayswater.

Did she "like Ike"? Would she be home in time for his inauguration on the twentieth? He touched on the Churchill-Truman meeting—all very casual, not trying to impress, as though American politics were as much a part of his thinking as British.

She was careful not to sound too informed. He could be trying to sound her out. She remembered Kelland's words: "sharp as a fox."

He had captured the ball. "Shall we play a game now?"

She made a face. "If you can bear it."

"I think you're very good for only a few months," he said without being patronizing. "If you would relax a little more. You seem . . . a bit tense."

She eyed him quickly, but it seemed just a throwaway remark. So would you be, she thought. Or perhaps you wouldn't. In your straw hat. Selling secrets to the Russians between dips. If you're the one, she conceded. Innocent until proven otherwise.

They played three games—three thwacking, rubber-squeaking, swiping, echoing games—by which time she was little more than a heap of wet clothing, and he was only mildly out of breath.

"Had enough?"

She nodded, pink-faced.

He checked his watch with a slight frown. "I have to go now anyway."

They left the court together. She had sensed his growing preoccupation during the last game. He was in a hurry to get away. That made what she had to do more difficult. She had to get him to date her—and soon, like tonight.

"Phew, that was fun. If I wasn't heading back home on Thursday I'd stick my neck out and ask you for another lesson." She laughed.

"What? Yes. Pity." There was no interest in his voice. He was looking in the direction of the elevator. Presumably he would shower in his apartment. "Well, have a safe flight." He extended his hand.

She wiped her own on her shirt before taking his. "Sticky! Well, I think a shower and then a nice long drink . . ."

"Good idea." He was backing away, the racket balanced on his shoulder.

Hell, she thought, I've lost him. On a brilliant impulse she added, "If I can find a towel, that is. Like an idiot I forgot to bring one."

He stopped out of politeness. "I'm afraid I didn't bring one down or . . ."

"Do they supply them here?"

"No."

"Oh Lord." She feigned dismay. "I *can't* change into my other clothes like this. I have to go on to a meeting!"

Anderson looked nonplussed. He shrugged and spread his hands apologetically and turned away.

She stood there defeated, watching the fish slide slowly from her net. He walked along to the elevator and pressed the button. As he waited he glanced back. She just stood there helplessly, a pathetic, sticky figure.

Then her heart leaped. He was coming back.

"Look," he said in his drawly way. "If you're really stuck, you could use my shower. Or at least borrow one of my towels and bring it down here."

Gail made her eyes look like saucers. "Oh, no. *Could* I?"

Anderson's apartment was very correct. Nice antiques, battle prints on the walls, miniature cannon on the big Regency desk. Like a stage set for a man-about-town movie.

"You go first," he said. "I have a call to make. Bedroom's through there, bathroom attached. You'll find a robe in the cupboard." He took up the mock-old-fashioned telephone and started to dial.

Gail went through and half closed the door. Now, how should she play it? Overtly sexy? Come out wearing just the robe? Give him a glimpse of her body? No, she decided. Shower first. Let him make the moves. Maybe he would come in to her. A warm flush started between her thighs. He was attractive. Playing Mata Hari wasn't so hard when the other party was desirable. Maybe he would strip down and they would shower together.

As she undressed she glanced around the room. Her attention slowly centered on the bed. It was large. A double. Something bothered her about it. The sheets. They were pink. She glanced at the dressing table. Bottles. Not at all like the other room. Feminine, almost.

Suddenly it came home to her. His lack of any kind of a play for her. He was queer! My God, that threw a real wrench into the operation. Why hadn't Kelland known?

She could hear him talking on the telephone. She moved to the door and put her ear to it.

"Thank God," she heard him say in relief. "I thought for a moment something had—" He broke off and listened for a moment. "Not me, laddie. You must've—" He broke off again. "Called it off?" Explosive: "My dear Tim, I've been waiting down there for half the bloody—" He listened again. Quickly, seriously: "Well, the message certainly didn't come from me. Slightly *American?*" Gail could almost hear his suspicions forming. When he spoke again it was so softly she could hardly hear him. "I think you better get along here. Now." A short silence. "I'll explain when you get here. Try and locate Tariq. Bring him with you."

Gail scooted away from the door. Damn Kelland! Of all the crazy, transparent . . .! Now what should she do? Put on her clothes and beat it? Or shower quickly and leave as naturally as she was able?

She opened the cupboard and snatched down the robe. Shower! She sped into the bathroom and turned on the taps. How could Kelland have been so lax as to have employed a tactic that could so easily be checked up on? She soaped herself rapidly, rinsed her body and jumped out, grabbing a towel.

"Almost through," she called out, as evenly as possible.

"Don't rush," Anderson's voice came back, entirely calm. "I had an appointment but I've decided to give it a miss. So no hurry. Take your time."

She hurried into the bedroom and started to dress. "Lovely place you have here."

"Thank you." Then after a moment, very casual: "Pity about your friend. I wonder what happened to her."

"So do I!" Panties . . . garter belt . . . Sharp as a *fox*. Nylons . . . bra . . .

In three minutes she was dressed. She came out into the sitting room. Anderson was standing by the bookcase, still in his sports clothes, thumbing through a volume.

"That was lovely. I'm so grateful."

"Not at all. I've prepared you that long drink." He pointed to a tall glass of something lemony standing on the open flap of the drinks cabinet.

"Oh. I—uh—really must hurry." She moved to the door and grasped the handle.

"You said a shower, then a drink." The dark eyes surveyed her calmly.

"Yes, well, I really haven't time now. The meeting, you know. You've been most awfully kind."

She turned the handle. The door was locked.

And he had removed the key.

She turned and stared at him, trying to keep the panic from her eyes.

Anderson closed the book unhurriedly and put it back on the shelf.

"I won't keep you long," he said. "There's just something I have to check up on before I let you go. I do apologize."

8

"BRING HER into the bedroom," Anderson said. "There's just one outside wall. The rest are contained in the flat. Bring the heavy chair."

He moved through ahead of them and shut the windows, drew the curtains. Grierson steered her in. Tariq brought the chair. They guided her bound wrists over the back of the chair and sat her down on it.

Gail was so terrified she thought she would wet her pants. The instant the one called Tariq had walked in the door, she knew she was done for. He was the man with the moustache. He identified her immediately.

Grierson closed the bedroom door and they gathered around her in the near darkness.

"No one will hear you scream," Anderson told her. "But just to be safe . . ." He was stripping the protective film off a big adhesive plaster. "Why did Kelland send you? It's an academic question. I'm sure he wouldn't mind you answering."

Gail shut her eyes. This just couldn't be happening. It was a horrible, impossible dream.

"Was it to identify me with the photograph? See, I know

about the photograph." One lump or two? There was no excitement or threat in his voice at all. He waited patiently.

"We'd rather you talked of your own accord," Tim Grierson put in. And he sounded concerned. He wore a pinstripe suit with an Old Etonian tie, and his face, despite the neatly trimmed beard, looked almost boyish. He was the third man in the photograph, Gail had realized. Why hadn't Kelland *known* that? God, what a mess he'd made of it all. He'd planned it in too damned much of a hurry.

"No matter," Anderson murmured. "What we really want is the photo back, as you can imagine. And the report in Russian that came with it. So, of course, we want from you the whereabouts of the house. We have the keys—from your handbag." He jingled them. "Now we want the address that goes with them." He added, "And we *are* in a hurry."

Again he waited. If she refused to talk, what would they do? Surely these people were far too civilized to . . .?

"Who has a cigarette?"

Tariq produced a pack of Turkish gold-tipped. Anderson lit one up with a grimace, leaning back to avoid the smoke.

"Tim . . ."

Grierson looked uneasy. He bent forward and started to unbutton Gail's shirt, but his hands were shaking so much that he ended by ripping it open. He tucked it well back under her armpits and pulled up her bra to free her breasts.

Oh God no. Let this be a dream. *Please* let it be a dream . . .

Grierson's face was close to hers. He said softly, "Hell, they're beautiful." He touched her breasts, cupping his hand under them fleetingly, thumbing her nipples. His hands were ice-cold.

The Turk made an animal sound and started forward, but Anderson interposed himself firmly.

"Stop it. That'll do. Now, Gail, the address. Just a few little words and you'll save yourself a lot of pain."

I'll never stand it, she thought. I know I won't. She really was wetting her pants now. She felt the urine, warm, between her thighs and buttocks. But this was her first real test of courage in the job she thought she could do as well as a man. She shook her head and prayed.

Anderson sighed. "When you're ready to talk, nod." In a sudden violent movement he snapped the plaster over her mouth. The cigarette glowed between his lips in the dimness. He passed it quickly to Grierson, who equally quickly pressed the glowing end to the tip of her left nipple.

The agony jolted through her whole body like an electric shock, zinging up through her nerve fibers to, somehow, her ears. Shark jaws of light clamped on her brain.

Grierson drew hard on the cigarette and applied it again— to the side of a nipple this time.

She screamed. It sounded no more than a buzz. The tears sprang from her eyes. She writhed and twisted. Grierson was drawing on the cigarette again. Again the agony, again, again—each time in a fresh place—the jaws of light champing in her brain. The stench of singeing flesh filling the room. A sudden movement from Anderson. He was reaching for the cigarette, breathing heavily. "Let me!" He was aroused. Getting an erection. She felt his fingers claw her breasts. His face came close, the cigarette in his mouth. Another searing pain, which went on and on and on as he drew again and again on the cigarette, keeping it in his mouth, moving it from place to place, the smoke choking him. She screamed and screamed against the gag, nodding her head frantically, jerking it about in a frenzy—she'd tell them anything, anything! But Anderson wouldn't stop. His fingernails were clawing into her other breast with a savagery that had Grierson suddenly grabbing at him, dragging at him.

"She's had enough, Mike. She's had enough!"

The car ride was just a haze of buildings and traffic and trees. Her breasts burned and throbbed against her bra. Every vibration of the suspension brought fresh pain. Anderson and Grierson sat close on either side of her in silence. The Turk was driving. At one point—it may have been in the apartment, she didn't know—they had guns in their hands, loading them, cocking them. All she knew was, she had broken, betrayed Kelland, the Agency, herself. Her future was in shreds. She wanted to die.

Suddenly they were no longer moving. She felt Anderson and Grierson vacate their seats, the car rock as they got out. Their faces appeared outside the window momentarily, and beyond them she recognized the plane tree with the boxer's limbs.

"Watch her," Anderson said to the Turk. "If she tries to give the alarm, kill her."

Their figures moved away from the car. Through tears of shame and chagrin she saw them slip toward the house. One of them shrank down the area steps. The other mounted to the porch. Then, like shadows, they were gone.

She sat there without moving, trying not to breathe, it hurt her so. The trees dripped on the car. The Turk lit a cigarette, his dark eyes on her through the mirror. The distant traffic whispered like the ghost sea that lives in cowrie shells. Time passed. There was a movement beside the car and a gun with a long silencer slid around the doorframe into the Turk's ear and a soft Wisconsin voice said, "Out."

The Turk moved out of the car like a man on a hydraulic lift. "Stay there, girlie." The heavy elfin face grinned in at her, but there was a look in the eyes that she had never seen before—an emptiness, the bleakness of crags where only the wind lives.

Then the two of them were moving away. They vanished down the area steps of the house.

More time passed. Suddenly Holz was back. He opened the door and looked at her. Just for a moment. Then he was reaching in, lifting her, carrying her in his arms with short steps—across the road and down into the house.

"You did well, baby," he was muttering. "I can tell you did—or you'd be up and walking. Hung on in there, didn't you. There's my girl. Holzie'll take care of you."

He laid her gently on his bed, then went away, and she heard him closing and bolting all the doors. When he came back, he said, "Now, what did they do to you?"

Gail just couldn't make sense of it. "What happened to them? Where did they go?"

"Go?" Holz smiled. "In there." He pointed to the outside cellar. "There'll be a couple of workmen around from the embassy in the morning to brick it up. Remove the door-frame, dragontooth the sides, match up the brickwork—no one'll know it was ever there."

Gail stared up at him. "You killed them?"

"What else?" He patted her head proudly. "You brought

them in just fine. Like birds onto a gun. Your tits, was it? I'll get some cold water. It'll stop the scars."

He went through to the sink and filled a bowl. She watched him tie on, bizarrely, a flowered apron.

"I don't understand . . ."

Holz came back with the bowl and set it down beside the bed. "It was the only way he could get all three of 'em in one swoop."

"Who? Kelland?"

"Mr. Wiz."

"He *knew* Anderson was our man?"

Holz nodded. "And the other one. His sidekick."

"You mean . . .!" Gail sat up with a jerk. Her mouth stretched open, her eyes squeezed shut. She uttered a sound far back in her throat. She had to wait for a long moment for the pain to go away. "You mean Kelland set me up?"

Holz nodded. "Dangled you. I couldn't'a done it. But then, who am I?"

Kelland had *known* she would break. "Bastard! *Bastard!*" she screamed. "Where is he?"

Holz made like an airplane with his hand. "Gone." He reached for the evening paper, dumped it in front of her. "The thing Anderson triggered—the thing in Moscow—it just blew up. Second page, third graph."

She found the item. It was short. The headline read: "Nine Moscow Doctors Arrested." The report said that they had been accused of murdering two Soviet leaders and plotting to kill others. There were no details.

She frowned up at Holz. "What does it mean?"

"Search me, sweetheart. All he said was, 'It's begun, Holz,' and booked on the first plane to Berlin."

Berlin? Gail suddenly felt totally exhausted. She closed her eyes and lay back, her brain spinning. She stiffened briefly as she felt Holz's hands open up her shirt.

"Don't be shy, baby," he murmured. "Old Holz has seen more tits than you've had hot dinners."

He raised her bra gently. She heard his soft intake of breath.

9

LIKE A great white army marching out to sea, watchtowers and ramparts bristling, the city of Cádiz gleamed in the winter sun. Fine shipping lay at anchor in the pincered haven of the outer bay. Gulls wheeled to vanish against the brightness of the whitewashed buildings. Far away, at the other end of the isthmus, the mainland spanned the horizon in misty hues—a B echelon, outstripped by the glorious advance.

As the bells of noon sang out across the Atlantic, a smart tender put out from shore and moved like a finger trailed in gelatin toward the handsome yacht anchored in the very center of the bay. The approaching boat flew a naval pennant; its crewmen were immaculate. Two civilians sat in the stern, one tall, one short. The taller, as though disdaining the environment, wore a blue serge topcoat and black homburg hat. The shorter sported a reefer with brass buttons and a rather jaunty naval cap. If he had been visiting a mountain resort he would have been wearing a Tyrolean hat with a ptarmigan feather. He had a thing about hats. Their names were Señor Don Eduardo Rafael Ruiz-Calderón and Señor Don Serafín Francisco Blas y Gallarza—the Minister for Foreign Affairs and the Minister of the Interior, respectively.

Reaching the yacht, they were helped aboard, to be

greeted by the captain. After a polite exchange they were led aft to the small sun deck. The boat was anchored in such a way that it would not swing, and a canvas screen had been erected on the Atlantic side of the sun deck to provide shelter from the light westerly breeze. The open side of the deck faced squarely onto the city. Standing at an easel was a portly man in his fifties. He wore a yachting cap and a white jersey streaked with pigment. He was painting the city's portrait.

"Gentlemen." He nodded briefly past the canvas to the visitors, who doffed their hats. He painted two more strokes, then laid down his palette and shook hands with each of them. "You've had a long trip. You must be weary." He signaled to two stewards lurking in the shadows.

Chairs were hustled forward. The tall one, Ruiz, ordered a dry sherry. The short one, Gallarza, said he would like a large beer. They both moved to inspect the canvas.

It was not a good painting, but the superb subject matter defied the onslaughts of the artist as it had, in its history, defied those of the Barbary Corsairs, the fleets of Buckingham, Blake, Rook and the Duke of Ormonde.

"Mm," Ruiz said, cocking his head critically.

"One of your best, Caudillo," cried Gallarza.

The Caudillo looked up at a burly security man leaning unobtrusively against the rail of the deck above. He dismissed him from view with a gesture. Now they were alone.

"I know why you've come," he said quietly. "When you wouldn't give your reasons over the telephone for wanting to see me, I knew immediately. And I may as well tell you now, my mind is made up. But by all means let me hear your views. Academic though they may be."

"May we talk right away, Caudillo?" Ruiz asked, with a glance at his watch. "I have to catch an early train back. I have an—"

"You'll stay for lunch, surely?"

"Lunch, yes. But—"

"Right. Let's get it over. While the women and children are occupied. Backgammon seems to be the latest craze." He lidded his rather bulbous eyes—a gesture of amusement. "Sit down, gentlemen. You don't mind if I daub a little? The blueness will soon be gone from the shadows."

"Of course," Ruiz conceded.

"We mustn't deprive the Prado of a masterpiece." Gallarza chuckled.

The drinks arrived and were served. The stewards departed. The Caudillo mixed a little copal oil with a touch of turpentine and made a rather clumsy wetness of color on his palette.

"Speak, gentlemen."

Ruiz and Gallarza looked at each other quickly to see who should begin. But the Caudillo forestalled them both.

"So that we don't waste each other's time, I think I should first make two points quite clear. It was the judiciary who sentenced Joaquín Cabeza to death in '39—or was it '38? Anyway, his execution is a legal matter—"

"But clemency is the head of state's prerogative."

"Ruiz, let me finish." The Caudillo eyed him sternly. "It's perfectly true that it's my prerogative. And that's my second point. I have no intention of exercising it."

Once bitten, Ruiz remained silent. He sipped his sherry and waited. Gallarza fidgeted, his own rationale, developed carefully during the journey, held in abeyance.

"My reasons for not doing so," the Caudillo went on, "are these. Forget that the man was a bandit, a firebrand, that he helped deny us Madrid for two years, that he destroyed three of my finest brigades at Teruel . . ."

Ruiz patted his lean thighs and nodded. "I know what you're going to say."

"The proclamation—yes. Remember only that proclamation he put out. Posted on every damn street corner of every town we captured. Offering a reward of two million pesetas for my head. My *head*, gentlemen! As though we were in the Middle Ages! I think he imagined it stuck on a pike! It was a personal affront—nothing to do with the war—an incitement to barbarism—and it is for that gross act that I propose not to interfere with his execution now."

There was a brief silence. He returned to his canvas, scowling.

Ruiz said quietly, "Now you want *his* head."

"Yes, I do!" The Caudillo daubed on a savage blob of color, regretted it, spread it with his thumb. After a moment he said in a more contained voice, "All right, gentlemen, now let's hear your objections."

Again Ruiz and Gallarza looked at each other to see who would speak. Gallarza gave way with a gesture.

"Our first objection is the timing," Ruiz began.

"Exactly. The timing." Gallarza nodded earnestly.

The Caudillo sighed. "Go on. But if you're going to wave European opinion in my face, you need not proceed. Do you think I haven't weighed all that up? Britain—you can forget her for a start. There's no appeasing her after Nazism—you know it, I know it. A black shirt will be like a red rag to her for decades. I could install Cabeza on the *throne,* it would make no difference to their prejudice. As for the rest of Europe—I've grown old in the face of their hostility, gentlemen. I'm still here, growing stronger. While they grow weaker."

"Exactly, Caudillo," Ruiz said. "We're growing stronger. We're on the edge of a new era. A new President in the United States . . ."

"Ah, here we go," the Caudillo murmured. "I thought this would be your argument."

"We are at this moment negotiating for Marshall Plan aid. The Americans are eager to lease bases on our soil—"

"Tell me one thing," the Caudillo cut in. "How a piece of non-news concerning a man they've long ago forgotten—and who will stay forgotten, the press having the strictest instructions—can conceivably affect the strategic and economic decisions of the White House."

Ruiz frowned and smiled. "It's hard to explain. But such news does get out—already I've heard rumors. And the Americans are a people who love to champion the underdog."

"And I'm sure"—Gallarza took up the baton—"that after a gap of fourteen years between, as it were, the crime and the execution, that's just how they'll see El Duro."

"As just an underprivileged peasant?" The Caudillo's voice was heavy with disbelief.

"Yes, Caudillo. Caught up in the ruthless wheels of state."

"And you are that state," Ruiz said. *"You.* His death will reflect on you personally. You're a Goliath, and he a David. And you know where the sympathies lie in that story." He paused to gauge the effect of his words.

The Caudillo eyed him past his canvas. He still looked a shade disbelieving, but he said quietly, "Go on."

"All I'm asking is, Is your revenge on this peasant worth the risk of souring our relations with the new President? Truman never liked us. Eisenhower, handled right, could become our friend. Even our savior." His eyes challenged the Caudillo directly as he said with emphasis, "I think it would be a good idea to convince him at the outset that both our countries are living in the same century."

The Caudillo stiffened. His eyes snapped anger. "Ruiz, that is impertinent."

"I'm sorry. But as you know, I'm deeply committed—"

"You're suggesting that my decision not to interfere with the course of the law is brutal and primitive?"

"I'm suggesting it might be *interpreted* as that."

"Look—" The Caudillo shoved aside his palette and faced them. "The man has returned to spread his old poison among the workers."

"Do we know that?" Gallarza popped his eyes back and forth between them.

Ruiz shook his head. "We have no evidence at all to that effect."

The Caudillo exploded his hands in the air. "Do you really believe the story that he came sneaking back here just to find his mother? Do you?" He laughed mirthlessly.

"I believe"—Ruiz picked his words carefully; it was no light matter to cross swords with the head of state—"that it is sufficiently unlikely as possibly to be true."

"He did suffer under the Russians," Gallarza said. "He may hold quite different views now. Anyway—"

"And if that's the case, Caudillo," Ruiz continued his line, "we should *use* rather than *abuse* him. That is the point I have come here to make."

"And I," Gallarza endorsed excitedly. "The man was a hero—"

"He was a murdering Moscow-paid revolutionary!" snapped the Caudillo.

"To the Republicans, I mean," the small man added quickly. "He still has a following among the Civil War generation."

"That is my fear, Gallarza!"

"It could be to your *advantage,* Caudillo," Ruiz pointed out quickly. "If he has changed—and can be seen to have changed . . . Do you follow me? It would be an object lesson to every leftist in Spain!"

The Caudillo eyed him in silence. He could have been digesting his words. He could have been debating his dismissal.

Ruiz made one last effort to home his point. "You are a devout man, Caudillo."

"I am indeed, Ruiz."

"Then you will know the Scriptures better than I. Where it says, roughly, that it's better for one sinner to be brought to repentance than for ninety and nine just men to enter the Kingdom of Heaven?"

"I remember it," the Caudillo replied. "It also says, if you remember: 'Vengeance is mine, saith the Lord.'"

"The *Lord,* yes," Ruiz replied. "Not the Caudillo. Or are you aspiring, sir, to deification, too?"

The Caudillo froze. Gallarza winced. Ruiz realized that this time he had gone too far. The "too" implied criticism of the absolute scope of the head of state's powers.

At this moment a small smocked projectile darted out from the saloon and fastened itself to the Caudillo's legs amid floods of tears.

"María hit me—María hit me!" it wailed. The Caudillo stooped, pried it loose and lifted it in the crook of his arm—and in his grandfatherly murmurings the reply he would have made to Ruiz was lost to posterity. Which was probably in itself an act of the Lord.

All he said later, when the weeping had abated, was, "I will bear your . . . heartfelt points of view in mind, gentlemen."

The date of this meeting, as entered in the ship's log, was January 15, 1953.

10

THE BOY was trotting along a dusty track, the can in his hand growing heavier with every step. It banged against his knee, and some of the hot soup spilled down onto his bare foot. As he stopped to scrape it off with his other heel, he heard the trucks.

They were coming along the plain behind him, growing out of the dawn dimness like metal dragons. He had to tumble into the ditch to escape their blind onslaught, holding the can away from him so it wouldn't spill, choking in their dust—one, two, three, four of them. And he saw with horror that they were filled with soldiers!

As they drew away toward the mine, he found himself scrambling up and running, no longer along the road but across the fields, his legs stumbling, the upper half of him gliding, to save what was left in the can. He had to reach his father and warn him.

But no matter how hard he ran, he could see the trucks would be there ahead of him. And when he came in sight of the buildings, they were stopped near the gate and the soldiers had spread out to face the picket line, their rifles at the ready.

His father stood among the strike leaders. He had on his

helmet and carried a pick in one hand and a stick of dynamite in the other. His eyes were tired—he had lived and slept on the line for three weeks—but the hatred that burned in them was undiminished. The pit conditions were appalling; men died at the coal face almost every day; the pay was close to starvation level. Yet the owner had refused even to negotiate. Now he had called in the monarchist soldiers to break the strike. An officer shouted an order. The soldiers charged the breeches of their rifles.

"No!" the boy cried and rushed forward.

His father saw him. "Keep away, son!" he shouted, and lit the dynamite fuse. Before everyone's astonished gaze, he walked toward where the mine owner sat in his Hispano-Suiza, with the charge held, hissing, above his head, calling to him to tell the soldiers to withdraw, then to meet the strike committee and negotiate, or he would blow him clean to pieces!

The owner, white-faced, shouted to the officer to pull back his men. But the officer only drew his pistol and aimed it at the boy's father. "Throw away the dynamite," he ordered. His father ignored him. The officer fired. The miner staggered and fell. The boy gave a howling cry. But his father was hoisting himself up again. He kept going forward, the dynamite still hissing in his hand. The officer shot him again . . . again. The line of soldiers started scattering then, the officer with them, as, crawling, dragging himself, his father reached the car. The owner had hastily locked the doors and windows and now crouched, petrified, in the back. The boy's father held the dynamite up in his hand against the window—until it exploded. The car, the owner, and his father were blasted to destruction.

The boy ran forward, his mouth gaping. All around him was pandemonium—the miners bellowing and rushing at the soldiers with their picks, the soldiers firing into them blindly as they fell back. He reached his father's body and threw himself down, cradling him in his arms.

Blood from the headless torso pumped all over him. Viscera oozed from the clothes. He clung to him fiercely, rocking him, rocking him.

Suddenly the army bugler began to blow a call—a long,

eerie call full of exhortation. And now around him the bodies of the dead began to rise. His father was struggling to rise, too, twisting horribly in his arms. He held on to him tightly, but he was only a child and his father was strong. As he struggled he began to vanish. All the dead were vanishing. The boy fought to hold on to his father, but after a moment there was nothing in his arms but bloody viscera. Then that, too, vanished and he was alone. "Come back!"

Cabeza struggled up with a cry, "Father, come back!" His voice echoed in the close emptiness. He stared around wildly, the sweat stinging his eyes as he tried to penetrate the darkness. His shirt clung, saturated, to his body. It stank of chemicals from the laundry. The bugle call somehow continued, exhorting the dead to rise. Harsh voices were shouting, *"Arriba! Arriba!"*

Madre! Cabeza swung his legs off the bunk and gripped his face. Had it been real? Where was he? The chill morning air struck through the wetness of the shirt, bringing him fully awake. And he knew where he was. *"Arriba! Arriba!"* "On your feet!" The commands were accompanied now by a metallic clanging.

He remained sitting on the bunk dully for several moments. It had been a long time since he had dreamed of his father's death. Presently he got up and groped for the end wall. He felt for the worn fingerholds between the stones. Now the toeholds. Reaching above him he could just grasp one of the bars. He pulled himself up to the tiny cell window and peered out.

Dawn was a saffron rent in the dark clouds beyond the quadrangle. Lights shone in the low buildings that formed the 200-meter square. Figures, galvanized, moved across their windows. The splashing sounds of water pouring into washbowls and buckets echoed from block to block—to all but his own. The solitaries were the last to be rousted.

But only by minutes. His light stabbed on blindingly. At the same instant a score of barred rectangles were projected onto the grit of the parade ground outside. He let himself hang by one hand and dropped unhurriedly to the stone floor. He moved to the stinking hole in the corner and undid the metal buttons in the gray army trousers and urinated.

He had two minutes now before they reached his cell. He moved back to the bunk, sat down and slowly put on his boots.

Cabeza was wise in prison routine. The secret was to space out your movements to match the dragging tempo. It saved energy and it filled out the time. He smoothed the socks carefully so there were no wrinkles under the feet. The boots were laceless. The first slid on easily. Precisely as he homed his foot in the second, the main door bolts in the central corridor cannoned back. *"Arriba!"* roared the sergeant's voice. Still forty-five more seconds . . .

He folded back the straw palliasse twice and flattened it. He folded the threadbare blanket neatly and laid it on top.

Precisely as he straightened, the cell-door lock snapped back. "Attention!" bawled the sergeant. Cabeza faced around, scowling but relaxed, arms akimbo.

The officer stepped in first. It was the one with the pockmarked face this morning. Neither he nor the sergeant who followed with his clipboard would meet Cabeza's eye. They inspected the cell, the sergeant ticked his name on the list, and Cabeza read their uneasiness in his presence. Falangist puppy dogs posturing before the ex-commander of a brigade. He was tempted to bang their heads together. Instead, he growled, "You know my complaint."

"Silence!" snarled the sergeant.

"I'm being held incommunicado. It's against the law. It's my right as a Spanish citizen to see a lawyer."

"I said 'Silence'!"

"You, Lieutenant—it's your duty to pass that on to the commandant, hear? Tell him El Duro wants—he *demands*—an interview."

"Two days' bread and water," the officer murmured as he went out. The sergeant wrote it down as he followed him. The door slammed shut.

Cabeza ground his teeth. He had been here five days. Each day he had voiced the complaint. Each day it had won him nothing but reduced rations. Well, to hell with the rations. He knew that if he didn't attract attention to himself in every way he could, the food would be useless to him anyway—he'd be dead.

It was obvious why they were keeping him under wraps,

why they'd moved him so fast and so secretly out of Granada. To be rushed for three hours in a closed van at night, hustled through the corridors here with a blanket over his head and thrown straight into solitary could mean only one thing. He was meant to vanish without a trace. Why a military prison? Because it was its own place of execution. A wall, a firing squad. With a bag over his head, the men wouldn't even know whom they'd shot.

There was a clatter outside. The cell door was opened by a guard, and old Jorge, the trusty, ducked in. As Cabeza bent forward to take from him the bucket containing a rag, scrubbing brush and bar of disinfectant soap, the old soldier murmured, "Underneath."

"Look lively!" the guard growled. Jorge scooted out. The door slammed shut again. The bolts were homed.

Cabeza waited until the clattering distribution of cleaning materials had moved on along the corridor. Then he shifted out of sight of the peephole and lifted the bucket. Tacked underneath by means of chewing gum were several sheets of writing paper, a pencil and, for good measure, four cigarettes and as many matches.

Cabeza hid them in the palliasse. He filled the bucket at the wall tap and got down on his knees and, with measured movements, began to scrub out his cell. He didn't have to. If he refused to lift a finger, there was nothing they could do about it. Kick him around maybe. In which case he'd kick them back. He had nothing to lose. But the work passed the time—one hour—until "breakfast." It gave him time to think what he would write on the paper and whom he would address it to.

He still must have many friends in the land. The problems were: Which to select? And where were they to be contacted now? The left-wing newspapers were an obvious first choice. They were all shut down now, but there was probably an underground sheet or two still circulating in Madrid. He decided he would have to return a note with the bucket, asking Jorge to tap some of his fellow prisoners for the necessary information. The main factor was time. Had he enough of it left to force these plans to fruition?

He managed to scrawl a short note in time for Jorge to take away with the bucket. "Breakfast" was shoved through under his door. He sat on his bunk and forced himself to eat the quarterloaf slowly, until he had finished the last crumb. Fifty chews per mouthful. A gulp of water between each.

He took one of the cigarettes and lit it, inhaled deeply. His senses swam. He sat and felt the heaviness creep through his limbs, quelling for a moment the yearnings of his stomach. He thought of Margarita and the *hacienda*. It was too early yet for her to have realized something had happened to him. He took two more drags and gouged out the tip, at the same time gouging her out of his mind. He hid the stub away.

"Left-right-left-right!" The crunch of trotting feet had started out on the parade ground. The files of men in full gear, with rocks stuffed in their packs, had begun to double back and forth, round and round, up and down—"Pick 'em up! Faster!" For the next four hours there would be no letup, the rocks getting heavier, the thighs weaker—"Brace up there, damn you!"—till by lunchtime the soldier prisoners would collapse, exhausted, on the benches, too tired even to eat.

Cabeza groped deep in the palliasse and brought out the broken spoon handle.

Four hours . . .

He climbed to the window and hooked his left arm through the bars.

He squinted for a moment at the doubling figures, the barking sergeants. They were too busy to pay him any attention. The sky was clearing. Soon the sweat would be pouring off them and they'd be even busier—just trying to stay on their feet. He dug the sharpened end of the spoon handle into the cement that secured the bars in the stone cell and started to scrape.

In five days he had cleared out a couple of centimeters or so from around the base of each of the three bars. It was slow work because he could hang there for only short periods, and he had no idea how deeply the bars were bedded in the stone. But it was a positive act toward survival.

He had been gouging away for two hours when, without warning, the cell door was flung back. The sergeant and two guards entered. They rushed forward and seized him, tearing him from his foothold. He fell heavily. They kicked him. He was dragged to his feet and rammed against the wall. At gunpoint they searched him from head to foot—then his bedding. The fragment of spoon, paper, pencil, cigarettes and matches were found and confiscated.

"Out!" The sergeant pointed to the corridor.

Cabeza stood there glowering. He did not move.

"I said 'Out'!" One of the guards hammered him in the kidney with the butt of his rifle.

Cabeza turned on him savagely, but the second guard quickly released the safety catch on his own weapon. Cabeza checked himself, staring down the muzzle.

For an instant he considered knocking aside the rifle and taking all three of them. But what would it win him—apart from satisfaction?

His eyes burned into the sergeant's for a long moment. Then he turned and limped from the cell.

They marched him out of the block, along the path that flanked the outer walls of the buildings. Cabeza got his first daylight glimpse of the high mesh-and-barbed-wire fence that enclosed the compound, the gun towers set at each corner. Beyond the wire stretched a barren red landscape, not a habitation in sight. It was his first clue as to the camp's location. Not a helpful one. And it hardly mattered. They were probably going to shoot him now, anyway.

They crossed a brand-new asphalt parking lot in the middle of which stood a builder's pickup and a Seat 1500, the commandant's probably, for the new, low building beyond it housed his office. Behind the office bungalow a further two-story administration building was under construction—at present little more than a shell.

A prison detail was tending the shrubs that surrounded the first building. As they approached, the sergeant bellowed, "About-turn!" The prisoners looked startled and turned their backs.

Cabeza was marched past them, straight in through the swinging doors. "Halt!" The sergeant moved on alone to a door marked COMMANDANT and knocked. He entered.

Cabeza looked around the small reception hall with its tiled floor and newly plastered walls. The place smelled of new paint. He was surprised. Instead of being stood blindfold before a firing squad, it looked as though he had got his interview with the commandant, after all.

The sergeant returned. He moved to another door on Cabeza's right and opened it. "In here!" he ordered.

Cabeza heaved himself away from the wall. Slowly, warily, he entered the room. He was given a final shove, and the door was pulled shut behind him.

The room was about twice the size of his cell, absolutely clean, absolutely bare, save for a portrait of Franco on one wall, a table and two chairs. On one of the chairs sat a tall, immaculately dressed man in his late forties, with a fine head of hair and proud, still-sharp features. He rose quickly and came forward, his hand outstretched. "Joaquín!"

Cabeza stared into the handsome dark eyes. He was incapable of movement for a moment. Then he grasped the hand and crushed it between his callused palms. "Don Miguel!"

11

Cabeza and Don Miguel stood together by the window and read the passing of time in each other's faces.

If he has suffered, Cabeza thought, he has taken it well. The other's eyes took in his scars and his unshaven state and then looked into him, as though seeking to discover how he had changed and what he had become. There was anxiety in his gaze. The answer seemed important.

"I'm glad to see you, my friend," Cabeza said. "How did you find me?"

"I work for the government now."

So that was it. He was a representative. Cabeza frowned. "For the Falangists? You work for the Falangists?"

"For the government." Miguel gave it subtle emphasis. "I am an under secretary in the Ministry of Agriculture."

"Ah. So you work for the land." Cabeza did not disguise his relief.

"The land, yes."

"And the rights of the peasants?"

Miguel nodded solemnly. "As you once did."

Cabeza grunted his satisfaction. "I'm glad. They have a good man on their side." So the government had sent him. No doubt because of their former acquaintance. Was it to

81

break good news or bad? He said deliberately, "And the *rancho?*"

Miguel looked sad. "It was destroyed in the war. Burned down."

Cabeza frowned. "By which side?"

Miguel hesitated. "I have forgotten about sides, Joaquín. Let's say it was burned by Spain, in her hour of agony."

Trying to gloss over their differences. Was it an olive branch he brought? He asked, "And the horses?"

"Slaughtered. For meat."

Cabeza shook his head. He blinked a little. "And the one horse." Even after all this time he found it hard to broach the subject. "I never . . ." He groped. "There are some things I have done that when I wake up at night I wish I could undo. The horse has been one of them."

Don Miguel smiled. "Such a small thing."

Cabeza shook his head. "No. It was a king among horses."

Miguel pretended to make light of it. "You were a child. I found out who was to blame. I wanted you to come back—to tell you I understood. But . . ."

"I was in jail."

"Yes, I heard that later. But when you got out . . ."

"There was too much shame in me. For that and for my father."

"Your father was driven to do what he did by the greed of my father."

"Yes. I had no shame for his act, only for your loss." He sighed and added, "So the *rancho* is no more."

"I put up some new buildings, turned it into a dairy farm." Miguel looked up with almost a shy smile. "Your mother is there."

The joy and relief that rose in Cabeza choked him. He just stared and laughed and shook his head. "Is she well?"

"She's fine."

"But . . . I was told she worked in Granada."

"I found her and took her from there."

Cabeza gripped him by the elbows and let him read his gratitude. "It seems I am always in your debt." He paused, then added levelly, "And now also?"

Miguel looked away, rocking slightly on his heels. "That depends."

"On what?"

Miguel turned away toward the table. He drew out a chair. "Sit down, Joaquín. Tell me about Russia."

"Russia?"

"I read that you had trouble there."

Cabeza made a gruff noise. "I don't want to talk about it."

"It was bad?"

"It was . . . a mistake."

"Go on."

"I prefer not. Just tell me what's going to happen, Miguel. Are they going to shoot me? Pardon me? Exile me? What?"

Miguel lidded his eyes. "As I've said—it depends. Things in Russia were not as you expected?"

Cabeza just couldn't fathom his line of thought and said so.

"Bear with me. Tell me what happened." Miguel sat down, very sleek and unreadable. He indicated the other chair.

Cabeza hesitated. He sat down slowly. The physical relief this brought startled him. He hadn't realized how weak the lack of food had made him. "Do you have a cigarette?"

"Forgive me." Miguel delved in his pocket. He pushed a pack and a box of matches toward him. "I brought them for you."

Cabeza stripped the wrapping and offered one to Miguel, who shook his head.

"*Qué va.* You want the story, here it is." He lit up and exhaled a cloud of smoke, thinking back.

"I escaped through France. A Russian ship took us off from Le Havre. As soon as I got on board I had a bad feeling. It was crawling with NKVD. They questioned us individually many times throughout the journey. They were rude, arrogant. They wanted every detail of our lives. What we thought about each other. Trying to get us to inform on our comrades. El Campesino was there. We both told them to take a jump. They didn't like it. Already they were making divisions among us. La Pasionaria, she was there—and Lister. They put themselves on *their* side. Spaniard against Spaniard. I thought we'd left all that behind."

Miguel shook his head sympathetically.

"In Moscow it was the same," Cabeza went on. "Oh, at first we were heroes. *Pravda, Izvestia*—full of us. We were feted. Stalin met us—but it was only for the photographs.

Propaganda. It was all propaganda. The whole place was run on falsehoods. There was nothing *real*, Miguel. Except for the poverty of the workers, their bad housing, the injustices they suffered."

"So?" Miguel looked disgusted.

"You know me—I spoke out. So did El Campesino. We were close at that time. Estremadurans. We'd fought all this before here, under the monarchy. Of course La Pasionaria thought it was paradise. Women see what they want to see. So they got her to warn us to keep our mouths shut or we'd be in trouble. We were no longer Spaniards, she told us—we were all members of the great Socialist International now. Like hell we were, I told her. I said, 'Woman, I am first a Spaniard, *then* a socialist!'"

"Bravo!"

"That was the end of me. She told them everything I'd said. I was arrested."

Miguel's eyes were riveted on his face. "And then?"

"Then was very bad."

"The face? The leg?"

"Yes. All that." Cabeza looked away, remembering. He looked back fiercely. "They're not like us, Miguel. They have no respect for a man's dignity."

"That must have hurt you most of all."

Cabeza nodded. "They tried to crush out what I am and make me something else. It was a close fight. But I won. I escaped. I am still my own man. And that is how I will die." He added grimly, "Soon, if you don't help me."

Miguel regarded him in silence for a moment. "I take it you're no longer a Communist."

"I did not say that."

"But surely . . .?"

"The ideals are still good."

"But in practice . . ."

"Because I have never seen it work doesn't mean it won't."

"I see." Miguel looked thoughtful. "But you've changed your attitude."

"Only a fool doesn't change with experience."

Miguel nodded. He leaned back. "Good. Then I think I can help you."

"That is good news," Cabeza said fervently. "To die here secretly is not my style. What must I do?"

"Sign a document."

"To say what?"

"That you renounce Communism."

Cabeza flinched. "It would not be true."

"Who would know?" Miguel made an easy gesture. "The important thing is to survive, isn't it?"

"The important thing is to survive with honor."

"There would be honor in it, I promise you."

"How?"

"You'd be allowed to live in Spain. After a period, when it's clear to everyone that you've changed, there'll be work for you. Important work."

"For the Falangists?"

"For Spain." Miguel sighed. "Forget the Falangists, Joaquín. Spain is one. All is either for Spain or not for Spain. Forget the old thinking. The world has moved on, my friend. Just think of the job. Being able to work again with your own people. Perhaps in the Ministry of Agriculture. Or Labor. It is not decided. But your talents for winning cooperation from the workers would be put to good use."

Cabeza digested his words. Don Miguel smiled at him encouragingly. Cabeza trusted his honesty and concern, but his landowning origins he could not trust. "I don't like it."

"Do you like the alternative?"

The steady gaze . . . The pressure—out of concern for him, but still pressure . . . Cabeza began to feel very uneasy. He wrenched himself off the chair. He took another cigarette, lit it, limped to the window. After a moment: "I'll tell you what I'll do. I'll set out my changed attitudes in a document of my own . . ."

"Not good enough." Miguel got up. "The document will be prepared by the Ministry of Home Affairs. It will not mince matters. It will call for your total public rejection of the communist credo. It will give your reasons for doing so in full detail."

"Prepared by Falangists?"

"Prepared by a lawyer."

"A Falangist lawyer."

"A *Spanish* lawyer!"

Cabeza inhaled from the cigarette slowly. He blew the smoke out with his words. "Then I will not sign. They'll take my document or go to hell."

"I think you've got your cases mixed. *You* will go to hell, my friend."

"Then so be it!" Cabeza said harshly and moved away.

"Think carefully what I'm offering. You have no audience. There's no one here to impress. All you have to do is sign one little piece of paper and you're free."

"That's what they said in Lubianka."

"You can stay on the farm. Be with your mother . . . You have no choice, man!"

"They said that, too."

Miguel made an impatient gesture. "Forget Lubianka. No, don't forget it—learn from it—that all political isms are just confidence tricks. Certainly not worth dying for, Joaquín. You can't let your life be snuffed out for a political abstract. Isms are brand names. They sound different, but the products all come out of the same machine. Its name is power. The process is called expediency. Power is what the politicians want. Expediency is how they get it. Expediency means lies. They lie to us every day. All you have to do now is lie back to them. They expect it. If you gave them a true answer they wouldn't know what hit them. Conviction isn't demanded of you, old friend—only your signature. So for God's sake be practical! String them along! Pay them lip service!"

"How can I serve with my lip what is stuck in my throat?"

Miguel ground his teeth. "Joaquín, listen to me—"

"You listen." Cabeza fixed him with a fierce gaze. "This document is a yoke. Remember what the Romans did to their conquered peoples? Well, this is the Caudillo's yoke for me. Whatever I do afterward—pay him lip service, escape back to Mexico, whatever I do—I have to pass under his yoke first. It is his revenge. He wants me to crawl!" He felt the energy that came from hate bringing strength to his weakened body. His eyes glowed feverishly.

Miguel had seen the same look before—in the eyes of the undernourished boy who had tried to drag him from his horse. He groped for the right words to calm him. "Don't make up your mind, I beg of you, before you've seen the document. I don't know what's going to be in it. It may be perfectly acceptable. You may find you can sign it with a clear conscience."

"Never." The red-rimmed eyes had locked into an implacable expression. "I have decided. I will never sign it!" Cabeza strode around the room repeating "Never. *Never!*" in a strange and terrible way.

He came suddenly to Miguel and clasped him in his arms, then held out his hand.

"You tried. You're a good man. I'm grateful. Go now. Quickly." He moved toward the door. He was nearing the end of his strength. If Miguel should sense it or see him falter, he knew he would start all over again.

"Old friend," Miguel said brokenly, "I don't know what to say. It's suicide—but you know that. Only two kinds of people refuse to compromise under threat of death—saints and madmen. But you are neither. I don't know what you are."

"You know well enough," Cabeza said. "I'm a peasant. And for men of the soil there are no compromises. A rock is a rock. A tree is a tree. If the rock says it's a tree, then the sky's an orange, men are turnips, the whole structure of it breaks down." He opened the door. "Do one thing for me."

"Anything."

"Give the Caudillo a message from me. Tell him to fuck his mother."

Cabeza limped out.

On his way back to his cell Cabeza felt the defiance in him turn to nausea and a great weariness. He had burned his bridges. But at least it was a clean smell they made. When the smoke cleared, it would show one simple course of action left open to him. He must escape.

And looking now at the layout of the compound, he knew how he would do it.

12

On that chill, dry January morning the city of Washington was busily preparing for the inauguration, in three days' time, of its new President, General Dwight D. Eisenhower. In the "pickle factory"'s rundown wooden buildings alongside the Reflecting Pool between the Lincoln and Washington monuments, the collection of intelligence and conducting of counterintelligence proceeded in routine fashion, with the exception that all Agency top-level decision-making was temporarily at a standstill. The offices of the DCI, the DDP and his deputy stood empty. Nor were their cars to be seen in the parking lot.

All three cars, plus a fourth, Kelland's, were parked alongside each other at a vantage point on the far edge of town. Though only ten minutes' drive from the White House, it was a remote spot. Nearby, sheep grazed. An old vineyard was still under cultivation. Southward, the River of Swans, as the Piscataway Indians called the Potomac, slid lazily toward the Francis Scott Key Bridge.

The Agency hierarchy stood together, huddled deep in their topcoats, stamping their feet against the cold: the Director of Central Intelligence, compact, casually neat, with a penetrating gaze; the Deputy Director of Plans, hulking, beetle-browed, deliberate; his deputy Redfern, square-jawed and pipe-smoking; Kelland, the central figure, relaxed, almost distant. They were all Ivy Leaguers, ex-OSS, liberals, hence an elite, sharing the same loyalties, speaking the same language—normally. But not this morning. Though only a close observer could have detected that they were in conflict. His clue: the white breath from their mouths, which indicated the tempo of their exchanges. The rapid puffs presently spurting from the DCI's lips would have made the Chattanooga Choo-Choo look like a subway train.

"Jesus, Dave"—his brown eyes bit into Kelland's angrily—"you take one helluva lot on yourself. What am I going to tell the Secretary of State? The British are still our allies, man!"

"Allies or not"—Kelland's breath responded in an easy flow—"if thy right arm offend thee, cut it off."

"Not if it's someone else's right arm, you don't," the DCI said sharply. "And not without authorization *at least* from George here." He indicated the DDP.

"'*At least* from George' means he'd have to clear it with you," Kelland replied. "And then you with—"

"Anyway, our charter is to advise," the DCI cut in severely. "Liquidating members of MI6 can only be a policy decision."

"Exactly. So you'd then have had to clear it with the National Security Council."

"Right. Right!" The DCI rolled his eyes.

"There wasn't time."

"Not time to send us a cable? Not one cable?"

"It wouldn't have been one cable, Frank," Kelland said calmly. "It would've been twenty cables—a pissing contest—ending with the Secretary of State turning chickenshit and informing the British, and Anderson and Grierson getting wind of it and defecting to Moscow with everything they know. A repeat of Burgess and Maclean."

There was a short silence. The DCI zigzagged his eyes from the DDP to Redfern, as if seeking their verbal support, but they remained curiously silent, pursing their lips, frowning at the ground.

Kelland pressed home his evident advantage. "Look at it

this way. If your house was on fire, Frank, and there was a door open fanning the blaze, would you call and ask the Fire Department's permission first before you slammed it shut?"

"If I didn't know the effect it would have, yes," the DCI countered quickly. "Dave, you know our basic MO—that the man on the spot never knows the whole picture. He's not in a position to make a unilateral decision. Never is."

"Uh—Frank . . ." The DDP stirred uneasily. "In all fairness . . . You're absolutely right in principle. But in this particular instance . . ."

Redfern nodded. "I agree. I think Dave *was* in a position to know the whole picture."

"And there were, and are, massive issues at stake," the DDP added.

"Calling for instant action," Redfern endorsed. "Action over and above—"

"Now, hold on!" The DCI cut them short, feeling betrayed by their lack of support, puzzled by it, suspicious. "I'm sorry, George, but I can't let that go by. A principle's a principle. Suppose the British were *aware* that Anderson and Grierson were working for the Russians—and were in fact feeding them with false information . . .? We fell into that one before, if you remember."

The DDP frowned and nodded his cropped gray head slowly. "True. You have a point there, Frank."

"But does he?" Redfern demanded.

Again, his expression gave the DCI the curious impression that this opposition was orchestrated.

Redfern went on: "The information they gave the Russians was *not* false. Dave *knew* it wasn't false. So in this instance . . ."

"In this instance"—the DCI clung to his point doggedly—"however you rationalize it, we have exceeded our charter. Even Section 102. We have acted without sanction of the NSC. And that is a dangerous precedent, gentlemen—it scares hell out of me—that's all I'm trying to say."

The DDP nodded his large head somberly. Redfern puffed on his pipe, rocking slightly in agreement. But conviction was strangely lacking.

Kelland himself made no sign of concession at all. He gazed

away to where, two miles to the south, the Washington Monument made like a bright sword in the sky. It provided a perfect symbol for what they all knew they were getting into—the limitations of their charter and how far the Agency could go along with it and still fight an effective war. For war it was—more deadly, more insidious than all the hot wars put together. The DCI knew it, yet here he was, feeling bound to argue procedure, protocol, mores—it was his job. But the Russians were not hampered by any such considerations. The MGB were deployed and working tirelessly in every corner of the globe, numbering tens of thousands, while the Agency, admittedly in its infancy, fielded some 1,200 souls. "Gentlemen," the DCI had just called them. It wasn't so long ago that Secretary of State Henry L. Stimson said, "Gentlemen do not read each other's mail." Well, he, Kelland, was here to bury that image once and for all. He had already managed to swing the DDP and Redfern to his side. Now, with their aid, he was about to bend the entire Agency to his will—on a path hitherto so unthinkable that even he was finding it hard to remain calm.

"Having said that . . ." The DCI modified his tone. "Let's get on to the more vital issue. That of the damage these two British agents have done."

More vital? It was the same issue. Kelland swung his gaze quickly to the DDP, who jumped as though he had been given a cue line.

"Hang on, Frank," the DDP said. "Do you mind if we square this away first? How far do you intend to take it? Are you going to play it by the book? Tell the NSC that we had to liquidate three MI6 agents?"

The DCI frowned. "I'd hoped you wouldn't ask that."

"Why?"

"Because I haven't made up my mind yet."

There was a silence for a moment. Three pairs of eyes rested casually on the DCI. Perhaps too casually, for it seemed to alert him to the trap he was being led into. He raised a palm toward them as if to say he needed more time.

"I really think we should decide now," Redfern prompted gently.

Another short silence.

"Understand, Frank," the DDP said, "there can be no question of hanging this episode on Dave personally, because of his special position. If we report the action, we report it as a department. If we get blasted—the same. Agreed?"

The DCI hesitated. He was being led in deeper. He turned to Kelland. "What are the chances of the British finding out what happened?"

"Nil," Kelland said. "Not for several years. And then they won't know why or by whom."

"And the safe house now?"

"Shut down."

"The Lessing girl?"

"On sick leave." Kelland added, "Even if MI6 managed to connect her with the disappearance of Anderson, there's no way they could either identify her or locate her."

The DCI digested this. He paced a little.

The DDP said, "It's not really the sort of decision we should hand on to new administration, Frank."

Redfern raised the stem of his pipe in support.

Kelland gazed away across the rooftops of Georgetown. He knew the DCI was well aware that he was being asked to set a dangerous precedent, that it was the thin end of an incalculable wedge, with incalculable consequences. Yet how could he refuse? The brilliance of his own stratagem almost caused Kelland to chuckle.

"Very well," the DCI said at length. "Your action is off the record, Dave. There'll be no report. So far as the Agency is concerned, it never happened. But if there's a comeback," he added, "God help us."

There was a sigh. Kelland and his fellow conspirators did not make the mistake of exchanging glances, but they knew that this cleared the decks for what was to come. For the killing of Anderson and Grierson was the direct result of their having passed information to the Russians, and that information had triggered off the Doctors' Plot, which had to be stopped at all costs. It was all interconnected. So if the first part was off the record, the second part would have to be also. Which was just what Kelland wanted. He and the DDP had planned the operation in rough already. And there was no way on earth that they could have gained sanction for it from the echelons above.

"It's hellish cold," the Deputy Director of Plans said. "Do you think we could sit in the car?"

Half an hour later, seated in the DCI's station wagon with the heater blowing softly, Kelland had come to the end of his interpretation of current events in Moscow. The DCI stared thoughtfully back at him from the front seat.

After a moment he said, "Let me recap. Anderson told the Russians that we have a mole in a key position in the Kremlin. That his code name is Omega. But he did not identify him."

"Because he couldn't," the DDP put in. "As his identity is not recorded anywhere but in the heads of four men—you, Dave, the Secretary of State and the President."

"And possibly the new President," the DCI said. "I shall have to check that out. So, Dave, you believe the Doctors' Plot is Stalin's way of flushing Omega out into the open?"

"It has to be," Kelland said. He did not add that Omega himself had confirmed it, that he had been in communication with him through mutual contacts in Berlin before returning to Washington.

"It's a typical Stalin ploy. In effect, he's set fire to the wheat field. Now he's standing back to see what pops out."

"We've already lost Khrylov," the DDP put in. "If he talks, six more deep covers will go with him—that's half our Moscow operation. Leningrad will be the domino."

"As the fire gets toward the center of the field," Kelland continued his analogy, "Omega's going to be left standing there in full view, singed pants and all."

The DCI looked shaken. "This is all just theory."

"I'll stake my career on its being fact."

"Me too," said the DDP.

Redfern tapped out his pipe in the ashtray and nodded.

The DCI blinked into space for a moment. "Then we have to stop this plot in its tracks, gentlemen." He glanced at the three of them shrewdly. "Am I wrong, or do I sense that you three have already conceived a plan?"

"You're not wrong, Frank." The DDP leaned forward. "This is what we propose to do."

And for the next ten minutes he outlined the plan Kelland had prepared in Berlin.

The DCI's eyes slowly hardened under his pale brows.

"Holy Jesus Christ!" he exploded when the DDP had finished. "Are you out of your minds? An idea like that wouldn't get to first base with the council, let alone the President, let alone the *new* President! There's a fresh deal coming up. No new administration in its right mind would . . ." His voice slowly trailed away as he read what their faces were telling him. That the administration wouldn't be asked.

He rubbed a hand across his brow, pinching his nose, squeezing his eyes shut, opening them. "You're not going to do this to me, gentlemen."

"We'll be doing it to ourselves, too, Frank," the DDP reminded him quietly. "If it backfires we all go."

"If it backfires we could be at war, George!"

"We *are* at war," Kelland said forcefully. "And if they get Omega, we've lost it. To hell with our jobs. To hell with the Agency. That man is our ear in the Presidium. He's worth a hundred deep-cover men. Without him, our cold-war goose is cooked. What was it Bill Stephenson said to Churchill?—'It's better to lose a *battle* than lose a source of secret intelligence.'"

There were murmurs of agreement from the other two. They were leaning forward. Closing in.

The DCI bared his teeth, moving his head from side to side. "There *has* to be another way!"

"If there is, tell us, Frank," the DDP said earnestly. "You're the chief. We'll listen to anything you say." He added, "But meanwhile—time is short. We'll have to start getting this thing together."

"No one's committed yet," his deputy reminded soothingly. "We'll keep our options open till the last minute. Maybe the plot'll collapse of its own accord. Let's hope to God it does."

"Amen," said the DCI fervently. He looked suddenly very white and tired.

By the end of the following week the plan was almost complete. Just one vital ingredient was lacking. Kelland, the DDP and Redfern rifled the files, sifting through every relevant item of intelligence to try to break the deadlock. If they could not find the element they were seeking, Kelland said, they would have to abort. The mere possibility sickened him, but he knew that his plan flirted too precariously with disaster to permit the inclusion of one piece that did not wholly fit.

Then one afternoon, while sorting, almost hopelessly now, through some recent reports from stations overseas, he hit on the snippet of news that ended their search.

It was so brief, so, at first glance, irrelevant, that he almost passed it over. Yet it was to change the history of the world.

13

"Arriba! Arriba!"

"Arriba! Arriba!"

Cabeza dragged himself from a shallow, haunted sleep. Another dawn. He filled his lungs a few times with the urine-tainted air, then forced himself up. There was a sick feeling behind his eyes and in his gut. But it was only lack of food, not despair.

Despair was an indulgence that killed more surely than even a firing-squad bullet. Even in his worst moments, and there had been more than he could count, he had never surrendered to it. He preferred to wait for the bullet. Papers had to be signed before there were bullets. Papers blew off desks; clerks left them "pending" to attend the funerals of their mothers; mailbags got stolen; time stretched; opportunities presented themselves. Opportunities like today. For today was the day he would escape.

The lights came on blindingly. He pulled on the laceless boots, taking his time. It would be the devil's luck if they came for him now. Don Miguel had told him a long time ago that there was no such thing as luck, that it was yourself making the thing happen. As a peasant, bred on superstition, he could never quite believe this. But if it were true, and thinking about it could make it happen, he wouldn't think about it.

He had filled the washbowl. Now he plunged his whole head in and blew into it. He knew from experience that the agitation of the water produced an energizing effect. But this morning it was only slight. His body had reached a low ebb. It made him wonder if he would have the strength to do what he planned. If he took it very slowly before the vital hour, perhaps it would be all right. He crossed out the "perhaps." It was no way to start—with a perhaps. He was damned if he was going to give the Caudillo the satisfaction of killing him here!—that was the way to start.

The cell door hammered back. "Attention!" The burly sergeant and pockmarked officer marched in. Cabeza scowled at them, searching their faces, seeking some difference of expression that would tell him whether this was to be the day.

The sergeant drew himself up to the window and snatched a look at the new cement that had been troweled into the bar sockets. He needn't have bothered. The repair had been done days ago and the *rápido* cement had set like a rock in the first hour. He dropped back to the floor with a grunt. But there was nothing different about his flat, broken-nosed face, save the redness of effort.

The officer's was averted from him as usual. The tick on the clipboard was as usual. They went out and slammed the door as usual.

Cabeza breathed a sigh, sat down on the bunk and listened to the clatter that accompanied the distribution of cleaning materials. Today was "polishing day"—the day he had been waiting for.

When the door opened again and old Jorge ducked in with the bucket, he also deposited a long-handled mop. A second trusty out in the corridor was scooping a mugful of wax out of the tub he was carrying. He handed it in to Jorge, who set it down beside the bucket and withdrew. The door was shut and bolted.

Cabeza quickly took the mug of soft white wax and sniffed it anxiously. The anxiety left him. Last week's issue had been no exception. There was spirit in it, not wholly absorbed by the wax. Definitely a petrochemical of some sort.

He covered it over carefully with his washbowl to prevent evaporation, and looked under the bucket. Nothing was attached there.

He was not surprised. It had become clear since the day of Miguel's visit that the source and manner of his supply of cigarettes, matches and writing paper had been discovered. No doubt Jorge had been hauled before the officer and given a drubbing for it, for since that day he had not volunteered so much as a conspiratorial glance. This had left Cabeza's written queries unanswered, and sealed off his last contact with the world outside his cell as surely as the stone slab of a tomb.

They had also confiscated the cigarettes and matches Miguel had brought him. This made his task of escape much harder. But still not impossible.

He got down and scrubbed the floor of his cell slowly, almost painfully. He let it dry a little, then, using as little of the wax as possible, gave it a polish with the mop. The remainder of the wax he put into the washbowl, which he jammed up under the boards of his bunk to prevent further evaporation.

When Jorge returned for the cleaning materials at breakfast time, Cabeza handed back the empty mug, and it was as though he had used it all. Everything was normal.

After the pitiful meal, he spread the blanket on the bare bunk boards, lay down and tried to move as little as possible while he went over in his mind every detail of what he would have to do. The exact sequence was important, and he thought himself through the actions many times, rearranging them till they flowed logically, at least so far as he could foresee them. But once outside the cell, he knew, he would have to shape his actions to the circumstances he found there.

Toward the end of the afternoon he bestirred himself. With measured movements he started to assemble the few props at his disposal. He had a full hour. The evening meal would not be around till six. Until that time the corridor was usually deserted. No guards to glance through his peephole—they would be on duty outside the block. He would have all the time he needed.

Keeping an ear cocked to the sporadic bellows of the drill sergeants out in the quadrangle, he dismantled the bunk. It provided him with a metal frame and three six-foot boards. He balanced the frame on its end in the middle of the floor and laid the planks from the top of it to the windowsill. The frame had two metal legs on one side, one of which helped to balance it upright. He now had a two-meter-high platform.

He climbed precariously up onto the rickety structure. From there he could reach the light fixture. The electric bulb was housed inside a flat metal container like a car headlight. Its glass door was held shut by a screw-headed bolt.

He picked off one of his metal fly buttons and, pressing the glass upward, used it as a screwdriver to loosen the thread. It wouldn't twist. The button bent, folded in half.

He tried again with a second button. But the thread was corroded solid. He needed to reach the bulb. He thought of breaking the glass with his boot, but the bulb was too close inside it. It might shatter and destroy the filament. Already the strain of his position was making him gasp and sweat. Easy does it, he told himself. There are a thousand ways to skin a horse.

He gripped the fixture and hung his weight on it experimentally. It moved. Encouraged, he struggled with it, twisting it back and forth.

Suddenly the bolts came out of the ceiling, bringing with them a hunk of plaster. The fixture sagged on the end of its pipe. The pipe was what brought the cable across the ceiling from the wall above the door. It was fixed to the ceiling by two simple clips. He bore down a little harder. The pipe bent and the clips broke.

Now Cabeza worked his way down off the structure, still gripping the fixture. The pipe bent all the way with him and in a moment he had the light assembly down to within a meter of the floor. He rested for a moment.

Then he worked the "headlight" off the pipe, till only the cable inside held it. A final wrench and it came away, leaving exposed the twin severed ends of the cable. Even better than he had planned.

He tweaked the naked ends of the electric cord together and that was that—phase one completed.

He paused for another rest. And while he was taking it, the sound from outside that he had been waiting for reached him: the sharp orders of dismissal that marked the end of afternoon parade. That made the time exactly four-thirty. Not having a watch, this was his only time reference. Now began the count, and it had to be as accurate as he could make it—second by second.

"One-and-two-and-three-and-four-and . . ."

At every count of sixty he scratched a digit on the wall with one of the bent fly buttons. He hoped that when he had clocked up thirty minutes it would be five o'clock. At five the lights came on. He had to be ready for them.

It was a tedious business, especially when his mind was brimming with the other things that had to be done. But it was the only way, and he had reached a tally of twenty-one minutes when he heard the unmistakable sounds of the main entrance door being unlocked. The door groaned open and there were voices, the stamp and scutter of boots, some strange, howling laughter. Cabeza felt the clutch of apprehension in his chest, but he continued to count evenly.

The footsteps passed his door. One glance through the peephole, he knew, and his whole plan would be discovered. "Twenty-nine-and-thirty-and-thirty-one-and-thirty-two . . ."

A cell door was unbolted farther along, followed by shouts and curses and scuffling. It sounded as though a drunken prisoner was resisting being thrown into solitary.

The noises continued in background accompaniment to his steady counting. It was difficult to concentrate. He almost lost track for a moment as another set of footsteps passed his door. Another guard coming to help, a part of his mind guessed. Maybe the officer himself.

Now there were some sharp words of command and very quickly after that the cell door was slammed shut. The cursing became more muffled. The footsteps began to return.

"And-fifty-eight-and-fifty-nine-and-sixty-and-one-and-two . . ." Cabeza marked up another minute and moved quickly to block the view through his peephole—just as the footsteps paused and there was an exchange of words right outside his cell.

For no particular reason he stretched up his arms and pretended to be doing some exercises, trying not to let the rhythm of the movements influence the regularity of his counting.

After several moments the footsteps moved on. He moved

back to the wall and marked up twenty-three minutes, still not pausing in the count.

The main door banged shut. The snap of the lock.

Keeping the count going, he now put the washbowl containing the wax under the bent pipe. He carried his blanket to the tap and soaked it thoroughly with water.

By the time his reckoning on the wall showed twenty-five minutes he was ready, standing with the bowl held under the pipe, the twisted ends of the cord almost touching the tiny amount of spirit that shone on the surface of the wax.

His heart thudded against his ribs as he waited, not knowing how accurately he had counted the time, how long he would have to crouch there poised for instant action. His life depended on the next short space of time. If he had been a religious man he would have prayed. But the nearest he had ever come to religious thinking was in believing that God helped those who helped themselves. He would know in a moment if that was true. In a moment. Any moment . . .

As the block lights came on, there was a sparking flash and a pop. The spirit whoofed into flame. The impregnated wax came ablaze. With a gruff laugh of exultation, Cabeza sprang to the door and slapped the basin over the spot where the outer boltguide rivets showed through the woodwork.

The wax adhered to the door. He slung the basin aside and snatched up one of the bunk boards, holding the flat end of it under the wax to stop it from drooling away down the door. Some of it escaped around the edges of the plank, but enough of it was held in position gradually to set fire to the woodwork.

Cabeza held it there, blowing on the flames, fanning them, muttering encouragement to them through bared teeth till they took hold. Then he got rid of the plank and took up the sodden blanket. To allow the whole door to catch fire so soon would be a mistake. The smoke might alert the guard before the flames had done their job. By damping continually around the bolt area, he was able to confine the fire to the one spot.

The door was thick and he could see it was going to take some time to burn through. No matter—so long as the corridor remained deserted . . . So long as . . . He clamped down on the conjectures and concentrated on the damping and blowing, the blowing and damping. The woodwork was beginning to crackle now. It sounded to his heightened senses like small-arms fire, but there was nothing he could do to stop it.

Presently the prisoner opposite began to shout that he could smell burning. Another took up the cry.

Cabeza called out to them harshly to keep their traps shut—that he was getting ready to barbecue the officer!

This got an appreciative laugh and seemed to reassure them that things were under control, for they stopped their noise.

The wood surrounding the bolt area was becoming charred. Now Cabeza stood back and let the fire have its way for a minute. When the whole door was blazing, he gave it a sharp tug.

The rivets stayed where they were, but the door wrenched free of them, swinging inward.

He suppressed a cry of triumph. He moved out into the corridor and looked through the smoke toward the main entrance. The grille set in the outer door showed only the gathering dusk and the corner of the next block outside—no faces. He started toward it, then changed his mind.

He turned back to the cells of the men who had shouted and unbolted their doors and tugged them open. He opened two more doors for good measure, telling the astonished soldier prisoners inside that he was getting out. What they did was up to them, but when he shouted "Fire!" they should all join in. Understood?

Without waiting for their replies, he limped to the main door and positioned himself against the wall beside it. Glancing back, he could see the prisoners standing confused in the doorways of their cells, clearly debating whether they should try to escape or not.

"Fire!" he bellowed. "Fire!"

They took up the cry, raggedly at first, then with a vengeance, using the opportunity to vent their frustration. Cell by cell, the whole block joined in.

Army boots came running. A couple of guards' faces appeared at the grille beside him. They took one startled look and vanished. A key rattled in the lock. As the door swung inward, a fire triangle began to jangle nearby. A guard came in through the door, his rifle at the ready. Seeing the prisoners—they ducked quickly back into their cells—he gave a shout to his mate and started along toward them.

Cabeza waited for the second guard to come through—but he didn't. He gave him several seconds. At any moment the first guard might turn and see him. He couldn't wait. He slipped out.

He spotted the second guard at once. He was at the corner of the building, rattling the triangle that hung from the eaves. His face was toward the door and he saw Cabeza instantly.

His jaw dropped. He let go the striker and started to unsling his rifle. He was the big, awkward fellow who had thumped him in the kidneys. Cabeza took four quick, limping steps toward him and kicked him in the balls with all his strength.

The man doubled up with a cry that was mostly breath. Even as he sank to the ground Cabeza had hold of the rifle and was pulling it off his arm. The man clung to the sling in pure reflex. Cabeza had to kick him again before the rifle came free. He turned with it and hurried away along the outside of the building toward the parking lot.

Running feet sounded from all directions, questions, replies, the opening and closing of doors. Almost immediately he met two NCO's running the other way. It was too late to turn aside, so he kept on toward them, beckoning and calling to them to hurry, pointing back toward the solitary block. They were past him before they realized the anomaly—a prisoner carrying a rifle!

Glancing back, he saw them turn and start to unholster their automatics. He slipped behind a building and pumped a round up the chamber.

He leaned out and snapped a shot in their direction. As they dived for cover, he ran on, the laceless boots slipping about on his feet, slowing him.

Now, in answer to the shot, the prison alarms began to ring. Their clamor rose from every part of the camp. A bullet cracked past his head. The post of a bulletin board ahead of him splintered. He dodged belatedly. Where was the damn parking lot?

Then he saw it—a black lake stretching in the dusk, the flints of its new surface glistening in the compound arcs. And there stood the car, the commandant's blue Seat, parked close to the path that led to his new office building. It was the only car standing between the new white lines—but it was enough.

Cabeza paused to gauge the positions of the gun towers before venturing across the open space. Luckily, they had been constructed to cover the perimeter wire and not the compound—and the parking lot was shielded from them by buildings in both directions. Luckily for now perhaps, he thought, as he started out toward the car, but not for in a few minutes' time when he would crash out in it through the mesh gates. He would have to run the full gauntlet of their fire. He hoped the Seat was a good starter.

He had lost a boot somewhere. And there went the other! The tarred surface was warm and even under his bare feet as he hobbled toward the car, gasping now, nearing the end of his strength.

The door of the office building was flung open suddenly and the fat commandant came hurrying out, putting on his coat.

Cabeza jerked up the gun and sent a bullet smacking into the wall close beside him. The commandant hauled up in his tracks, his mouth agape. He dashed back into the building.

Cabeza wrenched open the car door. As he slid in, a bullet whanged off the roof startlingly. He crouched low, fumbling for the ignition key, commanding it to be there. He ran his hands down beside the steering column and along the bottom of the dash, peering in the dimness. Where was it on these models? Another bullet careened off the pavement nearby, emitting a brilliant spark. He pressed both hands against the dash, feeling for the protuberance. He found it. No, it was the choke. At last he felt the slot—but the key was not in it.

Even as he reached under the dashboard for the wires, he knew there was no time left. The prison staff were converging on him from all sides. *Madre!* Now what?

He grabbed the rifle and tumbled out of the car. Keeping low, he ran barefooted toward the office building. What he must do had come to him in a flash. His last hope. For some reason no one fired at him. Maybe they were scared of hitting someone inside the building. He plunged in through the door, hearing the glass shatter behind him as, blinded by the sudden light, he headed for the commandant's office. A clerk's face appeared in his path. He put his whole hand over it and shoved it aside and heard the man fall heavily behind him as he grasped at the new brass handle of the commandant's door. He twisted it, rattled it—locked! The bastard had locked himself in!

Cabeza put his shoulder to it. But he was too exhausted now to force it open. He put the muzzle of the rifle to the lock, pointing it downward so as not to kill the man he was going to take hostage. But even as he took up the slack of the trigger, boots hammered the step of the porch outside and a sudden convergence of bodies jammed in the entrance.

Cabeza swung around, glimpsed an automatic swinging up to shoot him, sidestepped. There was a window. He went through it headfirst, shattering the glass. He fell heavily, rolling sideways to get his legs under him, kneeing himself up awkwardly. His legs would hardly function. He plunged forward onto his face, grazing it on a rock. Somehow he kneed himself up again. The world spun around him. The rifle—where was it? He grabbed it by the barrel. Amid the spinning he saw the black interior of the half-finished building ahead of him. He staggered toward it. Jagged rubble cut into his feet. His shoulder bit a scaffold pole as he cannoned into the cement-smelling blackness. His knee hit an empty drum and he stumbled. His outflung arm hit something vertical. A ladder. Without pausing to reason, he clawed his way up it blindly and flung himself down on the concrete floor of the upper story, his chest heaving.

He heard the guards close in around the building, their NCO's panting out orders. He scraped the rifle around till it was pointing downward and sent a shot crashing into the rooms below. It stopped them for a moment. He marshaled the last of his strength and, kneeling, got hold of the ladder and pulled it up after him.

Then he collapsed.

The whirling patterns in his head gradually slowed. He elbowed himself up and forced himself to take stock of his stronghold.

The gap in the floor, he guessed, was where the stairway would come. Across on the other side of it was a single big space where there would be rooms, only the partitions had not been built yet. The windows were just rectangular holes.

On his side of the gap was the same. Perforated bricks stood around in neat stacks.

"Resistir y fortificar es vencer," as the old Communist war slogan advised. "To hold out and fortify is to win." He started to build a low breastwork with the bricks.

As he worked he could hear voices talking below him outside the building. No doubt debating the quickest, safest way of recapturing him.

Well, he wasn't going to be recaptured. He would die here, if he had to. It was better than with a bag over his head against a wall. At least, this way, El Duro would die in action. Not exactly with his boots on, he was forced to admit, but fighting *some* sort of action against the fascists.

He had to believe the prison staff were fascists or it made no sense. The cell sergeant and pockmarked officer—they had to be fascists. If he could hold out till morning and by daylight spot those two in his sights, he would give them a free lift to hell. If he had enough ammunition.

He checked the clip. He had fired three. Two left. Maybe enough. He took another careful look around him, assessing his position for vulnerability to attack. There was no alternative way to where he was, except by a ladder put up to one of the windows.

He shouted a warning. He would blow off the first head that showed itself!

After a moment a reply came back. It sounded like the commandant's voice. It called on him to surrender. He was surrounded. There was not the slightest chance of escape.

Cabeza didn't bother to reply. He pushed himself along the floor till his back was to the end wall. He lay the cocked rifle across his legs and wished to God he had a steak inside him.

A little time passed. The brave beatings of his heart abated and he thought then: What a mess you have made for yourself, *hombre*. To die like a rat is not your style. You are a great disappointment. All your life you have made war and won only a few battles. All the important ones you have lost. You should have known this about yourself and taken the easy way out with Miguel.

Then he thought: If you die, your name will only be a small rumor on the tongues of prisoners to whom no one will listen. Margarita will never know what happened to you. And you will never yourself know whether the principles you fought for were true and worthwhile or just expressions of your own vanity and stubbornness. This was an uncomfortable thought. It brought home to him that the pattern of his life was incomplete. There was lacking the final encounter that would have resolved all such questions. A last battle remaining to be fought. And until it was, he was not ready for oblivion. He could not accept it.

14

CABEZA AWAKENED with a start, clutching up the gun instinctively. The air was acid-cold. His bare feet were like ice. His body inside the sweat-stiff clothes had the chill of near death on it. It was only by an act of will that he forced his mind to focus outside his own discomfort. His eyes probed the window spaces in search of a head, the horns of a ladder. But only the stars in unfathomable hosts met his gaze. Yet something had wakened him.

Then it came again. "Hey up there, General Cabeza—can you hear me?" A man's voice. Something strange about it. Coming from inside the building below him.

He sat up sharply—or tried. His body was almost locked in stiffness. He gripped the gun, feeling for the trigger. But there was practically no sensation in his fingers.

"I know you're up there," went on the voice. "Now, listen. I have nothing to do with the guard or this prison. Understand? I'm here on my own account. I have an official permit to speak to you. I'm alone and unarmed. I have a ladder and I'm coming up."

There was a scraping sound. The next moment the top section of a ladder appeared through the gap in the floor.

"Keep away!" Cabeza ordered hoarsely. He was still trying to figure what was strange about the voice.

"I'm coming up," the voice repeated calmly. "If you shoot

me you'll kiss good-bye to the last chance you have on this goddam earth."

The ladder shook as whoever it was started to climb. And Cabeza knew then what was different about his voice. He spoke in English. *Inglés inglés?* No, *americano inglés.* If it was a trick, it was a strange one. He aimed the gun at where the head would appear, at the same time keeping watch on the windows.

The head rose into his sights. It wore, of all things, a country gentleman's tweed hat. The features were in its shadow, but he caught the gleam of gold-rimmed glasses and the darkness of a moustache.

"Stop there!" Cabeza said in the same language.

The climber paused.

"Let me see the hands."

The man placed his empty hands on the horns of the ladder.

"Now, what do you want?" Cabeza demanded.

"Just to talk, General."

"Then talk. Make it quick."

"I'll talk when I'm up," the man said, with just a trace of iron in his voice. "I'll make it slow for you." And he climbed very deliberately to the top of the ladder and stepped off it.

He stood there in a patch of light from the arcs, seemingly unaware of how close to death he had been—and still was. He was very sure of himself. From where Cabeza sprawled he looked tall. He wore a handsome topcoat, which he slowly unbuttoned. The lining shone as he spread it open, doing the same with the jacket of the suit underneath. He pushed them away from his back and stood side view, so Cabeza could see between them and his body. Then he slapped all the pockets. They hung slack.

"There. No weapon—okay?"

The shirt under the suit would have cost a Spanish or Mexican peasant two months' wages. The shoes were made of some kind of reptile skin. They started forward.

"Stop!" Cabeza gestured with the gun. "Over there."

The man hesitated. He shrugged and moved to the far wall and sat down on a pile of bricks, facing him. He seemed quite unafraid.

"Keep the hands where I can see."

The American placed his hands on his knees, and for several moments the two men studied each other in silence. In his present condition Cabeza wasn't seeing so well, but the otherworldliness of his visitor came to him strongly. He was from a system where men trod smooth paths and spoke their minds and made decisions in comfort without fear. This made him no more trustworthy, but it confirmed that he was not from the prison. Curiosity began to take the place of suspicion in Cabeza's mind. But he kept the gun aimed at his chest.

"I've come a long way to see you, General. Seems I only just made it in time." The American gestured around. "But look—this is a helluva place to talk. Can't I get you down into an office or somewhere? I can guarantee you safe conduct."

Cabeza croaked a laugh. "So that is the game."

"No game, General. Just, what I have to say is confidential. I don't want for us to be overheard."

Cabeza growled, "Too bad. Here I am and—" He was seized by a fit of coughing. A long tremor convulsed him. He blinked away the tears, about to continue, "—and here I stay," but there was born in him then the sudden knowledge that he wouldn't. A way out of this rattrap had just presented itself. He could use this man as a hostage.

The eyes behind the glasses were watching his expression and Cabeza had the strange feeling the other was reading his mind. But the man said easily, "Well then, let me get them to bring you something. If I talk, you're not going to listen in the condition you're in. Say what you need, General. I'll tell them to get it."

Cabeza croaked a laugh. "You think they will obey? If I was on fire they would not piss on me."

The American did not laugh. "Like to bet?"

Cabeza's lips stretched in a mirthless grin. "A beefsteak—socks—a blanket."

The American leaned over the gap in the floor and relayed the requirements in quite passable Spanish.

"And boots," Cabeza added. "With laces." What the hell—if the request was granted, he would need them to walk out of here with his hostage.

A voice growled back from below that they didn't have such luxuries as beefsteak in the prisoners' cookhouse.

110

"Then get it from the commandant's kitchen," the American replied. "Quick as you can."

A grumbling discussion ensued outside—terminated by a reluctant order and the crunch of departing feet.

"Now," said the American, "maybe that entitles me to sit a bit closer?"

Cabeza thought about it. He waved him to a pile of cement bags two meters from him.

The American changed seats, lowering his voice.

"My name's Harman, General, but just call me John. Where I come from, who or what I work for, cannot feature in this conversation. So you'll have to accept that I know most things about you, while you know nothing about me—think you can do that?"

When Cabeza remained silent, he went on: "First let me say—maybe it's a cruel thing—that I'm reassured by the way I find you. The attempted crash-out, your holing up here, making a last stand of it. Shows you've got the iron in you still. If I had any misgivings, that was where they lay—that you'd have gone off the boil." He added, "And I don't mean that to sound patronizing."

Cabeza glowered at him. Was this some kind of joke?

Harman continued, "Because I admire your style, sir. I really do. Your file reads like a novel. Your character jumps right out of—"

"My file?" Cabeza's eyes had narrowed.

Harman nodded. His teeth gleamed luminously under the dark moustache. "You're used to featuring in people's files, surely? Madrid, Moscow, Mexico City . . . no doubt several others. A lot has been written about you. In the late thirties you were quite a media hero, for obvious reasons—the youngest brigade commander in the Civil War, despite the fact that at the time you could hardly read or write. Then when you surfaced from the Soviet Union after World War Two, your experiences were given a short blaze of publicity in the Western press—rather triumphantly in some cases, I guess, because the writers felt you'd been taught a lesson." He chuckled. "That you'd learned the hard way what the West has known all along—that Communism is a hoodwink, that it cares less about its workers than many Western democracies, that economically it can only stay in the ball park through having a vast unpaid slave labor force." He added amiably, "So when a dedicated socialist like yourself got chewed up in the machinery of his own convictions—well, I guess they thought it was kind of poetic."

Despite the almost amused lightness of his discourse, Cabeza felt the eyes boring into him from behind their glasses, measuring his reactions.

"But while I'm on the subject, don't get me wrong," the American continued. "It wasn't all a put-down. There was a lot of sympathy for you. Because the American people think a lot like you do, General. Like you, we hate to see injustice. Like you, we speak out and to hell with the consequences. Like you, this sometimes gets us roasted, but we soldier on, we don't give in. I guess we're both kind of stubborn. Ingenuous, even. We're simple enough to believe our way is right and the other guy's is wrong. Also like you, I think."

Cabeza ground his teeth. He wished the blanket would come. What in hell was this clown getting at?

He said harshly, "Get to the point."

"Señor Harman!" interrupted a voice from below.

The American moved to the top of the ladder. A blanket was tossed up to him. Then a pair of boots. Harman turned with them toward Cabeza.

Cabeza raised the gun sharply.

"Keep back. Put them down. Now push them over." He kept the gun hard on him.

Harman did as he was bid with a grim chuckle. He sat down again, nodding approvingly.

"Never trust anyone, General—that's the ticket."

There were socks in the boots. Cabeza pulled them on—one-handed. Then the boots, keeping the rifle aimed with the other. He drew the blanket gradually around him. "Ticket" was right. This man was his last ticket to survival. He wasn't going to lose him through a slack move.

"Ready to talk now?" Harman inquired. He rubbed his clean-cut jaw for a moment. "Now, how shall we play it?" He thought for a moment, "No, we won't play it. I hold all the cards. It wouldn't be fair. I'll level with you. You give me your reaction." He leaned forward, lowering his voice. "I have a job for you, General. A job only you can do."

Cabeza was startled. But he remained silent. He was not going to commit himself to a thing before he knew where all this was leading.

"You loathe and detest the Stalin regime—am I right, sir?"

"A job?" Cabeza said. "For a man trapped here? If you want me to understand, you speak plain. You can get me out? You are saying you have the power to get me out?"

"I have the power."

"You know I am to be shot?"

"Of course."

"That it is Franco's orders?"

"Of course."

"So you can stop the Caudillo's orders?"

"I can stop them, General," Harman said calmly.

Cabeza asked, "How?"

Harman lowered his head behind his raised palm. "Just accept I can do it."

Then he has to be with the U.S. government, Cabeza thought. He was important. And he had him under his rifle. Good. Things were beginning to look better.

"What is this job?"

"Ah." Harman made a butterfly gesture with his hand. "That I can't tell you. Not here."

Cabeza looked nonplussed. "You expect me to take the job without knowing what I have to do?"

"Well . . ." Harman huffed a laugh and encompassed their situation with a gesture. "Yes, I do."

"Because if I don't accept, I die?"

Harman hesitated for decency's sake. "Put bluntly—yes."

"Then, put bluntly, you're a fool."

Harman raised his head slowly. The glasses gleamed at him expressionlessly. "I may be a lot of things, General," he said quietly. "But a fool is not one of them."

The blood was beginning to circulate in Cabeza's veins again. A sweet, prickling agony spread through him. "If you know my file, you know I do not bend to threats. Already I have turned away one who came like you."

"Don Miguel de las Casas, I know. But this is different. I'm not asking you to renounce your beliefs," the American said very slowly. "Only avenge them."

15

GAIL LESSING stood entranced, the parcels of groceries weighing down her arms as she gazed along the Rue es Siaghin to where the sea made like a poppy field in the red evening light. Madame Garvi waited for her impatiently, her huge bosom lifting in a sigh—in her dark purple and red silk dress she looked like an enormous tulip. For her there was no beauty in Tangier, only an ugliness of human spirit.

They were in the Ville Ancienne, the Old City. The shops and stalls that lined the narrow street were already lit, people coming and going against their lighted fronts. The noise was unbelievable, tobacco and charcoal smoke writhing in the still air, vendors crying, *"Kikh!"* as they guided their trays through the crowds of Moroccans in cartwheel hats, and doe-eyed Muslim women in yashmaks and high heels, and French and Spaniards and Jews and Arabs. A couple of young Germans pushed by wheeling a Coca-Cola barrow. They wore Afrika Korps caps and desert khaki. Leftovers, Gail could only guess, from Rommel's army. The contrast with Boston, where she had been on leave with her mother until yesterday morning, was overwhelming. Dazed, she dragged her eyes back to her shopping list.

"Only cigarettes to get now."

"This way." Madame Garvi pointed her bosom down the hill. She was on loan from the consulate, where her husband was a porter—"Fully screened," the chargé d'affaires had assured Gail. "And one hell of a good cook, if you can just cut down on her supply of garlic and olive oil."

Just why she needed to be screened, indeed what this assignment was all about, Gail had only the vaguest idea. The coded cable that had reached her at home from the DDP's office in Washington had been unusually short and uninformative. Her role was to be the same as in London, it said. Which meant, presumably, that she was to be the administrator of a safe house. "Prepared to cater to up to a dozen. On arrival you will buy the following supplies . . ." And there had followed a rather odd list of, mainly, construction materials.

Gail had been dismayed by such an early termination of her leave. The wounds on her breasts were by no means healed. The wounds on her psyche even less so. But the reason she had been selected became clear the moment she stepped off the plane. Tangier was an international city. To deal adequately with the locals, an administrator here would need to speak Arabic, Spanish and French—in all of which she was fluent.

"There." Madame Garvi stood pointing to a tobacconist's window. It stood on the corner of a tiny square that was little more than an intersection of foot passages with a space in the middle—a space ringed by three rather downbeat cafés and a hotel. The small tables were packed with drinkers, bootblacks squabbling among them for custom, touts and hawkers plying in between. It was a picturesque scene, with the harbor visible below through the tousled palm heads of the Avenue d'Espagne, and the red Atlantic beyond.

"What a marvelous place."

"The Petit Socco." Madame Garvi waved a hand at it in disgust. "Full of criminals. Bad people." She pronounced it "bed." "They are smoking marijuana, you smell? Riffreff. From all over the world they are coming to a free city where they can be pigs. Drugging and meking their vicked deals for smuggling and gold. And vorse," she added darkly, tucking in her chins.

"Worse?" Gail wondered what could be worse.

The cook didn't know how to put it, but her heavily penciled eyes moved to where a crowd of bootblacks were scrambling for coins tossed by a group of men at one of the tables. The boys were aged from eight to twelve, undersized and graceful. The men were watching them lasciviously, discussing which they should take home as bed partners.

Gail shuddered. Madame Garvi looked down her large nose and compressed her lips.

"All is allowed here. It is the city of Satan."

Gail bought three cartons of American cigarettes at the little stall. As they turned to leave she glanced again quickly at the café table. One of the men had beckoned a boy to him and was flourishing a currency note under the ragged child's nose, propositioning him. At that moment, as though sensing her scrutiny, he glanced up and his eyes met Gail's. The leer in them died, and for an instant he looked at her intently— and Gail read recognition in his gaze.

It was an unpleasant face, quirky, with red lips and slanting eyes and an undershot jaw. European, perhaps Slavic. He wore a baggy gabardine suit and a large gold ring on his little finger.

His scrutiny lasted only an instant, then the eyes hooded themselves, and he went on talking to the boy.

Gail frowned as she started up the hill after Madame Garvi. She, too, had felt a stirring of recognition. Where had she seen him before?

A few paces farther on she turned for a second glance—to see him looking after her. The child was looking too, as if the man were talking about her.

Strange. As they walked back up toward the marketplace she wracked her memory, striving to place him.

Presently, pausing to glance in at the Monoprix department store window display, she caught a glimpse of the little bootblack trailing behind them. He carried his shoeshine box slung on his bony shoulder and appeared to be innocently plying for custom, sauntering among the crowds. She thought perhaps she was mistaken and it was a different boy. But when they moved on, he moved on too.

Damn, she thought. She guessed he had been sent along to observe where she went. That made it a professional "make." Well, now at least she knew in what area of her mind to look for the face. It took her only minutes then to conjure up a scene—a tiny cameo.

It was in New York. The United Nations building. When she had been on two months' detachment to the audio-translation department for a meeting of the General Assembly—September '50 that would have been. She was delivering some transcripts to the Soviet delegation, moving along a corridor, when she had heard raised voices coming from the Head of Delegation's office. The door flew open and out came Assistant Secretary General Alexei Koditsa. His normally bland face was red with anger. He started along the corridor, but a voice from inside the office called him back.

Koditsa stopped and turned slightly. He seemed torn between pride and compliance. Two men came to the doorway of his office—one heavyset, the other slighter in build. They beckoned him back inside.

"If you would be so kind, Alexei Alexeivich," the heavier man said quietly. "We had not finished." He opened the door wide and stood aside. "If you please."

She never saw whether Koditsa obeyed the "request," as she had felt it undiplomatic to look back. But she had wondered why he allowed two junior members of his delegation—for that is what she knew them to be—to confront him in this way.

It was not until later that she learned of the huge MGB infiltration into the United Nations—strictly against its rules and its charter. As many as 60 percent of the Soviet delegation were members of the secret police, according to Agency figures, using its offices almost overtly for espionage purposes. The key to the cameo she had witnessed then became clear. Koditsa was a bona fide diplomat. A figurehead. The real orders came from below. It was the Wehrmacht commanders and the SS all over again.

She had seen the two MGB men about the building several times after that. The thickset one, she learned, was a military adviser, Colonel Georgi Grechukha. The slighter one had some lesser job, she never discovered what, or his name. But he was the man she had just seen in the Petit Socco.

Reaching the market on top of the hill, Gail quickly hailed a mini-taxi. As the Spanish driver loaded their shopping into the trunk, she glanced around. The little bootblack was still with them, lurking behind the galabiehs of some women shopping nearby.

Gail bundled Madame Garvi in and piled in beside her, saying loudly, "Hotel Rif." It was the largest hotel in town—and the only one she knew.

Madame Garvi started and opened her mouth. Gail gripped her wrist, motioning her to silence.

The little cab sped away in the direction of the New Town and the seafront, leaving the boy staring after it with big brown eyes. He had overheard the destination. That should be worth fifty pesetas at least. In addition to what he would get for the other favors poverty would force him to perform for the Russian.

He turned and hurried back down the hill.

When they were well out of sight of the marketplace, Gail gave the driver fresh instructions. He turned back and took the road to Montagne.

Within minutes they were climbing past luxury villas in the gathering dusk, the coastline below becoming a signature of white surf between rock and ocean. The drained colors of afterglow still lay on the sea like a pale skin, but already the blackness of the deeps was beginning to show through— the blue-black deeps beyond the North African shelf, where the tuna ran and the dolphin tail-walked after feeding.

The villas grew ever more splendid as they approached the summit. Near the very top the cab stopped outside a fine wrought-iron gateway set in a high wall and blew its horn.

The instant baying of hounds greeted them, and within moments they were at the gate, baring their fangs—three huge red-black Dobermans. They were called to heel by a youngish pug-faced American in a red baseball cap. He opened the side gate.

Gail paid the driver. She and Madame Garvi and the dog handler, Jake, carried the parcels in.

The villa was large, Spanish and rambling, with cloistered patios, stabling and a pool. In addition to the high wall, there was a screen of cypresses that prevented it from being overlooked from any direction. Its owner was the son of a famous writer who was now dead. His custom was to rent it out during the winter months while he toured the fleshpots of

Europe on the accumulated royalties of his father's talent. It had been filled with Saracen armor and antique weaponry before her arrival, but that had been removed at the Agency's urgent request and stored in the loft above the stables.

Outside the stables now waited two Moroccans in cart-wheel hats, beside three mules loaded with timber—battens, planks, plywood sheets—plus a selection of adhesives, two bags of plaster and two sets of brand-new carpentry tools. Standing nearby, keeping an eye on them, was the ungainly figure of Holz.

Holz had been another of the surprises of this altogether puzzling assignment. The chances of their working together so soon had been remote. Yet this morning, before Gail was even up, the front-door knocker had echoed through the house, and going down in her robe, she had found him beaming there on the doorstep. He had come on the night flight from Washington.

Then by midmorning, the dog handler, Jake, had arrived from Berlin with the three Dobermans. It seemed the villa was being turned into a fortress!

Leaving Jake and Madame Garvi to carry the groceries to the kitchen quarters, Gail joined Holz, who shrugged and grinned. "Mules, would you believe! I couldn't tell 'em where to put the stuff. Well, I could've," he corrected, with a dirty chuckle, "only I don't know the Arabic for it. So I told 'em to wait for you."

Gail opened up one of the stables and told the men to stack the materials inside. While they were doing it, Holz took her arm and walked her along the terrace.

"What's it for, anyway?" he asked softly.

"What's any of this for?" Gail spread her hands. Then: "Surely they told you *something* in Washington? Who did you see?"

"Jason of 'dirty tricks.' All he said was what I told you—that we're supposed to be domestic staff and security for a Heinrich Schuster of Geneva, a rich industrialist who's decided to rent this little shack out here for the winter. 'What a corny old cover,' I says. 'Never mind how corny,' says Jason. 'Just get out there and help prepare the place for his arrival. And guard the setup with your life, Holzie, or your neck's on the block. This is a major operation.'"

"'Major operation . . .'" Gail looked thoughtful. "Schuster . . ."

"It has to be a cover."

Gail nodded. "But who for?"

Holz checked his watch. "Well, we'll soon know. I forgot to tell you. There was a call from the airport. The car's gone for him. He'll be here any minute."

Gail gasped. "Well, good heavens, what are we hanging about like *this* for?"

"I thought you loved me."

"Let me see. All the beds are ready. Drinks . . ."

"He's not a *real* industrialist, sweetie."

"Dinner . . ." Gail stood there debating.

"How're the tits?"

"Terrible."

"Have you tried acraflavian?"

"I've tried everything." She hurried off to warn Madame Garvi.

Holz smiled after her fondly, a little wistfully.

The blast of the car horn brought the dogs into full cry again. Jake hurried down to the gate, calling them to heel. Thirty seconds later the big Hertz Lincoln, with Madame Garvi's son Léon at the wheel, gritted to a stop before the villa entrance.

Gail and Holz came out onto the porch steps, peering curiously to catch a first glimpse of their new boss.

From the seat next to the driver a tall, stoutish, gray-haired and moustached man in a pearl-gray suit got out. Schuster. In the dim light of the porch lantern he looked to be in his late forties, distinguished, authoritarian.

At the same time, from each of the rear doors emerged two security men, neither of whom Gail had seen before. They stood back, waiting warily for a fourth man to get out.

He took his time. When finally he straightened out into the lamplight, Gail saw a swarthy, not tall but powerfully built man with cropped black hair that hugged his scalp like a cap. He wore a suit that barely buttoned across his barrel chest or reached his hairy wrists, yet there was dignity in his demeanor and a wary intelligence in the slitted eyes as they took rapid stock of the surroundings.

The dogs began to snarl and salivate. He turned and glowered at them and, strangely, they fell silent. His eyes moved slowly to rest on Gail's.

She shuddered. The animal vibes that assailed her were like breath from a furnace.

Then they were all moving through into the hall, Schuster leading the way, the security men bringing up the rear, their eyes fixed unwaveringly on the man they were escorting. As Gail stood back to let them past she nearly reeled with the odor that came off him. Though she had never smelled it before, she knew instinctively that it was the stench of prison.

"This is Joaquín Cabeza." Schuster was unbuttoning his jacket. He paused to wave a hand from one to the other. "General—Miss Lessing, Holz." He indicated the security men. "Laroche and Canfield." He unfastened something behind him and removed the padding from around his belly and slung it aside. Now he was tall and slim, looking like an older version of Harman. Then he peeled off the gray moustache and removed the wig and laid them on the hall chest. Gail froze.

"Thank Christ for that!" Kelland muttered. "If there's one goddam thing that sticks in my craw, it's playacting!"

16

CABEZA STOOD among the Americans in the hall and heard the young woman tell Harman—or was it Schuster?—that dinner would not be ready for another hour. His alert ear did not miss the hostility in her voice. He expected Harman to slap her down, but the man appeared to ignore her tone. Well, good. The slightest breach between these people could only be to his advantage.

That he had not already slipped from their grasp at Tangier airport had been due to the watchfulness of his dual escort—an element he had not foreseen when striking his bargain with "Harman" in the prison. When the American had finally obtained his release—it took two days instead of hours, as he had promised—and come to fetch him from the office where he'd been given temporary accommodation, Laroche and Canfield were at his shoulder. They had sat one on either side of him in the car to the private airfield, and the same in the plane. But guards had to sleep. They had their high and low concentration patterns, like anyone else. He would find a way past them. The dogs, though, they were a complication. And the one called Holz . . .

Cabeza eyed the grotesque fellow from under his brows. He was a bit like himself. With an added quality. Or perhaps minus one. It was hard to lay a finger on . . . He had seen a Tartar once, clowning as he cut a Soviet official's head off, aping the terror of his victim, aping him still as his head tumbled in the dust, sticking out his tongue and rolling his eyes. To a few people, killing meant nothing. Nothing at all. Less than the swatting of a fly. This man, he sensed, was one of these. Also, he was a peasant, or of peasant stock, and peasants were canny, hard to fool. He should know.

"Harman" was speaking, asking questions about the layout. Cabeza shifted his gaze to him, measuring him afresh in the light of his true age and appearance. There was still something false about him, as though this were a disguise too. The disguise of a leader, cool, authoritative, but beneath it—a presence, complex, dangerous, pursuing its own ends. He was inquiring about the alarm system.

"Both floors separate," the one called Holz told him.

"Well, as soon as the stuff is in from the car," "Harman" told him, "switch it on. Top and bottom. And the same every night—from dusk. We must organize our routine so no one has any business outside after that hour." He looked at the woman. "How does that work with the kitchen? The cook have to go outside for anything at night?"

"I don't think so."

"Go check. Then see all the windows are shut."

"The alarm doesn't work from the windows," the young woman said coolly. "It works from the outside shutters, so the house can be kept ventilated."

"So check them," Harman ordered. He motioned her to wait. "All of you . . ." He indicated Cabeza. "The General here is a great guy and I'm sure we're all going to get along just fine, but be warned: he's one of the world's most reluctant guests. So keep him happy, give him all he wants, but *don't let him out of your sight!*"

Cabeza eyed the faces turned curiously toward him, automatically comparing them with their Soviet equivalent. What he read heartened him. These people lacked the binding power of the state, the overtones of fear and accountability that made Soviet security such a force to be reckoned with. And another encouraging difference: this lot needed him alive.

The dog handler in the red cap was explaining, "No,

no—all I need to do is, before we lock up, give 'em the trigger word and set 'em loose. That kinda pulls the pin out." He grinned. "So to speak."

"Like a grenade . . ." "Harman" nodded, tonguing his cheek, not looking at Cabeza. "Right. That takes care of things for now. I'll hold a staff briefing session after we've eaten. Any questions?"

There was a moment's silence.

"Yes," Cabeza said. "What do I call you—Harman or Schuster?"

Kelland twisted a smile. "Confusing, I know. I'm Schuster so far as the outside world is concerned. But as I won't be setting foot outside these grounds while I'm here—nor will anyone else except Miss Lessing—call me Dave."

"Dave what?"

The American hesitated. "Kelland."

"All right, Kelland," Cabeza said. "I go now to my room. Someone will show me where. I want a bath and some clean clothes."

"Sure, General," Kelland said easily. "Anything you say."

Cabeza stood with Gail in the big ornate bedroom, watching her easy-to-look-at profile, aware of the almost imperceptible fragrance that followed her quick, light movements. She was a gleam of sunshine against the dark furniture. Again the contrast with the Russians came to him. They would have had some frozen bitch whose delight would have been to make him crawl.

He listened closely to her instructions—all very cool and self-assured and in good Castilian—about the windows. The outer shutters were to be kept closed, as they were linked to the alarm system. The windows themselves swung inward and could be opened or shut without fear of tripping the alarm. His escorts, Laroche and Canfield, had the rooms on either side of him, but his door would not be locked. He could move about the house if he wished, but, naturally, all exits were secured and linked to the system. And outside, of course, were the dogs . . .

"Your bathroom's through here." She opened a carved mahogany door and led him through.

It adjoined the bedroom—*qué lujo!*—and was all done out in Spanish tiles, with a bath to imitate a drinking fountain, lion's-head taps . . . !

"Clothing is a problem tonight, I'm afraid. I had no idea you were coming . . ." She kept at a slight distance while speaking, her eyes not quite meeting his. Not so cool. He amended his opinion. She was trying to establish a barrier of professionalism between them; trying too hard. That made her self-conscious, hence vulnerable. Another factor to remember.

"Tomorrow, I'll go out and buy what you need. Write down your measurements and let me have them at breakfast, would you? Which is at eight o'clock, by the way." She leaned over the bath and put the plug in—the backs of her knees were slim and beautiful—then turned on the fancy taps. "Oh yes, and if you have any trouble sleeping, there are capsules in here." She tapped a cabinet. "Also aspirin, stuff like that."

She went back into the bedroom.

Cabeza stood there bemused for a moment. He caught his expression in one of the mirrors. It was slightly incredulous. He shook his head and chuckled, then followed her.

There she was, turning back the sheets of the big four-poster bed. It had a carved and silvered back with gold-thread needlework on the headrest, tall twin candlesticks on either side. The dressing table had a triple mirror with porcelain birds and flowers around it. Big old chests and cabinets made monastic shapes against the white of the plaster walls.

Cabeza sighed. He was beginning to feel sorry for these people. All this expense to set up something that would never happen. He watched the slim figure busily folding back the damask counterpane and recalled the stinking camps on the way to Vorkuta, how the younger women were dragged off the packed trains and repeatedly raped by the guards, how their screams went unavenged by their listless, starving fellow prisoners, how the unheated, unsanitary buildings were so crowded there was no room even to lie down, how he had killed his first Russian on that nightmare journey just for a space in which to sleep.

"There. We'll be eating in half an hour," Gail said. Turning, she caught his expression.

It was so disturbing that she left quickly, without another word.

"Gail."

She paused at the head of the stairway.

Kelland was visible in the end bedroom, unpacking his things, putting them into drawers. He beckoned her along.

She went slowly, her face assuming a mask.

"Come in. Shut the door."

She pressed the heavy door shut and turned to face him in the room that was even larger and finer than the one she had just left. Kelland was hanging a suede jacket in the wardrobe. Or his body was. His mind, she could tell by his movements, was way ahead, working through the chicanes of their coming interview. She smelled sandalwood . . . and a faint trace of fear. Her own.

"How is he? How does he seem to you?" Almost casual.

"I wouldn't know. He hasn't spoken."

Kelland arranged the hang of the jacket and buttoned it automatically, flicking some dust with a fingernail.

"Are you wearing a gun?"

The question surprised her. Couldn't he see? "Hardly."

"Well, will you do so. Keep it loaded. Small of the back. Wear a cardigan." He took some ties from the case and spaced them out on the strap inside the wardrobe. "That's in case he tries to use you as a hostage."

"Is that all?"

Kelland closed the empty case, dropped it on the floor and toed it under the bed. He turned and looked at her for the first time. If he was nettled by her tone, he chose not to show it. He even smiled.

"Stop reproaching yourself."

"Reproaching *myself*?"

Kelland nodded calmly. "You did exactly as you were supposed to. In your position you're not expected to withstand torture. If there was any dereliction of duty, believe me, I wouldn't have asked for you on this mission."

She only just managed to check herself from an outburst that would have burned every bridge she had left in the business. She said coldly, "You knew what they would do to

126

me. It was part of your plan. You used me in—in the most . . ." She couldn't find the words.

"Wheels within wheels," Kelland said. "I had no option."

"No option? You could have briefed me. At least *prepared* me."

"That"—he turned back to the wardrobe—"might have been counterproductive."

"Why? You think I'd have chickened out? My God, don't you know *anything* about women? That having botched it once, I'd have gone barefoot through hell to redeem myself?"

"And overplayed the part?" He shook his head, pressed back the hangers and closed the door. "Maybe you wouldn't have. But I couldn't take the risk. Fact is, there was no time to analyze it from your angle."

It was a lie. Gail knew Kelland analyzed things from every angle—and still hadn't confided in her. Which could only mean that he hadn't trusted her in the first place.

She caught her breath. Suddenly she understood. He had used her, not in spite of her record but *because* of it! He regarded her as emotionally vulnerable. He had been relying on what happened in Santiago to repeat itself. And to her utter chagrin, she realized, it had—almost exactly!

Her mind sped back over the Chilean episode seeking just the smallest exonerating factor. When Tony had failed to show up at the rendezvous on three consecutive days, she had allowed her imagination to run riot—why? The answer was painfully clear: because she *cared* about him. Against every rule in the book, she had allowed those evening debriefing sessions to become torrid sexual interludes. It had been their solution to the pressures of loneliness, isolation and danger that surrounded them. And when he didn't show up, she had broken the rules again and gone out to look for him. The double game Tony was playing with De Baltra's Labor Action Group was a knife-walk. They could have penetrated his cover. He could be holed up somewhere, wounded, dying even, needing her . . .

She had gone first to his freight-yard hideout. And there had found him. His cover had indeed been blown, but he had escaped and was lying low, unscathed—at least until the moment she walked in. She squeezed her eyes shut at the memory. De Baltra had been watching her, waiting for her to make just this move, and before Tony could even close the warehouse door behind her, he was ripped apart by bullets. He had died at her feet, his dark eyes on hers, becoming darker and then empty as the young life ebbed from them.

No, there were no exonerating factors. She was flawed. She knew it. Kelland knew it. She just wanted to crawl away and be sick. No doubt he could read that too, for he said with what was meant to be a reassuring smile, "I repeat, stop reproaching yourself. Shut out the past. What happened can't be allowed to stand between us, or it'll screw up this whole operation. Sunflower, Miss Lessing, that's the code name. And it's the big one."

She stared back at him dully for a moment. "Why?"

"Why what?"

"Why include me on it?"

"I thought that was obvious. You run a good house, you speak—"

"Why," she repeated, "did you have them drag me back off sick leave when you could have had your pick of the girls at the 'factory'? Why me?"

His gaze flickered. "Okay. To put you back on your horse. I reckon I owe you that."

"Now tell me the real reason. What stinking role do you have me earmarked for this time?"

"I'll pretend I didn't hear that."

"Then I'll repeat it!"

Something like a flame licked through the blue eyes. He pulled her against him crushingly.

"Now listen"—his breath buffeted her face—"if you want to dig your professional grave, keep going. If not, watch that beautiful mouth and just thank your stars you've got what I *think* you have to offer, because—"

"Let go of me, please!"

"—we're running too tight on this one for grudges or hassles. So if we're going to have London rearing its head every five minutes, say so now and you can be on the first flight home tomorrow."

"I'd still *be* home," she gasped, "if I'd mailed the complaint against you I had drafted!"

"So that's the way you feel? Right."

"Not the way." He was holding her so tightly she could hardly breathe. "Or I'd have mailed it. You still haven't got the message, have you. I'm in the Agency to *stay.* Running to Papa every time I get pushed—even into a hot cigarette—isn't any way to prove it!"

Kelland eased the pressure a fraction. "Well, that's the first—"

"I haven't finished. Do you mind?" She pushed at him, trying to release herself, but he still kept his hold on her.

"Finish it."

"Being used, it seems, is part of the course. But not being trusted is something else. If I'm to work with you, I want to be told what I'm being let in for. If that's too much to ask, then—"

"You've got it." Kelland sounded relieved. "So we're partners?" He forced her chin up so he could read her expression. Her lack of conviction must have been plain to see, but he was measuring something deeper: maybe her need to make good, loyalty to the Agency, courage . . . for she felt his grip change subtly to an embrace. He said in a different voice, "Sorry I had to get tough. Just had to make sure . . ." He was suddenly stroking her hair, gentle as a lover, his body pressed to hers. She felt him go hard.

She wrenched herself free so violently she sat down on the bed. She regained her feet confusedly.

"Before I say yes, I want to know exactly why I'm here. You said, if I have to offer what you *think* I have . . . ?"

"You're to charm the General," Kelland said, his voice softly charged. "Raise his pulse rate—the same way you do mine! Object: to keep him sweet. So he doesn't go AWOL when he finds out what he's got to do."

"And what *has* he got to do?"

"For now, that's classified information."

"Who is he, anyway?"

"Classified."

"Why are we using an outsider?"

"Classified."

"In that case—" Gail began coldly.

"You'll be told," Kelland assured her, "just as soon as I deem it secure to give clearance."

Back to square one. Gail sighed. You couldn't win with this

129

man. Indeed, why bother? She told him then how she'd been recognized in the town. She almost hoped it would invalidate her for the mission.

Kelland went very still. "Describe him." When she had done so: "Sounds like Melnikov."

"It was a chance sighting, I'm certain of it."

"Chance or not, if it was him he'll follow it up, locate that cabdriver. And once they home in on this place we'll either have to shift or abort." A pause. "What's our Chief of Station's number here?"

"On that pad." She pointed to the night table. "But aren't we supposed to—"

"To keep communications silence? We'll have to break it, won't we. We're a minimal team. I can't spare anyone to go Commie-hunting. I'll have to rustle up some outside support."

He moved to the phone and flipped open the pad. "Thank you, Miss Lessing." It was a dismissal.

Dinner was served at the end of the massive living room. The dining room, Cabeza was told, had been earmarked for another purpose. So they ate in this fine room with shuttered French windows at one end, perhaps concealing a view across the city or the sea, and at the other end a sunken well of soft seats surrounding a stone fireplace that must have been many centuries older than the house. And opposite the fireplace was a carved mahogany bar with padded stools in front and shelves of drinks behind. No one touched the drinks. Just a little wine with the meal.

Everyone helped at the table, which, again, was not like the Russians. There, only the women would have served. Here the men got up and collected the plates and helped carry them out to the kitchen. Cabeza watched them from under his brows as he ate. And ate. He took three helpings of the excellent casserole and scraped up the gravy with the fine white bread. The young woman kept eyeing him curiously. There was an atmosphere around the table you could cut with a knife. Something must have happened—an emergency of some sort. Kelland said not a word. He seemed to be waiting for something. When presently the phone rang he got straight up and answered it in another room.

Cabeza took another helping of the gravy and scooped it up with some more bread. He wasn't bothered with their problems.

When Kelland came back, he told his team quietly that the matter was in hand. The COS was "tapping the grapevine" and would have their man located before morning.

Cabeza spread Gorgonzola cheese on the salted biscuits the Americans called crackers and wondered what good tapping a vine would do. When he had finished the cheese, he scooped out some more, ate that, and then washed it down with three cups of black coffee. He was beginning to enjoy himself.

After the plates had been cleared, the Americans gathered around the fireplace, although there was no fire, and by the way they looked at him Cabeza knew they wanted him to go. He poured himself more wine and drank it slowly. He had never heard of Moroccan wine being any good, but this had a sunny flavor that was comforting. When he had finished it, he removed the napkin from under his chin and wiped his mouth with it, folded it and poked it into the little ring that was provided. He got up and nodded to the men by the fireplace and limped out.

In his room, Cabeza opened the window and listened through the shutters to the distant sounds of the city. A plane passed overhead, very low. From the pitch of its engines he judged it to be heading in to land at the airport. When its thunder had died away he heard another sound—the thud of cantering feet and a cavernous snort in the garden below. The Dobermans, lacking anyone to tear to pieces, were chasing each other around in the dark.

Yes, they were a problem. He would have to give them some serious thought. He wished he could open the shutters, just to get the lie of the surrounding land. But that chance would come tomorrow, he guessed. No sense in rushing things. The food and wine felt good in his belly. The bed looked inviting.

He took off the uncomfortable clothes that Kelland had bought in too much of a hurry in Madrid—all except the shirt.

He lay down in the shirt and pulled the sheet up over him. In next to no time he was sound asleep.

17

KELLAND STOOD with his back to the empty fireplace and briefed his team on their duties for the initial few days. The Melnikov thing must not be allowed to distract them, he said. If the COS and his contacts couldn't contain him, he would cable Washington for reinforcements. Meanwhile . . .

Gail looked around at the other faces. Every eye was on Kelland. Like her, she guessed, they were trying like hell to glean some hint as to what they were all doing in this treasure-house tucked away in back of Tangier.

She had spoken to Laroche before the meal and gathered that he and Canfield knew even less than she did, except that Kelland had sprung the mysterious General from a Spanish military jail, where he had been under sentence of death.

It was a mild night and the French windows were ajar. So the first sound came to them clearly through the shutters. A sharp cry. It sounded like a woman's.

It was followed by a hair-raising series of bellows and thudding animal feet on the paving outside, interspersed with high-pitched screams that receded with the bellowing, which turned into the jerking snarls a beast makes when it gets its teeth into something.

The team leaped to their feet. Kelland bounded up the well steps and out into the hall.

"Jake, you go first—get them under control," Kelland said. He rattled the locked door of the under-stairs closet. "Keys."

Holz had them. While they unlocked the door and threw the alarm switch, Jake was grabbing the animals' leash chains from their hook and Gail and Canfield were unbolting the front door. By the time they had it open the screams had ceased, but the horrible snarling of the dogs continued unabated. Jake rushed out, roaring at them, calling them to heel.

The rest of them stood there waiting, peering out into the darkness, listening to his repeated commands. The snarling did not immediately stop. He was having trouble with them. But eventually the savage sounds took on a different quality —one of howling frustration. They heard Jake say, "Oh my Christ!"

"Get upstairs, keep an eye on the General!" Kelland told Laroche as he hurried out, Gail, Canfield and Holz behind him.

They found Jake in the middle of the lawn, struggling to hold the dogs in check. They were salivating, horribly excited, trying to reach something lying on the grass. It looked like a heap of old clothes. Kelland flashed a light.

It was alive—just. Blood pumped from the torn throat. A small hand groped among the severed arteries, as though trying to stem the flow. Even as they watched, the hand fell away. The undernourished body convulsed. A pitiful sound came from it and it died, quivering.

Gail felt her stomach heave. She sank to her knees, fighting the nausea, trying to communicate what she knew.

"It's the shoeshine boy!"

It took Kelland one cool instant to make the computation. "Gate keys."

Jake tossed them to him. Kelland strode down to the gate, Holz close behind him. His reasoning: the kid couldn't have scaled the wall on his own. If he had used a ladder, it would have needed transportation. But the road was deserted. Not a vehicle, not a movement. The surge of traffic whispered up to them from the city that glistened like gem dust four kilometers to the east. But up here, all was darkness and silence.

Kelland crossed the road and shone the torch down the steep slope on the far side. Nothing stirred among the graceful boles of the umbrella pines. He turned and panned the beam along the wall of the property. No sign of a ladder.

Holz had walked down the road a little way. He stopped.

"Chief." He was peering at the ground.

Kelland joined him with the flashlight.

There was a black tire mark on the pavement and a deep corresponding scuff in the verge close to the wall, as though a car had started away from there fast.

"That's how he got in, Chief. Off the top of a car."

Kelland gauged the height of the wall. "So how would he have got back?"

As if in reply Jake's voice called to them from behind the wall: "Hey—there's a ladder on this side!"

Kelland shot Holz a glance of concession. He led the way back uphill, to where Gail and Canfield were waiting in the gateway.

"Typically Russian," Kelland grunted. "To look us over by proxy."

"Melnikov?" Gail asked, striving to conceal from him that she was still shaking.

"Probably. He sent the kid in to smell us out, see who we are, what we're up to. Fortunately, the dogs didn't give him time to find out."

"So what do we do about him?" Canfield asked. "Lose him? Dump him in the sea?"

Kelland shook his head. "Call the police. Why not? He was trespassing. They'll think he was trying to steal something. Let's go." He headed back toward the house. "I'll have to make like Schuster. Stash your hardware and try to look like a household."

"What about Melnikov?" Holz asked hoarsely. Gail noticed his habitual grin was gone. His eyes looked strange.

"COS'll pick up on him." Kelland shot Holz a glance, adding, "When he gives us the word, there may be a small job for you."

Holz nodded. And now Gail could read the strange look. It was like a pang of hunger.

As the men went back into the house she thought, They're dehumanized. They can just swallow something like this happening and move on with it undigested.

She tried to picture how it had happened. She had to get it all straight, to understand it. But the more she thought back over it, the less sense it made. What possible information could an untrained Moroccan boy have gathered that would have been of the least use to the Russian? Even if he had been able to see into the house, he would have had neither the wit nor the vocabulary to describe the people he saw inside. And certainly he wouldn't have been capable of reporting any overheard conversation. Yet the first cry they had heard had come from almost outside the French windows.

She moved along the terrace thoughtfully and stood outside the living-room doors, trying to estimate where the boy had been when the dogs first attacked him.

Actually on the terrace, she reckoned. Well, there was nothing to be seen through the shutters . . . Though the windows were open on the inside . . .

She thought at first it was a bat. She moved forward very gingerly to peer at the dark blob hanging from one of the shutter louvers.

When she got close, there was enough light seeping through from inside to reveal that it was not a creature; it was an artifact.

Gail turned and raced noiselessly along the terrace, into the house.

In moments she returned, leading the men, motioning them to silence.

They approached the artifact on tiptoe, nobody speaking. Kelland shone the flashlight on it. Canfield peered at it knowledgeably. He nodded and made to detach the object, but Kelland caught his wrist and shook his head. He led them silently back into the hall.

He said quietly, "We have a live bug. Play it right, we can sucker this guy into a trap."

"We may not have to," Canfield said. "That's a vibrator bug, not a mike. It operates by beamed impulses. If he's listening, he's close."

Kelland asked sharply, "How close?"

"Half a kilometer maximum, I'd say."

There was a moment's startled silence.

Holz gave a sort of sigh. "Let me handle it."

"Slow down," Kelland said. "We're on thin ice with this one. Melnikov could just have heard something over that mike in the few moments between the kid putting it there and the dogs jumping him. What were we discussing, anyone remember?"

Gail was the first to answer. "House security and the General."

Kelland grunted. "Then he has to be stopped. Question is how. If we put a slug in him or mark him up, we'll have the MGB down here in droves."

"Let me just find him," Holz said. "While I'm doing that, you can be working out the ways and means. Okay?"

Kelland considered for a moment. He nodded.

"I'll go with him," Canfield said. "One of us can work uphill, the other down."

"You can save your shoe leather, Charlie," Holz said. "The skid marks point uphill."

He moved quickly out into the night.

For a heavy man, Holz could move like a shadow. This was the aspect of his work he took most pride in. More than pride, joy. It took him back to his Wisconsin youth, soft-footing it through the woods behind Willie Night-Owl. Willie was pure Winnebago. In summer he did odd jobs on the lonely and ramshackle Holz tenant farm, but his heart still lived in the woods of his forefathers. Sap flowed in his veins. He drew strength from clasping the boles of the forest giants. He could hear beyond hearing, see beyond seeing. He was more than a hunter. He was a mystic.

To the lonely youth haunted by family problems, he was a second father, but a stern one. Nature had her laws, he taught the boy. Respect them and the forest will flow into and through you. Ignore them and it will close its doors against you. When you take the life of one of its creatures, do so only for food, and in humility, for it is a gift. Another has died so you may live. Honor that gift, as you have been honored.

Holz had followed these teachings to the letter. Beyond the letter. All natural life to him became sacred. All, that is, save man. To Holz, as to the Indian, man was nature's most deadly enemy. He multiplied, filling the earth with his brats and his cities, his pollution and greed. And when the war came and Holz found he could legitimately redress this imbalance, he did so with such gruesome relish that he was transferred to the OSS for special duties. From there it had been a natural step to the ranks of the Agency. He was a psychopath, but an amiable and manageable enough one—so long as his talents were continually given full and rewarding scope.

Now he heel-toed it along the road, mouth slightly open to heighten his sense of hearing, eyes raised to the stars so as to detect the slightest movement with their sensitive lower edges. The umbrella pines balled past above him, giving the friendly illusion of forest. He was home again, Night-Owl just ahead on silent moccasins, the night flowing through them with freshness and vibrance.

He passed three large properties. They stood in darkness, their gates closed. There were no side roads, no tracks where a car could park concealed. Just ahead was the summit of the "mountain," where the road ended. Beyond that, there was just a steep declivity where olive trees made dark shapes against the constantly circling beam of the Cap Spartel lighthouse. On a site overlooking these groves they were building a new house.

A rough open driveway led between the pines to the unfinished front entrance. Holz paused behind a clump of oleander and peered toward it.

The new cement rendering of the construction provided a light background against which a parked car would have been visible. But there was none. And there was no way around to the rear of the building that he could see. Yet where else could the car have gone? Unless it had turned straight around and headed back to town?

There was no boundary wall. Holz slipped into the property, moving from tree to tree toward the house. He was about halfway there when the faintest gleam caught his eye. It came from behind a cluster of bushes to his right.

He circled around till he was behind it. And sure enough, it was a car. It had pulled off the drive and parked among the trees. It was facing away from him.

Keeping sufficiently to its side to avoid being seen in the rearview mirror, he edged nearer. But the background was too dark for him to see if there was anyone inside it.

He was about to creep closer when suddenly the interior was lit up. Holz caught the brief glimpse of a man seated behind the wheel peering at his wristwatch. The light flashed off immediately, leaving him with only the emblazoned image to examine. The features had been invisible, due to the angle. Hair neither dark nor blond, pressed flat by something across the top. A band of some sort. Headphones.

He had found his man.

As he made his way back to the villa, Holz was aware that it was not going to be easy. A man in a car, with the windows shut and—if he was a good professional—the doors locked, with the capability of instant mechanized flight at his fingertips, was a hard man to take.

He found Kelland, Gail and Canfield waiting for him in the hall. After he had made his report, Kelland said, "I want him brought back here in one piece. Can you do that alone or—?"

"I can do it," Holz said. "But I'll need a bit of help from this end." He outlined what he would like them to do.

"You've got it," Kelland said. "Fifteen minutes—sure that's enough?"

"Plenty." Holz sensed Gail staring at him and thought, Does it show, sweetheart? That I can't wait to get my hands on him? Does it shock you?

He gave her a little grin as he moved past her toward the kitchen, where he found a large raw potato. He put it in his pocket and returned to the hall.

"Zero watches," Kelland ordered.

They compared times briefly, then Holz went out and back up the hill, slowing as he neared the end of the road, his step growing more silent, his form melting into the shadows, till he became the trunk of a tree, a low bush, another tree, a footfall on pine needles, an empty space . . .

Gradually he worked his way around behind the car. Moments later he was crouching at the back of it. He lay down and took out the potato. Very, very gently, lest the least vibration convey itself to the occupant of the car, he pressed it hard into the exhaust pipe. Then he found a flat piece of bark and, squatting, braced it behind the potato with his knee. He crouched there and watched the luminous hand of his watch creep up to the appointed time.

Back in the villa Kelland was doing the same. Moments before the fifteen minutes elapsed, he and Canfield went out and around to the living-room French windows, walking this time without stealth.

"Ah, here it is," Kelland said as they reached the bug. "I see. Nice work, Canfield."

"What shall I do with it?" Canfield asked him, grinning.

"Better immobilize it. Sling it in the pond. Then we'll fan out and comb the area. Our Russian friend can't be far away. Maybe just up the road."

"I hope it doesn't kill the fishes," Canfield said, and dropped the bug into the bucket of water he was carrying.

From his position behind the car, Holz heard a sharp movement within. There was a clatter, as if the occupant had slung aside his headphones. The next moment the starter began to turn. The motor coughed and he felt a sudden explosive pressure against his knee. But the seal held. The motor died.

The occupant tried the starter again, again—with the same result.

A muffled curse. The door flew open and the man got out. As he strode forward to open up the hood, Holz moved up behind him, slipped his arms under his. He had snatched the gun from his shoulder holster almost before the Russian knew he was there.

The man's reflex came straight from the book. He turned, sweeping back with his right hand to knock the weapon aside before it could be used against him. But Holz was already a yard clear. He leveled the gun with a chuckle.

"No, wait!" The Russian put out a hand as if to fend off the bullet. He began to wheeze. He leaned sideways against the car, wheezing, fighting for breath.

Holz could see little of him beyond his general shape, the gleam of his high forehead. It could be a genuine attack of asthma; it could be a trick. His other hand could be groping for a weapon.

"Put both your hands on the car!"

The Russian seemed to struggle to comply, at the same time gasping for the breath to speak. "Wait!— Not yet— I—must prepare myself."

"Like hell you must," Holz growled. "Open up the trunk!"

"Will—will they find me?"

"Move!"

The Russian moved slowly, supporting himself against the car, the breath sawing in his throat. "If they do not—find me—my sister—in Leningrad—she will not understand . . ."

He paused at the trunk, crouching as if exhausted.

Holz peered at him suspiciously. "Open it."

"Do—I have time to—write a note?"

Holz's finger tensed on the trigger. He was certain the Russian was fumbling in his jacket. "Open it!"

The Russian fiddled with the release. "A personal note— nothing hidden—you have my word."

The trunk hood swung up.

"Get inside," Holz told him.

"I appeal to you. As a comrade enemy."

"Get in!"

The Russian leaned toward him, peering. "Do I know you, comrade enemy?"

Holz stepped back a pace. "Quit stalling, you Russian faggot, and get in there!"

"You are the one they call Holz?"

"In!"

The Russian gave a sigh. "Then I am dead," he said hopelessly. He got in the trunk.

Holz slammed the hood and locked it. He stooped and gouged out the potato with his jackknife. Pocketing the gun, he got in the car and switched on the lights. On the seat next to him he then saw the equipment the Russian had been using to energize the bug. It measured about two feet cubed, with something like a small radar dish on top. The electronics and instrumentation looked basic, rather clumsy.

Holz drove away through the trees and onto the drive and back down along the road to the villa. Outside the gate, he honked the horn.

Kelland appeared almost immediately, followed by Canfield and Gail. From another part of the gardens the dogs

started their bellowing, but they were leashed and Jake was
with them.

"You got him?"

For answer Holz got out and opened up the trunk.

Kelland shone his flashlight on the Russian. He gave a
grunt of recognition.

"So it *was* you, Melnikov."

The Russian shielded his eyes from the light, peering
toward the speaker. His eyes widened.

"Kelland! You are here?" he wheezed. "Then what you do
is important. My instincts are always good."

"Thanks," Kelland said dryly. "Get him out."

Holz and Canfield hauled the Russian out of the car and
hustled him through the gate.

Gail hung back. She had a sudden presentiment that what
was going to happen next she would not want to see. She
moved back toward the house, but her eyes were drawn in
fascination to the flashlit scene on the lawn. She stopped
despite herself.

Melnikov was led to where the child's body lay. He stared
down at the blanket, realizing what it concealed. His wheezing increased. He hunched his bony shoulders. From where
Gail stood he looked a pitiful figure. His high, distinctive
accent came to her clearly. "This was bad. Believe . . . I did
not mean . . . for this to happen."

"Take off the blanket. Take a look at your little bedmate,"
Kelland said.

Melnikov shook his head and backed away—to be thrust
forward again by Holz and Canfield.

"What're you scared of?" Kelland asked. He kicked the
blanket aside.

The Russian stood stock-still. A sound escaped him. He
turned his head away.

"What's that bit about the capitalists exploiting the poor
and underprivileged that your sort are always talking about?"
Kelland sneered. "You're full of shit, know that? Now pick
him up."

Melnikov shook his head violently and struggled to break
free. Holz and Canfield forced him close to the body.

"Do as he says."

Melnikov did everything he could to resist. But in the end he knelt down and gingerly picked up the torn and bloody corpse. He straightened with it in his arms questioningly.

"Now down to the car," Kelland told him.

Gail watched as the strange procession trooped back toward the gate. She had no idea what they intended to do with their prisoner. She didn't want to know. She went into the house quickly and shut the door.

Melnikov placed the body of the child in the trunk as he was bid. The front of his suit and his shirt were covered with blood. They sat him in the back while they removed the listening apparatus and searched the car thoroughly for any papers that would reveal the nature of his work in Tangier. They found nothing. Then they searched his person. His pockets were professionally empty, but clutched in his right hand they found a cyanide pellet. So that was what he had been fumbling for! Why hadn't he already swallowed it? Perhaps praying for a last-minute miracle—an error even the most hardened professionals are apt to make. When they tried to prize it from his grip he showed desperation for the first time, fighting frantically to retain it. But eventually, deprived of it, he sank down in the back and seemed to withdraw into himself.

Canfield carried the apparatus and the pellet up to the house and put them in the hall. He got out the Lincoln and drove it down to the road.

Kelland took the wheel of Melnikov's car. Holz got in beside him, facing back to cover the Russian. They drove away, the Lincoln following.

Then, minutes later, Kelland stopped the car in a lonely spot overlooking the sea. He applied the hand brake and switched off the lights. Canfield stopped a little way back along the road. He got out and joined them, and together they hauled Melnikov out and sat him in his own driving seat. His wheezing had stopped now. He made no resistance. He seemed utterly resigned to his fate.

Holz took out the Russian's gun and shot him through the right temple with it at contact range. He wiped his own prints off the weapon, squeezed it into Melnikov's hand and lay it loosely on his bloodstained lap.

They carefully wiped their prints off all the relevant parts of the car and stood back.

"Anything we've forgotten?" Kelland asked.

He strolled across the road and looked down into the black emptiness of the sea that surged and thumped below them. The wedge-shaped split in the darkness that was the Cap Spartel light passed over him ten times as he stood there. On the eleventh rotation, he turned back toward them.

"No? Then that's it."

When the news of Melnikov's death reached the Moscow headquarters of the MGB eight hours later, there were murmurs of disgust.

The report left the precise explanation of what had occurred to conjecture, but it was accepted by Deputy Director Likachev and his supergraders that he had taken his own life after some unspeakable excess. The general consensus was that when you employ a pervert such things must always be in the cards.

Doubt as to the accuracy of the report was not expressed until the following morning, when Likachev informed the now Deputy Minister of State Security, Colonel Georgi Grechukha, of the fate of his old UN assistant. Grechukha recalled that during their brief association Melnikov had confided in him his fear of death by violence, especially the gun. For this reason, he had told him, he always carried a cyanide pellet sewn into the lining of his jacket. So if he had killed himself voluntarily, Grechukha reasoned, would he not have used this method instead of blowing his brains out?

He got Likachev to send for the last report cabled by Melnikov before his death. They studied it together. It contained a summation of the agent's recent Agitprop activities. Added to which was a brief rider—to the effect that he had identified an Agency operator in the town and thought it possible the Americans might be intending to field a counter-Agitprop unit in the area. He was going to investigate.

Grechukha was thoughtful. So was Likachev. It could just be a coincidence, of course.

But long experience had taught both men that in a profession where so little is left to chance, coincidences are rare.

Certainly it could do no harm to follow it up.

18

CABEZA WAS awakened by the passing of a plane overhead. He squinted at his watch. It showed seven-twenty. Sunlight filtered through the shutters to glisten on the ceramic birds and flowers of the dressing-table mirror. Their reflection pricked the ornate ceiling with little points of lightness. *Arriba!*

He chuckled and swung his legs out of bed. That was about the tenth plane that had passed over since his arrival. *Bueno.* That placed the villa under their regular approach path. It could be useful.

He got up and limped to the window. He wondered whether the alarm was off. He was tempted to fling wide the shutters regardless, but thought better of it. They might think he was trying to escape and tighten their guard. That was the last thing he wanted today.

He went to the door and glanced out. The door to his left stood open. He moved along to it and looked in. Laroche was shaving by the window. He wore shirt and pants and a gun harness. He was a dark, erect man of around forty, with very black unsmiling eyes. The eyes spotted him in the mirror instantly and Cabeza saw his right hand free itself automatically, but he did not turn.

"Morning, General. Sleep well?"

"The alarm is off? I want to open the shutters."

Laroche shook his head. "Sorry, pal. The alarms on this floor stay on all day. Kelland's orders."

Son of a whore, Cabeza thought, as he went back to his room. He went in the bathroom and filled the basin and stuck his head in it. Then he confronted his dripping, battered countenance in the mirror and shaved it.

Kelland was more on the ball than he had anticipated. Well, no matter. It would take more than alarms and dogs to stop him.

The Americans had made two basic mistakes. The first was in bringing him to Tangier, a city he knew his way about. The second was in not confiscating the money the prison clerk had returned to him on his release—five thousand pesetas. Around ninety dollars.

That offered him four avenues of escape. There was a port full of ships, including the ferries to Marseilles, Casablanca and Port Vendres. There was the Tangier–Fez Railway, the airport and the road. Lack of a passport—they *had* confiscated that—complicated things a little.

Which avenue would they least expect? he wondered, as he went down the stairs. A soft tread behind him told him that Laroche was following him down. The port maybe. But he would think about it.

Kelland sat alone over coffee at the long living-room table. He was routing through a pile of international dailies, scanning the columns intently. He glanced up as Cabeza entered, his face unsmiling. "Morning, General." His eyes resumed what could only be their search. There were dark shadows under them, Cabeza noted.

The French windows were open and Gail stepped in from the terrace, where she had been talking to the car driver. She clattered down a coffee cup and saucer on the table. She looked brittle, impatient, as if she had been waiting for him. Nevertheless, she endeavored to smile.

"Your measurements, General."

Ah. Cabeza had forgotten them. He told her his size, noting that her smile was forced. Something has happened, he thought. He told her what he needed.

She grabbed some shopping bags and went out the terrace

way. "Okay, Léon," he heard her say to the driver. "You can drop me on your way to the airport."

Cabeza moved to the French windows and took his first look at the garden. It was mostly lawn, fringed with cypresses, a few neat flower beds, colorless at this time of year. He noted the high boundary wall. He took a pace outside to see if he could detect the gate. But it was beyond his line of vision.

A few meters along the terrace, Holz was seated in a white wrought-iron chair, his hands folded across his belly, his ugly face raised to the sun. His eyes were shut. He sat absolutely motionless, like a statue, but Cabeza sensed that he knew he was there all right.

"Cornflakes, General?" Laroche's voice asked pointedly behind him.

Cabeza ignored him. Presently, in his own time, he went back inside.

"Hell!" Kelland muttered. He had finally homed in on a news item relevant to his search. "Two more of our men went down in Moscow, according to Tass."

"Shit," Laroche said. "No names, I suppose?"

Kelland swept the paper onto the floor and retrieved his coffee, scowling thoughtfully. "We've got to get this show on the road, George—and fast. Where's Canfield?"

"Taking a horizontal shift. Catching up."

"I want that stuff brought in from the stable."

"I can get him," Laroche said, frowning. "Only you said last night you wanted him or me sharp right around the clock."

Kelland sighed. "Let him be."

"Holz is outside."

"He's catching up too. Forget it." Kelland paced, frustrated.

They *are* on edge this morning, Cabeza thought as he helped himself to more coffee.

"Heard the ruckus last night, I suppose, General?" Kelland said with his back to him.

Cabeza looked at him.

Kelland turned and saw the look. "No? You must sleep like a rock."

Cabeza waited.

"We had an intruder. A Moroccan. The dogs killed him."
Cabeza raised his brows. He said nothing.

"Just thought you might like to know," Kelland said, watching him.

Cabeza reached for a slice of toast. He laid three pats of the pale Moroccan butter on it, piled on the Seville marmalade.

He took a big bite and sat there munching audibly.

The car came back, bringing four more Agency men from the airport. They came in with their hand luggage, filling the hall with their bluff jargon as they shed their hats and topcoats.

Kelland led them along to the living room, calling to Madame Garvi to bring in more coffee.

"General, I want you to meet some more of our team. These are the experts."

Cabeza was just finishing breakfast. He sighed inwardly and hauled himself up.

The first was a Pole—Stefan. He was tall, with fair, thinning hair and a wispy moustache, aged about thirty-five. Next, a Russian, Gregori, with a cheerful meaty face, penetrating eyes, bushy eyebrows and the sharp black hairline of a young man, though he must have been well into his forties. They pumped Cabeza's hand heartily, greeting him in Russian, cocking their heads, listening to his replies in the same language.

"How's his accent?" Kelland asked.

"Good," cried Gregori. "He speaks more good Russian than I speak English!"

"But the accent?" Kelland asked.

"Accents do not matter in Moscow," the Pole assured him. "Every other person you meet there was born outside the Soviet Union."

The remaining two were American; one slim and bespectacled, wearing a bow tie—he could have been a lawyer or an architect. Kelland called him Cedric. The other a red-faced, balding man in his late fifties, Artie. Despite his sagging beer paunch, the grip of his hand was like the tread of an old motor tire with the canvas showing through. Cabeza guessed him to be a worker. Maybe a craftsman of some sort.

"This is an honor," chuckled the Russian. "In the late thirties you were a big trouble to us."

"Gregori was in the NKVD," Kelland said, watching for Cabeza's reaction.

Cabeza stiffened.

The Russian laughed. "Have no fear. Now I am American citizen. I defect in '48."

"And I also—in '47," said the Pole. "I was a flyer with the Soviet air force. I was a believer until Katyn, the massacre of all our officers by the Soviet military."

"That was never proven," Gregori said, frowning. Then he chuckled grimly. "But I believe it!" He added, his eyes twinkling, "For me it was the women. Our own were so—so . . ."

"Dowdy," supplied the Pole.

"Dowdy—it sounds a good word. Yes. My own wife was so 'dowdy.' My daughters—'dowdy.'" He made a face, adding dryly, "Of course, there were a few other little things I did not like."

"Gregori is now married to a beautiful American actress," Stefan said.

"Ah!" The Russian beamed. "Broadway. She sings, she dances." He kissed his fingers. "But you had a wife in Moscow, I think? Don't tell me . . ." He hammered his head. "Ludmilla Patolichev?"

Cabeza nodded somberly, his eyes narrowing. "You have a good memory."

The Russian laughed. "For your file only. I read your file—we both read your file—before we come from Washington." He added quickly, "But only for such details. The dissidence of El Duro was well known to us of the Moscow Division. You were a pain in our ass, my friend."

There were chuckles. Cabeza regarded him stonily, and presently, when the Russian shifted the focus of his wit elsewhere, slipped out into the garden. Laroche followed. Cabeza ignored him. Things were developing here faster than he had expected. He must make his move quickly.

He made a deliberate circuit of the house, getting a good look at the gate, the stables, the swimming pool, which was empty at this time of year. He pinpointed his own window. Underneath it was a paved terrace leading back to a covered patio with a barbecue chimney. He estimated the hanging drop from his sill. Three meters, give or take a little.

Kelland and the new arrivals remained talking in the living room for half an hour, their discussion becoming gradually more confidential in tone and substance.

After which they all trooped out to the stables and began to carry in the construction materials and tools, the Russian and Pole helping good-naturedly, as though to make it clear that such a menial task was not part of their job.

They ferried them into the empty dining room through the terrace doors. Artie laid a couple of the heavy sheets of plywood on the floor while Cedric opened up two portfolios of plans, drawings and photographs he had brought with him.

Cabeza observed this process while strolling around and around the terrace—with mounting curiosity. Using a steel rule, T square and set square, Cedric began marking out a ground plan on the plywood. Artie was already sawing lengths of timber, erecting them loose on top of the plan. He worked fast and precisely.

At lunchtime, Madame Garvi brought in beer and sandwiches. They took a break and sat around on the floor. Kelland joined them, and for a while they sat together swapping Agency talk, Gregori's distinctive laugh booming out across the garden, where Cabeza still strolled, debating his problem.

Seeing him pass, Gregori suddenly called, "Hey, General Tovarish! Come in. Come see."

Cabeza paused. The Russian indicated the base plan of the model. "You recognize?"

Cabeza picked his way through the littered tools and offcuts. He squatted down and ran his eye over the pattern of pencil marks and slats of wood.

Gregori took a swig of beer, looking around at the others, winking. "It is Moscow. No prizes for that. But let us see how good you remember the names."

Cabeza stiffened imperceptibly. Back in the prison, Kelland had told him he wanted him for an act of anti-Soviet sabotage, though for security reasons he couldn't tell him sabotage of what, or where. That the "where" would be Moscow, Cabeza had had little doubt, but this was the first positive confirmation he had received of this absurdity. He scowled across at Kelland, to find the American's gaze fixed on him perceptively.

Cabeza shook his head and tapped it insultingly. Nevertheless he returned his attention to the model ground plan. He was curious.

He had no idea as to the scale, but there was a blank strip along one edge of the board. That had to be the river.

He picked up a small handsaw to use as a pointer.

"The Moskva?"

Gregori nodded approvingly. "Go on."

"Then . . . this must be the south wall of the Kremlin."

"He's there," Cedric said.

"Let him do it alone," Kelland snapped.

Cabeza pointed to each of the breaks in the wall. "Uh—the Borovitzkiye Gate . . . Taynitzkiye . . . Spasskiye Gate . . ."

Gregori nodded silently.

Cabeza pointed inside the walls. "So this is . . . ah . . . the old Senate building . . . Kremlin Palace . . ." His voice trailed slowly away. He was looking beyond the walls for the Merchants' Quarter, the Kitai Gorod. But there were no marks outside the walls, other than the suggested beginning of Red Square. No marks at all.

He looked up at Kelland slowly. "This model is only of the Kremlin."

Kelland nodded, still watching him closely. The others looked surprised, as if they thought Cabeza would have known this.

"You are saying . . ." Cabeza found it hard to keep his voice even. "This sabotage you want me to do . . . is *inside the Kremlin?*"

Kelland spread his hands calmly.

"Can you think of a better place?"

Cabeza ate only a token lunch. Afterward he went up to his room.

Laroche followed him. He checked him in his doorway.

"For the book, General—you just popping in or staying in?"

"Siesta," Cabeza grunted, and shut the door.

He pressed his ear to the inner panels for a moment. He heard Laroche move along into his own room. He did not hear the door close.

Turning, he saw a heap of parcels on the bed. He ripped open a couple. Shirts, pants, underwear. So the woman was back.

He reached under his jacket and, from the waistband of his trousers, drew out the handsaw. He hoped the model makers wouldn't miss it. They had two of everything lying about down there, and the moment he had finished with it he would slip it back.

He moved to the shuttered window and estimated how many slats he would need to remove. He marked them with his thumbnail and stood listening. No sound of sawing reached him from the dining room below. He would have to wait.

The Kremlin! The trouble with Americans was they saw too many movies. The place was a sealed fortress, bristling with militia and MVD. Anyway, what could be the aim? What did they want him to do?—blow up the powerhouse? Block the drains? Disrupt telephonic communications? What would that achieve?

Ah—a plane was coming. He positioned the saw at the extremity of the top slat and waited.

When its thunder filled the house, he sawed rapidly, stopping just short of severing the slat from its frame, switching quickly to the next. He had all but amputated two of the louvers by the time the reverberation had died away. He stopped work and waited patiently.

Presently the sound of Artie's sawing came up to him. Cabeza timed his next cuts to coincide with the rasping strokes of the other saw. Jake was out there somewhere, he knew. There was a chance that he would make a distinction between the two sounds, but it was a chance he had to take. There was no way he could see into the garden. But he could see the terrace below through the slats—that was a help.

Anyway, no one gave the alarm, and one hour, two planes and several sawing sessions later, he had completed the job. The bulk of the louvers in the right-hand shutter were held in position now by mere filaments of wood. He stood back and surveyed his handiwork. Viewed from directly in front, the cuts in the louvers were all too visible against the brightness outside.

He went into the bathroom, ran a basin of hot water and softened up a bar of soap. He scraped the soap against the saw cuts until it filled them. He smoothed the result over with his finger, then wiped away the excess with a towel.

There. Unless one looked closely, the louvers now looked intact.

He tried on some of the new clothes. They weren't bad. He chose the darker Levis, a denim shirt and denim jacket. He laced and put on the blue canvas shoes. They had a white welt and bright cream rubber soles. He wasn't too happy about those. They would show up like a goat's behind at night. He must remember to dirty them as soon as possible. He inspected his reflection in the mirror.

Muchacho, he thought, no matter what you wear, you still look like a peasant on market day.

Six hours later, Cabeza was back in his room. He lay, fully clothed, on his bed and began to think over what he had to do.

The evening had dragged excruciatingly. The model builders had gone to bed first, followed at intervals by the others. Now the house was silent. Laroche was somewhere beyond the thick wall behind his head, hoping to "catch up" on the day's "sharpness." Canfield was on the other side of the bathroom, hoping to do the same. The young woman had gone to her room at the end of the corridor. Whom did she sleep with? he wondered. Kelland, presumably. So much the better; they would preoccupy each other.

He got up and moved to the door, opened it a fraction and listened. Not a sound. He stepped out. There was a light on downstairs somewhere. It was sufficient for him to see that both the neighboring doors were shut.

He tiptoed out and down the stairs. The light was coming from along the hall near the front door. He used its reflection to guide him to the kitchen. He went in, leaving the door open, so as to see his way across to the refrigerator.

He sensed the big room's spotlessness. Everything in its

place. Madame Garvi's small factory shut down for the night. The interior of the fridge was spotless too, cram-packed with food. *Madre,* they lived well, these Americans! As he had hoped, the joint of beef they had had for supper was in there—much diminished, but still with some meat on the bone.

He took it out and laid the dish on the table. He found a carving knife and cut three thick slices. He was just slipping them into his pocket when the light flared on. He froze.

Holz stood in the doorway.

He was fully dressed, had a folder or something under his arm. He was smiling his elfin smile.

"Still hungry, General?"

"Always," Cabeza said evenly. He poised the knife over the meat questioningly. "There is enough for two. You like the rare, or the outside?"

Holz shook his head, his grin looking a little fixed. "Never touch it. I'm a vegetarian."

How long had he been standing there? Cabeza wondered as he carved another slice. How much had he seen? He rolled the meat in his fingers and bit off a chunk.

"There is cheese." He waved his hand at the refrigerator, chewing.

Holz shook his head. He didn't move.

"A beer?"

Holz just smiled for a moment. "Okay, a beer." But he made no move.

Cabeza reached a can out of the fridge and tossed it to him.

Holz flicked the ring off the can. "Strange old life, ain't it?" He took a short, watchful swig. "You ain't leaving us, are you, General?"

Cabeza held his gaze without a flicker. "Why?"

Holz shrugged and took another swig. "Just, it'd be a shame. We ain't hardly got to know each other. Been hearing some pretty hairy things about you this evening."

"The Russian? He talks too much."

"Don't they all. But you're like me. You like to do, not talk. We got a lot in common, General."

Cabeza cut another slice of the meat.

"Holz," he mused. "Unusual name."

"Dutch. Me pa was Dutch."

"Ah."

"A Dutch prick," Holz said. "Full of religion. Full of horseshit."

Cabeza waited. When nothing further was forthcoming, he put the joint back in the fridge. He turned to encounter the almost lazy smile.

"You ain't full of horseshit, are you, General. Nor me. We know what life is all about, don't we. And death. We been there."

Cabeza tried to read what he was getting at, but the lidded clown's eyes were opaque. Was he trying to tell him something? Warn him? It occurred to him that Holz could possibly be a bit simple. But there was no comfort in the thought. So was the Tartar who had cut the official's head off.

"Well," Cabeza grunted. "I go back to bed."

He moved toward the door behind Holz.

Holz didn't move. His smile was almost fond, but Cabeza sensed a tiny change of gear as he approached. A tightening.

Cabeza knew where the American's gun was. He just watched his right hand and kept coming. As he made to step around him: "Not so fast, General." Holz put the hand out.

Cabeza stopped against it. One twist and he could have the man on the floor. But he waited first for whatever move the other would make.

Holz chuckled. "You know, you give me a funny feeling. Can't quite explain it. You sure you came down here just for something to eat?"

Cabeza said pleasantly, "That and maybe break your wrist."

Holz looked pained. "My my, we *are* touchy. I just wanted to show you something." He stepped to the table and flipped open the folder. In it was a drawing. "To ask what you think."

Cabeza moved to glance at the picture. Holz watched his face.

Carefully drawn in pencil and colored in crayon was a lion. A fierce lion with a fine mane. It was balanced on top of a spiky gooseberry bush, and all around the bush were little snapping creatures. They could have been jackals. They could have been Dobermans. The lion was bigger than they were, but it was outnumbered. It looked angry and uncomfortable. The gooseberries on the bush were all eyes and the stars above had eyes. There were eyes everywhere watching the lion.

"Ring any bells?" Holz inquired, smiling.

Cabeza chuckled. "Alarm bells?"

The massive face broke into wicked delight. "Oh yes!" he cried. "Oh yes, I like that! For that"—he tore the picture off its pad and handed it to Cabeza—"you get the prize." He stood aside, beaming. "Happy dreams, General."

Cabeza took it up to his room. He was half amused, half thoughtful. What had all that been about? He wasn't sure. Strange man, Mr. Holz. Where did he sleep? he wondered. Maybe he didn't. Maybe he wandered the house at night, snatching the odd forty winks in an easy chair. Well, he'd give him an hour or two to settle down. So long as he himself could be down at the Tangier docks around dawn . . .

He went straight through into the bathroom and got the bottle of barbiturates out of the cupboard. They were in pill form. He crushed all of them down to a fine powder on the edge of the bath and scooped them into a funnel of paper. He spread out the cuts of meat, sprinkled the powder on them, then rolled them up and tied them tight with bits of thread pulled from the carpet. Three tasty morsels.

He stretched out on the bed again and tried to relax.

The hour passed. He got up and, with a few silent cuts of the handsaw, removed the slats from the right-hand shutter. He peered out into the garden.

There was no moon, which was a blessing. And no sign of the dogs. He waited, listening.

It was not long before he sensed a shadowy movement on the far side of the pool. He hissed, as he had heard Jake do.

The dogs came around the pool, their feet thudding on the paving. They paused, staring about them, ears cocked, noses testing the air.

Cabeza hissed again. Their eyes snapped up toward him and they came toward the house in a loping rush. In a second they would start their bellowing. He quickly tossed out the rolls of meat—all at once, so as to be sure they each got one. So far as he could see, they did. Though in the darkness it was hard to tell, so fast did they wolf them down. Then they were staring up at his window, hungry for more.

Cabeza leaned back out of their view. He returned to the bed once more and stretched out. He had no idea whether it would work or, if it did, how long it would take. Maybe dogs were immune to barbiturates. Maybe it took more than the human dose to knock out those great, sleek bodies. All he could do was wait and see—and hope. "Pray" might be a better word.

He went to the window at intervals after that, but he didn't see the dogs again. Clearly they had wandered off to another part of the garden. But in what condition he could only surmise.

He gave it another hour. Then, pulling on a pair of dark socks over his luminous sneakers, he moved a chair to the window, climbed up and worked his body out sideways through the slatless shutter.

The tag ends of wood caught in his clothes, and to his heightened senses, it sounded like the breath of a steam locomotive. But taken very slowly . . . He squeezed out, inch by inch.

In a few moments he was hanging by his fingertips from the sill. Here it was. The moment of truth. If the dogs were still conscious, he was dead.

He hit the terrace with a loud thump. His bad leg buckled and he fell sideways. He rolled up and moved straight onto the lawn, limping quickly across the dewy grass. His eyes were everywhere, body braced to resist the instant rending attack that could come from the shadows without warning.

He passed behind the stables and the garage—no sense in trying to steal the car, there was no way of getting it out through the gate—and down behind the shrubbery that flanked the drive. Still no attack. It was beginning to look as though the drug had worked.

He pushed through the bushes onto the drive. Now all that lay between him and freedom was the massive double gate.

He gripped the ornate wrought-iron work and hauled himself up. The top was tricky—a row of gilded spikes. Don't rush it, he told himself. Lose a minute and save your *cojones*. Freedom without those would be a mockery!

He eased himself over and down the other side. Seconds later he was standing in the road. He was out!

He turned and headed away down the hill.

He had gone barely five yards when the night was filled with the sound he had been subconsciously dreading. Every alarm in the villa behind him started to ring!

19

EARLIER THAT night Gail had hurried through her chores, anxious not to be left alone with Kelland. She could smell a storm brewing and just couldn't face it. Her limbs felt heavy from too little sleep the night before and too much wine at dinner. The Russian had kept filling her glass, murmuring provocative little flatteries in her ear. The Pole had been attentive too. In another place, at another time, it might have been stimulating. But not with Kelland's cold eyes reminding her she should be concentrating solely on the General.

He should have got himself a Mata Hari, she thought bitterly, not a linguist. How did one even *begin* to turn the head of a man like Cabeza? Those slit eyes read your mind as surely as Kelland's blue ones. The animal potency of the man scared her. They both scared her. She was here to act as a catalyst between two men who not only gave her the willies but were as incompatible as fire and ice. She couldn't win! Fire, mercifully, had retired to his room, but Ice stood brooding on the hearth, eyes lidded against the smoke of one of his fancy cigarettes, just waiting, she knew, for the rest of the team to get the hell to bed so he could haul her over the coals. She raced to complete laying the breakfast things so she could exit with the others. But too late, they were already trooping out, the door closing.

A heavy silence ensued, broken only by the jingle of cutlery. Then, just as it seemed Kelland was about to speak, Holz popped his head in to say he was hitting the sack. Kelland turned. "Holz, I want you to sleep downstairs tonight. And not too soundly."

"The General?"

Kelland nodded, his gaze shifting to rest hard on Gail. "He's not ours yet. He's somewhere else. He has to be *ours*, Holz, or Sunflower is no-go."

Gail looked up, sharply defensive. "Will you tell me something? Why are we using a man who doesn't want any part of us? Why? Just tell me."

"Good question," Holz said.

Kelland crushed out his cigarette deliberately. "Are orders not enough? You want it spelled out?" He let them see they were way out of line before he answered. "General Cabeza is anticapitalist, anti-American—hence *the very last man the MVD would associate with Uncle Sam*. Added to that, he requires no conditioning. He already carries his own private motivation around in his head—revenge motivation, ideological motivation. So in the event of his ever getting picked up, the trail stops smack there, in Commieland, no comebacks." He watched them digest this for a moment. "Unfortunately, it's this mistrust of everything we stand for that's working against us. We've got to pull him over to our side more. And so far, Gail, all you've done is fart around like a high school virgin, when"—he stabbed a finger at her—"right now you should be up there in his bed!"

"That isn't true! I've *tried* to make contact with him . . ."

"Contact?" Kelland made it sound like child therapy.

"There's a culture gap. We're just not—"

"Bridge it, girl! Let your hair down. Get him horny. Appeal to him as a sex object!"

"Appeal to—to an ape? How do you do that?" Gail almost shouted.

Kelland met her anger unblinkingly. After a moment he pushed past them and strode from the room.

Gail exchanged uneasy glances with Holz. Had she come on too strong?

Presently Kelland returned with a folder.

"This is his file. Read it. *Tonight.* Wrap your brains around just what sort of a man we have here, what's locked up inside him, what makes him a *must* for this operation. Then, with your womanly intuition or whatever you've got, you'll be able to figure how to get under his skin. *Maybe.* I'm beginning to have doubts, but prove me wrong."

Stung by these words, Gail took the file upstairs. All she wanted to do was sleep, but if Sunflower was to be her way back in from the cold, she'd better get to grips with it. Maybe this folder would contain some clue as to what it was all about.

She began to read.

Two hours later she was still reading, riveted. The articles and documents that turned beneath her fingers, each was more disturbing and compelling than the last. She found it hard to imagine how anyone could have endured such hardships as the General and remain sane. Far from being an ape, he was a many-faceted man of incredible courage and resource, superior in so many ways to them, his jailers. More like a lion—captive in a cheap circus. Unwittingly she had hit on the same metaphor as Holz.

At last she turned out the light and tried to sleep. But her emotions kept on churning, churning. And when finally she dozed off, the churning continued into her dreams, bringing restlessness and a strange sense of foreboding.

After what might have been moments or hours, a sudden noise jerked her back to consciousness.

She lay there, puzzled, her mind replaying the sound for her awakened senses to interpret.

A heavy thump. Not from inside the house—*outside.*

She knew. Instantly. She struggled up and flapped into her robe. She was halfway to the door when she remembered her gun. Throwing herself across the bed, she grabbed it off the night table and thrust it into the robe pocket.

She ran to Cabeza's room. All was darkness. She widened the door until she was able to see the bed in the reflected light from her own room. It was empty! Then she saw the gaping shutter.

The next instant she was racing down through the house, calling to the men, banging on every door as she went.

"He's gone! He's got out! Quick!"

Down the stairs. Rushing to the front door, she came face-to-face with the startled Holz. He fired one question at her: "How?"

"Through his window." Then she was at the front door, throwing back the bolts. She hauled it open. The alarms began to jangle.

"Hold it!" Holz shouted, dragging her back. "The dogs!" He bellowed, *"Jake!"*

First down was Kelland, fully dressed and calm, and for an instant Gail entertained the absurd notion that he had been sitting in his room, waiting for this to happen. Then feet hammered the corridor above. Laroche and Canfield appeared in hastily donned shirts and jeans. They, too, came to a stop in the doorway. Everyone yelled for Jake.

"Knockout darts, Holz," Kelland said. He told Canfield to kill the alarm.

As Holz exchanged his pistol magazine for another, Jake came stumbling down, half asleep, zipping up his pants. He grabbed the leashes and hurried out, whistling for the dogs.

Kelland waited by the door, charged, silent. Presently he shouted, "Jake, what's going on?"

"I can't find them," came the reply.

Kelland waited another few moments, then said, "What the hell," and hurried out, Holz with him, Gail and the security men following, the Russian and Pole bringing up the rear.

As Kelland was unlocking the gate Jake appeared.

"I've found 'em," he panted. "They're out cold. Doped, by the looks of it."

"Then he's away," Kelland said, hauling the gate open. "Holz, tell us which direction."

Holz took the flashlight and shone it on the road. He indicated the wet blobs of footprints left by Cabeza's socks. They pointed downhill.

"Let's go," Kelland said.

"Hold it, Chief," Holz said. "You think it's going to be that simple? Get off the goddam road, all of you." He waved everyone back into the gateway. "Nothing's going to be the way it looks with that guy. Nothing."

He showed Kelland where the footsteps stopped.

"See? He got over to the side of the road." Holz shone the flashlight on the shoulder. There were faint scuff marks in the dust. They led back uphill. "What did I tell you?—he backtracked. He went that way." He pointed toward his hunting ground of the night before.

"Okay—go get him," Kelland said. "We'll follow."

Holz shook his head. "He'll go over the top and down, looking for a road. Get in the car quick. Go around, head him off!"

He started uphill at a trot.

"Remember," Kelland called after him. "This isn't a hit."

"It's whatever he makes it," Holz's voice shot back from the darkness.

Kelland turned and led the way up to the garage. Telling Jake to stay behind and hold the fort, he got in the car and backed it out. Canfield and Laroche piled in beside him. Gail, Stefan and Gregori into the back.

The wheels exploding gravel, the car spurted down to the gate, turned left and sped off down the hill.

Gail drew her robe about her against the rush of wind from Kelland's window. Curiously, she felt torn. A part of her knew that the General had to be stopped at all costs; the rest of her was whispering, "Run, lion, run!"

Holz ran up the now familiar road, making no effort to silence the thudding of his sneakers. The General had had a good start and he wouldn't hang about. He was a cool one. How had he done that with the dogs? The answer came to him as he ran. So his instincts back in the kitchen *had* been right. Holz cursed himself. Always listen to your instincts, Night-Owl had taught him. And he hadn't. Holzie, you're losing your edge, he told himself. Nothing short of peak form was good enough to hold the General. Nothing short of his very best. The fate of the whole mission lay in his hands now. He must not blow it.

Reaching the end of the road, he slowed. The new house? No. The last thing Cabeza would do was hole up. Unless he knew he had only one pursuer. Then he would become part of the landscape for just long enough to step out and kill him. But he wouldn't expect just one pursuer. He'd expect the whole pack after him. So he'd be down there, limping through the olive groves, scanning the country below him for the first flash of headlights that would indicate a road.

There was a road—the Spartel road—and he would find it. If he was lucky and caught a lift, he could be away westward and around Spartel on a big loop that would take him down past the Caves of Hercules and back to Tangier via Ziaten. But he wouldn't know that, so the chances were he'd try to grab a lift going east, straight back to Tangier—a mere five kilometers—knowing that once he hit the city they'd never find him. Kelland was heading around on that road now—to cut him off. But would he be in time?

Holz moved down among the olive trees and stopped again. He stood there, collecting his senses, listening, sweeping his lifted eyes back and forth, seeking the least disparity that would signify movement in that static wilderness.

God, it was lonely . . . beautiful. The sweet scents of the mountain herbs came to him. And as he inhaled them he knew suddenly by their very sweetness in his throat that he had been wrong and that Cabeza had not come that way at all! For the passage of a body through such herbs awakens in them a sharpness, a taint, that lingers for a while after the body has passed. And there was no such taint. The flora of the hillside smelled as sweet as a flower garden.

Holz turned, with almost the stamp of a wild buck, and raced back up the hill onto and down the road, sprinting as he had not sprinted in years.

He had told Kelland that it wouldn't be as simple as it appeared. What he hadn't allowed for was that, with the General, even a bluff was simple. Cabeza had pulled a *double bluff*. And the way he had pulled it came to Holz as he ran, and it was sheer genius. It was so beautiful it made his heart sing and his gut become a void, because it was clear now that if he couldn't reach the lower road in just a few minutes, they had lost El Duro completely and forever.

He could never make it on foot in time, he knew that. To steal a car in the village was his only hope. And people didn't leave their cars unlocked in Tangier, not unless they wanted them stripped to a shell overnight. He'd have to force one open and hotwire it. That could use up all the time he had.

He fairly tore down the road toward the village.

Kelland had driven down off Montagne and taken the west road, which wound up north again past the fine Djemma el Mokraa building before it turned due west along the valley that Holz had been overlooking minutes before.

He pulled onto the side of the road, parked, and killed the lights. He and the four men got out and stood, shifting a little, their feet crunching the grit as they peered up the slopes toward the distant olive grove.

Gail stayed in the car. She was cold in her robe with only the thin nightie under it, and she had on just bedroom slippers, which would have been quite hopeless on the rugged terrain she knew they intended to climb.

The men spaced themselves out along the road. Passing a silent signal from one to the other, they started up the slope slowly, like beaters at a shoot. They vanished into the darkness, to be picked out again by the rotating Spartel light—to vanish, reappear.

Gail shivered and wriggled down into the backseat, hugging herself. Would they catch him? If they did, she didn't want to see it. She was a fool to have come along.

She heard the trunk click up and felt a shift in the suspension. One of the men must have come back for something, she thought. Yes, there was a male figure moving outside the car. He came around to the driver's door, opened it and got in.

He shut the door quietly and started the engine. Gail sat up slowly.

He turned in his seat and backed the car around, and as the reversing lights came up against the edge of the road, their reflection lit up his features.

Gail gasped.

Cabeza was spinning the wheel, switching on the headlights. He snatched a quick, surprised look in the mirror before he drove away.

She wrenched a quick look back out of the window. The others must see the car taking off—what would they do?

What *could* they do? she concluded, as the car gathered speed in the direction of the city.

"That was very clever," she said evenly.

Cabeza chuckled.

"Only one thing you didn't allow for."

"Mm?" He was concentrating, putting the car not very expertly through the sharp bends.

"I have a gun," she said, raising it. "And it's pointing at the back of your neck."

Cabeza flicked a glance in the mirror and saw that it was so. He didn't bat an eyelid, just piled on more speed. The bends were getting sharper. Gail was thrown from side to side. She struggled to hold the gun steady.

"Stop the car, General! You hear? Stop it. Please!"

Cabeza laughed. "Why do you not shoot? Go ahead. We can have a big crash, big fire, and after, you can make the breakfast toast from our ashes."

His eyes mocked her in the mirror as he swerved the car about. He was a terrible driver. She clung to the strap, scared, trying to think coherently.

"Please, General," she cried. "I have to stop you, don't you see?"

Cabeza was hauling the car around a bend that just kept coming, getting sharper and sharper. The sharper it got, the more he seemed to be running off the road. The rear end broke away, slithering up onto the shoulder. Gail shut her eyes. When she opened them again, he had somehow regained control. The road had straightened out, and there, a couple of miles ahead of them, were the lights of Tangier. Silhouetted against the lights was something blocking the road.

Cabeza leaned forward, peering. The next instant he was stamping on the brakes. The wheels locked. The car corkscrewed, tires screaming. Gail was thrown forward. A vehicle loomed in their path—a battered red pickup, parked squarely across the road. There was no way around it—deep ditches lay on either side. They had to crash. But Cabeza somehow straightened the car out. The tires regained adhesion and he brought it to a stop less than a yard from the truck.

He scowled furiously and started to open the door. The

pickup appeared abandoned. He checked in sudden suspicion, his eyes springing intuitively to the roadside—just in time to see Holz rising like Mephistopheles from the ditch, Luger gripped in both hands, aimed directly at him.

Flame leaped from the muzzle and a projectile cracked through the open window to bury itself in the opposite side of the car. Cabeza had thrown himself flat across the seats.

Gail, shocked speechless, saw Holz spring out of the ditch toward the car, gun leveled for a second shot. She tried to shout to him that it was all right, she had the General covered, but before she could find the words the car shot into reverse. Cabeza was backing up blind. Holz flared into brilliance as the headlights caught him. He spread his legs and with both hands aimed the gun at the windshield. Gail threw herself down. The projectile cracked straight through the car and out of the rear window above her head. The car continued to shoot backward, virtually driverless. She expected at any moment to feel it keel over and crash into the ditch. But somehow it kept a straight course, and when she glanced up, Cabeza was upright again, leaning over her, watching out of the back as he continued to reverse along the road. The back window had a fist-sized hole in it, but it was still possible to see out, and he just kept on backing, backing. Beyond him she could see Holz following them on foot, sprinting, gun in hand, shielding his eyes against the headlights. But he was losing ground with every yard.

Presently they lost sight of him around the big bend. Cabeza still didn't stop. They passed several turning places, but he just kept going in reverse.

It was not until they had covered a good half mile that he pulled in to the side of the road and applied the hand brake, then twisted around in his seat and reached for her gun.

Gail was just too quick for him. She struggled across the car and out of the far door. She turned with the gun pointing.

"Out of the car, General. Put your hands up."

Cabeza got out, but as he faced her she saw a different man—a figure of urgent and overwhelming power. He came around the car, and his stature seemed now to dwarf her.

"Give me the gun."

She backed away quickly.

"Games are over. Give it to me."

The gun wobbled in her hand. She tried to steady it with the other. "Keep away. Please keep away." She felt absurd in her nightgown. The weapon seemed suddenly no protection against his advance.

She backed up, holding herself together with an effort, still keeping the gun on him.

He stopped a few feet from her, his eyes on hers compellingly.

"Give it, *muchacha*. He is coming. You are wasting time." It was an admonition—father to child. More than a father—an overlord. She was mere fluff and he had commanded armies—armies that had fought and died for him. And here she was, daring to stand between him and his rightful freedom.

She almost surrendered the weapon then. One thing alone prevented her. He wanted it so he could kill Holz.

She reaffirmed her stance. The distant patter of feet on the road came to her now. Or was it the beating of her own heart? No, it was Holz, and Cabeza had heard him too. He was even now moving forward to remove the gun from her fingers.

"General, stop! I'll shoot. Don't make me shoot." Her foot slid from her slipper into some thistles. The sharp agony threw her off balance. She fell back against a sloping rock. He was still coming. Thistles and flints all around her—she was powerless to sidestep.

"Stop!" The shrill command could have been a puff of wind. He reached out with fearless authority. His hand was less than a foot from the gun when she fired.

The impact of the bullet spun him backward. He dropped to one knee, clutching at his shoulder. A sound squeezed between his bared teeth. But already he was starting to rise.

She fired again, twice, the bullets exploding the grit on either side of him, whining away to smack into the opposite hillside.

The shock tumbled him backward onto the road. Before he could move again, she was standing over him, the gun aimed between his eyes.

Cabeza glowered up at her, surprised, hurting, assessing his chances still of making a lunge for the weapon.

But before he could act, Holz arrived.

Gail swayed for a moment. The shock of what she had done was almost as great as if she had done it to herself. A convulsion started low down inside her, working its way up through her like a gathering wave.

She stumbled aside and was sick.

20

CABEZA SAT on his bed while Gail dressed his shoulder. It was getting near dawn. He was surprised, a little impressed that she had found the courage to shoot, and angry at himself for having underestimated her.

The wound was nothing. The piffling little .32 bullet had passed through the deltoid muscle of his left upper arm. It had grazed the bone, which was turning his stomach a little. But the noise Artie was making outside his window as he nailed the steel mesh across his shutters was far more irritating.

Kelland had said very little, which had surprised and mystified him. Laroche and Canfield, more predictably, had manhandled him roughly—from a sense of guilt, he guessed. And rightly. In the MGB they would have been shot for negligence. Holz, of course, was still grinning all over his ugly face. But at the final count it had been this slender woman who had saved the day for them. And her mood was hard to define.

Having shaved the hairs off his shoulder, she had cleaned the wound and was now spreading on bandages, front and back. She still wore the nightgown, and as she leaned forward he could see the cleavage between her breasts. They looked

169

well developed but firm, and her skin had a sheen to it, like that of the girls of his own race who worked in the sun. Her hair, seen close like this, had mixed strands of gold and silver and brown in it, which seemed to him rare and becoming—and nothing whatever to do with the spot he was in, he reminded himself sharply, which now looked very bad. The first chance of escape was always the best. After that . . . But she was smoothing out the plasters, silky fingered, her breath catching softly in her nostrils the way his mother's used to when she had tucked him up in bed as a child, or helped him put on his clothes. *Qué va,* he thought angrily. Why do you heed such things when they are sealing you in like a barn rat? Yet he knew why. A shot fired between woman and man is not the same as between man and man. There are sexual connotations, hard to analyze, harder to ignore. Then she lifted her head to inspect her handiwork and, confound it if she wasn't weeping!

He tried to concentrate on his next move, but the tears worked on him as always, like acid in his gut. *"Qué pasa?"* He raised her chin impatiently.

She shook his hand away and plunged her head down. *"Nada.* Nothing, General. Nothing to do with you."

"Then stop your sniveling and let me think. You have landed me in a mess, *muchacha.* That should make you happy. It was a good shot." He added dryly, "Unless you meant to kill me."

"Oh, no!" Shocked. Then with more control: "You made me do it. I didn't want to hurt you. In fact . . ."

He waited. "In fact?"

Her eyes were on the window. "Nothing."

Artie was just finishing. When he had disappeared down the ladder, Cabeza prompted: "A woman's 'nothing' is usually her biggest 'something.'"

"If . . . it hadn't happened the way it did," she confessed, "I think I'd have let you get away."

He digested this revelation in slightly incredulous silence.

She went on brokenly, "You suffered such terrible things in Russia—and here we are forcing you back there. It's unforgivable!"

"You should tell that to Kelland."

She snuffled a bitter laugh.

Cabeza regarded her thoughtfully. A woman's tears are the oldest trap in the world. Could this be one of Kelland's? He weighed her present mood against what he had observed of the relationship between her and Kelland. It seemed to him consistent.

So as one door closes, another opens! he thought, amazed at his luck. For he knew from long experience that guilt among one's captors was an instrument that could be made to play many tunes. Gail needed to atone for her act of violence. Very well, he would help her! He would lead her on, twisting the knife a little more, a little more, till he had secured her connivance. Then . . .

He groaned, gripping his shoulder.

Gail reacted in instant concern. "It's hurting? Come, lie down. Here—" She pulled back the coverlet. Supporting him by his good arm, her breasts warm and mobile against him through the thin robe, she eased him down on the bed, pulled off his shoes and drew up the coverlet. She stood back, looking down at him agitatedly for a moment, then picked up the first-aid box. "Try and get some sleep."

"Wait."

"I must go now. It's—"

"Venga." He motioned her closer.

"What is it?"

He took her wrist and drew her down to sit beside him and, with his thumb, wiped the wetness from her cheeks. "You don't want Kelland to . . ."

"Oh, no." She smiled, quickly grateful, rubbing at her face.

"Cálmate. Be calm. You are very nervous, *muchacha."*

"I— Yes. I suppose it's the reaction."

"So. We will talk. When you have control of your reaction and there is nothing for Kelland to observe, then, if you wish, you may go."

"That's very—" She was about to say "thoughtful," but checked herself uncertainly. She glanced down at his hand, which was again on her wrist. "Talk—what about?"

Cabeza said heavily, "I will tell you of the freedom you have taken from me with that little bullet—of my *rancho* in Mexico, of the fine fighting bulls we breed for the *corrida*, of the saddle that awaits me, empty, while my *vaqueros* ride out, instructionless, into the early morning. And you, *muchacha*, will tell me how your friend Kelland proposes to get me to Moscow and what he plans for me to do there."

"I don't know what he plans. None of us knows yet. He hasn't—"

"Nevertheless," Cabeza said, "what little you know you will tell me." The dark slits of his eyes charged her compellingly. "You owe me at least that."

For a moment it seemed as if she would resist. Two distinct expressions crossed her face fleetingly—the first of a wild creature about to wheel and run, the second of its deciding, for some reason, to hold its ground.

She laid aside the medical kit meekly.

Kelland reached for another cigarette. He was still fully dressed, stretched out on his bed in the darkness, watching through his partly open door. He could see clear along to Cabeza's room that Gail was still in there, had been for almost an hour. He waited, the reflected tip of his cigarette glowing and fading on the polished surfaces around him, till the luminous hands of his watch made it one hour exactly— for no particular reason other than the sense that the period seemed to him conclusive. Then, smiling to himself, he sat up and, without turning on the light, made a phone call.

"Hal?" His voice was no more than a murmur in the silent house. "You can tell your guys to stand down now . . . All of them—the port, bus and train terminals . . . It's over, yeah. He bought it. We left things loose for him. He took off like a rocket. But we outsmarted him before he could reach you . . . Helluva risk, sure, but he needed to do it. Now let's hope he's got it out of his system . . . Right. Only remaining danger spot is when I brief him tomorrow. Any news of Haslar? . . . On his way? Good. Expected time of arrival? . . . Well, give me a buzz when you do. *Ciao.*" He hung up.

Stubbing out his cigarette, he got up and moved to the window. He stood thoughtfully for a while, watching the ashen world come up like a color print in the dawn light. Authoritarian? Pally? How should he play it? The way you broke news to a man like the General was vital. Every damn move you made within the radius of his observation was vital. Like Gail softening him up now, relaxing him.

That had worked well, the shooting. Piece of sheer luck. If it had been planned, it couldn't have fitted in better. His choice of her had turned out to be right on the nose. Likewise his fostering of her insecurity. Plus the fact that she only half understood what she was doing. On the nose. It was coming together like—like the manufacture of a Swiss watch . . .

The next evening Kelland summoned Cabeza to the dining room. The whole team was in there. They were gazing down at the completed model.

Cabeza joined them in their inspection. He had to admit it looked well made, almost real. He glanced around under his brows at the other faces. Expectancy, he could feel it. Gail shot him a tiny warning glance. She looked pale. Her hair was drawn back, emphasizing the long, slim line of her neck, and there was tension in the muscles. She wore a khaki drill shirt and slacks. Almost a uniform. He was reminded subtly that despite last night she was still one of "them."

Not that anything had "happened" between them. Cabeza had been careful to make no move she could interpret as a pass. To allow her, even if she was willing, to expunge her guilt in one sexual catharsis would have been a grave mistake. They had simply talked, she defensively, until he had got her to relax. Gradually he had drawn out her other, more candid, womanly side. But it had been hard work. That part of her seemed to be in retreat. This career she was chasing was wrong for her. In the end it would destroy her. That his plan to use her would hasten that process he had no doubt. But he had no option. In this game of life and death there was no room for sentiment.

Cabeza dragged his mind back to the present. Something was in the wind. He glanced alertly around—to encounter Kelland's intent scrutiny.

The intentness switched to a bland mask. "How's the arm, General?"

"It is with me. I am here. What do you care?"

"I care very much," Kelland said pleasantly and evenly. "So should you. Because in thirteen days' time you're going to have to hang your full weight from it. Think you'll be able to do that?"

All eyes turned to him, and for a moment Cabeza was

tempted to pretend disability. But playacting was not his style. He removed his arm from the sling Gail had made and flexed his fingers slowly, his eyes hard on Kelland. Suddenly he raised the arm high above his head, his face revealing by not a twitch the agony it cost him.

Kelland looked relieved. "Thank God for that."

"Now you will tell me," Cabeza said, returning his arm to the sling, "why in thirteen days?"

"Our deadline. You've had your fling, General." Still pleasantly. "Now we go to work. Your briefing starts tomorrow—crack of dawn."

Cabeza digested this expressionlessly. "If I attend."

Kelland inhaled through his nose, his glance sweeping across his team before coming back to Cabeza. "You will attend. One way or another, believe me, you will attend."

"I will decide," Cabeza told him calmly, "after you have told me what I am to be briefed *for*."

"The nature of the sabotage?"

"The *so-called* sabotage."

Kelland twisted a smile. "Touché."

"To merely demolish something you would use your own men."

"Correct. This is sabotage in its wider sense. Its political sense."

The team around them became very still.

"Meaning it has to do with people, not things."

"Again correct."

Cabeza said flatly, "I am to kill someone."

"You are to kill someone."

A murmur coursed through the gathering. Cabeza heard Gail gasp. A flush of anger darkened his face.

"This is what your files made of me—a cheap assassin?"

"No, a man with a grudge, General. A man with the fire and iron to *satisfy* that grudge."

"Meaning that we both want the same man dead."

"In a nutshell."

Cabeza waited for the revelation that had to come. The team craned forward expectantly. Kelland plunged his hands in his pockets, and for a moment the clink of small change was the only sound in the room. At length he said, "He sits on the Council of Ministers."

"No guessing games, Kelland!"

"Also on the Presidium."

"Now you listen—" Cabeza stabbed a fierce finger at him. "Go back to your files and read. You will see that before everything I am a survivor. Survivors risk their necks only to survive, not to gain revenge."

"Not even if it means they can change the Soviet system— the system you so despise—two birds with one stone?" Kelland hissed. "Don't bullshit me, General—you'd sell your mother for such a chance!"

"No chance, Kelland—an impossibility. You kill one of the Presidium, the others remain, the system goes on. You would have to kill the lot—Molotov, Kaganovich, Malenkov—"

"Small fry!" Kelland snapped.

"Khrushchev, Beria—"

"Forget them—*puppets!* There's only one man—when you pull him out the system collapses. *One man,* General!"

The exchange halted in its tracks, leaving Cabeza's fierceness to turn to incredulity. In the sudden sharp silence that followed, no one moved. Then everyone moved, excitement freeing their tongues in a torrent that swirled around the two protagonists where they stood, eyes locked, Cabeza's disbelieving, Kelland's hungry, avid for his first reaction.

"Got it now? We're offering to package you in and out, with every conceivable backup, expense no object. It's the chance you've been waiting for for half your life—tear the bastard apart!" Kelland hissed, his face so close Cabeza tasted his spittle.

Cabeza still couldn't quite digest it. Surely not even the Americans could be such fools?

"You . . ." he began, as if almost expecting a laugh, "want me to kill *Stalin?*"

Kelland's hands seemed to explode in front of him. "Who else, General, dammit? Who else d'you think we'd pull a man of your caliber in to assassinate?—Josef Vissarionovich Stalin!"

Book
TWO

21

THE CAPTIVE earth blundered on toward March, warm airstream pitted against cold, wind against rock, current against tide in the waywardness of oceans under a distracting moon. All was struggle.

Man, too, swarmed in his hives. In the United Nations, Cabot Lodge clashed with Vyshinsky about Russian involvement in the Korean fighting, which was still claiming lives, as was the war in Indochina. The North Sea claimed fifteen hundred more as it rushed into the lowlands of Holland and eastern England, flooding millions of acres and rendering a hundred thousand homeless. The British Queen lunched with Marshal Tito while her subjects prepared for her coronation in June, and the Department of Justice announced that it would continue to bar the return of Charles Chaplin to the United States. Burt Lancaster swashed and buckled his way through the movie houses as the Crimson Pirate. Field Marshal von Runstedt died. As did eight convicted Mau-Mau terrorists at the end of a rope. There had been an oil dispute in Persia and the Shah left the country. And then returned, at the instigation of the CIA.

In Russia the Doctors' Plot arrests and executions had reached purge proportions. *Pravda* almost daily announced the arrest of more Russians accused of spying for "foreign

179

powers." Most of them, curiously, were Jewish. There were violent anti-Jewish demonstrations and murders in Kazakhstan and an answering bomb blast in the Soviet embassy in Tel Aviv. Polgunov, head of Tass, vanished without a trace. Molotov's wife was arrested. Lev Zaharovich Mekhlis, member of the Communist Central Committee and Stalin's one-time friend and secretary, died in highly suspicious circumstances.

The "wheat field" was truly blazing. Omega sent a signal to the DCI, Washington, to say that if the Agency was going to move, it must move now—and fast.

The DCI informed the DDP, who immediately cabled Kelland in Tangier for a situation report.

Back came the coded reply: "Briefing complete in three days."

The DDP shut his eyes and prayed. The briefing in itself was useless, he knew, without the means of delivering Cabeza to Moscow. That means hung solely upon the arrival in Bilbao, Spain, of a certain letter. They had a street man waiting at the poste restante to collect it. It had not yet arrived.

The letter would be from Moscow, addressed to one Marcos Alfonso Montel. Montel was general secretary of the Spanish Iron and Steelworkers Union.

Montel and his wife were at this moment enjoying an unexpected vacation in a mountain chalet overlooking the picturesque Gorge of Pancorbo. There was not a great deal for them to do there, other than hike around the goat tracks in the appalling rain escorted by three armed Agency guards, or lounge in front of the log fire and plan what they would do with the very large sum of money they had been promised for their services and their silence. Being realists first and Communists second, they preferred the latter.

But without the missive from Moscow, operation Sunflower, upon which so much depended, was a nonstarter.

The DDP sat in his office and quietly sweated.

"Fingers crossed," he complained to the DCI, "is a helluva way to run an army!"

It was not until 9:00 A.M. on February 23, 1953, that he uncrossed them. The letter had arrived.

* * *

The morning of the twenty-seventh was a brilliant, rushing day, everything moving, flowing in Van Gogh brushstrokes, the cypresses bending in the wind's current, gulls blowing across the rich blue sky like paper; plants, grasses, shadows streamed around Kelland's ankles as he strode, his hair a cockscomb, around the villa garden on his morning walk.

Cabeza watched him through the mesh of his window as he dressed, thinking moodily, The briefing is over; there is confidence in his step, as of a man going to market with a glossy mule.

Well, you're not there yet, *americano*, he thought. You can lead a mule to market but still it shits where it pleases.

Nevertheless, Mule, he said to himself as he pulled his shirt down over his hairy chest, you have allowed him to lead you far. How could that have happened? It is very strange.

After learning that his task was to kill Stalin, he had told Kelland he was insane, that if such things were possible, Franco would have been long buried, as would Churchill and Truman; Stalin himself, for that matter. That he was permitting himself a daydream. One that he, Cabeza, wanted no part of. That they could bring what pressure to bear on him they liked, nothing would make him change his mind.

Yet he had changed it. Again he asked himself, How could it have happened?

Kelland's reaction had been—unexpected.

"A strike, General? I see." His voice had been quite calm. "You will be shut in your room, of course. No food. You understand that?"

Cabeza had said that he understood it. It would make no difference. "To die here or die there in Moscow is equal. I choose here."

Kelland had simply nodded. And gone off to telephone.

Cabeza, slightly puzzled, had stomped off to his room. Presently they had locked his door. And there he had stayed, settling down to develop a new, half-formed escape plan in his mind.

For how long? For some reason he was not sure. His memory of just what happened next, and when, was strangely hazy.

Someone else had arrived at the villa. An ugly man, fat and

short, with glasses. How could he know this, if he was locked in his room? There was no logical answer. Simply, the face was quite clear in his mind. Bending over him, smiling, the lenses magnifying his eyes. He could even remember the smell of his clothes. Faintly chemical. Was that before or after the coffee? Gail had broken the rules and brought him coffee. *Said* she had broken the rules. But women, though they practice much, make bad liars. She had been sent to reason with him; that much was clear from her opening words.

"Joaquín, *please* won't you reconsider?" Her manner and tone were beseeching. "You—can't—win. Not this way, believe me."

"If Kelland sent you here to tell me that, then I *am* winning." Cabeza chuckled grimly.

She shook her head quickly. "You don't understand." She cast about her for a moment. "Look—meet us halfway. *Pretend* to. Say you'll attend the briefing. Then go down and . . . just sit there."

"You are wasting your time, *muchacha*."

"Don't you see, we can't *force* you to listen. We—"

"You can't force me to do anything." Cabeza cut her off. "That is the truth."

"Don't be too sure," she said darkly, then continued quickly, as if to hide a blunder, "Have—have you forgotten that Kelland saved your life?"

"For what, ask yourself."

"But you did make a deal—right? You shook hands on it. I thought that in Spain, when you buy a donkey and you shake hands on it . . ."

"Then find the donkey is a viper?"

"You are still honor bound."

Cabeza laughed shortly. "You are dreaming, *muchacha*. We are not such fools."

Her expression took on a sort of desperation. She moved closer to him, lowering her voice.

"Joaquín, listen to me. I'm talking to you now as a friend—"

"As a friend"—Cabeza cut her off—"you are still an enemy." He raised a knuckle to her cheek and smiled. "Very beautiful, very convincing . . . but still an enemy." He added in a harder voice, "Until you prove otherwise."

"I'm trying to—you won't let me!"

"Tonight I will let you. Come to me when the others are asleep." He took the coffee from her and steered her to the door. "We will talk. About friendship. And its fruits."

"But—!"

"Now go and tell Kelland I will leave this room in my own way only, not his." And he had pushed her out.

Her heard her voice say, "Oh God, you stubborn . . . !" outside the door. She had stood there agitatedly for several moments, then gone. And he had drunk the coffee.

His next memory was of being back at the briefing. And of a great relief, as though many rocks had been removed from the river of his mind and it was flowing now as it had long ago in Siberia, with singular momentum toward a singular goal. That momentum was hate. The goal was Stalin.

When Gail had come to him that night—or it might even have been another night—her mood was different. Her eyes, as she had replaced the dressing on his wound, had searched his continually. She seemed to be waiting for something, yet not waiting, regretting that it wouldn't happen.

She had said, "You wanted to see me . . ."

Cabeza thought back. His head was crowded with the day's briefing.

"You don't remember?" Suddenly she put her arms under his and pressed her cheek to his naked chest, holding him tightly, murmuring, "It doesn't matter. It doesn't matter," nursing him as one would a child.

Her deep emotion mystified him, making him suspicious.

When she had finished his shoulder, she collected up the things and turned, watching him anxiously. "Is there anything I can do?" she inquired softly. "Anything at all?"

Cabeza told her she had done it. The arm was fine. Her behavior was making him even more suspicious.

Still she hesitated. "Would . . . would you like me to stay?"

Cabeza looked at the fresh, clean modeling of her face, the pink molding of her lips and shyly questioning eyes, at the supple figure, beautiful and full breasted beneath the thin robe, and wondered what it would be like to possess her. For a moment he was tempted. But there was something strange here.

He shook his head warily.

"I just thought . . . you might be feeling . . . lonely."

"Alone, *muchacha,* never lonely."

"I could sleep on the couch if you didn't . . ."

"Go, *muchacha.*" He said it gently but firmly.

She had gone, it seemed to him, sadly, though it could have been an act. Nothing in this world of Kelland's was to be trusted.

Since then, wherever he had gone, she was never far away, sitting beside him at the briefing, at mealtimes, bringing refreshments to his room. He had watched her face for some visible link, the briefest exchange of glances between her and Kelland that would have confirmed his suspicion that she had been set to spy on him, but she seemed always studiously to avoid her boss's eye.

Qué va, Cabeza thought now as he finished dressing. Neither she nor they are important anymore. Only Stalin is important. How I get to him. And how I dispose of him.

So the mule does *not* shit where it pleases, he thought wonderingly as he left his room and started down the stairs. Yet it does. How can that be?

Very simple, he told himself. Where I choose to shit is on Stalin. It is a decision made of my own free will.

And as if to endorse the origins of that decision, a picture came to him. A scene from his first winter in the Soviet Union.

The cold. *Mierda,* that terrible cold gnawing into his unaccustomed bones! The troops parading in Red Square. Domes and spires like sugar candy against a porridge sky. Stalin—there he was, the murderer—erect on top of Lenin's Tomb, surrounded by bemedaled generals with crab-shell faces.

When the parade was over, the Leader came on down toward where Cabeza and the other Comintern leaders waited half frozen below. He was laughing, eyes squeezed up, the frost of his breath crackling on the Satanic moustache. Playing the big man—in his two-inch lifts, the special topcoat trailing down by his boots to make him look taller.

"We meet again, comrades!" he cried, as he shook hands with each of them. "Enjoying our winter, are you? Be thankful for it. It is a wall against our enemies. Never forget that in your studies at the Military Academy. Winter is our mightiest army. Winter is a good Communist!" His chuckle was like the gurgling of an ice floe.

He came to Cabeza. The chunky, gloved hand grasped his as he said, "And you, Comrade Joaquín—are you becoming a good Communist?"

From the glint in his eyes, Cabeza realized he had heard something.

"I have never been anything else," he replied gruffly.

"Then you must try harder," rumbled Stalin. "Mere good is not enough. Perfect must be your goal. To build perfect Communism we need perfect leaders."

"However good the leaders," Cabeza told him evenly, "Communism can never be perfect while it allies itself to the dogs of fascism."

He was referring to Stalin's nonaggression pact with Hitler —the year was '39. This was open criticism, unheard of at these propaganda events, especially from a foreigner, a guest of the state. Cabeza felt those on either side of him move away from him slightly.

The great man's smile never wavered. Among the pockmarks, it might have been carved in stone.

"Wrong," he said flatly. "Communism *will* be made perfect. Because, with that pact, I have bought time for it to become so. And for us to build up our military strength." The slit-eyes remained hard on his, though he began to move on. "You have much to learn, Spaniard, about strategy." He added softly as he turned away, "And self-preservation."

Son of a whore! Cabeza snarled. And for a moment he was united in his determination to obliterate his enemy.

Then only part of him was; the other part was digging in its heels again.

It was very confusing.

He found himself staring down at the model. He had come down into the dining room, automatically.

They had served their purpose now—the little hardboard buildings. They looked worn. Ten days of prodding with pointers and dismantling of upper stories, of spilled coffee, of cigarette ash, had taken their toll. But nothing now could dim what they represented—the parks, the towers, the cathedrals, the administration buildings of the Kremlin. He had memorized them all, every courtyard and stairway and checkpoint. Especially . . .

His eyes were drawn to the former Senate building near the northern ramparts. In plan, the building resembled the triangular frame you place over the balls on a pool table, its center a courtyard. And tucked away in the northern corner of the first floor was Stalin's apartment. On the floor above was his Secretariat. Cabeza knew the layout, the furnishing of each room, what each cupboard and drawer contained, where the guards were positioned, at what intervals they were changed, Stalin's daily routine, his habits, even down to when he changed his linen.

Upstairs doors were slamming in the wind. Cases were being bumped downstairs to be stacked in the hall. Cabeza dragged himself away from the model by an effort of will.

He went into the living room to stake his claim on the coffee ahead of the mob, Canfield as ever hard on his heels. Laroche and Jake were already seated at the table, squint-eyed in the sunlight that glittered among the breakfast things.

He had scarcely grasped the pot in his scarred hands when they all came trooping in—Cedric, Gregori, Stefan, Artie, Holz—their faces closely shaven, beaming. They were catching a direct flight back to Washington.

Gail came in with their reservations. She looked quite different now with her hair dyed brunette, her freckles hidden under tan makeup. She gave him a little smile as he handed her a coffee and her hand rested on his arm for an instant, but the smile vanished as she took her place at the table. It had been four days since Kelland had told her that she, and she alone, was to accompany Cabeza to Moscow. Originally, his escort was to have been Canfield, but the only available cover identification, so Kelland had explained, was for a man and a *woman*. Gail's reaction to this had been marked—not at all what Cabeza would have expected from a loyal Agency operative. She had retired into herself from that moment on, becoming moody and uncommunicative.

Is it just that the project scares her? Cabeza wondered as he sat down beside her. Or does she know something that I do not? It is possible that there is much more to Sunflower than I have been told, that I am only a thread in a huge and complicated tapestry of cold-war intrigue.

In which case here came the Master Weaver himself, bursting in from the garden, almost blown in, hammering the French doors shut behind him, combing down his hair with his fingers, surveying them with charged eyes.

And suddenly there they were—the whole team—together for the last time.

Sitting there, listening to their cross talk between munches of toast, Cabeza could almost hear the mutter of guns. It was so like the atmosphere before a battle, when those who were being relieved and would soon be on their way back to safety and a comfortable bed, with perhaps a woman in it, were full of high spirits, and those who would remain and fight trying to share their mood and not quite succeeding. He and Kelland and Gail and the three security men would stay on here—for how long, no one was quite sure. There had been complications. Something to do with his and Gail's new identification and the Moscow flight arrangements.

Flying to the USSR was no easy thing, apparently. There was no air access to Moscow from the West, except aboard a Russian plane, and then from only a handful of airports. Tangier was not one of them.

Well, good, he had thought. This meant a broken journey. An opportunity for escape. And no sooner had he thought it than a strange sensation started in his gut—a sort of sickness, a pushing back, as if his body were recoiling from the edge of a precipice.

Kelland's eyes kept dabbing at his fine gold wristwatch.

"Where the hell's Léon got to? He's late."

"Wasn't that the car?" Holz lifted a finger.

Kelland froze, listening.

To Cabeza it was just the gunfire, the battle drawing closer. The battle for which he had been fully briefed, yet still had no plan. How many times had he dreamed that in his life? And now, here it was—a reality.

Or was it? He was no longer certain. Reality was a sharp thing. Its paths all led toward one goal—survival. But now that goal lay masked in fog. Other directions rang in his ears. This way or that? He stood confused at the fork.

Either he would soon awaken or the Americans had achieved in just ten days what the Russians had failed to do in five years. They had divided him. Without deprivation, without torture. If true, it was very impressive. And very alarming.

Cálmate, he thought. It will resolve itself. Take it as it comes. Eat your breakfast.

"Stalin—breakfast: 7:50 A.M. Starts with quarter-pint of vodka. Two salt herrings with chopped raw onion. More vodka—in one swig. Two lamb chops or rare steak or Wiener schnitzel, roast potatoes. White bread, butter, jam, smoked salmon, pastries and lemon tea sweetened with strawberry or raspberry jam. Does not read newspaper, rarely talks. Overall time: 20 minutes."

In came Léon with the mail and newspapers. Kelland was on his feet at once. He claimed several packages addressed to him, selecting one unerringly. It bore no stamp and no postmark. That meant it had come via the U.S. legation diplomatic bag.

The conversation halted as he slit it open and drew out two passports and some documentation. He sat down, studying each item closely, taking his time.

Eventually he passed one passport to Gail; the other, plus documentation, to Cabeza.

"Well, that's it," he told them. "That's your cover."

And he said it with the air of a soldier who unbuckles his pack after a long and difficult approach march.

The passport was in the name of Marcos Alfonso Montel, general secretary of the Spanish Iron and Steelworkers Union. Gail's was in the name of Susana Montel, his wife.

They contained tourist visas valid in the Soviet Union until March 10, 1953, specifying Moscow as the point of entry and listing the half-dozen or so towns they would be allowed to visit during their stay.

In addition, there were Spanish identity cards, a union membership card and two letters typed in rather clumsy Spanish.

The first bore the letterhead of the Central Council of Soviet Trade Unions in Leninsky Prospekt and was an invitation to "an honored comrade and his wife" to visit the Soviet Union as their guests, together with a party of other leading international trade unionists. The Aeroflot flight would leave Schönefeld Airport, East Berlin, on the twenty-fifth of February 1953. Travelers should make their own way to Berlin, but thereafter all expenses would be met by their comrade hosts.

The second missive bore the letterhead of the Intourist Central Office in Marksa Prospekt and said that they had just heard from the Central Council of Trade Unions that Comrade Montel had been prevented by illness from joining the Berlin-Moscow flight as scheduled, but understood that he was now fit to travel. It gave the time and number of an alternative flight leaving Berlin on March 1, and hoped he would be on it.

Cabeza glanced up at Kelland questioningly.

"The date of the first flight cut us too fine," Kelland explained. "We had to get Montel to apply for a later booking." He added, "That was our cliff-hanger—whether it would get here in time."

"So they are real people?"

"The Montels? Sure. Why invent people when the world's crawling with the bastards? Real ID, real passports. Just your photos and descriptions added."

Cabeza pursed his lips. "And the Montels?" But he could guess the answer.

"As of this moment they've outlived their usefulness."

Cabeza eyed Gail. She looked down at her passport expressionlessly.

"These other trade unionists—we will meet them in Moscow, yes?"

"Probably."

"What if they know Montel?"

"They don't. We've done our homework, General. There are no loopholes, you have my word."

Your word, Cabeza thought, is loophole enough. But the ID seemed convincing. Entirely plausible, in fact.

Kelland drew out two small objects from a remaining package. He passed one to Gail, one to Cabeza. They were wedding rings.

He watched them put them on. They fitted perfectly. (How had he managed *that?*) Kelland said dryly, "I pronounce you man and wife. Now go work into your characters. Create a

credible relationship. And I suggest you snap into it because
we take off for Berlin in"—he checked his watch—"just
twenty-six hours."

"Joaquín, you're not trying!" Gail exclaimed, halting irrita-
bly, striving to capture her flailing hair.

Cabeza sauntered on absently around the lawn. Her wind-
blown voice followed him edgily.

"You heard what he said—it's no earthly use our passports
saying we're married if we haven't rehearsed a domestic
scenario to back it up. What I'm suggesting . . ."

Cabeza barely listened. "Scenario." The very word used in
relation to marriage was a mockery. To play at such things
was not in him. Not today, with the strangeness in his head
and the guns coming closer. Especially not to ease the
misgivings of this Agency woman. What did she know of
marriage, anyway?

Then he thought bitterly, And you, Mule, what do *you*
know? As a husband you were a great disaster. You had
everything in your saddlebag—an honored position at the
Moscow Military Academy, a beautiful and intelligent wife
who loved you and was bearing your child. What did you do?
You took the life she and you were making and crushed it in
your stubborn peasant hands!

"Listen—" Gail said, catching up with him. "The Montels
have three children—right?" She began to outline a possible
conflict between their having to attend a Catholic school and
their parents' Communist convictions.

Cabeza pushed on against the wind. Its turmoil was
everywhere—in the tossing trees, his head. Ludmilla's image
danced before him, her big eyes fiery, sharing his disgust at
the wretched living conditions of the Soviet workers, the
corruption and injustice that plagued the nation, yet caution-
ing him against any action that would destroy their lives
together. She had had a lot to lose—him, her career as a
doctor at the Golitsin Hospital, their hard-won apartment,
the future of their child-to-be, her father's reputation—he
was General Patolichev, one of the most respected tutors at
the academy.

But, as ever, the Mule had not listened. He had spoken his
mind and found himself before a tribunal, spoken it again and

been arrested. Ludmilla was arrested too, and interrogated. They had threatened her with torture, but she would tell them nothing; not one word that would incriminate him.

Cabeza writhed at the recollection. This was no time to be remembering such things, he told himself. His mind seemed to be running wild, and there were vital decisions to be made. Like, was he really going to kill Stalin? Like, why was Kelland sending this woman with him instead of a man who could hold a gun to his head if he tried to escape? Was Kelland really so sure of him? Or had he something up his sleeve? Yet Ludmilla's image, having been invoked, would not leave him. Was she still there in Moscow? he wondered.

She had survived the interrogations, he knew that. After a fruitless month they had released her. But they had taken away her job. She found employment in a shop, then in the streets clearing snow. Five months pregnant, shoveling snow high onto the backs of trucks! But she had kept the child inside her. She would, he thought. She would cling to it with all her small but awesome strength. Then she had gone away somewhere—to a relative in Georgia, rumor had it—and there given birth to a baby girl.

As to what had happened then, he had never been sure. Word filtered to him in Vorkuta that she had returned to Moscow, that she was back working in the Golitsin. It seemed unlikely. But the war was raging. Doctors were in short supply. In those desperate days, he supposed, anything was possible.

And here was Gail concocting scenarios about marriage!

He was about to turn on her fiercely when Holz appeared, ambling toward them across the lawn. He looked wrong somehow in a collar and tie. He was carrying a folder. Beyond him Cabeza saw the other travelers assembling on the terrace with their baggage.

"We're off now," Holz announced.

"Ah!" Gail strove to focus. "I have some letters I'd like you to mail when you get back, d'you mind?" She hurried away toward the house.

Holz beamed at Cabeza. "Well, good luck, General. Make sure you kill the bastard."

Cabeza barely bothered to mask his hostility. "What happens to you now?"

Holz shrugged and grinned. "If I'm lucky, a spot of furlough. If not, another assignment."

Cabeza took his hand perfunctorily. It was almost flaccid. Holz was too secure in his talent to need to match strength. But he said softly, "Pity we never had our showdown." He tilted back his large head and grinned, squeezing up his eyes till the ripples ran all the way up into his hair, his thick lips spreading and opening and tucking up at the corners.

But somehow it was only his outer skin that was grinning. From deep inside him something cold looked out at Cabeza and imagined him dead.

"A little good-bye present." Holz handed him the folder. "So long, General." He headed back toward the house.

Cabeza watched him go for a moment. The wind tugged at the folder in his hand. He opened it. Inside was a sketch.

It showed a red lion and a huge red bear locked in mortal combat. The bear had a Stalin moustache. They were fighting on the ice, but the ice had broken and they were falling through, still locked in each other's arms. On the shore a giraffe was pushing out its long neck along the ice to try to rescue them, but they were out of reach. All around them the snow was falling. The flakes were eyes—all eyes—watching the two creatures anxiously. But the pair of them were doomed, it was plain to see.

22

Two AND a half thousand miles to the north, the low, weak sun made little impact on the snowy murk that hung over Moscow. The city lay in the winter's thrall, its rivers frozen, its lights burning, its traffic gritting through icy streets.

Muffled crowds thronged the shopping centers, and lined up in the department stores, bought ice cream outside the metro stations, slid and skated in the fairground atmosphere of Gorky Park under the great poster faces that exhorted and cautioned them, heralded the forthcoming elections, Red Army holidays . . .

It was a kaleidoscope, almost an illusion, trapped in the ripples of a once-flung stone. For the streets, buildings, all were fashioned in concentric rings around the ancient Kremlin, whose giant ruby stars glowed like silent sentinels in the sky above its center, the spires that supported them rooted in another world—a world at once the heart, and the stake in the heart, of the Soviet peoples.

Behind heavily guarded ramparts, the Kremlin, with its cathedrals and bell towers, palaces and administration buildings, was a forbidden city within a city, accessible only to government personnel and those with special passes signed by the commandant.

MVD boots scrunched to attention in the snow as Colonel Georgi Feodor Grechukha, Deputy Minister of State Security, came briskly out of the old Senate building. His tough, clown's face looked thoughtful as, bull neck hunched against the searing cold, back straight, belly extended, he moved to the pastel-colored Zim parked under the frozen lashes of the Kremlin trees.

Already his police escort were piling into their Pobedas, starting up. Their officer stepped toward him questioningly.

"Back to the Lubianka," Grechukha muttered into the astrakhan of his collar. He got into the car.

Zapotkin barely had time to swing his meager knees aside as the Deputy Minister plumped in beside him and spread himself, purposely squeezing his aide into the corner. The heater was going full blast, the inside of the car like an oven. Grechukha threw open his coat. The man had the blood of a fish, he thought, as well as the face of one.

Already they were moving, the two police cars leading the way. Feeling the other's eyes on him, Grechukha turned away to gaze out of the window. The fish was trying to gauge his mood, find out how the meeting had gone. Well, let him stew for a bit in his own fishy juices. Zapotkin's job was to watch him, report his every move, Grechukha had no doubt. Though to whom, he was never quite certain. In the Soviet Union even the watchdogs of state had their fleas. It didn't bother him; he was in a particularly strong position right now. That this could change overnight, he was well aware. But only if he played the cards wrong. In which case he would have only himself to blame.

So how *had* it gone? he asked himself as they swung past the Presidium building toward the Redeemer Gate. He was never quite sure until well after these meetings with Stalin were over—sometimes days after. The Old Man's mind was so devious, and getting worse as the years went by.

The main thing was that he had managed to keep his head—that had real meaning when you were dealing with Josef Vissarionovich—and stall him. A lesser man would have panicked and shown all his cards. And that would have been fatal. You had to have an ace up your sleeve if you hoped to stay in the top game.

They were passing out into Red Square now, the taillights of the police cars speeding ahead toward Twenty-fifth of October Street, flashing their headlights and blasting their horns as a warning to the police posted at the snowy intersections to stop all traffic.

To the right, a host of snowplows and trucks were parked in the shadow of Saint Basil's Cathedral, their crews kicking their heels, waiting for the next snow to fall. Beyond them the billboards advertising champagne and caviar and cheese stood out in garish contrast to the somber battlements of the citadel.

Grechukha leaned his face close to the car window so that the crowds lining up outside Lenin's Tomb should see who it was who was driving out of the Kremlin. He liked to be recognized, liked the distinction of having the traffic stopped for him; in fact, he insisted on it. "When you live like a wolf, howl like a wolf"—one of the Old Man's favorite sayings. The howling part was his perk—the pale green Zim, the summer *dacha*, the toadying of almost everyone he came in contact with, the power over life and death that he enjoyed as the boss of State Security . . . For he *was* the boss, let there be no mistake. The Minister himself was just a figurehead. Interchangeable, as Stalin had shown only four days ago—by firing Abakumov and replacing him with Semyon Denisovich Ignatiev. He had confirmed it further when he had called Grechukha to the Secretariat and broken the news to him.

"Don't be alarmed, Georgi Feodor," Stalin had told him. "Regard it purely as a domestic measure. Part of a stratagem which need not concern you. Our relationship still stands. You will continue to conduct the purge and interrogations of doctors and Jews as I direct, reporting to me, as always, personally."

"Personally" . . . Grechukha smiled to himself. It had a nice confidential ring to it. Then the smile died as he remembered that Pauker, too, had shared just such a special relationship with the Old Man. So had Ordzhonikidze and Yenukidze and, up until only the other day, Mekhlis. And they were dead. And now, today, Stalin had not been *all* that pleased with him, he recalled.

After inquiring how the roundup of Jews was going, how

many he had executed, how many had died in the bloody demonstrations still going on in the Ukraine, he asked how the interrogations were shaping.

His tone was the same as if he had been inquiring about the health of the Deputy Minister's wife. It reminded Grechukha of his divisional commander during the war, who used to ask of his forward troops whenever he visited them: "How many Germans have you killed today?" Only, these were not Germans; they were fellow Russians. Innocent fellow Russians, at that; their only crime that they were Jewish.

But neither he nor Stalin was a sentimentalist. They had long ago abandoned scruple for strategy. Each understood this of the other—the stocky Georgian with his handsome pockmarked face, becoming fleshy now at seventy-three but still with the shiny cheeks and full hair of a young man, and the tough, grinning, fidgeting ex-MGB agent with the butcher's hands and spread nose and balding forehead that swept up and back into his stiff hair like a rapidly narrowing road. They were a good match.

Grechukha had said carefully that the interrogations were not going quite as well as he had hoped.

Stalin regarded him expressionlessly for a long moment. It took a strong man to meet that gaze. Grechukha only just qualified.

The Leader raised a stubby forefinger.

"Sit still for a moment."

Grechukha stopped rubbing his thighs and sat still.

"Listen."

Grechukha listened, watching him alertly.

A typewriter was clacking in the secretary's office next door. Other than that, there was silence in the high room with its gray-striped wallpaper and plush drapes and comfortable furniture. Stalin remained motionless behind his desk, sucking on his empty pipe; he had given up smoking.

What is this—a war of nerves? Grechukha wondered. Well, it was a game he used to play with his prisoners and he was adept at it. He mirrored the other's stillness.

Stalin said, "Hear him?"

"Hear who, Comrade Josef Vissarionovich?"

"Our traitor. Our American spy, whom they call Omega."

Grechukha stared at him, puzzled.

"He is here in this building. Now. *Here.* Can't you feel him? Working against us?"

Ah, it was a joke. Grechukha chuckled. "Yes, Josef Vissarionovich, I can hear him."

Stalin did not smile. "I gave you the order to find him. I have given you a purge to help you with your arrests and to mask your true reason for making them. Yet still you do not come up with his name. I want to know the reason."

Grechukha groped for an excuse that would stall him without incurring his wrath. "Perhaps . . ."

"'Perhaps' is no answer." Stalin cut him off.

Grechukha tried again. "The purge, with all respect, may—I say *may*—be self-defeating. My detainees are mostly Jews. It could be that our spy has no Jewish connections." If his present findings were proven correct, this was not true, but he said it without a qualm.

"Nonsense!" Stalin thumped the desk. "The entire Jewish Zionist movement in the Soviet Union has sold out to American Intelligence. They are positively committed to creating a fifth column both here and in the people's democracies!"

Word for word, Grechukha thought. There had been an article in the *New Times* in January saying exactly that. Now he knew who had dictated it!

Stalin went on, "It stands to reason, then, that Omega is part of this conspiracy. He is directing it, Georgi Feodor. He is in close contact with the Jews." He added softly, "If he is not one himself."

Grechukha glanced at him sharply, but the slit-eyes were lidded. Was that a hint? Did Stalin suspect the same man he did? He had had this impression more than once, that this crackdown on the Jews was not a blind at all. That Stalin had opened a path for him to follow. And he was appearing not to follow it! The possibility created a sudden hairline fracture in his determination to withhold his ace.

He decided to reveal just the tip of it. "Have no fear, Comrade Josef Vissarionovich. If our spy is here as you say, then my men are at this moment watching him. He is all but in our hands."

Stalin's eyes narrowed. He sat forward a little.

"What are you saying?"

197

"I—" He hadn't meant to tell him this; he hoped he wouldn't regret it. "I have taken the precaution of putting every member of the Presidium under full surveillance. Their homes and offices are bugged, their communications monitored, their contacts recorded and investigated."

He searched the slit-eyes for their reaction.

The slit-eyes searched him back. They seemed to smolder.

"*Every* member?"

"Every member, Josef Vissarionovich," Grechukha said bravely.

"That is a lie!"

"A lie?" The hairline became a fault line now under the fierce gaze.

"Stalin is not under surveillance. Or he would know it."

Grechukha let his breath go in a relieved laugh. So it was a joke. "No, no. All but you, Leader Comrade!"

"Why all but me?" The fierce look remained. "You are too trusting. How do you know I am not the spy? How? Tell me."

"If you are the spy," Grechukha groped for a punch line in the right vein, "then we are all spies, so it wouldn't matter."

Stalin liked that. He laughed heartily.

"Good!" He contemplated his churched thumbs for a moment, then looked up slyly. "I take it you have done this with the consent of Kremlin Security?"

Grechukha's grin faded. "No."

"Bravo." Stalin chuckled approvingly.

Grechukha felt suddenly encouraged. "I thought it best if only my team knew what was happening."

"A wise precaution. And what is happening?"

"Excuse me?"

"Among my Presidium, my ministers. What are they up to? What have you found out?"

"Nothing." Grechukha forced himself to look happy to say this.

"Come now." Half playful. "Speak out. That's an order."

Grechukha laughed uneasily. It was hard to keep any suspicions to yourself when you were dealing with a paranoid. The Old Man had been convinced for years that one or the other of those closest to him was plotting to overthrow him. And now, at last, if the readings his men were beginning to feed him were correct, it was true! Whether Omega's intentions were to overthrow or simply to betray Stalin he had no means of knowing, but he held a position of such power that he, Grechukha, knew he would be placing himself squarely before a firing squad if he showed his hand one moment before he had a cast-iron case against him. So he said, "We've uncovered a few irregularities, of course. But all under the heading of domestic. Mainly sexual."

"Is that all? No conspiracies against me?"

"No, no, Comrade Josef Vissarionovich. No one would dare."

"No?" Stalin's eyes bored into his for a moment. "Well, when you spot something, you're to report it straight to me, understand?"

"Of course, of course. Instantly."

Stalin grunted. He resumed the study of his thumbs for a moment. "And when this is all over, I will want to know the names of the men you have used on this operation."

"If you wish. You'll want to reward them, of course."

"To silence them."

Grechukha stared at him, the smile wiped from his face. It came back—like a well-trained dog—but only just. He nodded.

Stalin said matter-of-factly, "We can't allow them to remain at liberty with such intimate knowledge in their heads."

"No, I agree." But Grechukha's voice lacked its usual conviction. Not out of concern for his men. He had suddenly seen a second, chilling danger to himself.

"Very well, Georgi Feodor." Stalin placed both hands flat on the desk, a signal that the meeting was over. "By the way, how is your head?"

"My head?" Grechukha inquired, getting up.

"Today is the twenty-seventh of February. Our first trial is scheduled for the fifth of next month. I want Omega's identity to emerge clearly from the cross-examinations, the finger pointed squarely at him. Or I will have your head in front of me on this desk."

Grechukha froze for a split second, searching his face. With the permanent crow's-feet around the eyes, the slight uptilt at the corners of the moustache, it was always hard to see if the Leader was smiling.

* * *

Now he was returning to speed up the interrogations. If he could forge a link between some of those already in custody and the man he was beginning to suspect, his problem would be half solved.

They were circling the vastness of Dzerzhinsky Square. Away to their left stood Dietsky Mir, the Children's World store. Ahead loomed the gray façade of the most feared building in the whole of Moscow—Lubianka prison. It housed also the headquarters of the MVD, under the less evocative title of Ministry of the Interior.

The Zim drove into the yard. Grechukha went straight up to his office. As deputy head of both the MVD internal Security and MGB external Military Intelligence, he had an office both here and in the MGB building. It was a bad arrangement: two separate organizations, with separate files, under separate roofs. But steps were being taken to combine both services in one—under the title KGB. But right now, Grechukha was the wearer of two hats. He recalled Stalin's words when he had first been promoted from the UN delegation to his present position.

"Remember, Georgi Feodor, the man who wears two hats also has two heads!"

A typical Stalinism. Grechukha had chuckled confidently at the time, thinking he had meant that he would need to be doubly intelligent. Now he was not so sure. In view of the Leader's recent remark, perhaps he had meant he would be doubly at risk.

Yes, that seemed more in keeping with the Old Man's Wagnerian sense of humor, he thought grimly as he entered his office suite. He was beginning to feel much less sanguine about the tenor of the meeting than he had on leaving the Kremlin. If he was going to come out of this in one piece, he would have to produce this Omega out of one of these hats pretty fast. Even then there was no guarantee.

And there was Boris Likachev's powerful form eclipsing the window of his outer office. He was gazing out at the snow-muted traffic below, puffing on his pipe, his handsome, muscular features composed in an expression that said, Problems. As if he hadn't enough already! Boris was Deputy Director of the MGB.

"Comrade!" They did some elbow slapping. "Come in,

come in." Grechukha led him through into his lofty office, shutting the door firmly in Zapotkin's fishy face.

"I haven't much time, but take a seat. Fine party the other night. Ah, and I've been saving some tobacco for you." He took a couple of tins from his desk drawer and pushed them across. He kept a regular supply for his friends, confiscated from the prisoners. He began taking off his coat and hat.

Likachev pocketed the tobacco with a nod. "I've been going through some First Division reports." He sat himself on the window ledge, extending his long legs. He was a regular film star, no more than forty, with piercing blue eyes under black lashes. "Anderson. You know. Our London man who told us about this spy."

"Yes?"

"He and Grierson—you know they disappeared."

"Of course, yes. They've turned up?"

Likachev shook his head. "MI6 have now written them off as dead."

Grechukha paused fractionally in hanging up his coat, waiting for the significance of this to reach him. It didn't. He moved to his desk and started rummaging in the drawers for the files he needed.

"Go on."

"Nothing strikes you?"

"Boris, I have a lot on my mind."

"Well, who eliminated them?" Likachev waited. "Not MI6—not their style. And not us."

"The Americans?" Grechukha ventured.

"Seems logical. See what it means?"

"Ah." The kopek dropped at last. "They know that we know about their spy. Would you like a quick glass of coffee?"

"Forget coffee, Georgi—this is important. Yes. They know that *we* know, and that we must now be busy trying to uncover him. Therefore, that the Doctors' Plot was devised for that purpose. Logical?"

Grechukha nodded, preoccupied.

"I don't think we should underestimate them," Likachev said.

"What can they do?"

Likachev drew in a breath. "Well . . . They can either try to pull him out. Or kill him. Or . . ."

"Or what? Come on, man, what are you getting at?"

"Well, Anderson's report said the man is a Russian, a member of the hierarchy. That could even mean one of the inner circle."

Grechukha looked at him sharply. "Yes?"

"This purge of yours is creating a bit of a rift in the Presidium, Georgi—we've all seen the signs."

Grechukha looked startled. He placed a finger to his lips.

Likachev looked puzzled. "We bugged?"

Grechukha shook his head and pointed toward the connecting door.

Likachev lowered his voice. "I mean, Molotov is furious about his wife's arrest—who wouldn't be? Kaganovich has spoken out more than once against what's going on. Even Beria, the Old Man's most devoted puppy dog, isn't exactly laughing and scratching about it. I mean, you know all this. Simply—"

"Do I?" Grechukha stood very still. "But go on."

"Simply it wouldn't take much to exploit such a disagreement. Turn it into a coup. That's all I'm saying. In which case, Omega could actually wind up in the seat of power!"

Grechukha affected a dismissive laugh. "You're not serious."

"About that?—no. I'm just outlining some American alternatives."

"Well, let me outline yours," Grechukha said evenly. "Leave internal security to the MVD. Will you do that? Just accept that I've taken steps that rule out your last idea completely. With regard to the other two . . ." He closed his eyes and considered them.

"I'm convinced"—Likachev slapped his thigh—"that the Americans are up to *something*. I have good instincts, Georgi."

"You have, you have," Grechukha cried. "And I'm very grateful for your pointing this out. I will bear it—"

But Likachev had not finished. "You remember Gregori Kazakov?"

"The traitor?" Grechukha sighed. "Do I not. He was on a mission for me when he defected."

"So he was. And Stefan Pescovitch?"

"The Pole? Of course I do. Another defector."

"They are both attached to the CIA now. We've kept them under constant surveillance. They've recently left the States. Something that under normal circumstances they wouldn't dare do. They're in Tangier. I've had that confirmed by our airport watchers from both ends. Where they went to in Tangier I haven't yet found out."

"Tangier . . ." Grechukha began to show interest. "Melnikov . . ."

"Exactly."

"Melnikov cabled a report that he was on to something, didn't he? Some American operation . . ."

Likachev sighed. "You're there. At last. Comrades Gregori and Stefan are the CIA's foremost experts on our intelligence system, Georgi. Stefan worked for two years in Kremlin Security."

Grechukha came to his feet sharply. He plunged his hands in his pockets and started to pace.

He asked, "Melnikov's replacement—did he ever pick up the threads?"

"No. He's still trying. But he says the CIA station there is containing him. His every move is watched. He has been involved in two traffic accidents—rigged, he says—either of which could have killed him. He says, whatever it is he is being kept from, it has to be big." Likachev's blue eyes were very serious.

"I believe that Gregori and Stefan are being briefed, or are briefing someone else, for some counteraction *here in Moscow,* Georgi. That's all I came here to tell you."

Grechukha sat in deep thought long after the MGB man had gone. Suppose the Americans *were* planning a penetration—what could they be after? Killing Omega made no sense at all. Nor did pulling him out. If it was the man he suspected, he would no more leave the country than fly; he didn't even like the Americans, was simply using them to advance his own ends. No, it would be to achieve something vastly more subtle and devastating.

Well, his first move must be to make sure they never got in. He would order an airport and frontier alert immediately;

every visitor checked and rechecked, his papers examined under a microscope.

But in case they did get through, he would also have to alert Kremlin Security. Which would make the undercover work of his own men there that much harder. Damn! He was under pressure from both sides now—Uncle Joe *and* Uncle Sam. *And there was a deadline.*

23

THE WINKING star approaching Berlin from the southwest materialized into a sleek, privately owned Lockheed Constellation. It circled twice in the overcast, then came skimming in to land on the central runway of Tempelhof Airport in the American sector. The time by its cabin clock was just after 6:00 P.M.

Cabeza stared out at the broken skyline of the city. It was almost dark, raining, the runways and lanes seething with traffic. The sudden lights and noise galvanized his exhausted mind to one last effort. He *still* had not reached a decision. Each time he seemed to arrive at one his brain balked, like one of Don Miguel's horses faced with an impossible fence. Fragments of the briefing churned in his head. Images of Stalin . . . Now he strove again to burst through the block.

Kelland was looking at him, unclipping his seat belt— giving a casual look, or perceiving his inner turmoil? It must show, he felt. It had to show. His upper lip was sweating, his mouth dry as chalk. And this strange nausea . . .

The plane taxiing now, Gail beside him reaching down to collect her things, Laroche and Canfield seated fore and aft of him, alert as mountain cats with a hare between them.

Where would they take him? To a house, no doubt, in the American sector. Would it be easier from there or from inside the crowded terminal building? He couldn't decide. Stalin's face . . . *Concentrate.* Passport. Kelland had his Montel passport. But he would have to give it back to him before they passed through immigration control. Have to. So he would make his escape after the control desk—*bien?* Yes or no? Answer!

A bus braked alongside them almost before they were in the parking bay. The navigator came aft and opened up the cabin door. They were all on their feet now, Canfield and Laroche closing on either side of him, Kelland shaking hands with the pilot, then leading the way out.

A prickle of rain and lungful of fumes later they were all standing in the near-empty bus and it was rolling, tracing a dizzy pattern between the taxiing aircraft. Yes or no?

Before he could elicit an answer, the bus was stopping. The door jackknifed and they passed through into a passageway streaming with people, Canfield and Laroche practically hugging him, Kelland striding ahead, Gail eyeing him sidelong, almost as though sensing the turmoil in his mind.

The crowd slowed gradually into a line that shuffled steadily forward into the immigration hall, where it divided to file past two desks. Kelland still in front. Still with his passport.

He reached the desk first and passed through. Then Canfield. Now him. How . . . ? Mere seconds before he stepped empty-handed to the desk, Kelland slipped him the passport. Cabeza presented it. A flick—a glance—a stamp. The official pushed it back. Kelland's hand retrieved it.

Cabeza watched it disappear into his pocket, dazed. So quick! He knew now that whatever he was going to do he would have to do it without a passport, in a strange city, where he did not know the language. Was or *wasn't* going to do? Gail was still watching him. She appeared hypnotized. They were moving through into customs now. The thought of drawing official attention to the guns carried by his escort glowed in his mind—and died. This was the American sector. Where the Agency ruled supreme.

His eyes fastened on the crowd waiting beyond the barrier.

A large crowd. Ah. Outside there would be buses, taxis, cars, confusion . . .

The mere thought he was entertaining brought acid to his throat. He gulped it back and, when they had reclaimed their baggage, endeavored to lead the way out. Suddenly it was happening. He had the sensation of bursting through an invisible wall. He cut Laroche off against the exit doorframe as he walked through. He outpaced Canfield into the surging crowd. His adrenaline peaked. He prepared to run . . .

Two large men barred his way, embracing him and then the others in welcome. They must have been watching over the barrier and seen that the five of them were together.

The setback was only fractional, but enough to destroy his impetus and his advantage. They were back in a group again, Kelland's gaze boring into him suspiciously as he gripped the men's hands.

"Franz, Rudi, hi. Meet the Montels—Marcos, Susana."

The two pairs of eyes snapped them up curiously. Franz was dark and built like a butcher; Rudi like a beer waiter, blond and thinning on top. Mid-thirties, identical raincoats.

The acid choked him then. He reeled, fighting back the desire to throw up. Vaguely he became aware of Laroche and Canfield stepping toward him. Each gripped his hand.

"Good luck, uh—Marcos. Mind you make it."

"We'll be watching the newscasts."

Then they shook hands all around. He saw Gail's startled expression. Hands aloft, the two American agents turned and moved away along the hall toward the check-in desks.

"You didn't tell me they were leaving us." Gail's voice came to Cabeza from far away. She sounded almost accusing. His head was swimming.

Stalin . . .

The slit-eyed image loomed before him. There was softness all around, but the image was sharp and clear. He heard voices. The slam of a cell door. Hands were gripping his arms. He was being steered out of the airport.

The rain brought back an echo of reality. Wetness everywhere. Cabs fizzing past, wheel to wheel with their reflections. A car door stood open. His case was prized from his hand. He was bundled in. Heavy bodies crushed in on either side of him. Gail and Kelland were getting in the front, Gail looking back at him, intuitive, agonized. The trunk slammed. A driver got in . . .

Streets, ruins . . . They were weaving their way through the city's maze. Great gaps between the buildings. Decelerating now, coming to a stop. Armed guards. One poked his head in the window. Kelland was speaking in German, handing out some papers. The guard went away. Gail's face—he caught it in profile for an instant. It registered sharp bewilderment. Back came the guard. The papers were returned. They drove on.

The strangeness was ebbing from him at last. They were crossing a bridge. He stared out across the water at the stilettos of light reflected from the buildings on the far bank. What river? The Spree? Berlin on the Spree. He knew virtually nothing about the city except that it was on the Spree.

That and one other thing: the Spree was in the Russian sector!

"Why?" he demanded. "Why?"

"You're not concentrating, Marcos," Kelland said. He stood with his back to the coal-fire in the high, ugly room, Franz and Rudi roaming around him restlessly. "How does it fit?"

Fit? Fit? Cabeza stared blindly at his reflection in the full-length mirror Rudi had brought down from one of the bedrooms. The heavy topcoat fitted him perfectly. Why wouldn't it fit? Everything Kelland organized fitted. Fitted him like a coffin.

"It makes me look like a banker."

"Good," Kelland said. "You'll be wearing that into the Kremlin. They all look like bankers in the Kremlin. Now the hat."

Cabeza fumbled with it, tucking up the earflaps. He put it on.

"So why? Why you bring us to this sector, where there is danger? Why not stay on the other side till morning?"

Kelland exchanged a look with the Germans. "I have my reasons."

Claro, you do, Cabeza thought. You are full of reasons.

And empty of information. You play the same blind game with us the Central Committee played at Teruel. And that was a sellout!

The house they had brought him to was large and of a past century, sparsely furnished and smelling of damp—one of a row of eight spared by the wartime bombing. The rest of the road was flat, the rubble cleared, waiting for reconstruction. It would wait a long time, he thought, remembering the dearth of such dwellings in Moscow. The dead hand of the Soviet was already on this part of the city. It was in this house, with its dim lighting and unheated rooms. And here he was, already parading like a shopper in Revolution Place.

"This fur at the edges . . . ?"

"To give the impression it's fur-lined. Which it normally would be. But, as we know, the lining isn't normal. It has a dual purpose."

As we know. Cabeza pulled down the earflaps of the hat. He stared at his reflection in the mirror. The horror of Siberia came to him. He tore it off.

Feet hammered the hall. Gail came in quickly, shutting the door with a shiver.

"God, it's cold up there!" She deposited an armful of clothing on the worn settee and turned to inspect him, his secret in her eyes. "Are you feeling any better, Joaquín?"

"Worse," Cabeza said.

She was wearing a green worsted frock with black trimmings.

Kelland circled her slowly. "What do you think, Marcos?"

Cabeza shrugged and nodded. Catholic colors. She was beginning to look the part now. On the settee was a dark red dress—that was right too—plus some sweaters, cardigans, skirts and a cheap coney fur coat.

Gail grimaced at her reflection in the mirror. She was still uneasy and mystified at having been whisked over into this sector without warning, Cabeza sensed.

"Can't say I think too much of the workmanship." She fingered some crooked stitching.

"You made it yourself," Kelland told her. "Some of the sweaters too. If you look in the sewing repair kit in the suitcase, you'll see we've included—"

"I know—who thought of that?—thread and wool to match."

"Not to match," Kelland said. "The *same*. Actual leftovers from the dressmaking. And every item bought in Bilbao. Same for your stuff, Marcos."

Gail's look of uneasiness deepened. "You really think we're going to come under such close inspection?"

"You might. What with the purge—the security shake-up . . ."

"Shake-up?" Cabeza and Gail turned simultaneously.

"Stalin switched ministers."

"When?" Gail demanded. "That wasn't in any of the Agency reports."

"You must have missed it."

"Hardly. I'm not that—"

"Well, it's a fact—accept it." He cut her off. "Stalin said 'Jump,' and the guy who really runs that outfit, Grechukha, is a jumper. New brooms sweep clean, but old brooms scared for their jobs sweep cleanest. So I'm taking no chances, that's all. Now, let's get on with—" He broke off, looking at Cabeza. "What bothers you?"

"Grechukha? Georgi Feodor Grechukha?"

"You know him?"

Cabeza nodded slowly, his brow darkening. "My interrogator. In the Lubianka."

Kelland pinched his lip for a moment. "Well, you're not likely to run into him. Not in the short while you'll be there. So . . ."

Cabeza thought he would very much like to run into him. If he could somehow do it without going to Moscow. He would like to work him over very slowly with something quite obscene—like a blowtorch.

The fire had shriveled in its grate and there was no more coal. In the gathering chill the remaining props were allocated, examined, and relevant queries dealt with. Then, at a glance from Kelland, the Germans collected their cans of beer and removed themselves to the communications room next door. What remained to be said now was for Cabeza's and Gail's ears alone. They had reached the final and most secret phase of the briefing.

They sat around the central table. Kelland talked deliberately, his eyes, which never left them, skull-like under the single pathetic overhead bulb.

He explained about the equipment Cabeza would need, how there was no way he could carry it through customs, that therefore it would be delivered to him in the Moscow hotel. How, need not concern them. It would be done discreetly, exposing them to no danger.

He went over the assassination plan for the final time, move by move. Voiced meticulously in the remoteness of this East German suburb devoid of outside traffic and all sounds save the faint stutter of Morse from the room next door, the hiss of Gail's nylons as she crossed and recrossed her legs with ever-increasing nervousness, it seemed to Cabeza suddenly and utterly preposterous.

When the last lethal instruction had fallen from Kelland's lips, Gail launched into a host of questions, all of them searching, demanding his reassurance. Kelland answered her evenly at first, but as she persisted, a warning chill crept into his tone, which finally silenced her. He turned to Cabeza.

"And my pass?" Cabeza asked.

"No pass," Kelland said.

Cabeza sighed. What then? The Kremlin was a sealed fortress. No one could . . .

Kelland withdrew something from his briefcase. A black leather folder. He opened it and handed it across. Under the gleam of the plastic Cabeza saw a card bearing his photograph. It was one of the prints they had taken of him in Tangier. The lettering was Cyrillic. He peered to decipher the heading: "OOKK." Gail leaned close to do likewise.

Under the photo was his description. His identity was shown as Sergei Nikolai Kovich. There was an oval stamp encircling a signature. Around its periphery were the words "Ossoby Otdel Kemlyovskoi Kommandatury."

Kelland was watching him almost wolfishly for his reaction.

Gail said, "OOKK—what's that?"

Cabeza had seen such a card just once before in his life. He had been under interrogation in an office at NKVD headquarters. A man had walked in and shown this card, then proceeded to rifle the security filing system. The NKVD officers had stood meekly by and watched him remove a score of secret files from their cabinets and march off with them without a word of explanation.

"Can you tell her, Marcos?"

Cabeza peered at the fine yellow print, then at the bold signature across the stamp. He deciphered it with difficulty: "Poskrebyechev." It just *had* to be a forgery. Yet he knew that it was not. "No chances," Kelland had said. The card, then—the signature, the stamp—was genuine. His particulars had simply been filled in in the normal manner.

The significance of this took his breath away. It meant the Agency had a man working at the very heart of the Soviet machine!

"It is an elite," he managed to say evenly. "A very small security elite. Responsible only to Stalin."

Kelland nodded his confirmation. "They can walk in any-where. Literally. They can search, audit, interrogate, execute. And the only authority they need is the possession of this card. You read the signature?"

"Poskrebyechev."

"He's the commissar. Big Brother himself. The only man in the Soviet Union with direct day-and-night access to Stalin. Or was, till the Old Man purged him a couple of months back—he's purging *everyone,* and that's what you're going up there to stop." He added, "But his signature's still valid—till the end of the year." He poked out a finger. "So put that away in your pocket. Guard it with your life. Your *life.*"

Cabeza flipped it against his thumb, thinking, So *that* is why I am to murder Stalin. Bit by bit the animal reveals itself.

"So he just shows this at the gate and they'll let him in?" Gail sounded disbelieving.

"Having given the password, yes," Kelland told her, with a hard look. "I'll cable it to you both at your Moscow hotel."

Cabeza looked at him incredulously.

"You'll what?" Gail said.

"There's no other way," Kelland informed them. "Kremlin Security coin their passwords pretty much off the cuff—sometimes just an hour or two before they come into force. There's no way I can get the one you'll need before it's been invented. But the moment it has, it'll be radioed to me in minutes. Chances are you'll be airborne by then, so I'll cable it straight to your hotel."

"Kelland," Cabeza said with a sigh. "You will be here, in the Soviet sector, *de veras?*"

"Correct."

"Do you have any idea how long it takes to pass something through the Soviet cable system?"

"Hours," Gail hissed.

"Fifteen minutes," Kelland said. "If you know their priority code." He smiled thinly. "Of course, what's in the message may fox them a bit, because it'll be just plain domestic. But only if they understand Spanish. And it's not one of their disciplines." His gaze hardened as he switched it to Gail. "I take it you'll be able to decipher a K4 coded in Spanish?"

"I should think so."

"A positive answer."

"Yes."

"Just as well. Because that's why I'm sending you to Moscow—to decode that cable."

Gail looked startled. "But you said—"

"And to flesh out Marcos' cover—sure. But that wasn't the priority. He could make out just as well without you. I trust him completely." He added dryly, "But not to the point of teaching him how to decipher our codes for himself. Got it?"

He was lying, Cabeza knew. Kelland didn't trust him as far as the washroom. If so, why had he kept him under such tight escort? Why all the alarm circuitry on every window and outside door of this house?—brand new and fully activated; he had seen Kelland throw the switch the moment they had entered. No. Gail's inclusion had some additional purpose. A purpose not even she knew—hence her jumpiness. And this intimate link Kelland seemed to have—and was advertising he had—with the Kremlin . . . He was throwing coils like a snake.

Cabeza suddenly began to review the whole operation again, focusing particularly on the arrangements for their escape. If there was a sting, that was where it would lie—in the tail, the job having been done.

After he killed Stalin, he was to go straight from the Kremlin to an address in Moscow. There he would meet an Agency man, a Russian, who would hand him two fresh sets of identification and plane tickets to match. Then he, Cabeza, would collect Gail from a street rendezvous and drive with her to the airport. They would board the flight and be flown out of Russia—practically within the hour.

Where they would be flown to, Kelland was keeping a secret. Also the nature of promised fresh ID's. Because if they knew that, he had explained, Cabeza might be tempted to bail straight out again without having completed his mission.

Not an unreasonable precaution, Cabeza had to admit. Though, again, it made a complete lie of Kelland's claim to trust him. It left too many loose ends. Suppose the agent just wasn't there at the rendezvous? Suppose the cover he provided wasn't adequate? Or there was a flight cancellation? And Kelland had told them there were no loopholes! The tail end was like a *colander*. Why hadn't he seen this before?

He began to lay his objections on the line. And he didn't pull his punches.

Kelland listened expressionlessly. He lit a cigarette, then shifted to his feet.

"Marcos, if what you're suggesting was possible, I'd be laying Susana's life smack on the line beside yours. My own operative? I wouldn't do that. She's your guarantee, man. She's your cast-iron guarantee that the escape plan will work."

Cabeza weighed this in his mind—and was not impressed. Kelland, he knew, would feed his own mother through a band saw if the stakes were high enough—and these were astronomical. He glanced at Gail and in her eyes read the same misgiving.

He got up and faced Kelland squarely. "If that is my one guarantee, it is not enough. I will not commit my life—our two lives—to such a plan."

Kelland stood very still.

"Because a few paltry details don't add up to total immunity from risk, you telling me now you're refusing to go?"

Cabeza opened his mouth to say "Yes." Before he could speak, a sharp pain convulsed him. It was as if all his intestines had twisted themselves into one agonizing knot.

Kelland watched him try to master his distress. Gradually Cabeza began to move again. He even smiled.

"Marcos, you're not going to let a small throw of the dice

stand between you and the sonofabitch who put you in the Lubianka, are you? Those green cell walls, the stink of excrement, those icy jets of the water torture hitting you like steel needles—think of them—and those fat cats grilling you at all hours of the night, the confession sheets, the P90's, the pens they kept pushing in your hand—blunt-ended so you couldn't ram them between your ribs and kill yourself. Just think of them. Of the big shot behind it all. That you're going to strew his guts around half the Kremlin!"

Cabeza stared slowly up at him. Where had he gained such knowledge of the Lubianka? Certainly not from him.

"Why not sleep on it?" Kelland said. "We're all through now, anyway, and you have one helluva day ahead of you tomorrow. You need to be in peak form. You're going to make history, dammit!"

Cabeza found himself stumbling up the stairs like an obedient zombie. He forced himself to stop. The pain in his belly urged him on, but he resisted it stubbornly, knowing its origins, defying it. How had Kelland known those things? And there was something else. Something had been said that had given him a sudden glimpse of the card up Kelland's sleeve.

It was something he had said himself. "I will not commit my life—our *two* lives . . ." He had included Gail in his protest, as if somehow she was his responsibility. And that was the card—she *was*.

He was awed by the subtle way Kelland had achieved this. By means of a thousand small devices he had gradually nudged her into Cabeza's boat. Now he was launching them both into limbo, with Cabeza at the helm, Gail as his passenger. Knowing that an armed male escort would never get his gun through the Soviet security screen, that, anyway, Cabeza would make mincemeat of him, Kelland had simply hung this unprotected girl around his neck, with the warning that to abort in Moscow would be to abandon her to the MVD wolves!

Blackmail. It was sheer moral blackmail. But now that he was wise to it . . . Cabeza began to chuckle, then stopped. What difference did it make whether he was wise to it or not?

Under no circumstances, he realized, would he abandon Gail or anyone else to the MVD, having suffered at their hands himself. Kelland had read him, as ever, right down to the small print.

Madre, Cabeza thought. If that is the play, how do I beat it?

24

KELLAND HAD motioned Gail to remain with him in the living room. He gave her a cold stare, then paced for a moment. She waited on tenterhooks, half guessing what was coming.

He swung to face her. "Look, your brief was to pull him to our side, not go over to his. So the plan scares you. You don't have to spell it out in front of him. You triggered him off, you know that. He dug his heels in. He's not supposed to dig his heels in. Haslar said he wouldn't."

"Haslar"—the very name raised her hackles—"didn't know the kind of man he was dealing with. His guinea pigs were all skid-row drunks. He—"

"I agree." Kelland cut her off. "I think he undercooked him. But that's all the more reason for you not to rock the boat, because, get Marcos' juices working again, we could have a flyer. And if we do, girlie, you're up shit creek, make no mistake."

"So you've already said."

"So back me up. Stop filling his ear with your doubts. Make him feel he's the big macho and you're Little Orphan Annie. You'll be in his bed tonight—right?"

"I—"

"So let your body tell him how much you care, how much you need him. Keep your mouth shut and your legs open."

"You don't have to be crude," Gail countered, to hide her confusion. She had purposely fostered the impression that she was on intimate terms with Joaquín to keep Kelland off her back.

"If crude brings it home to you that this is life or death—*your* life, *your* death, Susana, then crude I'll—"

"You mean the *plan's* life, the *plan's* death."

"That, too."

"That you don't want me stuck in Moscow because if the MVD get me you're scared I'll talk, like I did in London."

"That, too. Everything."

"Then why not say so? Why—?"

"I just did. The whole thing is interlocking."

"You don't think it would interlock better if instead of insulting and haranguing me, you tried to ease my mind a little, live up to that promise you made in Tangier?"

"Be specific."

"He's gone to bed now. We're alone—maybe for the last time. It would be a nice gesture if you took me into your confidence, filled in some of the blank spots for me."

Kelland met her gaze with a slight flicker. He shook his head. "You and he have gotten too close for that."

"Meaning you still don't trust me."

"Meaning," Kelland said carefully, "that I trust you within the context of your briefing as it stands. The plan has been designed for you to know that much and no more. Its provisions—"

"Good night." Gail turned on her heel and made for the door.

Kelland said quietly and dangerously, "Come back here."

Gail paused, too afraid of him to complete the move.

"I'm waiting."

She came back slowly, not looking at him.

"Over and above that," Kelland said evenly, "I'll tell you one thing. Orders will reach you while you're in Moscow. They will be Agency orders. And you're to obey them *implicitly. Whatever they may be.* Understand?"

"Is that all?"

"Do—you—understand?" His eyes bored into hers.

"Yes. May I go now?"

The eyes continued to bore until he was quite sure she had got the message. He nodded and held out his hand. "When you have given me your gun."

She stared at him.

"No sense in my arranging little things like dressmaking thread if they find a .32 on you, is there?"

Gail drew the gun slowly. She began the routine unload, but he took it from her, ejected the cartridge himself.

"Besides, tonight being the last night . . ." He flicked a meaningful glance at her as he replaced the cartridge in the clip. "Which reminds me. If, when you've both used the bathroom and are shacked up together, you hear someone lock your door, take no notice. I'll be around most of the night. Franz'll be next door to you, Rudi down in the hall. All exits are wired. If he makes any kind of a wrong move, yell." Kelland added softly, with a flirt of his eyes, "Though with you under him, he'd have to be crazy."

As Gail went upstairs she had to tell herself forcibly that it was Kelland's policy to provoke her, that somewhere along the line he had made the assessment that she worked better when aroused. And he could be right. Nevertheless, she could quietly kill him for the barrel he had put her over. Now she *had* to sleep with Joaquín, whether he wanted her or not.

How should she approach it? His door was slightly ajar. She tapped on it and looked in. The room was empty. In the bathroom, clearly. She gave a little sigh for the reprieve, went into her own room—it was freezing, not even a blow-heater— and undressed convulsively. Of all the Godforsaken places to make love in, *have* to make love in! She had never felt less like it in her life.

Wearing the fur coat over her "Susana" nightdress—that was a turn-off for a start!—she returned to Joaquín's room. He wasn't back yet. Should she get straight to bed? No, that was out of character. *He* was supposed to call the shots. The easy chair. She curled up in it to wait. If worst came to worst, she would sleep in it—rather than face Kelland's ire in the morning. And she knew she might well have to. The Haslar thing had changed Joaquín's attitude toward her. "Possible paranoid side effects," Haslar had warned. She shuddered. Gruesome. It was an unspeakable thing to have done.

She had seen a film once. Electrical contacts had been clipped to parts of the open brain of a man. They had activated the current through one contact, and a hand had moved; through the other, and he had lifted the opposing arm. Only he hadn't. He had but *he* hadn't. It had been confusing, obscene.

Yet she had actually shared in the relief when Dr. Haslar had arrived at the villa. Joaquín was locked in his room; the whole operation in jeopardy. But the moment she had laid eyes on the doctor, she changed her mind. He was a ghoul—small and chubby, with one of those smiles that appear toothless and eyes like bottled olives. Full of his own track record.

"Of course, we're still experimenting," he admitted to Kelland in her presence. "Artichoke has a long way to go yet. But between us—the OSI, Medical Services, Technical Services—we're beginning to get a system. A real system that'll work for you fellows in the field. Switch on, switch off. Think of it. The intelligence agency that operates full mind control dominates the world!"

Kelland said he wasn't concerned with the world, just—

But Haslar was away. He described his new method of de-patterning—how by intensive electroshock combined with drug-induced sleep, he could wipe any mind completely, then recondition it, "for any purpose, you name it"—by the technique known as psychic-driving.

Kelland had cut him off. "Let's get to the case in hand, shall we?"

"Ah yes. He's up in his room, right? You want me to ferret him out."

"I want you," Kelland had said carefully, "to get him to come out of his own accord, raring to go."

"Itching to kill."

"Itching to kill."

Haslar chuckled. "Love it. Well, let's diagnose. Your man has survived some very nasty experiences in Russia, right? The operative word here clearly being 'survived.' Meaning he

has learned to live with them—his experiences. In a word, he
has *digested* them."

"Yes?" Kelland waited, frowning.

"So we give him *indigestion,*" Haslar said.

"Stir up his memories?"

"Yes. With the emphasis on Stalin. Always on Stalin. I'll
open up his mind, make him more receptive for briefing
purposes. You fill it with Stalin."

"And will that stop him from trying to escape?"

"I'll seed in a revulsion to the whole idea of escape."

Kelland looked doubtful. "You'll have to seed it in pretty
hard. He has a will of iron."

"Then he'll need full medication. A couple of two-hour
sessions should do the trick."

"Sessions of what?"

"Narcohypnosis."

"That means drug-assisted?"

"Of course."

"No electroshock?"

"No, no. Unnecessary. No time, anyway."

Kelland looked relieved. Then: "Would he remember?"

"Not a thing."

"But he'd see the needle mark."

"He'll see it and ignore it."

"How will you make the injection?"

"Sedate him first. What does he drink?"

And that had resulted in her taking the coffee to Joaquín.
Kelland had wanted to send Madame Garvi in with it, but
Gail had pleaded for a last chance to talk the General down
before they resorted to such a hideous measure.

For all the good it had achieved, she thought miserably.
God, it was cold. Where *was* he? Tomorrow terrified her,
reaching into her insides with icy fingers. She needed something warm inside her. Yes, all right, she smiled, but before
that. A cup of hot tea. Better still, a pot between them.

She got up and went down the stairs. Explosive passages of
Morse and static reaching her through the communications-
room door as she passed. She heard Kelland's voice exclaim
in German, "It *is* them—that's the relay! Switch on the
recorder."

She went on into the kitchen. She lit the gas, frowning. She filled the kettle and put it on, then moved back a few paces toward the door, inclining her ear.

The rush of Morse continued unabated. The rate of sending was fantastic.

Presently there was a break in transmission. Kelland said, "Okay, acknowledge."

She heard the brief rattle of the key. It was followed by Morseless static. The relay station had instantly shut down.

She heard the whir of a recorder rewind, followed by a playback of the message at half-speed. She could picture Kelland starting to decode it, the Germans at his shoulders.

She heard him mutter, "Looks good."

"From the Ivanovskys?"

"Who else?"

Some more silence—terminated by the triumphant scrape of a chair.

"That's it, then—we've got the green!"

She slipped quickly back into the kitchen. But no one came out into the hall. And minutes later when she started up the stairs with the tea, the men were still in there, conversing quietly in German.

Joaquín's room was still empty. She put down the tray. The Ivanovskys? Who were they? They had given the "green." She was bursting to discuss with Joaquín what this could mean. Where the hell *was* Joaquín?

The bathroom was over on the other landing. She moved out and glanced across the stairwell. The bathroom door had a frosted glass panel. The room was unlit.

She moved around the stairwell to make sure. The bathroom was empty. Well, he hadn't been downstairs. She glanced in the other two rooms on that side. Also empty.

She came back and tried the room next to hers. Some things were in there belonging to one of the Germans—but no Cabeza.

The room next to that was a spare. She poked her head in and switched on the light. It was like *ice,* bare—no bed, no wardrobe. Just a table in one corner. On it was a chair. Above the chair was a hatchway into the roof space. It was open.

She moved forward and peered up into the blackness.

"Joaquín?"

She turned off the light and peered again. Now dimly she could see a rectangle of sky, as if some tiles had been removed from the roof.

She remained stock-still for a moment, then switched off the light, shut the door and returned to his room.

She stood there debating what she should do, fighting to suppress the utter relief and, at the same time, utter emptiness that overwhelmed her. He had beaten them. Despite all Haslar's efforts, the marvelous, wonderful General had managed to break free—purging her of all guilt, her fears of tomorrow, Kelland . . . Kelland! The thought sobered her. If she failed to give the alarm now, this *instant*, she was done for! As was Sunflower, with all its historic and international ramifications—ramifications she could only guess at—affecting the security, maybe even the very survival of the United States as a free nation! Here it was, the conflict of her life, heart versus head, brought to the final crunch.

And as if to precipitate her decision, footsteps were approaching the door. The lock clicked home. The footsteps started away again.

It was now or never. Joaquín, she knew, couldn't have gotten far. The Germans, if they moved fast, could still bring him back.

Her duty was crystal clear.

Cabeza stood in the road, knowing that of all the battles he had had to win, this was going to be the hardest. Even by the time he had clambered to the ground his head was swarming with images, fragments of his briefing, memories of his suffering in Russia. It was like a beehive, with the honey pouring down his throat—poisoned honey, turning his stomach.

Valor, hombre, he muttered, gritting his teeth. Remember, it is only in your head—put there by Kelland. And it is not alone; *I* am in there. And I am stronger than anything Kelland can devise. Concentrate only on me, obey *my* orders. See, I will begin counting. At each count, place one foot before the other.

He turned himself in the direction from which they had brought him and commanded himself: One! No, not those voices, *my* voice! Two . . . Steady as you go. Three . . . He built up speed till he was limping along the deserted road, his eyes focused on the sidewalk ahead, picturing each number there, placing his advancing foot on it—quickening now, the beehive sealed—past the drab old houses, aware that most of them stood in darkness, that there were gaps between them left by the wartime bombing, that the rain had stopped, that . . .

But there—already his mind was drifting and the babble had recommenced. The compulsion to vomit convulsed him. He strove to regain his concentration, but a boot with two-inch lifts jammed itself in the doorway of his mind. *"You have much to learn, Spaniard, about strategy—and self-preservation!"*

Watch me, Georgian! Cabeza gasped. You taught me well. Watch the mule shit where it pleases. Watch it survive!

Walk on the numbers—they lead to the bridge. His consuming thought was to get back to the bridge. Once across it, he would be out of the Russian sector. Then . . . He had no plan for then; just an instinct for now, and a half-formed intention that had to do with seeking sanctuary in the Mexican embassy.

The numbers faded and up loomed the vision of his cell in the Lubianka, the drained, skull-like face of Stanislav as he sat on the bunk opposite, his feverish eyes fixed on the peephole. He toppled sideways and lay still. In rushed the guards. They beat at him with their rifle butts. Cabeza could hear the zap of the metal butt-plates striking dead tissue. Stanislav had defeated them at last. He had escaped in the only way he knew.

The image had scarcely faded when he was down the mine, and brave Tatanya, the only woman on his shift, lay dying at the coal face, blood oozing from her loins, black and frightening in the candlelight, her eyes lifted to his in terror and despair.

He hit a lamppost with his shoulder, spun and dropped to his knees. For an instant he crouched there clutching his belly, his forehead on the cold pavement.

"Nadiezhda," Stefan's voice whispered in his ear. *"Stalin poisoned her—his own beautiful and intelligent wife. And when his girlfriend Yolka Andreievna accused him of it, she vanished without a trace. As did Rosa, his second wife, and after her Anya Chernikhova, his mistress. After the war he beat up his commonlaw wife Yevgeniye Movshina and ordered her shot."*

The bridge, the bridge! Cabeza forced himself to his feet and onward. But the voice followed him. *"He is mad, General—a master of poisons. He keeps them always by him—in his Secretariat, in his apartment—poisons that kill with natural symptoms, developed for him by Yagoda and his chemists."*

But how would he find the bridge? It must lie to the west, but where was west? His eyes raked the overcast in vain. The street signs meant nothing. He would have to ask. But what would he ask for?

"Stalin—the great famine . . ." Gregori's voice now.

Stalin does not provoke me! Cabeza cried aloud. He would ask for the Spree. But how was it pronounced in German?

"But listen, General, sixteen million people died from starvation—the direct result of his agricultural policies, forced collectivization. In addition, between '34 and '38 he had seven hundred thousand people shot or tortured to death. Five million were in labor camps . . ."

The bridge! I will use the OOKK pass to get through the checkpoint. And when I am through—

"Add it up, General! Think of it—he has killed more innocent people than Hitler ever did—more than the whole population of a country like Yugoslavia . . ."

They made their revolution, Cabeza cried harshly. Now they must lie in it—I am not responsible!

The road was giving way to a thoroughfare of sorts. A car swam by. Stay away, Grigori, he begged. *Por Dios,* keep out of my head while I think which way to turn . . .

"The peasants called on God to deliver them. They called for a miracle . . ."

I cry also, Grigori. Tell me, *hombre,* left or right?

"So you know what Stalin did? He ordered a five-year plan to wipe God from their minds. He destroyed the churches, told the NKVD to kill off all the religious families—whole families, General, shot while they prayed!"

Cabeza turned right. A young couple were coming toward him—lovers, their arms about each other, their heads close.

He tried to straighten up his body. It cost him agony. Sweat sprang from his brow. Lovers . . .

"Stalin's daughter Svetlana had a lover—Alexis Kapler . . ." Stefan's voice again.

"Favor." Cabeza halted the couple, blinking, striving to clear his mind.

"Stalin disapproved of Kapler. Kapler vanished."

"You—you speak English?"

The Germans shook their heads, staring at him curiously, a little fearfully.

"The Spree. Which way to the Spree?" Cabeza made signs. He was almost fainting with the effort to appear normal.

"Stalin's friend Ordzhonikidze vanished in the same way . . ."

"The river!" Cabeza cried. *"Rivière? Río? Spree?"* He tried every language and pronunciation he could think of.

The girl was tugging at the youth's arm. They began to sidle past.

"Rivière—ach!" The young man nodded quickly. He pointed in the direction Cabeza was going, giving him hurried directions in a mixture of German and French, backing away from him.

Cabeza nodded. The indications were sufficient. He limped on, aware of their following stares, trying to pick up his count.

"Yenukidze was the next to go. Of all Stalin's friends, he was the closest and most loyal. But the old man had him arrested and shot."

Then he was a fool! Cabeza cried. Only a fool befriends a tiger. Don't fill my head with fools.

"Lenin wasn't a fool. Stalin killed him, too."

That is a lie. Lenin died of a sickness.

"He died of poison. Sent to him by Stalin via Grigorevich."

Who said so?

"Trotsky said so, in his book. And he killed Trotsky. He had him murdered. Stalin killed both the great founders of the Revolution!"

Cabeza blundered aside into a shop doorway and was sick. The repeated convulsions drove him to his knees. He was weakening, he knew. He was listening to the voices, arguing with them. It was an argument he would lose. He must not care about the Revolution, only about the bridge. But he must hurry now, or he would never have the strength to get there.

He dragged himself to his feet and kept going. And now there was a big intersection with traffic lights glinting on the tramlines and a statue and over on the far side some people leaving a bar, one of them trying to sing, the others trying to hush him up. The bar was closing. Which way had the young man pointed?

More cars now, their headlights flashing across the unlit shopfronts. It was Saturday night, but the city was dead. Dead. Left, was it? Yes, left.

He reeled across the intersection, the voices haranguing him, the sickness knotting his belly muscles. Into a long, straight avenue now.

Squinting ahead, he could just see a bridge. *The* bridge? Could it really be? *Madre*, he was getting there! He was going to make it!

Then between him and the bridge he saw two police. They were patrolling toward him along the sidewalk. What should he do—bluff it out, keep going? Presently he would have to submit to the scrutiny of the checkpoint anyway. *Qué va*, he would make it a test.

Qué pasa? What test was this—in a dark alley? Why had he turned aside? This cramp . . . ! Cinema posters on shadowy walls, a fire exit, trash cans . . . He stumbled among the trash cans and sat down involuntarily. A dog started to bark. He rolled on the ground, trying to hollow his back, to stretch out his locked belly muscles. The dog kept on barking.

"It had woken Stalin in the night," said Grigori's voice.

No, Cabeza groaned. Not the dog story.

"Howling and barking—yes. Stalin called out to the guard to go find it and shoot it. This was down near Sochi on the Black Sea."

I remember it, Cabeza thought, and it disgusts me. He tried to shut his mind to it as he fought with the cramp, at the same time watching for the police. But the story went on in his head—how Stalin the next day asked the guard if he had shot the dog and the guard said that it had gone and would not bother him again.

"But did you shoot it?" Stalin asked again.

And the guard admitted, no—because it was a special guide dog belonging to a blind old Bolshevik. Stalin was very angry and said that when he gave an order it was to be obeyed. He told the guard to find the dog and bring it back and carry out his order.

So the guard telephoned along the coast and eventually the coast guards located the old man. They brought him and his dog back. And when they arrived at the villa, Stalin came out to see. He told the guards to take the dog away and shoot it. But when they went to get hold of the animal, it snarled so much they were afraid to touch it. So in the end they got the old man to take the dog away himself. The guards went with them—and shot them both.

Cabeza moaned. The act was an obscenity. Everything about Stalin was an obscenity. He felt the old rage stir in him. But this was what Kelland wanted. If he let it get a grip on him, he was done for. The police were passing the mouth of the alley now. He would think only of them and the bridge and the fact that he had for the moment conquered the cramp. See, now he was getting to his feet, brushing off the filth, straightening his clothes. Now moving back into the street and now limping, still in pain but quite quickly, toward the bridge.

And here he was at the bridge, starting across it . . .

He stopped suddenly and stared over the parapet. He almost gave up then. Below him was a railway line, not a river!

He gripped the parapet, looking at the platform below. Warschauerstrasse Station. Then he looked on along the road and at the far end saw what looked like another bridge.

Even as he started toward it, there began in his head another story—and it was the one he least of all wanted to remember.

"It happened also by the Black Sea, near Batum," Stefan's voice said.

Cabeza began to count again. His footsteps were wandering.

"Stalin—he eats good. He likes good food. And, very much, fish. One night he is eating fish and he says, 'Is very nice, but not so nice as the so-and-so fish that the Georgian cooks throw alive into the pan . . .'"

Cabeza had lost count altogether now. The picture of Stalin seated at table with his minions in the holiday villa rose in front of him.

"So Pauker—you remember Pauker, his ass-licker?—he says that nearby in the mountains is a lake where such fish can be found, and he will get some. He promises Stalin that he will have his special fish for dinner tomorrow night."

Cabeza thought hopelessly, Yes, I remember every word of it; how Pauker and the guards went out early, only to find that the fish could not be caught in winter, because they lay on the bottom, deep in the lake. But Stalin must have his fish! Pauker cried. So they threw in hand grenades.

Cabeza could see the scene quite clearly—the explosions lifting and shattering the water in the early light, the fish dying, their white bellies coming to the surface, first in their scores, then their hundreds, the guards out in their boats, poking about, looking for the rare and special fish for their Leader's supper.

Now down the track came the local villagers—in force, men, women, children, shouting, very angry. The lake is their only source of food; now they will starve, they cry. They beg the guards to go away. But the guards take no notice. They throw in more grenades. More explosions . . .

Then in desperation the villagers attack them—with staves, pitchforks. At last they drive the guards away. When they arrive back at Stalin's villa, the guards all have bruises—and a lot of fish, but only two of the kind Stalin likes.

When he hears what has happened, Stalin is furious. He shouts that this is a rebellion against the Soviet government. "We will show them whose lake it is!" he cries. And orders the NKVD to arrest the villagers and deport them all to Kazakhstan.

Cabeza had reeled to a halt by some railings. He gripped them then feverishly, willing it, willing it not to happen. But now, however fiercely he told himself that the rage that choked him was Kelland's weapon, he could hold it in check no longer.

Magma seethed in a thunder of images, torn faces, hoof-beats, the rasp of weaponry, planes over Guernica, his father's headless body . . . They had all of them fought for a glittering ideal. They had offered their lives for it gladly. And in its very birthplace the ideal had been betrayed—betrayed by the Leader himself, Josef Vissarionovich Stalin! And he, Cabeza, *did* care. The Revolution meant to him what the Crucifixion meant to others. It had given his life a purpose. If it was rendered meaningless, then his whole life became meaningless and he might as well not have been born!

After a sleepless night, terminated by the audible unlocking of the door, Gail dragged herself out of bed, dressed and prepared to meet her doom. Though terrified of what Kelland would have to say, she had had time to adjust to the prospect of dismissal with ignominy and, strangely, felt more at peace with herself than she had for a long, long time.

Descending the stairs, she paused outside the kitchen door and consciously relaxed herself. Chin held high, she marched in.

Kelland and the Germans sat at the table, munching absently while they studied the latest news reports monitored from Radio Moscow. With them, moodily grimacing at the *ersatz* coffee, was Cabeza.

25

UNTIL THE Russians took it over in 1945, Schönefeld Airport had been a works-maintenance airfield. It still showed. The main buildings were small and functional. Numerous Soviet medium-range bombers were visible inside the hangars undergoing conversion to civil use. In the parking bays stood half a dozen already converted Ilyushin passenger transports belonging to Eastern bloc airlines.

Out on the runway a silver twin-engined Il-14 bearing CCCP coding and Aeroflot insignia waited to receive its payload of twenty-seven Moscow-bound passengers, who were even now straggling toward it, heads bent, hats and collars clutched against the chill wind that swept across the field. Gail and Cabeza were among them.

They wore their Moscow clothing, fur hats, heavy coats— the Montels en route to their Mecca.

Kelland's eyes followed them intently from the observation lounge, never leaving them till they were safely aboard the plane.

The steps were removed. The motors spun to life. Franz and Rudi, beside him, turned away, relaxing. Not so Kelland. He continued to watch and, as the plane taxied away, scanned every figure and piece of equipment left within reasonable radius of where the aircraft had stood. His scrutiny was almost superstitious in its thoroughness. Even then he did not move, but remained to watch the plane take off, his gaze following it into the sky.

Only when it had melted into the overcast did he relax his vigil. 0905 hours precisely. He made a mental calculation: 214 mph at 9,840 feet . . . Given no excessive headwinds, they should reach Moscow at around 1400 hours German time—1600 hours Russian time. 4:00 P.M. It was tight, but within acceptable limits.

"So far so good," Kelland said. "Next move. Franz, I want you to fix me a meeting with Tofik Gorokshov."

"He's been purged."

"So who's their spymaster here now?"

"Yuri Krashenko."

"Yuri? I thought he was dead."

"No such luck."

"Well, I want a word with him. Feed it into the grapevine."

"You, meaning Schuster or Kelland?"

"Kelland. We don't want any links with Tangier."

"Time and place?"

"This evening. As far from the smell of Uncle Sam as possible."

One minute they were descending through murky cloud; the next there was Moscow below them, stretching as far as the eye could see. The pattern of its lights against the snow was of spokes and concentric circles, like a great spider web spangled with dew. The eye of the web was the Kremlin. The similarity was uncanny, breathtaking, and heightened her already sickening apprehension. She glanced at Cabeza, but he was still entombed in his thoughts.

Apart from a whispered flurry of questions from her and a grunted answer or two from him as they packed their bags before leaving, there had been virtually no communication between them all day. Cabeza seemed anesthetized, his eyes glazed and distant. She had managed to learn that on returning to the house and finding his door locked and the men still about, he had rolled up in a blanket in one of the spare rooms. Though why he had returned at all remained a mystery. Her information that she had purposely not sounded the alarm had drawn a long, searching stare from him, but no comment. Hardly a just reward, she felt, for having laid her all on the line for him!

But more than his gratitude right now, she needed his reassurance, to know what his intentions were. For all she knew, he might be intending to escape again the moment they stepped off the plane!

They landed at Sheremetyevo Airport, the cold blue world swinging up to meet them with a burp and the sudden roar of reverse thrust. Mountains of cleared snow and echelons of snowplows spun past, followed by the usual schools of parked aircraft. They reminded Gail sharply of the closed nature of the world they were now entering, for every plane in sight bore CCCP or Eastern bloc markings.

All except one. She peered at it as they swung by. It was an American DC-6, bearing the white-on-blue star and USAF insignia. What was *that* doing here? She glanced at Joaquín to see if he had noticed. It was impossible to tell.

As they unbelted, the stewardess told them to remain in their seats. She collected their passports and immigration cards and waited until two plainclothes MVD came aboard. They took a slow look around, then took charge of the passports and returned to their car and drove away.

"There will be a slight delay," the stewardess announced. "Remain seated, please."

She appeared unperturbed, but by the reactions of the other passengers Gail realized this was not normal procedure. She glanced again at Cabeza.

He evinced nothing.

They waited a full twenty minutes. Luggage was unloaded from the under compartment and trailered away. The cabin grew colder by the second and the passengers more restless. Gail checked her watch. This was bad. They had to be at the hotel by five-thirty at the latest.

At last the captain came through from the control cabin and spoke to the stewardess.

"You may leave now," she announced.

Cabeza suddenly seemed to come alive. Grasping Gail by the arm, he drew her up and along the aisle while the other passengers were still fumbling to put on their coats. They were out of the plane first, and it was like stepping into a meat locker that had blown its thermostat. The searing cold was like nothing Gail had ever experienced in her life. She paused, gasping, on the steps, while Cabeza helped her into her coney.

"Vámonos." He hustled her toward the reception building, shrugging into his own coat as they went. "There will be a big line. We will be first."

He was right: there was a line in the immigration hall. But they were not first. The passengers of another plane were ahead of them. And the passport officials were spending not seconds but minutes questioning each one of them. There were three of them in the kiosk, plus an MVD man. They were conducting what amounted to a screening process.

Cabeza grasped her arm. "Come." He pushed his way in front of a middle-aged couple, firmly and without apology. The couple opened their mouths to protest, then closed them again. Cabeza knew the Russian character well, that they would be reluctant to make a scene in the presence of the MVD. Within minutes they were at the desk.

"Montel," Cabeza said loudly, so the sorters in back should hear. He spelled it out in Russian and gave the number of their flight.

The immigration staff spent two abortive minutes searching through the wrong pile of passports. The official told him he was ahead of his flight. They would have to get further back in the line.

Cabeza seemed not to understand. Mixing Spanish with purposely bad Russian, he managed so to confuse the issue that eventually, in exasperation, the officials dug out his and Gail's passports from the other pile.

They proceeded to check them against a dossier. A blacklist, presumably. They took their time. The official at the window stared out at them bleakly.

Now their visas. Gail could feel the crowd behind becoming restive. The armed police posted around the hall watched through deceptively bored eyes. Next it was the MVD man's turn. He went through all their documentation again, for discrepancies this time. Gail watched him peering at the stamp across each of their photographs and her heart sank. Now he was comparing their passport and visa photos. He came to the window, frowning.

"Do you have other means of identification, Señor Montel?"

He asked it in Russian. Cabeza again seemed to have difficulty in understanding, but at last produced the Intourist letter and Montel's union card.

The MVD man examined these in silence. He seemed in doubt about something. But either this was just a routine ploy, or he couldn't face the communications gap, for after a few moments he shrugged and handed them back, with a nod at the control official, who stamped their visas and passports and pushed them across.

The hall clock as they hurried through into customs showed four-forty. Gail felt the tanklike drive of the man beside her, but was it Haslar's conditioning or was he powering her in some direction of his own? She had no means of knowing. She was completely in his hands.

They found their luggage had already been searched and was waiting for them. Cabeza flicked his signature to the declaration held out to them, hefted the cases and turned toward the exit—to come face-to-face with a neatly dressed woman. She addressed them in passable Spanish.

"Excuse me, please, you are Señor and Señora Montel?" She waved a gloved hand toward the yellow stars on their flight labels. "Yes? Ah. I am Anya Petrovna here to meet you." She tapped an Intourist button pinned to her prominent bosom.

There was no escaping her. They had to stop.

She was of medium height, with a skin like magnolia petals, stout and compact in her smart coat and fur hat.

"Did you have a good journey? You wish for a trolley? No? I have a car here for you. I am sorry, but because you arrive just the two of you there is no one from the Committee of Trade Unions to meet you, so I must welcome you on their behalf to the USSR and wish you an enjoyable and memorable stay." She smiled with a nice blend of cordiality and reserve. The effect was pleasant, professional—and time-consuming.

Cabeza, surprisingly, slowed right down. He took off his glove and shook her hand and said in a rough, shy way that was perfectly in character, "I bring you in return the salutations of the Executive Committee and workers of the Spanish

Iron and Steelworkers Union. We are honored to be guests in your great country." Then he picked up the cases and turned sideways, inviting her to lead on.

The woman hesitated fractionally, and Gail could see that as a guide she was used to calling the shots. Nevertheless, she accepted the cue, leading them briskly in her small high-heeled boots.

"Has there been some trouble here?" Gail ventured. "All these police . . . And we were—"

"One does not ask such things," Anya said shortly over her shoulder. "The police are for criminals only." A moment later she seemed to regret her tone, for she turned to her just inside the main entrance. "You must . . ." She tucked up Gail's collar for her in a firm, motherly gesture. "For you it will be very cold. We suffer much from our winter here—and we are used to it. But you from your warm country . . ." She led the way out.

Cabeza gave Gail a warning look that said, Keep her moving. Give her no excuse to stop and talk.

But Anya didn't need one, and no sooner were they outside than she drew their attention to the architecture of the building. When they reached their car she launched into a labored introduction to their muffled driver.

Cabeza dropped a case briefly to clap the man's shoulder. "Comrade." He moved straight around to the trunk and loaded the luggage himself.

In moments he had somehow hustled them into the car and they were driving out of the airport.

It was an agonizing journey. Anya and the driver worked as a team. Whenever she pointed out of the window, he slowed down. There were many places of interest, and she was determined that they should miss none of them.

"Now we are entering the Leningradsky Prospekt. It is very fine, no? And there is the racecourse, observe?—where race the horses in summer."

They crawled past the buildings and stands and Anya pointed out the stabling—for five hundred horses, she told them proudly.

Gail felt Cabeza's impatience building to a head beside her.

"And there you will see Petrovsky Castle built 1776 where the czars used to stop on their way to Moscow from Saint

Petersburg. Napoleon took refuge here in 1812 when the city was burning."

Again they slowed, to view the former Petrovsky Park, which was now the famous Dynamo Stadium.

Cabeza groaned.

Anya glanced back at him, frowning. "You are not well, comrade?"

Gail took the cue swiftly. "Here, *caro*, lean on me."

"What is the matter with him?" Anya asked.

"It is his hip. From an accident."

"Accident?"

"Why we were delayed in coming. A rail swung from a crane. It struck his hip. The bone was cracked."

Anya clicked her tongue sympathetically. "I noticed that he was limping. You would like to visit a doctor?"

"No, no, *gracias*. It is only when he sits for a long time. Today all day he has been sitting."

"Then we must get quickly to the hotel." Anya spoke to the driver.

A little glance from Cabeza said, Bravo, *muchacha*.

"I will show you the places of interest when we return to Sheremetyevo at the end of your stay," Anya promised.

"Bueno," Cabeza gasped. "That would be most kind. We would not like to miss them."

As they drew up outside the rather shabby baroque entrance of the Hotel Metropole the clock in the Redeemer Tower of the nearby Kremlin was just striking five-thirty.

They were still on schedule.

26

THE METROPOLE was clearly something of an institution, old-fashioned to the point of Edwardianism, with a large art nouveau ceramic of a nude woman at the entrance and shades of the Palm Court inside. One expected to hear elderly musicians playing in the tea lounge. And one was not altogether disappointed, though they played at a slightly later hour—during dinner.

Into this hall of respectability marched Anya Petrovna with her new arrivals. She escorted them to the desk and handed in their passports. While they were signing the register she crossed to the Intourist desk for a word with a youngish, rather sullen-looking colleague, no doubt to report their arrival.

Gail looked around, shyly, as befitted her role. This was Susana's first trip into the international big time. She would be out of her depth, nervous. The way she felt right now, this took no great act of imagination.

While Cabeza scrawled his carefully practiced imitation of Montel's signature in the book, her eyes roved the lofty roof, the décor, the well-heeled clientele—foreign visitors mostly, she guessed, plus a sprinkling of resident news correspondents, their Russian friends, contacts. A man sat behind a newspaper in the corner. MVD perhaps. She knew they must assume that one way or another they would be under constant surveillance during the brief time they were here. Their room would almost certainly be bugged. The hotel servants would be part of the network. Even now, Anya's Intourist colleague was eyeing them, memorizing them. If they tried to leave the hotel, they would be discouraged, escorted or followed. Stalin's Moscow was a paranoid institution, and neither of them must forget that for one instant.

What looked like members of a Chinese trade delegation were entering the hotel, unmuffling themselves, conversing in their high-pitched way. No, she decided, catching their intonation—North Koreans. Russia was still fostering their conflict, squeezing the last drop of American and UN blood out of it before finally suing for peace. The Koreans were glancing toward the desk, frowning, muttering together.

Shifting slightly, she was surprised to see a rugged red-faced man in USAF uniform standing right behind her, sorting through some postcards. He wore the stripes of a flight sergeant and exuded an air of physical potency that seemed totally out of place in these surroundings.

She remembered the DC-6 she had seen at the airport. Perhaps he was one of the crew.

As she watched, a second man in USAF uniform came out of the gift shop and sauntered over.

"Hell, Mac," she heard him begin. She missed the next bit, then heard: "For kids' stuff she says try Dietsky Mir in Marksa Prospekt. You reckon we have time to look in there?"

The sergeant checked his watch and shook his head. "Cut it too close." He added something she couldn't hear, then the two of them moved toward the elevator.

Anya arrived back with some literature—vouchers, guidebooks and a syllabus of the places they would visit during their stay.

Reaching for their room key, the reception clerk uttered an exclamation. He produced an envelope from their pigeonhole. He had almost forgotten. A cable had arrived for them.

Gail reacted sharply, then made it look like apprehension. For working folk like the Montels, she knew, such a communication would usually mean bad news.

Mirroring her uneasiness, Cabeza opened it up. The point of origin was shown as Bilbao, Spain. (How had Kelland managed that?) The message was in Spanish and read: "Bianca has given birth to twins. Boy and girl. Mother and babies doing well. Enjoy your holiday. Alberto."

Cabeza chuckled. He read it aloud to Gail, who almost sobbed with joy and relief. They embraced each other emotionally.

Anya smiled. Learning that Bianca was Susana's younger sister, she shook them both by the hand.

"Then you are uncle and aunt—congratulations! For the first time, yes?"

"No," Gail ad-libbed, "the fifth."

Minutes later, having exchanged some pesetas for rubles in the gift shop, they were riding up in the elevator, escorted by the porter. He led them along lofty corridors to a high-ceilinged room containing twin beds and utilitarian furniture. On the cream-painted wall above the beds hung a painting of charging Cossacks. The large many-paned window was double-glazed, with an opening pane in the center. There was a bathroom attached.

The porter lingered hopefully, but Cabeza made no move to tip him.

Gail rewarded him with a smile. *"Spaseba."*

The man gave them a sour look and withdrew.

Cabeza signaled to remind her that anything they said might be overheard. She threw off her coat with a happy chuckle.

"Twins, Marcos, imagine that! Isn't it wonderful? Can I see the cable?" She went to him and squeezed his hand, reaching his eyes mutely for a second as she took it. She read in them nothing but concentration. A good sign, she decided, as she got out a pad and pencil and sat down on the bed. He was on course, following the plan as though last night had never happened.

The door was slightly ajar, and now it suddenly swung inward—to reveal the USAF sergeant. He looked quickly to the right and left before leaning in. He pointed mutely to the cupboard, then immediately withdrew. His footfalls made no sound as he strode away.

Cabeza froze for a moment in surprise. Then he closed the door and went to the cupboard. Tucked away at the back was a bulging briefcase. He lifted it out—it was heavy—and opened it on the bed.

It contained a folded carpetbag and some tools—wrenches, screwdrivers, a small blowtorch, a hacksaw, a large spool of measuring tape and a clipboard, to which was attached a plain Russian identity card in the name of Mikhail Alexei Babayev, and a work order for maintenance repairs handwritten in Russian.

Gail glanced up to measure his reaction. He nodded, preoccupied. Selecting two of the largest screwdrivers, he began to unscrew their handles.

Gail continued rearranging the words of the message, regrouping the letters into short sequences.

Cabeza gingerly withdrew from the largest handle a four-ounce stick of plastic gelignite. He squeezed it experimentally. It had the color and consistency of rich, dark Spanish marzipan.

From the other handle he produced two unusually designed firing caps. The ends of each were sealed like an electric detonator, but where the wires would normally have protruded there were simply perforations.

Gail read his satisfaction as he packed them back gently and returned the screwdrivers to his briefcase. Well, that's two of the beyond-our-control elements taken care of, she thought. Kelland had not let them down so far.

"Now I will bathe," Cabeza said loudly. He went into the bathroom and turned on the taps.

Gail followed him in. She had decoded the password. It read:

"*Krasny krasny.*" "Red is red." Or, in the older sense of the word, "Red is beautiful." She held it up for him to memorize. She pointed to the second part of the message: "Valid until seven P.M."

Cabeza checked his watch. It was now ten to six. He had just one hour and ten minutes in which to complete his mission.

Gail eased open the door to the service stairs. It gave onto concrete steps leading down into the dim lower regions. She listened for footsteps and heard none—just distant kitchen noises.

She nodded to Cabeza, who quickly slipped through and turned. For a moment they looked at each other.

"Complete the bath," he ordered quietly. "Make noises with the water. Talk like I am still there."

"I'll be waiting for you at the junction of Gorky and Ogareva from seven-fifteen."

He nodded. His eyes were like black diamonds.

She remembered the gruesome electrical experiment with a pang. Joaquín was going out to kill Stalin. He was but *he* wasn't. Even here, Kelland's fingers were remorselessly jerking the strings . . . She moved to Cabeza impulsively, clutching his arms, pressing her face to the roughness of his cheek. "Take care, *caro. Please?*"

Someone was coming down the steps.

She stood back quickly. The unnaturally bright eyes stared into hers, and in that fleeting instant she read everything she hungered for—recognition, gratitude, reassurance. Then the awareness went from his gaze as his mind sped on ahead down the stairs. His body followed.

It was snowing lightly as he stepped from the side entrance of the hotel into Revolution Square. He paused to turn up his collar, glancing around.

The heart of the great city was pulsing with Sunday evening life. Crowds were window-shopping, silhouetted against the lighted storefronts, circulating, hobnobbing around the kiosks that sold Eskimo pies and soft drinks, getting on and off trolleybuses, thronging to cross at the intersections.

Beyond the frozen trees and fountains of Sverdlov Square he could see the towering columns of the Bolshoi Theater; near it the Children's Theater and TSUM general store. Marksa Prospekt teemed with traffic.

The bizarre nature of what he was about to do came to him suddenly and strongly. He was going to strike at the very heart of this mighty nation going so peaceably about its business. There was not the least sign of terror, even apprehensiveness, on the faces that passed him. He found it almost impossible to believe that a bloody purge was in progress, that Jews and other victims were being rounded up hourly, imprisoned without trial, tortured, executed.

Nevertheless it was a fact. Therefore everything he was looking at was a lie—the same lie the Germans had lived under Hitler. The war had exposed Hitler's lie, but Stalin's just went on—and on.

He turned resolutely left and, tucking the heavy briefcase under his arm, walked quickly toward Red Square. Gail's parting embrace lingered in his mind. It and the sacrifice she had been prepared to make for him last night had swept away his last mistrust of her as Kelland's tool, permitting the reservoir of his own emotions to flow toward her in his mind. And it was a good feeling, a warm feeling under his coat, strengthening his resolve to carry out this mission without error so as to ensure her safety and escape. Which was precisely as Kelland had intended. Even in defiance, Cabeza realized, they were still moving to his design. He was in them and around them, encompassing every permutation—a godhead, a devil. Cabeza had never feared any man. But he was close at that moment, he was forced to admit, very close, to fearing Kelland.

He was passing the Lenin Museum. Opposite loomed the State History Museum. He braced himself as he turned up the steep ramp into Red Square.

The wind met him icily. And there it was, the timeless scene.

"Magnificent" was a poor word. "Haunting" was nearer the mark. The vastness of the square, the battlements looming beyond it, towers spiking the snowy darkness, the domes and cupolas of Saint Basil's Cathedral like a handful of gaudy Easter eggs held up to the sky.

In the old days Cabeza had often wondered why the sight of the Kremlin moved him so. Now suddenly he knew. It was like all the Moorishness of his own beloved Spain gathered together and transformed into a winter's tale.

Fixing his eyes on the ruby star glowing atop the Redeemer Tower, he limped along the square toward it—past the great GUM department store to his left. To his right, the bronze doors of the Lenin Mausoleum stood shut, guarded by two sentinels, motionless as statues. Above it, inside the walls of the Kremlin, he could see the great dome of the building that was his objective—the former Senate—but to reach it he must pass along outside the walls as far as Saint Basil's in order to enter via the Redeemer Gate.

The snow swirled, freezing on his lashes, blinding him, so that the cathedral grew toward him only as a shape, a redness against the darkness where the frozen river lay. The murmur of traffic came to him from the far shore. It mingled with the hollow sound the wind made in the cupolas above—a sound that sobbed ever more eerily as he drew closer.

Suddenly the first bars of the "Internationale" chimed overhead. He squinted upward sharply. The great Redeemer clock was beginning to strike six. *Bueno*. He was right on schedule. Stalin's suppertime had crept from six-thirty to a quarter to seven in recent months, according to his briefing. If that was correct, it gave him a clear three-quarters of an hour to do what he had to do. *If* it was correct.

And if the OOKK identification stood up to inspection. The ifs were bunching now. He was approaching the moment of truth. Kelland's plan was about to be put to its first—and last—test.

With no pause at all in his stride, he turned into the Redeemer Gate.

The tower was so huge that the entrance was like a tunnel. Armed sentries stood under the dim electric lanterns, stamping their feet. Cabeza headed straight on with all the authority he could muster, stopping only when one of them stepped out in front of him.

He hung the OOKK card in front of the man's face.

"*Krasny krasny,*" he muttered, staring past him impatiently, as if on urgent business.

The man peered at the card. He stepped back smartly. But before Cabeza could move on, an officer appeared in the doorway of the guardroom. "Stop!" He stepped down toward them and took the folder. He was tall and hulking, with a flat face and Asiatic eyes.

He peered at the card with the beginnings of officiousness. But they were magically stillborn. He returned the folder and, too, stepped back.

Cabeza evinced no relief. Giving the man a hard look, he limped on.

He emerged from the tower into the wide lamplit darkness of the Kremlin. In keeping with the square outside, the spaces were enormous. To his left stretched formal gardens with walks and birches and ornamental shrubs. Ahead lay Cathedral Square. To his right loomed the façade of the little theater that was incorporated in the Presidium building.

Cabeza skirted this and turned right. Ahead now he could see the corner of his objective—and a two-man guard patrol. They were moving toward him along the path, rifles slung.

He limped on, preparing himself for their challenge. As he drew level they halted and peered at him. He paused straight by them with a confident *"Dobrye vyecher."*

They made no effort to stop him.

Within moments he was rounding the flattened end of the former Senate, heading along the front of the building toward the entrance arch. He inspected the enormous façade curiously, gauging its height, comparing it with the Tangier model.

No scribbles on hardboard now, but the real thing. The depth of the cornice that ran around the top of the building was far more than he had been given to imagine, overhanging the walls by perhaps a meter and a half. He eyed it in some dismay. That could present a real problem.

The windows, too. All of them appeared sealed, with just a single opening pane. He hoped to heaven Cedric's information about Stalin's apartment windows was correct.

Every room in the building appeared to be lit and busy. Several official cars stood outside the entrance. To his left, beyond the snow-covered trees of Kaliayev Square, he could make out the massive, severe lines of the Arsenal building. All was exactly as he had been briefed.

As no doubt would be the checkpoint under the arch. "Here you will come under the closest scrutiny," Stefan had warned him. "You will be at the very core of the Soviet—the building in which the Leader himself works and lives. And the Leader is a paranoid. The security surrounding him will reflect that."

Well, here he was. Four great columns flanked the triumphal entrance, which was not actually an archway but a flat-topped portal under a shell-like relief. He marched straight on in.

Another tunnel, penetrating the whole depth of the building to the inner courtyard. There was a guardroom with two armed sentries standing outside and more guards visible within.

Cabeza stopped by the first sentry and again hung out his identification.

"Krasny krasny."

The man took one look, nodded and waved him on.

Cabeza could hardly believe it. Paranoid security? He limped on through into the courtyard. Ahead was the handsome circular building topped by the dome that was visible from Red Square. It stood in the apex of the triangularity, approached by a path flanked by grass and small trees. This was the mighty Sverdlov Hall, where the Council of Ministers held their meetings.

He followed the path, the beginnings of uneasiness stirring in him. His peasant nature was ever mistrustful of handouts. Penetrating this far had been almost too easy. Could he possibly be walking into a trap? The Agency had a man within these walls. Suppose he had been caught and talked?

Asking questions in your head only weakens resolve, he told himself. If he has talked, it is too late, anyway.

He glanced away to his left, but the windows of Stalin's apartment were not visible from here. A gallery crossed the central space between him and the corner angle of the building. Stalin's windows overlooked the small additional courtyard this provided.

Cabeza crossed the broad walk at the end of the path and mounted the seven circular steps. Facing him was a high doorway. He tried it. It opened.

He found himself in a curving hallway. It acted clearly as both a foyer to the great hall and linkage between the two wings of the building. Government personnel were passing on their way from one block to the other. They barely glanced at him. There was no sign of a security check.

He turned left and moved around till he came to an ornate lobby. Groups of dark-suited men stood talking. "Bankers," Kelland had said. "They all look like bankers in the Kremlin." Cabeza moved confidently among them. The lobby served a lofty corridor and a palatial stairway. He made for the stairway.

Before he could set foot on it, a Kremlin Security guard stepped in front of him. "A moment, please."

Cabeza knew instantly that he had been spotted as an unfamiliar face. He halted with a scowl.

"Who do you want to see?" The inquiry was polite but authoritative.

Cabeza showed his card in meaningful silence, giving the man just long enough to absorb its import before hurrying on up the stairs. He half expected to be called back, but the man let him go without a murmur.

Reaching the first floor, he turned right, into a corridor similar to the one below. The doors on either hand served offices, conference rooms. Typewriters clacked. A bunch of gossiping secretaries stood in his way. He limped purposefully around them. A red-faced man in a marshal's uniform came out of an office, almost bumping into him. Cabeza paused politely for a moment and their eyes met. It was Voroshilov!

Cabeza had met the marshal once—on that winter's day in Red Square—but though he searched the bloodshot eyes for a sign of recognition, there wasn't a glimmer. The ex-blacksmith-turned-Bolshevik lumbered away—in the direction of Stalin's Secretariat.

Cabeza heaved a sigh. Two doors further down he found the washroom. He pushed straight in, entered a cubicle and locked the door.

He opened up the briefcase, took out the carpetbag and began to transfer the tools into it. He had barely begun when someone came in—two men, by the sound of it. He froze.

He listened to their monosyllabic talk—something to do with the coming elections—as they urinated. The taps gushed. The towel dispenser screeched. The door huffed open, then shut.

He quickly completed the transfer. Rolling up the thin leather briefcase, he stuffed it under the tools. He took off his topcoat and hat, shook the snow off them, turned them inside out and put them on again. He pocketed the Babayev ID card and tucked the clipboard under his arm.

It was done. He emerged quickly and inspected himself in the mirror. Now he was a Kremlin worker, dressed in a greasy, well-worn coat and cheap hat. He unbuttoned the flaps and let them dangle about his ears to make himself appear even more scruffy.

He left the washroom, went back to the stairway and climbed to the top floor.

Its layout was much the same as the two below, but not quite so grand. Fairly busy, but no sign of Security. He skirted the stairwell to a small door set near the end wall. Dead accurate, there was no other way to describe Cedric's model. A quick glance around and he was through it, sneaking up a flight of narrow steps to the roof.

The roof door was bolted from inside, but not locked. He shot the bolts back and stepped out into the icy night.

It had stopped snowing, for which he was thankful. He was right beside the upper elevation of the Sverdlov Hall, a vast merry-go-round of arched windows topped by a molded cornice from which the dome curved away upward out of sight. High above him the Soviet flag snapped and bickered in the darkness.

Immediately behind him the shallow pantiled roof stretched away on the first leg of its vast triangle. There was a walkway around the edge, bordered by a low parapet and metal handrail—constructed no doubt to facilitate snow clearance. And the snow had been cleared—*bueno!* There was only the recent light fall to impede his progress.

Cedric had calculated it all most carefully, measuring both of his feet, allowing an extra few millimeters for the thick boots he would be wearing. Two hundred and fifty-four—the number was indelibly printed on his mind. But he would have to concentrate. There was no room for the slightest error.

Aligning his right heel with the start of the pantiles, he placed his left foot in front of it.

"Two, three, four . . ." He toe-heeled it slowly along the walkway, keeping his balance by means of the handrail.

His mind kept leaping ahead to what he must do next. He kept dragging it back.

"Fifty-seven, fifty-eight . . ."

He was passing the gallery now. Presently he would arrive above the small northern courtyard.

"Two hundred!" He paused and looked down into it.

No human shape marred its snowy whiteness. He could see into some of the offices of the front building—figures moving, a girl working a duplicator. Some of the windows were shaded. Others were in darkness. Even as he looked, two lights went out in succession.

The staff is going home, he thought. But the Presidium meeting will continue until six-forty-five. Providing it remains true to its schedule. Suppose for some reason it had been canceled and Stalin had already returned to his apartment? The thought chilled him.

"Two hundred and one . . ."

At the count of two hundred and fifty-four he stopped and heeled a mark in the snow. He checked his watch. Six-twenty-six. He was running slow now.

He had rehearsed the next move many times at the villa. First the measuring tape . . . He wound it out of its sprung spool—fully—till its fifteen meters were snaked out on the snow in front of him. It lay rather stiffly for tape. It was in fact a dozen strands of nylon gut sweated flat and coated with fabric—breaking strain one hundred sixty kilos. Cabeza applied the brake to the spool, then, fitting a pair of angle brackets to the studs on its stout metal casing, he hooked it to the parapet.

He passed the other end of the line out under the handrail and back over the top of it, clipping its ring to an attachment on his belt.

Now came the part he didn't like. He had never been a climber, except over the rocks in his guerrilla days. Sheer heights disturbed him. But it had to be done.

He climbed over the rail and clung there while he passed the line over his shoulder and under his thigh, as Laroche had taught him—outside his overcoat, so it should not cut into his flesh. He released the spool brake, hooked his arm through the handles of the tool bag, and leaned out and tried to gauge the positions of the windows immediately beneath. Though he knew they belonged to Stalin's Secretariat and were both bulletproof and frosted, he did not want to be silhouetted against them as he descended.

The extreme depth of the cornice made this almost impossible. His stomach turned as he leaned out further. He was just able to glimpse the lower windows.

Adjusting his position slightly, he eased himself over the cornice and hung there, double-checking. Yes, he was clear of the windows. But he was dangling way out from the building, like a spider on a thread, just as he had feared. *Qué va.* He let the line slip through his gloved hand.

The huge corbels that supported the cornice butted him in the belly. Then he was swiveling down between the top windows.

Yes, they were frosted, thank God. Cedric was right yet again. Behind them, he hoped, Stalin was still presiding over the Presidium meeting.

He spun down in fits and starts to the floor below. Here the heavy molding above the ground-floor windows stepped out to meet him—at least, most of the way. He could just reach it with his foot. He gave a kick. He swung out and swung back. At the second try he made it. The ledge was just wide enough to stand on.

Stalin's living-room window to his right was in darkness. But, *mierda,* the housekeeper's window to his left was lit!

On Sundays at this time she should be visiting her bedridden mother. What could have happened?

Cabeza glanced behind him to make sure no one had entered the courtyard below. He looked across at the windows opposite. No curious faces peered out at him. Yet.

He edged his way along the ledge until he could see in through the window.

A middle-aged woman sat writing a letter at the table in the small, cheerless room. A chunky radio was playing classical music beside her. He could just hear it.

She had scraped-back gray hair, rimless glasses. Stout-bodied. She fitted the housekeeper's description, all right.

Cabeza crouched on the ledge and quickly ran through the ramifications. Her presence must affect Stalin's supper arrangements, he reckoned. On her evenings off, the meal was supplied, together with serving staff, direct from the canteen kitchens. But now . . . perhaps she was cooking the meal herself. In which case she was liable to start moving around the flat at any minute.

He backed along to the living-room window. Cedric's information had been that Stalin liked to be able to throw open his windows whenever the spirit moved him—a habit originating from his pipe-smoking days. It followed, there-fore, that his living-room window would not be sealed, as were most others in the building. Cedric had been so sure, that Kelland had based his whole plan on it. Cabeza was about to learn whether this faith was well founded.

Balancing precariously, he pulled off a glove and took out a switchblade. He slipped it up between the top and bottom sashes and felt for the latch. The blade encountered something. He tried to move it. Nothing happened.

He reversed the direction of the blade and tried again. Still nothing. He applied more pressure. The catch snapped open.

Now to raise the sash. But though he dragged at it, it refused to move. Was it sealed after all? Maybe it was just frozen. He ran the knife around the frame and tried again. Still the sash would not move.

Valuable moments were slipping by. He dug the blade savagely between the window and its frame and dragged it around with all his strength.

He gripped the frame and heaved.

The sash came up with a jerk.

Cabeza froze and listened, his ear to the gap. When he was satisfied that the sound had not been heard, he put away the knife and heaved the window up half a meter. He swung the tool bag in and lowered it to the floor very gently. Then climbed in himself.

The sound of the housekeeper's radio reached him faintly. She had it turned up quite high—good.

He unclipped the line from his belt and, reaching out of the window, gave it a little tug and let go.

It sprang away upward—to vanish, he hoped, into its spool on the parapet.

He had passed the point of no return.

27

DESPITE THE gusting rain, the gaunt man crossed the forecourt of the tavern slowly. The wind blew his raincoat against his almost skeletal form, like hung washing against a pole. He entered the steamy bar and looked around with hooded eyes.

It was too early for the beer drinkers. From the half-dozen or so customers seated at the tables it took him only a moment to spot his man. He moved first to the bar.

"Coffee coffee," he ordered with a hard look. "No *ersatz*." Then he slid onto a bench at the wall table where Kelland sat.

"David. How are you keeping these days?" He spoke English with an American accent and a Russian roll of the *r*'s.

Kelland stared at him. "Yuri." It was almost a question, so incredibly had the man changed. The once broad cheeks were sunken, the bushy hair now tinder-dry and in retreat. The nose, marooned by the depletion, had become a beak. Only the eyes and mouth remained as landmarks of the man he knew—the wire armature poking through the clay—metallic, intelligent, unrelenting.

"What happened to you?"

"Nothing. A small accident."

"Accident?"

"Oh . . ." Krashenko made a dismissive gesture. "Some spray. From a cyanide projector."

Kelland almost chuckled. "I thought you fellows took an antidote before and after you used that stuff."

"I was not using it," Krashenko grunted. "It was used against me."

"The biter bitten. Well, well."

"For four months I was in hospital. Saved only by our medical expertise."

"Now maybe you know what your victims feel like."

"Strange." The Russian's mouth curled grimly. "I do not remember you as a humanitarian."

"I'm just addicted to old rituals—weekly target practice, the moment in a dark alley when you screw on the silencer, you know."

"So bulky to conceal, with newspapers going tabloid."

"Buy *The New York Times*."

"The advertisements for consumer goods are bad for our agents' morale."

Kelland laughed. "Gas versus gas."

"We prefer our own." The Russian toyed with the ketchup dispenser for a moment. "You wanted to see me?"

Kelland paused while the barman delivered Krashenko's coffee. "It may be nothing. But I give it to you for what it's worth."

"And what is it worth?" The hooded eyes surveyed him cynically.

Kelland lifted his shoulders. "I may have a favor to ask you sometime. 'Build up credit where you can' is my motto."

"I can make no promises."

"As I say, this may not be anything."

Krashenko tasted the coffee. He grimaced and shot a fierce look toward the barman. "I am listening."

"One of our Mediterranean street men picked up a buzz—around Thursday. I'm not saying where. Just bar talk. Nothing to substantiate it. No details."

Krashenko raised his brows. He waited.

"Seems an old enemy of your system is on his way to assassinate your General Secretary."

The Russian made a small explosion with his coffee. He took out a handkerchief, dried his lips carefully.

"Go on."

"Our man tried to find out his affiliations. He drew a blank. So it would seem that his motive is personal. And who can blame him? He simply wants to change your lousy system."

"And who is this revisionist?"

"How's your Spanish history?"

Cabeza crossed the darkened living room of Stalin's apartment and eased open the door.

The hall was lit by a single light. The entrance door was to his immediate right. To his left was a passageway with six doors—three bedrooms, dining room, bathroom, kitchen, according to Cedric's model. The décor was commonplace for the Leader of the Soviet peoples; not ascetic, like Lenin's old apartment in this building—just uninspired. The proportions, too, were far from grand, save for the high vaulted ceiling, which was bisected by the room partitions in a way that showed the flat to be a conversion. Before Stalin's time this area had been the end section of a corridor.

Testing the air, Cabeza could detect no smell of cooking. This suggested that the canteen arrangement had been allowed to stand. If so, that lessened his chances of discovery—providing he moved fast.

He tiptoed past the housekeeper's room. The music was rising to a climax, working for him nicely. The bathroom was at the extreme end of the passage. He went in and closed the door behind him silently. There was a small brass bolt. He homed it for good measure, kicked the bath mat against the gap underneath and switched on the light.

The room was of medium size, very clean and polished-looking, and again exactly as described by Cedric—enameled bath, washbasin, lavatory, bidet, two cabinets on the walls. One small window, frosted, curtainless.

Cabeza opened up the carpetbag on the floor and slipped the explosive and detonators out of their containers. He pressed the detonators one into either end of the gelignite, leaving just their perforated ends exposed. One would have been enough; the second was a backup.

He had practiced the following routine many times under Kelland's exacting eye. First the taps—make sure they are well turned off and not leaking. Now the basin—feel it is quite dry.

Now down on his knees. Locate the S-bend of the waste pipe. There was no pedestal to impede him as there had been at the villa. He found the pipe easily. Then running his fingers down, he got his first shock.

There was no S-bend! The pipe went straight into the wall.

For Cabeza, plumbing was a luxury of recent years. He had never mastered the principle of it, and now he was at a loss.

The rehearsals at the villa had been based on the assumption that all systems would incorporate an S-bend. For without it, and the U of water it contained, he was told, the smell of sewerage would rise unimpeded into the bathroom. And in order that it could be drained, there would inevitably be a screw plug at the lowest point of the S, which he would be able to remove, making sure first that there was a receptacle underneath to catch the water. He was to let it drain fully, then dry out the inside of the pipe with cotton waste. He must do this thoroughly, and then, as a guard against any remaining beads of water, work an absorbent rubber-lined sleeve up through the trap. Only then would it be safe to install the explosive, elongating the plastic sausage till it fitted through the trap into the sleeve. Pack the base with more dry cotton waste. Then screw back the plug.

The detonator was sensitized to explode only under direct contact with substances of over 50 percent moisture content on the Ventner Scale.

"Stalin—Ablutions: Washes vigorously before every meal . . ."

The device had been designed by Agency scientists to meet Kelland's requirement of "maximum success potential from minimal materials through localization"—his own jargon.

Now, Cabeza thought grimly, he would have to invent another way to skin his horse. If there wasn't a trap, he must make one.

He got out the hacksaw and proceeded to try to cut a wedge out of the underside of the pipe. It was then that he got his second shock.

Unlike the waste pipe at the villa, this one was made not of lead but of galvanized iron.

There was no way he could saw through iron in time. Certainly not without alerting the housekeeper.

Perhaps, if he could prize the waste fitting out of the basin itself . . .

He tried, but it was sweated in there solidly.

The nut underneath, then, that attached the pipe to the basin. If he could loosen that and pull it free—bed the explosive in the top of it . . .

He applied the wrench to it. It was coated with layers of cream gloss paint. He scratched around the paintwork with his knife and tried again.

Though he strained till his face was crimson, the nut would not shift.

He straightened and stared around. The lavatory?

He climbed up and removed the lid of the flush tank and peered in. If he could somehow attach the explosive to the arm, then when the chain was pulled and the arm plunged into the water . . .

He found that the arm was of the submerged type. No part of it showed above the surface. *Mierda!*

He stepped down again and checked his watch. It was twenty-five to seven. At any moment now the housekeeper might become mobile. Or Stalin's supper arrive from the canteen. Or Stalin himself . . . and he had exhausted his last alternative.

A wild bird began to spread its wings inside him.

On the floor above, in the Secretariat, Stalin was at this moment locked in a battle of wills with his Presidium. It was unprecedented—an open revolt!

Lazar Kaganovich, never a humanitarian, had startlingly proposed that a committee be formed to examine the case of the doctors, for whose arrest, he protested, there was still not a shred of evidence.

The rest of them—from Chairman Shvernik, through Molotov, Bulganin to Kosygin—all backed him up. Only Khrushchev and Beria supported Stalin.

Stalin stormed and ranted. Their raised voices echoed along the corridor, causing the Security guards and the Leader's bodyguard, Rusakov, to exchange frowning glances.

Suddenly Kaganovich tore up his Party card and threw it in

Stalin's face. Stalin, purple with rage, leaped toward him. His colleagues had difficulty in preventing him from attacking his old colleague.

The meeting was coming to a premature and angry end.

Cabeza stood absolutely still, eyes closed, and reviewed the whole of his briefing. Every detail of Stalin's habits, of the apartment, the rooms, their furniture, the contents of the furniture paraded through his mind. Did they offer any other means of harnessing the explosive?

The kitchen sink? Stalin would never go near it. Liquid . . . The watering of the living-room plant? What would he drink for supper?

"Stalin—drinking habits: Breakfast—"

Forget breakfast—supper!

"Supper: Starts with a glass of brandy . . ."

There was no way he could attach the explosive to brandy. How about his medicines? Cabeza had no information about his taking any medicines. Anyway, the same applied to *any* bottle. Even— He stared at the bathroom cabinets.

"Stalin—the criminal: Expert in poisons. Yagoda and the NKVD developed several sophisticated poisons for his use. Some fast, some slow—each with a different natural symptom: heart attack, hemorrhage . . . Keeps these in two places. In Secretariat, the cabinet immediately inside the door. In apartment, bathroom cabinet to left of window."

Cabeza stared at the cabinet. The list of its contents sprang before his eyes: *"Poison (two bottles), Band-Aids, bottle of antiseptic, bottle of iodine, spare razor blades, denture adhesive, hypodermic . . ."*

He grabbed a screwdriver and prized the cabinet open, muffling the sound with a towel.

There they were—two bottles, a dark blue and a dark brown. Which was which? Did they kill fast or slow? It didn't matter. He found the hypodermic and filled it from the blue bottle.

He shut the cupboard door, collected the bag of tools and left the bathroom.

Still no sound of movement from the housekeeper's room. He crept into the dining room. The table was neatly laid for dinner—one place.

"Sideboard, lower shelf."

He opened it up and found the brandy—two bottles. One almost empty, the other brand new and sealed.

He took the sealed one and very carefully, so as not to break the needle, pressed the hypodermic through the cork. He injected the poison, gave the bottle a shake and replaced it.

He closed the cupboard and left the room quickly. As he did so, above the sound of the radio he heard the faint strains of the "Internationale." Six-forty-five!

He tiptoed back past the housekeeper's room to the front door. He opened it silently. If there was a guard posted outside he was a dead man.

"Only when Stalin is in his apartment is it guarded," Stefan had told him.

Stefan was right. The short visible area of corridor outside was deserted.

Cabeza went out and started to pull the door shut behind him. He paused. It had a spring latch. If there was one sound the housekeeper would be listening for, it was that.

He delved in the tool bag, found a bit of cotton waste, stuffed it in the latch housing.

He pulled the door shut. It made only a dull sound.

He picked up the bag and turned—to come face-to-face with Josef Stalin!

28

STALIN, ACCOMPANIED by bodyguard Rusakov, was striding toward his apartment in a furious temper. Seeing Cabeza coming out, he stopped abruptly, his every instinct leaping to self-preservation. The whole world right now was plotting his overthrow. This man could be part of it!

Rusakov's hand blurred to his gun. Like Stefan, he was an ex-fighter pilot, selected for his reflexes and intuition. Many ambiguous moves were made around Stalin every day; a reach for a handkerchief could be a reach for a gun. His job was to make a lightning assessment of every such move and, if in doubt, shoot.

But Cabeza's assessment was faster. His dismay became awestruck apology in the blink of an eye. He spread his free hand well clear of his body, his eyes not on Stalin but on the bodyguard.

He read Rusakov's changed response, saw the striking snake of his hand freeze. But it remained on the gun, poised for instant reappraisal.

"Who are you?" Stalin shouted, his eyes squeezed tight, body braced. Was this how it would happen—confronted in a lonely corridor by a hireling? "What were you doing in my apartment?" he bellowed. "Who sent you?"

Cabeza read his danger in the other's fear. His own fierce immediate instinct was to self-protect, attack before Stalin could give the order to kill him. It was like a gas-filled mine. One spark . . . ! So move first—do it—to hell with your own life—this was the man—the switchblade—strike! His mind countered simultaneously with the image of the lion and the bear dying, locked in each other's arms. Ah—*that* was the trap. The only trap. Inside himself. His own animal instincts. The hatred fostered in him by Kelland. He must not fall prey to it. *He must not.*

He clamped down hard, purging himself of all violent response. "The Works Department, Comrade General Secretary," he mumbled. And very slowly, so as not to excite Rusakov's reflexes, he reached in the tool bag and brought out the clipboard with the work order. Eyes lowered, he offered it toward Stalin humbly. "They sent me to fix a tap washer."

Stalin barely glanced at the authorization. "Why with no escort?" The paranoia raged in his eyes, undiminished.

"There—there was an escort, Comrade General Secretary," Cabeza stuttered. "They were called away. Some emergency—they didn't say what. But the—your housekeeper—she was in there."

Cabeza hoped fervently that she still had her radio going and could hear none of this. He couldn't trust himself to even look at Stalin, but he felt the power of the vibes coming from him begin to waver. He continued to offer the clipboard, eyes fixed on the floor.

Stalin's suspicions switched off as suddenly as they had switched on. He scowled at Cabeza for a further moment, but he was impatient to make some lethal phone calls. With a grunt and a dismissive gesture he strode past and let himself into the apartment.

Rusakov hesitated. He wasn't satisfied. He took the clipboard and studied the work order.

Cabeza stood quite still, listening for the emergence of the housekeeper from her room, for Stalin's question concerning the presence of an unaccompanied worker in his flat. He heard a door snap open and slam. He slipped his hand in his pocket, felt the handle of the knife. He pressed the button with his thumb, felt the blade come open against the lining.

The bodyguard's right hand still hovered near his gun. He wore a civilian suit, sharp-shouldered. His face was sharp-featured. His gun hand sharp-knuckled. Everything about him was sharp, wary. No voices behind him yet. Now another door opening.

"*Propusk*," the bodyguard ordered.

Identification. Cabeza still held the tool bag in his left hand. The card was in his right inner pocket. Without letting go of the knife, he put down the bag and felt for the card as quickly as he dared.

Now a telephone pinged inside the flat. He heard Stalin's voice demanding a number. The bodyguard was examining the identity card. Cabeza stole a glance behind him.

Through the open doorway of the apartment he saw the housekeeper hovering outside the living-room door. She was looking out at them curiously. Stalin must have gone straight into the living room. Now she was turning away, moving toward the dining room.

"All right. Go." Rusakov was thrusting the card and the clipboard back at him.

As he stooped to retrieve the bag, Stalin's raised voice came to them from the living room, shouting into the phone.

The bodyguard left him without another word, went into the apartment and shut the door.

Cabeza almost ran. Reaching the more populous part of the building, he threaded his way back toward the washroom, which was on the same floor. At any moment, he knew, the alarm could be given, the whole building could come alive with Security guards. Rusakov had only to mention him to the housekeeper and the cat would be out of the bag.

He found the washroom and locked himself again in the same cubicle. The other two were, mercifully, unoccupied.

He reversed his clothing and returned the tools to the briefcase, his ear keening for the first intimations of alarm, running feet . . .

He heard the Redeemer clock strike seven. Now the password was defunct! Would he need it in order to get out of the Kremlin? Stefan had said that frankly he didn't know. It depended on who was the guard commander.

Cabeza, once again in his guise as an OOKK man, left the washroom and hurried, still unchallenged, from the building.

As he retraced his steps, cars came streaming past—government personnel heading for home.

He rounded the end of the Presidium building. The Redeemer Gate in sight now, the lights green, the cars flowing through. By the steady way they were moving, it seemed that the guards weren't checking them. But they would know the cars, he reminded himself, recognize the drivers. Him they would not recognize. The guard had changed at seven.

As he passed the theater, some people came out of it—a group of several men and women, chatting together, laughing. They headed for the gate on foot. He quickened his pace till he was close behind them. As they entered the tunnel, seemingly all one party, Cabeza saw that the two guards and their officer commander were indeed checking every vehicle as it went out, ducking down to glance at its occupants before waving it on.

The theater group took the walkway. Cabeza stuck close to them. They were still in high spirits, their talk echoing in the tunnel. They pushed past the guards, calling out, "Good night."

The guards barely glanced at them. Another vehicle was coming through and they were stooping down to see who was inside. Cabeza flipped a casual hand. The officer's eyes passed over him, but no awareness sparked in them.

The next instant they were through, and Cabeza was striding away across Red Square!

He could scarcely believe it. What could have happened in the apartment? Why no alarm? Had he been so convincing that neither the bodyguard nor Stalin had given him another thought?

An enormous weight seemed to lift from his shoulders. If no sinister import had been attached to his presence in the apartment, Stalin would settle down to supper as usual . . .

Drink his brandy as usual . . .

He swung off the trolleybus in Solyanka Street and paused to get his bearings. He backtracked a block, turned down a side street and followed Cedric's instructions through a maze of back alleys to Vorny Street.

Shabby old buildings, uncleared snow, backyards, trash bags. He had to look for the old Turkish baths.

There was a solitary streetlight. As he passed under it he checked his watch. Seven-thirty-two! Gail had been waiting for him for fifteen minutes already.

He began to walk faster, then warned himself, don't rush it. You don't know what to expect here. This is the dark side of the plan.

There ahead was the sign, BANYA, barely legible beside a peeling door. He slowed, eyeing the high unlighted windows on either side. Their smashed panes showed up like giant ink splotches. He came to a halt, glancing up and down the street.

Deserted. The steady whine of factory machinery came from one of the blank-looking buildings nearby. The sound of traffic on Solyanka was no more than a rumor on the chill air. For some reason he took off his gloves and pocketed them.

As he pushed open the door, it grated on rubble and stuck. He squeezed around it and stood inside, waiting for his eyes to get used to the darkness.

In the sickly light seeping through the windows he was able to make out a sort of lobby with doorways opening off it. Ahead, through what had once been a pair of glassed doors, was a large area of lighter dark.

He scrunched his way forward till he found himself in a big central room under a high, semicollapsed dome. The wall was ringed with vandalized shower cubicles. Twisted piping and debris were everywhere. He stood listening. The place seemed utterly deserted.

No, not quite. A sliver of light showed on the far side of the space.

He crossed toward it as silently as he was able, and saw that it came from a doorway over which had been hung a blanket.

He put his eye to the chink.

In what had evidently once been the steam room, a man was seated on a junk chair with his back toward him. He wore a heavy coat and fur hat and seemed to be writing something on his knee by the light of a battery lantern. By his very stillness it was evident that he knew he was being observed.

"It's all right, General, don't be shy. Come on in."

Cabeza started. The vaulted ceiling gave off an echo, but all the distortion in the world could not have disguised that voice.

He pushed his head in, glancing left and right to make sure

the man was alone, before he swept the blanket aside and entered.

The man still did not turn, and now Cabeza could see that he was sketching in pencil on a small pad.

Cabeza moved toward him quickly, to close the gap and the other's action time in case he was concealing a gun.

"What are you doing in Moscow?"

The man chuckled. He tore off the sheet, crumpled it and tossed it away. He came to his feet, turning, stretching his arms. His hands were empty save for the pad, which he slipped into a pocket.

"They rerouted me, the bastards," Holz said. "There was I, all set for a vacation. The DDP, he says to me, 'Not so fast, Holzie. Why not keep it all in the family? You and the General being such good buddies and all. Just pop along there and sign him off like a good boy, before you put your feet up.'" He chuckled fondly. "Hey, you're looking great. Like a goddam Muscovite." He peeled off a glove and stuck out his hand.

Cabeza took it warily, testing it in his own. But could detect no tension in it.

"You are lucky it was me," he growled. "With your back to the door. How could you know I was not dead?"

"Dead?" Holz shook his head, smiling. "Not you, General. These Russkies had their chance at you before and never got to first base. They ain't in your league. 'Cause you got something they don't. Blood with iron in it, not misery. And you got the hunger—that special fighter's hunger that never lets up. I even had money on you, know that? Fifty bucks. And I don't fling that much around 'less I'm—"

"*Basta.*" Cabeza cut him off impatiently. "Give me the papers and I go."

"Not so fast, General. I'll need a few details first." Holz moved away slightly. "Did you actually hear the stuff go off? Brief me."

Cabeza briefed him, moving after him, keeping the same distance between them. Holz digested in silence, then nodded approvingly.

"That'll twist the fucker's gut." He added, "Though we don't know when. Well, great. It's better. Gives me that much more time to get clear."

Cabeza held out his hand. "The papers. *Dámelos.*"

"Papers?" Holz eyed him, the grin still on his face. He seemed to be balancing himself.

"The new identification."

"Come again?" The grin faded to a questioning blankness.

Cabeza's eyes narrowed to slits in the lamplight. His heart kicked over and lay still for a second.

Suddenly Holz relaxed and burst out laughing. He punched Cabeza's shoulder. "Your face! Sorry, General. My little joke. I have them all right here."

He reached into an inner pocket. Cabeza stepped suddenly close to him. Holz froze fractionally, then slowly produced a passport and an ID card from his inner pocket.

Cabeza snatched them with a scowl. They looked curiously familiar. He dropped the briefcase and opened them up.

They were his own! From Mexico. Giving his true name openly: "Joaquín Cabeza." No false cover, no plane tickets.

Cabeza's mind crashed into a different time scale, spinning through all the permutations. He was expendable—a Communist Spaniard with personal motives for killing Stalin, totally unconnected with the Americans. If he was caught under his own name, any investigation would stop right there. Case solved. Except for one thing. He would talk. Holz, he realized, had been preparing to take him moments ago, but he had stayed too close. He hadn't trusted his speed against the General's. So he had passed him the documentation to shock and divert him.

His mind had computed all this milliseconds before Holz took his final backward step. He moved simultaneously, his muscles bunching, lungs sucking in air, thighs thrusting, arms reaching out, his eyes perceiving the other's raised elbow and plunging hand—in—out of the heavy coat on the same axis so as not to snag the silencer in the lining. It was the strike of a snake, the counterstrike of a mongoose, in delayed action. He felt his toe catch against the heavy briefcase, felt his trajectory lower a fraction, saw the gun emerging, long as a freight train from its tunnel, saw it turn toward him, reached to grasp it, knew he wasn't going to make it, saw the spurting flame, felt the impact as the bullet crashed into his chest.

Now he had the gun in his fingers, hot in his fingers, twisting it aside, casting his other arm behind Holz's head and crooking it around Holz's neck, holding the head viselike as he forced the gun on around toward him, saw the clown's eyes widen, felt the grunting breath on his face and the sudden flexing of all Holz's muscles as he fought to divert the steady turn of the weapon, sensed Holz's mounting terror as he realized he hadn't the strength, that this man who should be dead was doing with one hand what he could not prevent with two, his frenzy growing, his gasps becoming cries of stricken protest as the silencer rotated to settle its cold steel between his eyes.

The explosion blew half the back of Holz's head off.

The echoes whacking around him, Cabeza staggered. Lethal things were happening inside his chest. A feeling of suffocation. A desire to sleep. He resisted it fiercely, his mind still endeavoring to compute the elements of survival. He had only moments of consciousness left.

Gasping, he knelt beside the body and rifled the pockets, hoping, hoping . . . But—no, Holz had not been withholding the fake documents. They had never existed. He found only Holz's own identification, his cover for the mission.

He pocketed it, pocketed everything he could find, including money, replacing it with the Mexican passport and ID he had just been given. He and Holz were of the same build, not unalike. Maybe, just maybe, someone would think . . . Last of all, he pocketed the gun.

Only a part of him was functioning clearly now—that last stronghold, very close to the soul. It ordered him to his feet. Somehow his body obeyed.

Now go, it said. Go as far from this place as you can drag yourself. Go!

He made it somehow to the doorway. A deadness was spreading up through his lower limbs. He ripped the blanket aside and reeled out across the domed space, clawing himself over the debris. The deadness was spreading even faster, creeping up his body like a cold shadow.

When it reached his head, he knew, he would pass into oblivion.

29

GAIL SAT on the bed, eyes closed, trying to keep abreast of Joaquín's movements in her mind. She had sat like this for an hour—the most emotionally punishing hour of her life.

Hearing at last the distant chimes of the Redeemer clock, she surfaced slowly. But there was no feeling of relief. Seven o'clock simply meant that his assignment should now be complete *one way or the other*. If he had failed—unthinkable. Jail. Interrogation. Trial. Massive sentence or execution. If he had succeeded, she would not know about it till they met at the rendezvous. But at least now she could get moving.

Opening up her case, she transferred the few personal things she would need on the journey into her sling bag.

A slight scratching sound behind her spun her attention to the door. A folded note was being pushed underneath.

She stared at it, startled, listening to the faint creak of someone moving away.

She moved to the door and retrieved it: "See you main stairs—ready to move—5 mins."

The heavy scrawl was unmistakably male. The USAF sergeant, it had to be. But why? Her heart missed a beat. It was about Joaquín. Something had happened!

Scarcely able to contain her apprehension, she put on her coat and hat and sat waiting, her eyes dabbing at her watch.

She would allow thirty seconds to get to the stairs. *Cálmate*, as Joaquín would say. Remember your training. It could be a trap. She sat inhaling through her nose, out through her mouth, counting the breaths.

Now. She left the room silently and went along to the stairs.

Her timing was perfect. And it was he, the sergeant, coming along from the other corridor. He had on his great-coat and cap and carried a small valise.

They reached the stairs simultaneously and started down, slowing a little. He spoke in a cool monotone without looking at her.

"Turn right at the bottom here. Take the service stairs. I'll go out the front way. My buddy has a cab. We'll pick you up."

Gail was so surprised she stopped in her tracks.

"We take off at eight sharp," he added.

It didn't make sense. On inspiration she let her bag slip from her shoulder. It tumbled down the steps, spilling some of its contents. He stooped to help her.

"What's happened?" she demanded quietly.

"Nothing." His hard gray eyes made a question mark.

"So . . . you mean . . . that's the plan? We fly out on your plane?"

"You were briefed."

"Not for that. We were told Marcos had to go to Vorny Street, pick up the fresh ID and plane reservations there."

"What the hell for? All I have to do is smuggle you aboard. We have a spot ready for you in the baggage compartment."

"Then someone has his wires crossed. By eight o'clock? Can't be done. Look—we have to talk." She straightened, adding loudly, *"Muchás gracias, señor."*

She continued down the stairs to the small mezzanine. There was no one about. She drew back out of sight of the stairwell and waited for him to join her.

"Now tell me exactly—what were your orders?"

The agent sighed. "To fly the tools in and you out—period."

"And whose orders were they?"

"DDP's."

"He knew takeoff would be at eight o'clock?"

"He knew."

Gail ran a hand through her hair. "I don't understand! There's no way Marcos could get to Vorny Street and back and then out to the airport by eight o'clock."

The hard eyes surveyed her, puzzled. "Marcos isn't going to the airport, sweetheart—you are. Just you."

Gail stepped back involuntarily.

"Look—" The Agency man spoke quickly. "I'll say this just once, then we must get started. This is an air force plane on a government mission. It's here to collect seven U.S. POW's from the Korean War. Some exchange deal. The DDP picked up on it last week, twisted some arms and got me aboard as one of the flight crew. He gave me my orders personally, and believe me, they included your boyfriend *out*. So if you've got any beef about it, lay it on him when we get back, okay? Now let's move."

"Oh my God." She caught his arm as he turned away. "But don't you see? It's a communications gap, between Kelland in Europe and the DDP in—"

"Kelland?" The operative shrugged. "From what I hear, he doesn't leave gaps. And those are the orders—your partner stays."

Gail felt her knees go. She leaned her head back against the wall. "You will obey those orders *implicitly*," Kelland had said. *"Whatever they may be."*

"Maybe there's a separate brief waiting for him at the RV, I wouldn't know." The operative glanced about him uneasily. "Relax, sweetheart, the DDP's not going to throw him to the wolves."

Gail blinked and rolled her eyes. There were tears in them. "How long have *you* been in the Agency?"

"Long enough to go where I'm pointed. I suggest you do the same. The service stairs are along there. See you outside."

Gail remained motionless for several seconds after he had gone. Suddenly she could see it all in one piece—Kelland's blueprint. Every little twist and nuance fell into place now with the precision of a steel jigsaw. There was just one gap

269

left unfilled—what Joaquín would find at the rendezvous. And just one piece to fit it. It was coffin-shaped.

She made for the service stairs. As soon as she was out of the Agency man's sight, she ran. Two maids were coming up the stairs. There was no time for deception. She pushed past them and hurried down. They shouted after her to stop, that to exit that way was forbidden. She ignored them. Moments later she was heading quickly out across Revolution Square.

She had not gone far when, glancing back, she saw a taxicab circling so as to come in against the curb outside the Metropole service entrance. She turned up her collar and plunged into the crowds.

The guard now posted outside Stalin's apartment stepped aside with a click of his heels as Colonel Georgi Feodor Grechukha strode self-importantly to the door and knocked.

It was opened almost immediately by the bodyguard, Rusakov. He pointed toward the dining room.

Grechukha shot him an inquiring look as he deposited his coat and hat, but Rusakov was giving nothing away. He was Stalin's man, and Stalin's man only.

Grechukha straightened his jacket, subdued the bushy hair bordering the motorway of his skull and, belly extended bravely, strode to meet whatever fate had in store for him.

"Come," rumbled Stalin's voice at his knock.

He was seated alone at the supper table, eating voraciously. Behind him the housekeeper was stooping over the trolley that had been sent up by the canteen, preparing his next course. An unopened bottle of brandy stood on the sideboard. An empty bottle and a quarter-filled tumbler were by Stalin's right hand.

"You sent for me, Comrade Josef Vissarionovich?"

"Don't ask fool questions, and sit down." Stalin pointed to a chair with his fork. His brows were rucked, as though someone had snagged a thread running through them, and the complexion of his bulging cheeks as they masticated was unusually dark.

Grechukha read the signs and was not comforted. He sat down, stiff-backed, and began rubbing his thighs.

"Well, we know now," Stalin growled indistinctly through

his food. "Have we enough on him to arrest him?—that's all I want to know."

Grechukha's eagerness to reply affirmatively was handicapped by the fact that he didn't know what the Leader was talking about.

"Uh—who, Josef Vissar—?"

Stalin thumped the table. "Lazar Kaganovich, who else!" He drained the last of the old brandy at a gulp. "Answer the question!" He transferred his gaze to the remaining salt herring on his plate, attacking it savagely.

Grechukha tried to remember the question. Luckily, he succeeded. "Have we enough evidence to arrest him? Meaning that—that"—Grechukha could hardly bring himself to utter the absurd notion—"you think he is the American agent Omega?" He only just managed to keep the derision from his voice.

Stalin's complexion darkened still further. "Isn't it obvious? Why else would he be so eager to stop the arrests? Do you think he gives a damn for these doctors and Jews? Do you? He's my late wife's brother and I know him. He wouldn't care if we wiped out the whole population, providing his own skin remained intact. No, Georgi Feodor, he sees us creeping closer. Attack was always his defense—by plotting, stirring, lobbying. He even set his family at one another's throats as a child. But never openly. Never before." He pushed his plate away and signaled for the next course. "Which means one thing—that he's desperate. And in his desperation he has managed to hoodwink those other fools into supporting him. But in doing so, Georgi Feodor, he has exposed himself, forewarning us. If we move quickly now, we can get him. *If we have the evidence.* So I am asking you—have we?"

Grechukha was over a barrel. He had a strong suspicion who Omega was, and it was not Kaganovich. It was someone even bigger. So big that if he denounced him to Stalin without full supporting testimony, he was a dead man. And despite the interrogation and torture of many prisoners, he still did not have that testimony.

"I would need time to collate what we have before I—"

"There *is* no time."

"But you've just said," Grechukha reminded him cunningly, "that the others are behind him. So we can't afford to make any mistakes, can we? Not a single one."

Stalin considered this, becoming slightly calmer. "I'm glad you say 'we.' It shows awareness of the fact that the ax that falls on me will take your head with it."

"It will, it will," Grechukha cried, almost enthusiastic in his relief. "We are together in this." He almost added, "as always," but thought it might sound a bit too matey.

"Good." Stalin got up and went to the sideboard. He stripped open the fresh bottle of brandy and poured two glasses. He plumped one in front of Grechukha, carried the other back to his place and resumed his seat.

"Down that, then go. Check your files, examine your evidence. If you have any legal queries, call on Minister of Justice Gorshenin. I will expect your answer tonight. And tomorrow we'll finish him!"

Grechukha took up the brandy, about to raise it in a false toast to these sentiments. But the prospect of having to concoct a way out of this by morning was so daunting that he put the glass down again. "No. I do not wish to insult, Josef Vissarionovich, but I will need a clear head for all this."

Stalin made a gesture of slightly surprised acceptance.

Grechukha hurried out.

Stalin looked after him thoughtfully. In the scramble for sudden gold, sometimes one had to grab the first tool at hand. He hoped this one was adequate for the vital task. If not, he would have to use force . . . unleash the OOKK and purge his whole Presidium!

He grabbed the brandy and drained it at one gulp.

Gail stared from the blood-spattered wall to the bluish powder burn surrounding the bullet hole, the ashen features and sagging jaw. So sure was she that it was Joaquín that it took her several full moments to realize it couldn't be.

The relief was so great that she had to support herself for a moment. Holz? She had to retrieve the lamp, still glaring among the rubble, and force herself to shine it on his face before she could be sure. Kelland had risked Holz way up here? So far from his element? With not two words of Russian to rub together? She realized then just how vital

Joaquín's death must be to Kelland's plan. And how highly he respected Joaquín's prowess. Even so, he had miscalculated. When the chips were down, Holz had been no match for the General.

Grief constricted her throat. Poor, strange Holz.

But his death meant Joaquín was alive, that was the main, wonderful thing! With or without their escape ID? she wondered. And did they still have time to use it? There was no sign of the gun—so he was armed. That was something. Where would he make for? The rendezvous, of course. And he would get there ahead of her, she realized. The thought of losing contact with him brought her quickly to her feet.

Then she saw the briefcase. She shone the flashlight inside it. No sign of the explosive. That meant— She froze. It was still there!

Her mind seething with possible explanations, she started to put the gelignite back, then changed her mind and slipped it into her sling bag. It was a weapon—of sorts. Safe enough to carry, so long as she kept it dry. At worst, it provided an option to being caught by the MVD!

The street was deserted. Solyanka Street was her best bet for a trolleybus. She began to run.

Reaching the first of the alleyways, she slid to a stop. Directly ahead were two armed militiamen. Backs to her, they were bending over a drunk lying in the snow.

She withdrew quickly. Was there another way to Solyanka?

"Come on, comrade—on your feet!" she heard one of the men say.

"Rub some snow on his face," said the other.

There was another leg to the alley. She headed across into it. As she stole away she heard a familiar word behind her. It was uttered groaningly, under duress. *"Mierda!"*

The militiamen had dragged the man to his feet and were slapping the snow off his coat. He clutched on to them, swaying drunkenly.

"Think he'll make it?" The militiamen stared at him doubtfully. "Where do you live, comrade?"

They shook him for an answer. His head lolled back. And then Gail knew who it was for sure.

"You sure he's drunk?" the one supporting him muttered suspiciously. "He looks sick to me. Get his *propusk.*"

The other prepared to feel in Cabeza's coat for his identity card.

Gail rushed toward them, crying in Russian, "Ivan? Is that you?"

She pushed the men aside and took charge of Cabeza angrily.

"So this is where you are! I wait—I wait—I become worried—and where are you? Drunk is where you are!" The militiamen began to laugh. She turned on them furiously. "It is not funny. That a man should be so in love with the bottle is a crime. You should arrest him!"

"If we arrested every drunk we found on the street, we'd be running a ferry service," chuckled one.

"You better keep a closer eye on him," the other warned severely. "Or one morning you'll find he's been cleared away with the snow."

They turned and continued on their beat.

Gail hung on tightly to Cabeza, feeling him sag, guessing the truth, but unable to detect any sign of blood.

She eased him to the nearest wall and supported him with her shoulder while she felt under his coat. Nothing. Then inside his jacket. Yes, dear Christ! Warm, sticky blood was oozing from the region of his heart!

Shocked and frightened, she held him there, wondering what to do.

The militiamen were glancing back. She quickly dragged his arm around her shoulders and turned him the other way and started to walk.

His legs helped her—just. But he was on automatic pilot, she could feel. Barely conscious. Was he going to die? If he was done for, so was she. Kelland . . . A confusion of agonies tortured her as she labored under his weight between the close, dark buildings. Don't die, *amado. Please don't die.*

It was beginning to snow, the flakes drifting down in slow motion, huge as cotton bolls. A door opened somewhere ahead. She hesitated as the scutter of corrugated sheeting being wrenched aside reached her, the sound already losing its edge in the snowfall. The ensuing hump of firewood into a box softened to a dull mutter as the whiteness closed in around them.

Thankful for it, Gail leaned Joaquín against a wall. There

was a sack of something—it looked like trash. She dragged it under him and he slid down onto it, his features ashen in the reflected light of a window high above. She rubbed at the frozen snow on his face with her gloves, then pressed her cheek to his fiercely, trying to warm him.

"What happened?" she whispered. "Did—did you do it?" She felt him nod. *"Sí . . ."*

She wondered how he had managed it without the explosive, but it didn't matter. "I've got to get you to—" Her voice faltered. Get him where? Where in this whole city could they go? This whole *world . . . ?*

The answer sounded in her ear hoarsely. "The airport."

She drew back, peering at him. "In your state? How? How? Do you have the escape identification?"

The breath rattled wetly in his throat for a moment. "The . . . OOKK pass . . . use it . . . to board a plane."

With his eyes closed, his brows and lashes frozen white, it was like hearing a corpse speak. But there was something still there in control, still giving orders.

Impossible orders. There was no way she could get him past the airport MVD—no story she could concoct that would . . . Not enough money, even, to buy a ticket.

The U.S. embassy? The thought glowed, then faded. The CIA station was based there. They were the enemy now. Another possibility came to her. Would the OOKK pass work in a hospital? *Shot while on a security mission—vital to be treated in the utmost security?*

It might work in the States. But in Moscow? If only she knew how their health system operated. Channels— everything was channels in the socialist countries. A private doctor might be a better bet.

Then a star shell seemed to explode in her mind.

Stalin shucked through another of the diaries, tearing the pages in his impatience. The living room was littered with them—all open. He shifted from volume to volume, entry to entry, like a dog confronted by a dozen scents and none of them the one he is after.

What *was* he after? He wasn't sure. All he knew was that Rosa had scribbled her heart out in these diaries—written a book from them—that somewhere among the references to

Lazar Kaganovich, her brother, there must be a clue—just the smallest chance observation—that would reveal his first contact with the Americans.

It was here somewhere, he was convinced, hidden in some innocent sentence. Why was his vision blurring? He ripped at the pages blindly.

Suddenly he swept the whole lot to the floor and staggered back into his chair. He was allowing himself to become overwrought. Why was he so afraid? Because he had cleaved his way to power in the same cunning, ruthless way Kaganovich was using against him now? Live like a wolf, howl like a wolf, *die* like a wolf! He had set the pattern. He knew it backwards—every vicious, lying ploy that would be used against him if he didn't act first.

His heart was hammering. He had had a bad shock. Seventy-three. He needed his pipe. His old "nose-warmer." Something to calm him.

Kaganovich's guts were the only thing that would calm him. Well, he would have them tomorrow. Tonight . . .

He felt strange.

The mess on the floor . . . the fool pictures on the walls, the ornaments—womanless—all a reflection of himself now that his wives and mistresses were gone. Only those child virgins from the typing pool to cavort in front of him when he ordered. Served up to him like plump white potatoes. Just more reflections of himself. Nothing real. Nothing real in this whole damn czarist fortress but lies and intrigue and memories—Lenin's ghost. He had to get out.

Yes, go to Blizhny. That was the answer. Sleep off his rage in peace. If he felt any worse he would call his specialist, Vinogradov. No, he couldn't—Vinogradov was in jail, swept up in the purge. Well, Valechka would have some remedy. Yes, he would go to the *dacha*, play some of his Georgian folk music, roll up on his old couch . . .

He called for Rusakov.

"Warn Security—I'm going to Kuntsevo. Fifteen minutes."

"At once, Josef Vissarionovich!"

"Wait. Tell the switchboard that Colonel Grechukha will telephone. I want his call put through to me at the *dacha*—no matter what the hour. Make sure they understand that."

"I'll make sure, Josef Vissarionovich." Rusakov went out and closed the door.

Stalin leaned his head back, breathing deeply. The vaulted ceiling danced before his eyes. It was full of speckles. A steady whining sounded in his ears.

"I'll see you in hell, Lazar Moiseyevich Kaganovich," he promised softly.

30

IN THE MVD building, Colonel Grechukha was pacing his office with short, erect steps, his muscular mouth flexing and pursing silently. He was conducting an inner dialogue of considerable importance to his survival in office, even in life.

Following the arrest and execution of his old army commander General Vlasov after the war, he had come to a bitter conclusion: that dedication to the Motherland and Communism was a load of manure, that life in the Soviet Union was no more than a game of *gorodki*, a row of skittles and a ball. In which case he had better be smart and decide right away whether he wanted to be a skittle or the ball. He chose, fairly predictably, to be the ball.

Now, as a ball, he was being rolled helplessly against a very large skittle indeed—and the wrong one, to boot. Kaganovich was not Omega. But how did you tell the Old Man that without the necessary evidence to convince him?

To stay in the *gorodki* park without rolling up against the First Deputy Chairman called for a ploy of exceptional duplicity and swiftness. He had thought of one. It was coming together nicely, despite an irritating number of interruptions, all in the form of Zapotkin.

The aide had been curiously active since Grechukha's return from the Kremlin, entering his office on a host of trivial excuses, glancing longingly at the UTMOST SECRECY files the Deputy Minister had taken from his private safe.

Now, as Zapotkin knocked and came in again, Grechukha swung toward him angrily. "What *now*? What *is* it?"

"Uh—beg pardon, Deputy Minister, but Reception says that Boris Likachev is on his way up."

"Boris?" Grechukha scowled. "What the hell does he want?"

His aide shrugged. "I'm afraid you so seldom take me into your confidence I cannot hazard a guess. Shall I phone the canteen to send up some coffee?"

"No." Grechukha was reminded that he hadn't eaten yet. He added, "But when he's gone, you can order me some sandwiches. I shall be working late tonight."

"May I be of any assistance?"

"No, thank you."

The fish eyes searched his quite boldly. "I don't have to remind you, Deputy Minister, that I am fully cleared to handle *all* grades of top-secret information. I would deem it an honor to work late with you."

I'm sure you would, Grechukha thought. And who would you report it all back to?

He said aloud, "That won't be necessary."

The handsome Likachev entered the suite, his purposeful manner broadcasting that this was more than just a visit in passing.

Grechukha dismissed Zapotkin and ushered his friend in with a tight smile, shutting the door.

"Boris, good to see you. Do you mind very much being brief?"

"Brief? Certainly. Joaquín Cabeza—remember him?"

"Cabeza . . ." Grechukha waved him to a chair, searching his memory banks.

Likachev chose his favorite window ledge. "You ought to. You had him next door for a year." He was referring to the Lubianka.

"The Spaniard? El . . . El Duro?"

"That's the one. We've had a communication from Berlin, unconfirmed, that he could be routed in our direction."

"El Duro . . ." Grechukha half closed his eyes, remembering, his mouth hardening.

"His objective, the rumor says, to assassinate the General Secretary."

Grechukha opened his eyes again slowly. His mouth began to twist. He uttered a laugh from the belly.

"You're a month early."

"What?"

"This is the first of March, not April."

Likachev smiled. He shrugged slightly. "I thought I better pass it on. Though there's nothing supportive, it's such a crazy one, I thought . . . Well, I'd hate for there to be something in it and not to have taken action." Levelly: "Wouldn't you?"

Grechukha huffed a sigh. As if he hadn't enough on his plate already! He went to the door and told Zapotkin to find Cabeza's file.

"'39 to '43? That'll be down in Records, Deputy Minister."

"I don't care if it's down your pants—get it sent up!"

Grechukha returned thoughtfully. It was beginning to come back to him now—the jail-ravaged face with the burning eyes, the iron willpower that had resisted all his interrogations. Where had the fellow been sent to—Siberia, wasn't it? But hadn't he died there? No, he thought grimly, his type wouldn't die; they wouldn't do you the favor.

Likachev said intuitively, "We gave him the motive, I think."

Grechukha grunted. The possibility of Cabeza's killing the Old Man galvanized him. He began to pace again. Just suppose El Duro had managed to squeeze through his point-of-entry security screen, how would he tackle the job? To start with, he would need shelter, a base to work from, a weapon . . . So first, look up all his old contacts. The Spanish community—Lister, La Pasionaria . . . And hadn't he been married to a Russian woman? Where was she now? Find out. Have her put under immediate surveillance.

He barked through to Zapotkin, "Get me Kremlin Security —Vasily Khrustalyov! Then tell Major Modin and Roman Dygay I want them up here. And when Cabeza's file comes up, print me some copies of his photograph, say a hundred, for limited distribution."

Likachev watched him curiously.

"So you are taking it seriously."

"No choice, is there?"

"Suppose not." The MGB man heaved to his feet. "But, as I say, it's only a rumor. You don't have to go mad."

Grechukha said, as evenly as possible, "If he *is* here, I want him, that's all. Call it unfinished business."

"How about Josef Vissarionovich himself—you going to warn him?"

"Not at this stage. No sense in crying wolf."

"Especially *to* a wolf. His howling might keep us awake at night." Likachev gave one of his rare grins. "Well, I'll leave you to your . . . vendetta. Good hunting."

The taxi slowed, scuffing the banked snow of a residential side street.

"Which number, comrade?"

Gail hesitated. She had given the driver, an enormously fat woman muffled to the eyes, quite enough cause to remember her already without letting her know the house number.

"This will do."

She withdrew her arm from behind Joaquín, peering at him, making sure there was no blood on his lips in case the driver should decide to take a closer look at him. To say that the woman was curious was an understatement. She was fairly bursting with chatty camaraderie and concern. Knowing that most of the Moscow drivers were part of the network, Gail had spun her a yarn about their being at an employees' reunion, how her friend had had a turn, that she wasn't sure how much was due to an old head injury and how much to drink. Anyway, she was taking him home. His family would know what to do.

The cab stopped. She got out quickly. "Wait, would you? Don't touch him, please. He seems to be sleeping."

She hurried along the dimly lit street, looking for the address she had obtained from the Golitsin Hospital. Joaquín's wife, Ludmilla, was still in practice there, she had learned over the phone—a marvelous stroke of luck.

The houses were wooden, very Russian, with windows and doors decorated in the chunky eighteenth-century style. They had once been painted in gay colors but, over the years, had deteriorated to downright shabbiness. Icicles hung in glassy spears from rotting sills and broken guttering.

She had only the vaguest idea where they were in the city. They had crossed the Yauza River and were somewhere southeast of the Kotyelnicheskaya Embankment, that was all she knew.

Anyway, here it was—No. 64—quite a large building, as ill-kempt as the rest. She entered warily.

She found herself in a bleak, empty hall. There was a row of mailboxes on the wall. She found the name Patolichev quickly. Apartment 8.

As she went up the stairs a door opened below her and a woman looked out. She had several scarves wound around her neck, a pouchy face, hair like a disemboweled sofa.

Gail cursed inwardly. No doubt the concierge. They were nearly always either Party members or informers.

Apartment 8 was on the second floor. As she approached the door she heard music, voices, laughter. It sounded as if a party was in progress.

She hesitated for a moment, but desperation gave her courage.

She had to knock twice before she was heard. There was a sudden hush within, and she could hear plainly the thumping of her heart.

A small, pretty woman with enormous eyes and cropped dark hair opened the door. She wore a voluminous turtleneck sweater and had tiny pearl studs in the lobes of her ears.

"Yes?"

Past her, Gail could see the room was full of people, flushed, their gaiety suspended in sudden apprehension. A phonograph was playing, of all things, Stan Kenton's "Peanut Vendor," the very latest in Western progressive jazz. At that moment someone removed the needle from the disc.

Gail said whom she was looking for. The woman nodded rather warily. "That's me."

Gail almost collapsed with relief. But there was no absolute guarantee that she was the right person. The guests were all listening. Gail told her that a man was outside, badly injured.

Ludmilla shook her head. It was not practical for her to treat anyone in the flat, she said, when the hospitals were so handy and so much better equipped. She gave her the address of the nearest emergency room and started to close the door.

She must have read the dismay in Gail's expression, for she never completed the action. Casting a reassuring look back at her guests, she came out onto the landing.

Gail whispered, "Does the name Cabeza mean anything to you?"

The big eyes didn't actually widen, but their expression changed in a way that told Gail all she needed to know.

"He's badly hurt. Perhaps dying."

The choke in her voice drew a sharp, perceptive look from the Russian. It seemed to establish her bona fides beyond question, for without a word, Ludmilla turned and went back into the flat. Gail heard her speaking to her guests quietly, urgently. From her tone and their reaction it was clear they were all close friends. There were no protests, no questions, just a few murmurs of disappointment followed by a general move to retrieve coats and hats.

They came out past Gail. Aware professional faces regarded her curiously, one or two of them nodding almost as if they knew her.

Minutes later Ludmilla accompanied Gail out to the cab. She kept murmuring, "I can't believe it, I can't believe it." The driver was standing beside her vehicle, looking like a captive balloon in her multiple clothing.

"Ah, there you are," cried the woman. "So you found his house."

"Is he all right?"

"Hasn't moved, comrade. I'll give you a hand."

"No." Gail headed her off, taking out her wallet. "How much do we owe you?"

"It's on the meter, comrade."

Ludmilla got straight into the back and bent over Cabeza.

Gail paid the driver, thinking, Suppose he has leaked blood all over her taxi? She added a sizable tip.

She helped Ludmilla out with Cabeza, peering back at the seat, but there was no stain that she could see.

They struggled under Joaquín's dead weight toward the apartment house. Behind them they heard the taxi drive away.

"How on earth are we going to get him up all those stairs?"

"We'll manage," Ludmilla told her quietly.

"What about the woman on the ground floor?"

"Leave her to me."

They had barely supported him inside when a black Pobeda appeared along the road. It stopped to deposit two men on the curb opposite, then drove on.

After eyeing No. 64 for a moment, the men pulled down their earflaps, turned up their collars and moved to a less obtrusive position in the yard of a disused church a few meters farther along the road.

31

LUDMILLA BOLTED the door and immediately spread an old rug over the settee. She and Gail heaved Cabeza's unconscious form onto it.

"He has changed," Ludmilla murmured, fetching a table lamp and standing it on a chair close by. "His nose, and the scars . . ." Her tone was flat, to hide her deep emotion. She took off her coat. "My people spared him nothing."

"Ludmilla, forgive me for bringing him here. I didn't know what else to do!"

"He is in bad trouble?"

"Yes."

"Well, you were not followed here—I looked. So there is time for me to do something. Afterwards we must talk." She began to unbutton Cabeza's overcoat and spread it back. "How did you find me?"

"The hospital. I—" Gail sucked in her breath. The whole front of his jacket was caked with blood.

"Help me." Ludmilla eased him up while Gail pulled the topcoat out from under him. "We will need hot water. Not from the tap. There is a kettle." She indicated the kitchenette.

The flat was small. Just the sitting room and a bedroom and a tiny space for cooking. Gail lit the gas, filled the kettle from the single tap and put it on.

Ludmilla unbuttoned Cabeza's jacket and shirt and peeled them back gently. Gail watched, mesmerized. His chest was a bloody, hairy mess.

"In the bedroom closet you will find some sheets. One is torn. Bring it, please."

Gail did as she was bid, glad to be kept busy.

The bedroom was even smaller than the sitting room. There were two beds, some white-painted furniture. Scattered on their surfaces were wooden animals, a model warship, some children's books. Children's drawings were pinned to the walls, several of ships. She found the sheet and brought it back.

"We are lucky," Ludmilla said. "The bleeding has stopped."

"Thank God."

"Tear the sheet in strips—what is your name?"

"Gail."

"You are not Russian?" Ludmilla was feeling around under Cabeza's back. She frowned.

"American." Gail tore up the sheet.

Ludmilla slipped on her stethoscope and listened to Cabeza's chest, at the same time feeling his pulse. After a moment: "He has lost a great deal of blood." She added softly, "But he can make do on very little, my Spaniard. The heart is shocked but fighting. The lung is damaged."

"That . . . is very bad?"

"Not good. The kettle is boiling."

Gail fetched it, and a bowl and a towel.

Ludmilla washed the blood from the wound and now for the first time they could see the bullet hole. It was close to the middle of his chest, a little to the left.

Ludmilla uttered an exclamation. She reached into her bag.

"What is it?"

"The bullet looks to be in his heart. How is he still alive?" She fitted a lens to her eye and studied the wound.

The hole wasn't neat, as one would have expected. Its edges appeared ragged, contused.

Ludmilla probed with a pair of tweezers. "Ah." She laid

some tiny fragments on her palm and turned the outside of his jacket toward Gail. "Yes. See? A button. The bullet hit a button. Then a rib. It was deflected from the heart—just."

She continued to probe. She picked out all the fragments of button and bone she could find. Then she shaved the hair from around the wound and gave it a final clean-up. She applied a dressing, and got Gail to help her wind the strips of sheet tightly around Cabeza's chest to splint the shattered rib. Finally she covered him well, lit a heater and placed it near him.

She ran her hand back through her hair and stood looking down at him, the short hair sticking up between her fingers like grass. She was debating something and Gail could feel her emotion. When she turned, her eyes were dark with concern.

"Now, listen," Ludmilla said. "There are things that should be done for him and done quickly. The bullet is still in his chest. First he needs a transfusion, then an X-ray, after that an operation to remove the bullet. For all these he should go to the hospital. Think carefully now. Is this quite impossible?"

Gail shook her head emphatically. "Absolutely impossible."

"Even if the alternative is that he dies?"

"If he's caught, they'll kill him anyway. His last words were to get him on a plane. If—if you could just patch him up, I may still be able to do that. He has a pass and that was his decision. He doesn't make decisions lightly."

"No," Ludmilla agreed. "But there are many ways to skin a horse—does he still say this?"

Gail laughed and nodded. Sudden tears sprang to her eyes. Ludmilla touched her arm gently. "I see you know my Spaniard. Listen, I will make some tea and you will tell me what he has got himself into. Then we will try to find a way of getting him to the hospital."

As Gail explained as much of the circumstances as she dared she noted Ludmilla's mounting agitation.

"Yet you cannot tell me what it is he has done?" The Russian's voice was sharp. "You think I have not the right to know?"

"The right, oh yes." Gail moved to her impulsively. "Just—it's better for you *not* to."

Ludmilla appeared slightly mollified. "So serious?" A fierce little gleam showed in her eyes. "So he is still putting the world to rights. They could not destroy that part of him!" Then she said, "You seem in doubt whether the police are looking for him."

"Well, if they're not, they soon will be. But not by name."

"Ah. Not by name. You are sure?"

"I don't see how they can be."

"You must think hard. This is very important."

"I know—vital."

"Because if they look for him by name, here is the first place they will come. I have my husband and children to think of."

"Yes, I—" Gail checked herself. "Your husband? You're—you remarried?"

"Of course." Ludmilla smiled wryly. "You think because once I was married to this rare, strange man, I should die in a convent? I am not made that way. Anyway," she added with characteristic practicality, "there are no convents in Russia."

"I didn't mean that." Gail felt a deep sense of release. She realized then that she had been subconsciously watching Ludmilla's every move, admiring her, resigning herself to the conviction that she could never hope to compete with anyone so right for Joaquín. And now suddenly it was a no contest! "It was just . . . I hadn't really thought about it. *Into* it . . ."

"Hadn't you?" Ludmilla eyed her perceptively.

"Well . . ." Gail lidded her eyes.

"You are not his woman?"

". . . No."

"Yet you are. I see." Ludmilla smiled faintly. "This is a condition I recognize. He is not very quick in these matters. For me, it was clear from the first moment you spoke of him at the door." She added softly, "And I approve."

Gail smiled. "But you hardly know me. And he and I—we're so utterly different."

"Perhaps. But, like me, you are independent, I think. He respects that."

Gail looked unconvinced. "He calls me *muchacha*—girl!"

"With him, a disparagement can become an endearment. It is a good sign."

"Oh?" Gail looked relieved. She changed the subject tactfully. "But your husband—I didn't realize. When do you expect him back?"

"April." Ludmilla smiled. "He is a naval officer with the Baltic Fleet. A very fine person. He married me when I was still under a cloud after Joaquín. It was a very courageous thing to do in a country where revenge is taken on the family."

"Very."

"So you see my fear—that he will lose the mother of his children, his career, the children put in a state institution—all because we underestimated the ability of the police to connect Joaquín with the crime he has committed."

"I understand." Gail gave it her full concentration. "He came to Moscow under three different identities . . ."

"Three?"

"And none of them is connected in any way with the name Cabeza."

"In that case, there can be no immediate danger." Ludmilla added, "And he is here now. The next danger will not be until he leaves this apartment."

"But what about the woman downstairs?"

"Yes, she is a problem. But I am a doctor. To treat an accident case here is nothing very strange. If I tell her in the morning that after treating him I sent him to the hospital, that he was fetched from here very late in the night . . ."

"Suppose she sees him when he does leave?"

"Then there is another way. Even Party members can be bribed."

"You'll offer her money? Suppose she won't take it?"

"Not money. There are things more valuable than money in the Soviet Union. Drugs. Pain-killing drugs. She suffers much from her back."

"You're sure that will work?"

"No. But there are still other ways . . . a thousand ways to skin a—" She broke off abruptly as the doorknob rattled. It was followed by a thumping on the panels.

Gail recovered first. She moved fast to Cabeza's overcoat, reached in it for Holz's gun.

Ludmilla moved to the door. "Who is it?"

"Us!" cried youthful voices.

The next moment two children breezed in—a sturdy boy of about seven and an attractive girl of twelve. They stopped in astonishment as they saw Cabeza, then Gail.

Ludmilla quietly rebolted the door.

"Darlings, this—this poor man has had an accident. He's very ill. I'm keeping him here for the night. So we'll have to be rather quiet, all right? This is his friend, Ga—Galina."

Gail put down the overcoat. Her hands were shaking.

"This is Mikki," Ludmilla said proudly. "And Tineka."

The boy came forward directly, holding out his hand.

"*Zdrastvidye.*"

"*Zdrastvidye.*" Gail shook it solemnly.

"What did you do upstairs?" Ludmilla asked them.

"Oh, we played some records."

"Anna tried to teach him chess," Tineka said.

"Really? How did you get on?"

"They're getting a kitten," Mikki said. "Can we have a kitten?"

Ludmilla laughed. "We'll have to see."

"What happened to him?" Tineka asked, gazing curiously at Cabeza.

"He was . . . hit by a car."

"Didn't he look?" the boy said.

"What?"

"Left, then right, you know."

"I don't know, darling. Ask Galina."

"Did he?" Mikki turned to Gail.

"Uh—yes, he did. But the car skidded," Gail said. "On the ice."

"Now off to bed, children," Ludmilla told them. "Or you'll be late for school in the morning."

"Where are you going to sleep?" Mikki wanted to know. "That man has Papa's and your bed."

"Galina and I will use the mattresses. Now off you go."

The boy went through into the bedroom. Tineka did not immediately follow. She remained looking down at Cabeza in obvious concern.

She was small, darker than her mother. Studying her profile, Gail noticed the familiar high, flat cheekbones, the spread lips. Her likeness to the man she was gazing at was unmistakable.

"He looks very pale," the child whispered. "Is he going to be all right?"

"We don't know, darling," Ludmilla said. "I expect so. Now hurry along. If you've been to the bathroom, you can use the sink to clean your teeth tonight."

"I hope he doesn't die," Tineka said softly. She dragged her gaze away and followed her brother into the bedroom.

Ludmilla turned to meet Gail's questioning look. She nodded.

"She doesn't know," she murmured. "She thinks Konstantin is her father. Please be careful."

"Of course." Gail added gently, "What lovely children." She agonized for a moment. "The more I think about the terrible position I've put you in . . ."

Ludmilla made a firm chin. "The mattresses are in the roof space—through the children's room. We'd better get them now. Then I will tell you what I propose."

32

GRECHUKHA WAS sitting in at the interrogation of a Jewish woman whose confession was going to enable him to arrest Lazar Kaganovich—not as Omega but on a corruption charge. This was the clever solution he had hit on to satisfy Stalin's immediate craving, while at the same time still keeping his options open with regard to the real American spy.

Of course her confession would be false, but that was hardly relevant. Nor was the fact that she was pissing where she stood and might well discharge other body functions before finally signing. But such assaults on his blunted sensibilities were a small price to pay for getting himself off the hook.

The red telephone light flickered on the table in front of him. He answered it convulsively, keeping his voice low so as not to break the fine web of terror Nikolayev was spinning around their victim.

Zapotkin's voice came to him excitedly over the line. He had in the end managed to find an excuse to work late and was speaking from Grechukha's office.

The information he imparted was so startling that despite

the imminent climax of the questioning, Grechukha breathed a quiet word in Nikolayev's ear and departed.

Fifteen minutes later he was standing with MVD's Major Modin and several police officials in the tiled mortuary attached to the Eastern District Police HQ. An attendant was holding back the sheet while Grechukha gazed at Holz's dead countenance.

"You knew him, I believe," Modin murmured, waiting confidently for his nod of recognition.

Grechukha did not reply. He looked several times from the distorted gray features to the identification found on the body: the Mexican passport in the name of Joaquín Cabeza, the Spanish union card in the name of Marcos Montel, the Russian *propusk* claiming he was Babayev, a worker in the Kremlin. The photographs more resembled the prisoner he remembered than the corpse did. But death brought changes, he was well aware. And the fact that the countenance before him was now beardless further confused the issue. Yes, they *could* be the same man . . .

But if so, where was his *satisfaction?*—the triumphant kick he ought to feel at seeing the bastard dead? Try as he would, he couldn't get it. This left him oddly cheated.

But one thing there could be no doubt about. The Cabeza rumor from Berlin had been fact. And the Spaniard's objective was fact. So the question was, If this *was* he, had he died before or after achieving that objective? Before, obviously, or the city would be in an uproar. Wouldn't it?

"Have you checked out either of these cover identities?" he asked Modin.

The gray-haired major nodded. "A Marcos Montel and his wife arrived in Moscow on the four P.M. plane from Berlin."

"And his *wife?*" Grechukha registered surprise.

"They checked in at the Metropole, where their passports and baggage still are—but they are not. Intourist says they must have slipped out the back way."

"At what time?"

"Not before seven."

"And this *propusk?*" Grechukha tapped the Babayev card.

"No such worker exists in the Kremlin."

"Of course no such worker exists!" Grechukha snapped.

"Did Cabeza use it, that's what I want to know. Was it produced at any Kremlin checkpoint?"

Modin said he would have to inquire.

"Well, do it and quickly!" Grechukha turned to the woman police doctor. "Time of death?"

"Before eight o'clock, Deputy Minister."

Grechukha calculated. Allowing only fifteen minutes between the Kremlin and where the corpse was found, that left Cabeza forty-five minutes, at maximum, in which to have carried out his mission. Such speed of operation would have been impossible.

He felt a great load slip from his shoulders. Then he reminded himself: Providing this *is* Cabeza.

He studied the briefcase full of tools. Clearly they were just props, to add credence to the worker identity.

He asked about the weapon. The fact that it had not been found suggested murder, did it not? He told Modin to get the "wife's" passport photo printed and circulated. He returned to the corpse and studied it for a further few moments.

He wanted very much to believe that it was Cabeza. But conviction still eluded him. He turned to Modin. "I'll get my aide to bring you Cabeza's file. It has his fingerprints. I want you to check them against the dead man's. You are to notify me the moment you know the result."

Then, just to thoroughly ease his mind, Grechukha went up into an office and telephoned Kremlin Security. He asked if they had anything to report.

Nothing, he was told. The General Secretary had gone home to Kuntsevo for the night. The guards both there and in the Kremlin had been doubled as per his instructions. All was well.

Grechukha hung up—reassured, but not entirely. It was only by an act of will that he forced himself to leave the matter in the hands of the MVD and return to the Lubianka interrogation.

By 2:45 A.M. not only the woman but also her husband had signed statements thoroughly incriminating their close friend Lazar Kaganovich. Grechukha returned to his office, his old ebullience beginning to resurface. He had solved a tricky problem, and the Cabeza threat had been removed. The corpse had to be his. Who else's could it be?

He sent Zapotkin off on a fool's errand (after all, he might even be Kaganovich's man!) and telephoned Stalin at his *dacha*.

One of the guards answered. The Leader was asleep in his study, he said, but he had left orders to be awakened when the Deputy Minister called.

Grechukha waited. He was confident that Stalin would be well satisfied with what he had done.

He was kept waiting for some time. There sounded some sort of commotion at the other end.

At last the guard picked up the phone again. "I'm afraid something terrible has happened, Deputy Minister," he cried in a choking voice. "Comrade Stalin has had a stroke!"

33

GAIL WAS awakened by the vibration of the children tiptoeing past her, their stage whispers. A hissing sound was coming from the kitchenette. She peered at her watch. Nearly eight!

Sitting up, she saw that outside it was still quite dark. Ludmilla's mattress was stripped and leaning against the wall. She was already dressed and making breakfast.

Gail got up and, pulling her coat on over her underwear, moved anxiously to look at Joaquín. He was still unconscious, still breathing wheezily. Occasional shudders wracked him. She felt his forehead. Cool—almost chilled.

"He is holding his own," Ludmilla said cheerfully, coming into the room. She gave Gail's wrist a reassuring squeeze. "You will forgive me while I feed the children and get them off to school. There is tea in the samovar."

Gail dressed quickly, the fur coat her only privacy, answering the children's questions as they moved about her collecting their books, lying to them about where she lived and what she did.

When the children were ready to go—Tineka in a black pinafore over a brown dress, with the red neckerchief of the Pioneers; Mikki in a gray suit with a mandarin collar and brass buttons—Ludmilla made them stand still and face her.

"Now, darlings," she said in a stern voice, "I want you to swear—with no questions—that however much you are tempted, you will not tell a *single living soul* that Galina and—and her friend are staying with us. Pioneers' honor?"

Wide-eyed, the children raised their clenched right hands.

As the car entered Kuntsevo, Grechukha noted the gradual thickening of police along the roadside. He caught the glint of radiator grilles in darkened sideroads. His insides were a void of apprehension. Could this, after all, be Cabeza's doing?

Lights and figures thronged the *dacha* gateway. Beyond them he could see the building, lit up like a fairground, cars choking the driveway. He told his driver to park outside and approached the house on foot.

He had been summoned here to Blizhny only a couple of times—once in the springtime, when it was at its best. Stalin had received him on the glassed veranda, virtually among the cherry blossoms. But Grechukha didn't like the house. Too many bits and pieces added on—a manifestation of the Old Man's inner restlessness, his loneliness now that his wives and mistresses were all "gone" and his children had flown the nest.

An official car scrunched by him. It stopped up ahead, and a dark, clean-shaven, soft-bodied man got out. Malenkov. He went up the steps and into the house.

Grechukha followed him in.

Inside, all was muted chaos—staff hurrying about, doctors, nurses. No one questioned his right to enter. It seemed to be open house.

He followed the general flow into a large room that looked more like a dining room than a bedroom, with a big table for eating and chairs and settees set around the walls and a fire crackling in one corner, flickering and winking between the massed bodies of—of just about everyone: Voroshilov, Molotov, Kaganovich, Bulganin, Khrushchev, doctors (whose faces were unfamiliar to him, all the old hands like Vinogradov being under arrest), housekeeper Valechka, chief of bodyguard Khrustalyov, his own boss Ignatiev . . .

In the center of all this, almost invisible, Josef Stalin lay on his sofa bed in a coma. Two doctors were applying something to the back of his head and neck. Leeches? Surely not!

Grechukha couldn't be sure, as Beria was in the way, hovering close to his master in a curiously excited, almost jealous manner.

Grechukha buttonholed a passing woman doctor and asked her for a report on the patient's condition.

"Very grave," she told him. There was a cerebral hemorrhage affecting vital areas of the brain. The right arm and leg were paralyzed.

"Caused by what?" Grechukha asked, trying to keep the anxiety from his voice.

The young woman shrugged. "Pressure of office. Overwork."

"I see. Purely natural causes."

"Why, of course." She gave him a curious look before hurrying to assist at the bedside.

Grechukha experienced profound relief. So it was all a coincidence.

He glanced across at Kaganovich. Well, there he stood—the "pressure of office" that had brought this on. The coarse features showed no awareness, no regret. Too busy figuring what all the others were figuring, he guessed—where this would leave *him,* which of them would come to power if and when the Old Man died.

He switched his gaze to the man he believed was Omega. Oh yes, he was here, paying his respects, feigning grief. What were his plans now, Grechukha wondered. More important, what are *my* plans?

He sensed someone edging closer to him. It was Vasily Khrustalyov, the chief bodyguard, glum-faced.

"Doesn't look too good, eh?"

Grechukha shook his head, dutifully sad.

Khrustalyov murmured on for a few moments in mournful praise of their Leader. Then he whispered, "By the way, Modin was onto me last night, asking if we'd had cause to check the identity of a Kremlin worker called Babayev . . ."

Grechukha stiffened slightly. He nodded.

"The answer," Khrustalyov murmured, "is yes."

The ground seemed to tremble. The columns wobbled. The whole edifice of Grechukha's newfound confidence came tumbling about his head.

Khrustalyov went on, "Apparently Rusakov ran into him coming out of Comrade Stalin's apartment. He'd just been in to do a repair job."

"In . . . the apartment?" Grechukha's words were almost soundless. "What time was this?"

"Around six-forty-five last night."

Grechukha stood motionless among the ruins. So the stroke *wasn't* a coincidence. Somehow the Spaniard had beaten them all!

"I'd have reported it earlier," Khrustalyov was whispering, "only Rusakov went off duty. I didn't see him till an hour ago." He eyed the other's expression. "Was it important? Modin didn't explain."

Grechukha's mind was already springing to salvage all it could from the debris. "Natural causes," the doctor had said. A poison, evidently. But the doctors weren't suspicious. And this man obviously hadn't made the connection. Not even Modin knew the whole story. So, for as long as he, Grechukha, was able to keep all these elements apart, the cat would remain in the bag.

"No, not important," he whispered. "Don't bother to contact Modin. I'll tell him when I see him."

He excused himself abruptly and threaded his way out.

He had not proceeded more than a few meters down the drive when one of the *dacha* staff called after him. He was wanted on the telephone.

The voice on the line was Zapotkin's—with another bombshell.

"The fingerprints don't match, Deputy Minister," he cried. "The body in the morgue is not Cabeza's!"

Grechukha digested this in silence for a long moment. He glanced at the throng around him and lowered his voice.

"This is what you do. Make more prints of Cabeza's picture, and the woman's. Circulate them first to the airports, then to every exit point in the west USSR. Copies to all precincts, street patrols. Checkpoints to be established on all major routes out of the city."

"At once!" Zapotkin cried. "And that ex-wife of his—shall I have her brought in for questioning?"

"Good thinking," Grechukha began. Then he thought, Too

good. It was the sort of move he should make himself—and reap the credit for. "But I will go personally. Do you have the address?"

"Right here, comrade." And Zapotkin read it out to him as if he already had it in his hand.

Grechukha hung up, mystified. He had at no time confided anything about Cabeza's mission to Zapotkin. So how could he know it was so urgent?

He strode, slithering, out to his car. That bastard El Duro! How had he done it? How the devil had he managed it? Twelve hours. He'd had twelve whole hours to get himself clear. There was no way he'd still be in Moscow. Unless . . . something had gone wrong. Well, if he'd been near that ex-wife of his, she'd tell him about it, all about it—his escape route, his contacts—if he had to break her over a *wheel*. And when she'd told him, he'd have her shot!

The children having left for school, Ludmilla was putting their night things away before departing for the hospital. Gail helped her, conscious of her mounting tension and the position she had put her in, wracking her brains for a solution. She was keeping an eye on Joaquín for any signs of returning consciousness and an ear on the little radio, which she had turned on so as to catch the newscast.

When presently the news was announced, she stopped in her work, listening. The first item concerned the upcoming elections. She knew immediately that no revelation about Stalin would be forthcoming. Puzzled, she was about to turn off the set when, out of the corner of her eye, she saw a vehicle come to a stop across the street. She paused by the window to watch it.

It was a black car resembling an old Packard. Two men got out, to be immediately joined by two others from the yard of the old church nearby. Both pairs stood in conversation for a moment, their gaze wandering toward No. 64.

She stepped back quickly. From behind the curtain she watched the second two get into the car and drive away and the first two take over their position in the churchyard.

Ludmilla had sensed something from her movement. "What is it?"

Gail switched off the radio. "We're being watched."

Ludmilla strode toward the window, but Gail pulled her back.

"Quickly—we can't stay here another second—it's too dangerous for you. Is there anywhere else in the building—an empty apartment, a storeroom, an attic?"

Ludmilla shook her head.

"A cellar?"

"No."

"The roof space."

"No, they'd look there. Besides—"

"Not if you hid the door. It's a small door. Hang something over it."

"But it's freezing in there. Just tiles and rafters. It would kill him!"

"Not with the heater." Gail moved to grab it. "Bring the mattresses."

Without waiting for her to agree, Gail carried the heater through into the bedroom. She opened the small door. Ducking, she carried the stove through into the icy compartment. There was no stand-up space—just rafters sloping down from six feet to nothing. Length—maybe nine feet. It was filled with toys, boxes, empty luggage. She started stacking everything into the far end.

Ludmilla brought the mattresses. She was shaking, still groping desperately in her mind for an alternative.

They laid the mattresses side by side on the floor.

"We'll need water, towels, a bucket, any old overcoats . . ."

"How will you see?"

"A flashlight—got one?"

Ludmilla hurried away. Gail emerged. She grabbed a child's chamber pot from under one of the beds and pushed it through. She fetched Joaquín's and her coats, hats, dumped them on the mattresses. She bundled all the blood-soaked strips of sheet and swabs together. "Where?"

"Into my medical bag."

Gail crammed them in. "What will you hang over the door?"

"Uh—there, that little Bokhara rug."

"You'll need a hammer, some tacks."

In minutes they had completed the preparations. Now to move Joaquín.

"Wait." Ludmilla stood debating for a moment. "Gail, we will have to do this *very* carefully."

"In the rug?"

"Yes. One either side. Keep it as taut as you can."

The pale green Zim came fast along the street. It slithered to a stop outside No. 64.

Grechukha got out quickly. "Blow the horn," he told the driver.

The man had scarcely touched the button when the two MVD men appeared from the churchyard.

Grechukha beckoned them over impatiently. They appeared startled by this unheralded visit from the top brass.

"Come with me!" Grechukha strode briskly into the building.

They climbed the stairs to the apartment. Grechukha tried the door. Locked. He raised his fist to hammer on it, but the door opened and a small woman dressed for the street and carrying a black bag almost walked into his fist. She stopped with a startled gasp.

"Ludmilla Patolichev?" Grechukha pushed her back into the room. His hot eyes snapped up the interior, registering the lack of space, the layout, and that no one else was visible. He swung her aside, signaling the men toward the two inner doors, taking quick note of her expression: shock, mostly, and outrage.

"How dare you force your—! Who—who are you?"

"State Security—and no injured innocence, please—you're in trouble, Doctor." Grechukha heeled shut the door. Strike hard while they're in shock. "Where is he?—talk fast." He pushed his belly at her.

She tried to step back, but hit the wall behind her.

"Who? No one's here. Who are you looking for?"

Her fear was beautiful—but under the circumstances, normal. His eyes dredged hers for something deeper. Yes, he saw it.

"I want him, I want him," he breathed into her face. "And you are going to give him to me."

"Who—who?" she almost screamed at him.

Yes, there it was again. But immediately he saw a screen drop down behind her eyes. Her defenses coming into play—already, too quick—she was intelligent—damn!

"Well?" he called to his men.

One could be heard opening and closing the bedroom closet. The other emerged from the kitchenette with a shrug.

Damn again. He turned toward her, saw her listening. She was on tenterhooks—why? Waiting for the other man to reappear from the bedroom?

After a moment, he did, with a shake of his head.

Ah yes—very strong then—relief: it came off her like an odor.

Grechukha strode past him into the bedroom to look for himself.

Tiny. Children—he must remember that—at school, probably. But a rabbit hutch! And she a doctor. (He thought of his own spacious apartment, his *dacha*.) Nowhere to hide even a mouse. His eyes raked the walls. One decent rug. The rest sticks—sticks of furniture one had to wait in line for hours to buy in drab shops where the staff was either rude or half asleep. Yes, doctors weren't much in the Soviet Union. But don't waste time.

He came striding back. "So he's gone, has he? How long ago?" He watched for a repeat of the relief in her eyes, but now there was nothing. She had mastered herself. He cursed. She just kept crying "Who?" to his questions.

"Your ex-husband," he told her at last. "Joaquín Cabeza. He's been here—you know it, I know it—so the quicker you—" His voice trailed away.

She was *laughing!* Her eyes had widened, then squeezed up, and now she dropped helplessly back onto the settee, utter relief tinged with hysteria taking hold of her.

"*Cabeza?*" she cried. "I . . . I thought . . ."

"You thought what?" He paced to stand over her.

"That you were here on some . . ."

"What? Out with it, woman."

"Some serious charge."

Grechukha was nonplussed. Her relief sounded genuine. She sat forward with a bewildered shake of her head. "He's dead," she said, as if incredulous that anyone should make such a mistake. "He died ten *years* ago."

"Wrong, Doctor. Stop bluffing."

"Dammit," she cried, "he died in Siberia—look it up. You must have a file on him somewhere."

Grechukha told her that Cabeza was not only alive but here in Moscow. "He's been here in this room! I can *smell* him!" He dragged the air into his nostrils savagely.

The young woman stared at him—and there it was again—a flash of real apprehension, as though she somehow feared he might actually smell the man.

He tested the air in his nostrils again. He got a faintly chemical smell.

"You—you mean he survived and has been released?"

"He escaped, during the war—fled the country."

"And now you're telling me he's back? I don't believe it. If he escaped, he wouldn't *come* back. He wouldn't come near Moscow. It doesn't make sense!"

Grechukha had to admit that if she was innocent, it wouldn't. He tried to probe behind the mask of puzzlement she was presenting—and couldn't. He flexed his lips awkwardly and took a short step, to reestablish his physical mastery of the situation. But it only served to confirm his uncertainty.

The two men were moving about the room, fingering things, poking into drawers. He saw she was watching them. She stood up suddenly.

"Look, what can I say to convince you? If he really was in Moscow, do you really believe—"

One of the men had straightened from behind the settee with a grunt. He dangled something in front of her eyes. A blood-stained medical swab! "What's this?"

"Oh, thank you." She reached out calmly to take it.

But Grechukha had caught the sudden look again. Was this it—the proof he was seeking? Had Cabeza come here wounded? He ordered her to answer the question.

She tried to shrug it off, saying it was nothing. She had had an accident case. But the look was still there.

He demanded details.

"Oh, it was last night. A man. He had been stabbed.

Someone brought him up. I dressed his wounds and sent him on to the hospital."

"You're lying."

"Why should I? Ask anyone." Evenly: "Ask your woman downstairs."

"Give me his name." Grechukha signaled one of the men to take it down.

"Uh—Petrovsky, I think."

"Petrovsky. Which hospital did you send him to?"

"I didn't."

"You said you did." Good. She was beginning to lose her accuracy.

"There was a woman with him."

"Woman?" Grechukha's heart gave a little kick. "What woman?"

"His wife, I suppose. I told her to take him to the hospital. I didn't actually send him myself."

Her fear was becoming more visible with every moment.

"How did she take him?"

"A taxi, I think."

"You *think?*"

"I know. Yes. Yes, come to think of it, I saw it drive away."

"You're lying. Why? Why are you afraid?"

"Afraid?"

"It was him, wasn't it?" Grechukha demanded.

"Him? Who?" Incredulously: "Cabeza?"

"Cabeza. Why else would you be terrified?"

She seemed to collapse then. She turned away, raising her hands to her face.

"Look—" she said brokenly. "I was tired. I'd had a long day at the hospital . . ."

"So what? What are you saying?"

"I know you're looking for an excuse—any excuse—to arrest me. I really was worn out. I left it for the hospital to do. I know it's against the law, but—"

"What? Make sense, woman!"

Ludmilla turned back toward him miserably. "I should have reported it straight to the police. It's the regulation—report all woundings to the police." Her eyes filled with tears. "There. You've got your excuse now. You've got it!" She collapsed, weeping, on the settee.

Grechukha stared at her. He felt as though he had just snapped at a minute steak and got a mouthful of fluff. Was *that* all she had been scared of?

The men were looking at him uncertainly. He turned to them with a scowl.

"Get your department to check her story—the woman downstairs, the hospitals, Petrovsky, the taxi—I want it verified—a full report—to be on my desk by noon."

He looked down again at the weeping woman. Arrest her? No. She was more useful as bait.

"If you're lying," he muttered, "I'll soon know. Then . . . heaven help you."

He turned on his heel and stomped out. The men followed.

The door did not slam behind them—just clicked shut.

For the moment, she had won.

34

Gail sat propped beside Joaquín in the stove-lit darkness of the roof space. Her feet were roasting, her head freezing. She had poked a hole through the tiles and snow to get rid of the fumes, but the oily stink still sickened her.

Four hours had passed since the MVD and, slightly later, Ludmilla had left the apartment—four hours of claustrophobic silence, relieved only by Joaquín's increasingly alarming breathing. She had talked to him, to herself. She had reviewed their position a hundred times. And each time she had been left feeling even more trapped and helpless than before.

A door banged. Footsteps, movement. In a daze she clutched the gun. She heard the chest being dragged aside.

"It's me!" Ludmilla's voice.

The next moment there was light and fresh air. Gail crawled out, blinking, and stood up, filling her lungs gratefully, questioningly.

Ludmilla's manner was abrupt, intent. The softness had gone from her eyes. "How is he?"

"He's been coughing."

"Any blood?"

"No."

307

"Good. Now we have to be quick."

"Are they still out there?"

"Yes. And I'm being followed. But they didn't stop me. Presumably they've had no orders yet. But it can only be a matter of time." She produced a liter of blood and transfusion equipment from her bag. "Now, shall we do it out here or in there?" She answered herself, "In there," and hurried away.

"What can I do?"

"Take off his jacket, bare his arm."

"Which arm?"

"It doesn't matter."

Gail ducked back into the roof space and did as she was bid.

Ludmilla came back with the hammer and some nails. Squeezing almost on top of Gail, she banged a nail into one of the rafters and began to suspend the equipment.

Within minutes the needle was in his arm and the blood gravity-feeding through it into a vein. Ludmilla adjusted the flow against her watch to sixty drops a minute. She pricked his finger, took a smear of blood, matched it against a Talquist test card.

"Hemoglobin eight . . ."

"You had no problem getting the right group?"

Ludmilla shook her head. "He is a universal recipient." She added with a touch of wryness, "A true man of the people."

Presently they stood out in the bedroom together. Ludmilla lit a cigarette, inhaling deeply, blowing out a long plume.

"You were wonderful this morning," Gail whispered. "Wonderful."

"I nearly died."

"I keep trying to work out how they were so sure Joaquín's in Moscow." Then: "Did you hear any . . . news at the hospital?"

"News?"

"Any . . . important news?"

"No . . . ?"

Gail slowly shook her head. "I just don't understand it."

"I don't understand it," Kelland muttered as the newscast ended. He took a turn out along the hall of the Berlin house.

A bad feeling was beginning to stir deep inside him. "Moscow should be buzzing with it by now!"

"Maybe the Presidium is sitting on it," Franz suggested.

"Then why no word from Holz?" Kelland glared toward him. "Why no completion report? Not a word from the Ivanovskys!" The scrubbing of his rubber soles on the worn linoleum increased in tempo as his mind cast about for some hook to hang the blame on. Someone, some *bastard*, had fucked up! He checked his watch. "What time is Holz's plane due in Budapest?"

"Three."

"Two more hours." He ground his teeth. This had to be the cliff-hanger of all time!

"Herr Kelland." The operator glanced up, both hands pressed to his headphones. "Someone is using your call sign, asking us to acknowledge."

"Strength?"

"Five. Close. American sector, maybe."

Kelland stood torn. Determined not to get caught up in Washington's eleventh-hour shits, he had vowed not to surface till Sunflower was in the bag. But now . . . He nodded.

The operator rattled his key briefly, then listened. He began to jot down a message.

Kelland sat quickly beside him and decoded it as he went, reading: *"Point woman not on return flight. Where the hell are you? Report position and sit-rep soonest. Repeat soonest."*

Kelland rose to his feet, the message clutched in his hand.

The operator looked up at him curiously. Any reply would have to be extremely brief, he reminded, to escape the attention of the Russian radio location units.

Kelland shook his head. "Don't acknowledge." His sharp features had drawn into a tight mask. So Gail hadn't made it back to Washington!

It was coming apart. How? Something he had missed out on? That wasn't possible. He had planned Sunflower to perfection—*perfection*.

By two o'clock, Grechukha could wait no longer. He told Zapotkin to chase up the report that he had ordered to be on his desk by noon.

It took his aide half an hour of steady wading through inter-departmental ineptitude to get to the lieutenant concerned with the investigation. In the bureaucracy-ridden MVD this was by no means unusual. Nor was the lieutenant's reply. Which was to the effect that the report was not yet complete.

Grechukha grabbed the phone himself, said tensely, "Give me what you've got!"

The lieutenant told him that they had located the wounded man, Petrovsky—in the Golitsin Hospital.

This was a knock on the head for Grechukha's expectations.

"Did he actually confirm that Dr. Patolichev treated him in her flat last night?"

"Well, no," the lieutenant admitted. "He can't confirm anything—he's in a coma."

"From knife wounds?"

"Correct."

"But he *was* admitted last night."

"Yes. According to the register, he was brought in shortly after midnight."

So her story checked out. Grechukha sighed inwardly. Then something clicked in his mind.

"The Golitsin . . . Isn't that where Dr. Patolichev herself works?"

The lieutenant said it was.

So it was possible, Grechukha suggested, that she had known Petrovsky was a patient and had built her story around that fact.

The lieutenant reminded him that when she was questioned she had not yet been to the hospital and so could not have known that Petrovsky had been admitted.

"Unless he was admitted previously and she altered the register immediately on her arrival this morning," Grechukha said. "You thought of that?"

"But there was no alteration," said the other. "I myself checked the entry."

"And did you check further back? To see if his admission had been crossed off a previous page and added on at the end?"

The lieutenant admitted that he hadn't, but—but surely all

the evidence supported Patolichev's story? The concierge at No. 64 had already confirmed that a man was treated in her flat last night. The times tallied . . .

"A man, yes." Grechukha was becoming impatient. "But which man? *Which* man? Did you show her the photographs?"

"Photographs, Deputy Minister?"

"Of Cabeza and the woman."

"None have been issued."

Grechukha gave a great bellow of frustration. He turned and conducted a furious exchange with Zapotkin. He resumed the line: "More are being printed. As soon as they are ready they will come to you by hand. Take them to the concierge—see if she recognizes either of them. At once, understand?"

It was just past seven that night when Ludmilla again opened up the roof space. Gail crawled out excitedly.

"He came around!" she cried. "About an hour ago. He looked at me. I told him where we were. He seemed to understand. But he was in pain, so I injected him with the morphine as you told me. He's sleeping now. But *sleeping*, Ludmilla."

Ludmilla took the flashlight and went in and shone it on his face. His color was almost normal. The strong features looked more composed. She thumbed back his eyelids, sounded his heart for a moment.

As she came ducking out again she said, "Yes, he is much stronger. But now comes the hard part. The dangerous part." She added, "In more ways than one."

She told Gail that there was an MVD car outside. Two men were with the concierge, showing her photographs; she had seen them through the door as she came in.

Gail's newly awakened optimism vanished. "Then quick— you'd better shut us in again!"

Ludmilla shook her head fatalistically. "If she tells them the truth, we are sunk anyway."

"You gave her the pain-killer?"

"At lunchtime." Grimly: "Let us pray that it worked for her. Come, help me bring in the table."

How could she be so calm? Gail followed her into the other room. She glanced around.

"Where are the children?"

"I left them with my mother-in-law."

"Was that wise?"

"They are better away from all this."

"But a break in your normal routine . . ."

"It is normal. They go to her from school every day. I collect them on my way home. Sometimes they stay there the night. We are wasting time."

They moved the dining table through into the bedroom. Getting Joaquín onto it promised to be no easy feat. But as they started to lift him his eyes opened. Just his eyes, as though someone had opened two upper windows in a still house. They gazed up into Ludmilla's face unseeingly for a moment. Awareness grew in them, as an image grows under the photo developer. "Ludmilla . . . !"

"Hola," she replied softly in Spanish. *"Qué tal, hombre?"*

"Bien."

"Muy bien." She took his face in her hands and bent her lips to his—just a touch, very tender. "Now we are going to move you. Will you help us?"

Cabeza nodded. And though his effort was only token, it eased the deadness of his weight, and presently he was stretched out on the table in the bedroom.

Together the two women stripped off his jacket and shirt. He watched them, smiling, though it was evident he was in pain. Ludmilla lowered her face close to his.

"There is a bullet, you know this?"

He nodded.

"I am going to put you back to sleep. When you wake up you will be either alive or dead, *comprendes?"*

Cabeza grimaced.

Ludmilla took one arm and applied a tourniquet, then injected into a vein a quarter grain of morphine.

She rubbed the arm for a moment and stroked his brow until his eyes closed peacefully.

It was perhaps the strangest thing Gail had ever watched in her life.

"If I probe," Ludmilla had told her, "I may kill him—the

wound is so close to the heart. And we have no X-ray." And she had taken off her wedding ring and tied a short length of thread to it. "Shave all the left side of his chest, please."

Gail had done so. Then she watched in near disbelief as Ludmilla suspended the little pendulum above his body. It began to rotate quite violently.

She moved the pendulum steadily back and forth until she had covered the whole of that side of his chest. Its rotation slowed twice—on different sweeps, but over the same area. She concentrated above this area till she had established the precise point of smallest rotation. She marked this with a cross of lipstick.

"Help me turn him, please."

After Gail had run the razor over the left side of his back, Ludmilla continued the process. When she reached a point between his shoulder blade and his spine, the pendulum slowed to a stop. Then slowly reversed its motion. Presently it was spinning strongly in the opposite direction. Ludmilla marked that spot too.

She pulled Cabeza to the edge of the table and ducked down so as to align the two marked spots with her eye. They seemed to tally, for she immediately pushed him back and, without further ado, began to operate.

She worked from a small incision made at the center of the cross, cutting a little, separating the muscles, probing a little. Gail had to steel herself to watch as the probe sank deeper, deeper into the split she had opened up in the powerful rhomboideus muscles.

When the probe was buried a third of its length, suddenly Ludmilla looked up with a tight little smile. She jiggled the instrument and, very faintly, Gail could hear the sound of metal on metal.

At this moment there came a loud knocking at the outer door.

35

LUDMILLA'S HANDS froze for an instant. Then, shaking slightly, they went on working, as she prepared to extract the bullet.

The knocking continued. The light was on in the sitting room. Whoever was out there must know someone was home. That it was the MVD from downstairs Gail had no doubt. She knew she must handle them alone. Her insides a void, she darted to get the gun.

"Ludmilla, you there?" A woman's voice.

Gail stopped short, staring at Ludmilla. She was working delicately with the forceps, gripping, easing, withdrawing. Her face showed only concentration, but she murmured, "It is Tamara Voyvodsky from upstairs."

A second later it came—a small, chewed-up, bloody lump of metal. The forceps released it into a dish with a clatter.

Gail stood confused, not quite able to grasp that it was not the MVD. She moved to the window and peered out. The street was empty. The official car had gone!

Ludmilla hurried to the door. In a daze of relief, Gail heard her call through that she was busy and would be up in a minute. The woman called back that she had run out of tea. If

Ludmilla would lend her some, she would get it herself if she would just open the door.

Ludmilla repeated firmly that she would be up in a minute. She came back to the table and disinfected the wound, stitched, dressed it.

"How did you do that with your wedding ring?"

Ludmilla gave a little shrug. "It doesn't matter what you use. Divining is just . . . *you* yourself, what you sense." She moved away into the kitchenette and fetched a packet of tea. "A pendulum, a rod, they just make the tiny changes inside you more easy to recognize."

"You can divine water?"

"Anything." Ludmilla smiled ruefully. "Except the future. Now I must take her some tea and invent some excuse why I had my door locked. They are very inquisitive, my neighbors. I must leave them no room for suspicion."

She went out.

Gail returned slowly to Joaquín. Anything but the future . . . Yes, Ludmilla, she thought uneasily. If only you could divine that.

The evening passed slowly, agonizingly. Neither Gail nor Ludmilla could relax. Every sound in the street outside took one of them to the window. Every voice, footfall in the house brought them upright in their chairs, Gail ready to bolt into the roof space where Joaquín already lay, Ludmilla ready to seal them in.

They listened to the radio newscast. Still there was no news of Stalin.

And while they sat and discussed means of getting Joaquín out of Moscow, the MVD scoured the city streets for him and stopped vehicles on lonely roads and searched trains and double-checked on every person leaving the Soviet Union by plane, road, or boat in a huge coordinated, yet still low-profile manhunt. Other units looked in vain for the taxi driver who, according to Ludmilla, had driven Petrovsky from her apartment to the hospital. Until he or she was located, Grechukha refused to abandon the possibility that it had been Cabeza whom Ludmilla had treated and that he was still concealed somewhere in the vicinity of No. 64. There was another taxi driver whom, unknowingly, they had so far not interviewed—the cheery woman who had delivered Gail and Cabeza to that address. As fate would have it, she was temporarily in Gorky, where her father was on his deathbed. He had only hours to live. And when those hours elapsed, no doubt she would return to the capital.

Long after Gail had retired to her mattress beside Cabeza in the roof space, Kelland paced the lower rooms of the Berlin house, ruining cigarette after cigarette. Fresh scenarios crowded through his mind as he strove to adjust his future plans to the collapse of Sunflower.

Excluded now were his hopes for the house on Lake Nahuel Huapi in the Argentinean Andes. The old woman wouldn't honor the option much longer. He could cable her for an extension, but what would be the use? His deal with Omega specified payment on completion, and now there would be no completion. If one element of his plan had come apart, it would all come apart, so finely was it integrated.

So that skiing in winter, fishing the 25-pound rainbow trout in summer, the rebuilding of the old *hacienda,* the fashioning of his environment to meet his needs against the backdrop of lakes and islands and forest, paradise within paradise—*gone!* Snatched from him—by whom? Who had done it—that girl? Dammit, hadn't he read her correctly? Sure he had—like a book! Holz, then? He was a little crazy, but he had allowed for that. He had allowed for *everything!*

"Herr Kelland!"

Even as the operator called he caught the unmistakable explosion of Morse from his headphones. At last! The spools were rotating as he entered. He waited on tenterhooks for the signal to end. Now at least he would know the *facts,* however bitter.

The rewind now . . . the half-speed playback. His eyes chased the operator's pencil hungrily across the pad. He snatched the message, sat down to decode.

It was in Russian, which he translated easily. The first four words brought him to the edge of his seat: *"Stalin dying. Suspect poison . . ."*

He uttered a cry of exultation—short-lived.

"Point man alive. Manhunt in progress . . ." Cabeza alive
—Jesus! *"Your immediate intercession imperative."*

Imperative—they weren't kidding! Kelland bounded up the
stairs. Stalin still alive, so Omega wouldn't have made his
move yet. There was still a chance he could find and silence
Cabeza in time! He threw his fine clothes together—creases,
forget it—cover disguise—gun—aftershave—cigarettes. He
didn't try to figure any of it out. There would be plenty of
time for that on the plane.

36

CABEZA CAME around within half an hour of the operation. To the women's astonishment and alarm, with face set, he very slowly sat up and swung his legs to the floor. It cost him dearly in both pain and scolding, but he had proved something to himself and was grimly satisfied.

After that, he permitted the women to help him into the roof space, where he stretched out and slept until far into the night, when he woke again and, despite the morphine that clouded his thoughts, forced his mind to consider the position.

It was then that the true extent of the sacrifices made by Gail and Ludmilla came to him. Though Ludmilla's was perhaps the greater, without Gail's rapid intercession in the first place Ludmilla would never have had the opportunity to use her medical skills. Gail, he realized, had abandoned her own chances of escape to rescue him. It was an act of devotion that moved him profoundly.

He eased onto his good shoulder and studied her in the bluish light where she lay on the mattress beside his, her full molded lips parting with silent words, her eyes moving under their closed lids, keeping watch over him, it would seem, even in sleep.

As his body stirred, her eyes opened wide and met his. With an intake of breath, she started to raise herself, then lay still—and for a timeless moment they looked at and into each other. Then, impulsively, despite the agony of his chest and back, Cabeza reached out, lifted the coverings that separated them and drew her to him, letting them fall so that the two of them were in the one cocoon, their clothed bodies pressed together.

There is nothing of her, he thought, but courage and slimness, almost like a child's. His hand moved down over her back, her hips, drawing her still closer, feeling her yield toward him in a way that—yes, even in his weakened state— stirred his manhood. Her head went back and her mouth came up to his, as a flower opens to the sun, and Cabeza gave to it his gratitude, gently at first and then fiercely, ignoring the pain that seared and burned through him as he turned slowly onto her, thinking, She gives me strength that cannot be there. Her eyes flared and the lips under his fought to free themselves as she shook her head.

"No, *amado*, you mustn't!"

"*Cálmate.*"

"No—you could start the bleeding—I forbid it!"

"*Cálmate.*"

"Joaquín—!" Her eyes searched his wildly, then disbelievingly, fading increasingly as he pressed his hardness to the mound between her thighs.

Her protestations grew less and less certain, her breathing shorter, as he bore down upon her, her arms emerging to encircle his neck, careful to avoid his wound. He was in a dream, the drug clouding his mind, yet strangely not his body, miraculously not his body. The fibrous Spanish stockings under the thick skirt made a breathtaking contrast of the smooth, rounded thigh above, smooth as wax, then warm wax, warmer . . . Gail drew down her arms and moved this way and that under him, he helping her, then himself, the fire scorching across his back, till their lower bodies at last met free of impediment, his nakedness against hers, his nerves fighting through the dulling effects of the drug to drink in the contact with the hunger of long abstinence and deep affection that banished finally all pain, all weakness.

The last protestation of her eyes melted to a smoky

darkness that became opaque as she sank under him like a swimmer drawn into the deep, surrendering herself to sweet drowning.

Cabeza's last sensation was of entering a soft furnace. Then he passed out.

In the room that was like a dining room, the man who had dominated the Communist world for over a quarter of a century remained comatose, his pulse rate 60. The hemorrhage in the left hemisphere had extended into the deeper structures of the brain. His respiratory and circulatory functions were deteriorating.

To regulate his respiration and the action of his heart vessels, his team of physicians was administering oxygen and drugs. A session of the Academy of Sciences was being held elsewhere to decide what more could be done to save him. An artificial respirator had already been supplied, but it stood idly by. None of the doctors in attendance knew how to use it.

Grechukha, on his second morning visit, observed this scene. Members of the hierarchy came and stood awhile in silence and went. Beria alone seemed a fixture. He alternately stood and sat beside the bed, his eyes riveted on his master's, as though he wanted to avail himself of their first glance should they open, or was praying that they would never open again.

Stalin's daughter Svetlana sat on a sofa, her face convulsed with grief, clinging to the hand of a woman doctor.

Bulganin and Malenkov stood uneasily nearby, turning occasionally to stare blindly at the blown-up magazine photos and framed reproductions of Yar-Kravchenko's drawings on the walls. Higher up, above all these, hung a portrait of Lenin. His enigmatic eyes seemed to be focused on his old enemy where he lay dying—perhaps of the very same poison that had ended his own life!

Zapotkin meanwhile sat at work in the State Security office. A dispatch rider arrived with an UTMOST SECRET envelope. He signed for it. It was marked "For Deputy Minister's eyes only."

From the identity of the rider and the nature of the seal, he knew this to be one of the daily reports submitted by the special team that was monitoring the activities of the Presidium hierarchy. He was not supposed to know that this team even existed. But Zapotkin knew a lot of things he wasn't supposed to.

He took the envelope through into Grechukha's empty office, neatly peeled off the seal with a razor blade and studied its contents.

He was glad he did. It contained a bombshell—the first positive intelligence that could lead to the exposure of Omega!

Stalin was dying. The vital question was, How much longer could he cling to life? Hours or days? He decided he would have to take a chance on hours. For, whatever happened, Comrade Grechukha must not be allowed to see this report.

He folded it tightly and put it into his inner pocket and returned to his desk. He would destroy it during the lunch hour.

Though punctuated by lack of breath and occasional bouts of pain, Cabeza's questions were relentless. From Gail's answers he was piecing together every detail of what had happened before and after the shooting, as well as building a practical picture of their environment—in this house and in the city. Despite the dreamlike emotional experience of last night, he had forced a breakfast down his throat and now sat propped in the semidarkness of the roof space, Gail close to him, touching him sometimes as she talked, methodically regaining mastery of his situation.

They discussed the strangely swift involvement of the police, Kelland, his plan, what action he might take to remedy what had gone wrong, Holz . . .

Holz . . . Cabeza's thoughts circled him musingly, then with sharpening attention as he remembered: I am Holz, I have his identification. Kelland clearly intended Holz to escape after completing his mission. What is to prevent us from escaping by the same means?

Gail had Holz's wallet. She opened it for him under the flashlight. She had already considered that possibility, she told him. "But we've missed out." She showed him the return air ticket for Budapest in the name of Matya Revai, a businessman. "We're a day too late. The flight left yesterday."

The light wandered as she made to return the ticket to the wallet, but Cabeza caught her wrist and steadied it. "Not so fast, *muchacha*." He had glimpsed something penciled lightly on the reverse. It had been smudged out purposely and they were able to decipher it only with difficulty.

"Klimenti Ivanovsky, Pokhoronnoe Buro, 4 Volga Street."

Pokhoronnoe meant "burial." Cabeza mused quizzically, How wise it was of Holz to have recognized that he would need the services of a burial bureau! Then he thought more seriously, But in what context?

It was Gail who supplied the answer. She had placed the name and now told him of the radio message Kelland had received in Berlin from "the Ivanovskys."

"Then they must be Agency people, *muchacha!*"

"It looks that way."

Cabeza leaned back and closed his eyes. He needed to sleep, but a course of action had to be decided on now.

After some minutes of thought, he said, "*Cómo no?* I have an idea."

They were listening to the midday news on the radio when Ludmilla returned from the hospital. There was still no revelation about Stalin. But even so, this was predictable, Cabeza told Gail. "The Russian leaders do not like to make a clean announcement of anything. They must distill it first for their private purposes. And if there is no purpose, they must find one. And if they cannot find one, they suppress it anyway, as their privilege. The news will come, *muchacha*. It will come." He said it confidently, but in his heart there were the beginnings of doubt.

While they were eating the stew Ludmilla had prepared for them, the roof-space door open between them and where Ludmilla sat in the bedroom, he voiced his idea.

Ludmilla looked startled. She eyed Gail's appearance for a long moment before answering.

"Yes, I do know someone. But . . ." She looked doubtful. "It would be asking her to take such a risk!"

"What sort of woman?" Cabeza asked her.

322

"An intellectual. Her husband is an architect." She added thoughtfully, "Also a dissident. Perhaps because of how she feels about the regime, she might agree. For when would you like it arranged?"

"Tonight. You must make the call from a public phone. The line from this building and from the hospital will be listened to." He added, "And you should bring the children home with you. To leave them away longer will be to start the MVD thinking."

Ludmilla hesitated, and Cabeza guessed what was in her mind. But she said quietly, "I will bring them."

That night, back came the children hand in hand with their mother, their footsteps dogged through the darkened streets by the MVD shadow—past a car that was parked now with its lights out at the intersection of their street, past the surveillance team in the churchyard—and safely home, still without challenge.

Ludmilla heaved a deep sigh. They still, it seemed, had not been able to break her story about Petrovsky. They only had to check the page numbers in the hospital register to realize that she had removed three of them and copied them out again, with Petrovsky's admission closer to the end. But the MVD, for all their vaunted efficiency, were poor detectives.

The children were delighted to see that Cabeza was recovering, though mystified by his and Gail's accommodations. No, they hadn't told anyone, but why were their two visitors hiding in the roof space? Ludmilla explained that they were not supposed to be in Moscow and the authorities would be very cross if they found out. This seemed to satisfy them and made it all rather exciting and adventurous. Tineka crept in to sit beside Cabeza.

"What would they do to you if they caught you?" she wanted to know anxiously.

Cabeza was studying the small, earnest face with the big serious eyes for the first time. He took in the trim figure under the black pinafore. Her breasts were forming. Her legs were surprisingly long and slender for her height. He felt a pang of contrasting emotions—love, wonder, pride, fear. *You have killed us all!* It was an effort to steady his voice. "How old are you now?"

"Nearly thirteen—why?"

"And how are you at school?"

"Oh. That depends. I'm best at biology, nature studies, you know. But we don't get enough of it. The teacher says it's for the peasants, that we should help build Communism by taking up physics, engineering. I think I'd rather work in the countryside."

Cabeza said, "Peasants, eh. They do not like peasants at your school? It is a strange kind of communism they build." Then he answered her levelly, "They would put me in prison."

Tineka's eyes widened in alarm. "Oh, no! Well, you needn't worry. *We* won't tell anyone. I'll make sure Mikki doesn't. And I certainly won't."

"Even if the police ask you?"

"No, I swear." Then, reading his silence as disbelief: "Really. You can trust me."

Cabeza studied her earnest expression for a long moment. Then he smiled. "I trust you." His voice choked a little. He held out his hand.

Tineka placed her own solemnly in it. The square, dark, scarred hand closed over the small, pale one for a moment. "We have a secret."

"Yes." Then she shivered and pulled away. "It's cold in here! How can you stand it?"

"Go and get warm."

Tineka returned to the sitting room, and presently there came a knock at the outer door. The bedroom door was pulled shut, excluding Cabeza from what happened next, but he had already given Gail her instructions and they had embraced wordlessly, for there was danger for them all in what she was about to do.

A woman came in quickly. She embraced Ludmilla silently, smiled at the children, then turned to inspect Gail.

"Anya, this is Galina," Ludmilla said.

"Zdrastvidye."

Gail realized Anya was one of the guests she had seen come out of Ludmilla's party. She was attractive, in her early thirties, similar in build and appearance to herself. Her nose was longer, her cheekbones higher. But in all, not a bad match.

"Were you stopped?" Ludmilla asked.

"Yes. They asked where I was going. I said to visit a friend in apartment twelve."

"You told them Tamara?" Ludmilla looked surprised. "I must warn her, in case they check."

"They won't check," Anya said contemptuously. "They couldn't even be bothered to get their hands cold looking at my *propusk*." She added, "I thought it best not to mention your name." She started taking off her coat.

"That was quick thinking, Anya. It's very brave of you to do this."

"Darling, I don't know what it's about, and I'm not going to ask. But we all have to help each other in these frightening times." She took off her coat and helped Gail on with it. It was gray, rather striking, with a big fur collar.

Now she put her hat on Gail's head, pulling it well down, as she wore it herself. She handed over her gloves and handbag.

"My *propusk*." She opened the bag and showed her where she kept it.

Gail took it out and studied it, especially her expression in the photograph. She composed her face in the mirror in an attempt to match it.

The children watched, but Ludmilla's glances kept them silent.

Boots—Gail's were sufficiently similar to make a change unnecessary. She pocketed Holz's documents and turned to face her benefactress.

Anya looked her over critically. She nodded. "Good luck. Be careful."

Minutes later, apprehension like a cold stone inside her, Gail stepped out into the freezing night. She tucked the collar well up around her face and turned toward Taganskaya Square.

The street appeared deserted. But as she neared the intersection a light was suddenly flashed in her face from a doorway. She shielded her eyes, slowing naturally. She could see nothing for the glare.

"It's me again," she said.

After a moment's inspection the flashlight was switched off and she could see two muffled figures standing in the doorway. They waved her on without a word.

Crossing the intersection, she noticed the car parked just around the corner. Its lights were out. A copy of *Pravda* was spread across the windshield to keep it from icing over. Whether anyone was inside it she couldn't see.

She walked on to Taganskaya Square, where she caught a trolleybus. No one got on behind her. She rode up Chkalovskaya Street, across the river and on around the Sadovaya Circle as far as Lermontskaya Square. There she got off and walked past the Soviet Navy Exhibition to the address on the back of the flight ticket.

It was long past office hours and she knew the Muscovites, despite a lunch break lasting up to three hours, went home promptly at six. But if the undertaker Klimenti Ivanovsky was what she believed him to be, she was confident there would be some way of contacting him.

Volga Street, she found, was a tiny side street lined with shops. They had the Spartan, anonymous look of military supply depots—all in darkness. There was a steamy-windowed cafeteria with a small line of people outside—hunched figures hugging themselves in silhouette against the cold fluorescent lighting. Sandwiched between this and a *camisiony magazeen*—a commission agency for secondhand articles—she found No. 4.

It was little more than a doorway, unlit but open. There was a confusion of boards and cards on the wall inside, showing what offices were to be found within. She was peering at these when a man with a heavy moustache and dangling earflaps pushed in past her carrying a wooden box filled with chunks of ice. He was followed by a lanky youth carrying a sack. They kicked their way through the inner door and disappeared along the hallway toward a dim light showing in the nether regions. Gail could hear distant sounds of commotion coming from this direction.

She found the sign: POKHORONNOE BURO. It was written in chalk on what looked like a school slate, which seemed to show a rather offhand attitude to death.

She moved along the hall and had not gone more than a few steps when the man came back, his box now empty. He was scowling and muttering. He slammed out of the building, evidently in a foul temper.

Gail made for the light and presently found herself in a

small space with a counter. Behind the counter was an office, with nothing to distinguish it from any other—no traditional flowers, drapes, urns. It could as well have been where you applied for travel documents or a change of apartment, except perhaps it was even more dingy. And there was a smell—a sickly, sharp, horrible smell.

As there was no one in attendance, she went on through.

The rear of the premises was clearly an extension, fairly large, absolutely bare, cold and lit by a single staring bulb. Coffins stood around on trestles—maybe eight or nine. The lanky youth and three women were fussing around one, packing ice around the corpse inside, holding handkerchiefs to their noses, dabbing their eyes emotionally, at the same time rebuking a tall, dour-faced man and a dumpy woman who stood uncooperatively by.

Gail cringed from the stench. No one took the least notice of her. She was buffeted in the back by the moustached man returning with yet more ice. It seemed he was gathering it from the street, breaking off icicles from the windowsills.

Presently it was done. Still gesticulating and remonstrating, the outraged family took tearful leave of their loved one and departed, their voices receding to the street.

The dour-faced man seemed to notice Gail for the first time.

"We are closed," he said flatly and turned his back.

"I am looking for Klimenti Ivanovsky," Gail said through her handkerchief.

The woman glanced up from her sweeping. She had a fat, nondescript face and a body to match. She nodded toward the man as if to say, That's him, and went on with her work.

The man headed past Gail into his office. Gail followed and, taking out Holz's return air ticket, held it in front of him, showing first Holz's cover name, then the scrawled address on the back. She watched his expression.

Not a flicker. He moved away from her around the office, putting things away, packing up for the night.

Gail curbed her annoyance. She asked very softly, "Can I talk freely in here, or . . . ?"

The man shrugged and repeated, "We are closed."

She followed him and showed him the Hungarian passport with Holz's photo. He barely glanced at it.

She decided then she would have to go for broke. "He missed his flight," she said. "There was a shooting. He was hurt. He needs help to get away. Both of us—we're in a desperate position."

She might as well have been talking to the furniture.

"Listen," she said evenly. "I'm not the MVD. I'm an American. I can't prove my identity here and now, but I'll give you my full details and you can check them out either through our mission at the embassy or direct with Kelland." She watched for a reaction to the name.

The man sat down and began to pull on a pair of overshoes. The woman had come in and was putting on her coat. They seemed entirely preoccupied with what they were doing.

Gail brought out Holz's wallet. "If you want proof that he's been injured, look at this!" She showed them Cabeza's blood on it, on some of the notes inside. "Do you think the MVD would have the imagination to invent that? Do you? For God's sake, can't you see I'm telling the truth?"

But the outburst won her nothing. The man and woman just continued to get themselves ready to go home.

Gail flapped her hands in despair. She turned and walked out.

"Wait." It was the woman who spoke. She came to the counter, took a blank card from a box and pushed it and a pencil in front of her.

"Your details," she said quietly. "We'll check them and be in touch."

Relieved, Gail shook her head. "You won't be able to reach me. We're on the move and we're being watched." Seeing her expression: "Oh, it's all right, I wasn't followed. But whichever way you're going to check, can't you do it now?"

The woman shook her head.

"Well, I can't come back."

"You will have to. For one thing, there will be documents."

"What kind of documents?"

"Travel passes."

"Needing photographs?"

"No."

"How long will they take?"

"A few hours, but—"

"Can't you deliver them—to a drop?"

"A drop—no. Because someone will have to clear you personally."

"Personally?"

"To debrief you. Look," the woman said severely, "you missed your plane. They will want to know why. And why you are in contact with this man"—she tapped Holz's wallet —"when it was not part of your orders. They will want to know details of the shooting. It is standard procedure when things go wrong, you must know that."

Gail knew then that Joaquín had been absolutely right; these people were involved in Sunflower to the hilt. She played her next card as he had instructed, speaking urgently.

"Listen—Montel double-crossed us and now we're stuck. Every second we remain in this city puts the operation more at risk—and that includes the pair of you, because if we're caught we'll be made to talk, and the MVD are breathing down our necks right now. So your first priority is to get rid of us fast. But fast!"

The woman glanced back over her shoulder at the man. He frowned at his overshoes.

"I'll give you my report now," Gail continued. "Then you process it, do what you like, but there can be no further contact between us. You'll deliver the travel passes to a drop at this address."

She scrawled down Ludmilla's mother-in-law's flat number in Dobryn Square. The other two were silent.

At length the man said, "Write it all down—your report. We'll see what can be done."

Gail sighed. She and Joaquín had worked out a convincing story. It was beginning to look now as though their bluff was going to work.

37

THE NEWS came through suddenly at eight o'clock the next morning. The children had just left for school. Cabeza was sitting in the bedroom, cautiously exercising his shoulder while the women tidied the apartment. The music on the radio died abruptly and a voice warned that news of national importance was about to be broadcast.

Then the reader, in terms of deep solemnity, announced that Josef Vissarionovich Stalin had been taken gravely ill.

Cabeza became as stone, his face transfigured. Ludmilla hurried to turn up the volume.

The announcer went on to say that Stalin had been stricken by a brain hemorrhage on Sunday night in his Kremlin apartment, that so far he had not responded to medical treatment. The full clinical details were then given—in a bulletin signed, the announcer said, by ten doctors headed by the new Health Minister, A. F. Tretyakov.

Ludmilla stood by the set, her mind following the announcement, her gaze on Cabeza's and Gail's reaction. Her eyes widened to rifle targets of shock.

Daily bulletins would be broadcast, the announcer was saying. The medical opinion was that Stalin would not be able to participate in government for some considerable time.

Cabeza emitted a deep rumble of sound, his face lifting, fists balling. An emotion of almost orgasmic intensity convulsed him.

Then, before Ludmilla could pour out her questions, he heaved himself up and supported himself shakily toward the roof-space door, beckoning Gail to follow, telling Ludmilla to shut them in quickly.

She obeyed, puzzled at first. Then she heard what he had anticipated—the sudden sounds of movement throughout the house. She just managed to close up the bolt-hole and unlock the outer door in time.

Her neighbors were coming out of their apartments, knocking on doors, calling to each other asking if they had heard the news. Eyes searched eyes for a lead. No one knew whether to be glad or sad; whether they *were* glad or sad; they had suppressed their true emotions for so long that they were no longer able to recognize them. Ludmilla was no exception. Cabeza's revelation had left her completely dazed.

An old man upstairs began to sing the "Internationale" in a choking voice. This triggered tears from some of the women, but whether they were tears of grief or relief, who could tell?

In the streets it was the same. The news swept through the city like a flash fire. People clustered at street corners, outside the metro stations, their faces sealed, unreadable.

Grechukha observed them from his car as he sped behind his outriders along Dzerzhinsky Street. Well, that's one cat out, he thought moodily. Time was ticking away for him and there was still no news of Cabeza or Omega. Which reminded him. He did not seem to have received yesterday's report from his Presidium surveillance team.

When he got to his office he mentioned this fact to Zapotkin.

For Zapotkin, time was running the other way. There was too much of it. Stalin was hanging on, and until he died, he, Zapotkin, was still answerable to this idiot.

"What report was that, Comrade Deputy Minister?" he inquired innocently.

"Come on," Grechukha growled. "Your eyes have been burning holes in those envelopes every day for a month!"

"Oh, *those* reports. You say there wasn't one yesterday? Strange. Would you like me to look into it?"

Grechukha said no, he would chase it up himself that afternoon. "No news of Cabeza, I suppose?"

Zapotkin shook his head. Grechukha hurried away toward the Lubianka, where yet another interrogation was due to begin.

Zapotkin knew that he had until this afternoon before the report business backfired on him. It was no use relying on Stalin to die by then. So he would have to devise some evasive action. He came to the conclusion that it was time to throw a sizable monkey wrench into Comrade Grechukha's works.

He went along to the elevator and rode up to the third floor, where State Security Minister Ignatiev had his offices.

Ignatiev still knew nothing about Grechukha's secret surveillance of the Presidium. Zapotkin thought it was about time someone slipped him the word.

Throughout the morning, Cabeza sat beside Gail in the roof space listening, somehow without listening, to the pronouncements that punctuated the radio programs every hour or so, and to Gail's quiet comments. He was back in his jail routine, conserving his energies, psyching himself for the demanding thing that was approaching. And all the while he rolled his left shoulder gently, willing the muscles to knit, the blood to circulate, the pain to lessen.

They learned that the temporary direction of the nation's affairs had been taken over by Stalin's deputy, Georgi Malenkov, in conjunction with other members of the "inner circle"—Molotov, Beria, Khrushchev, Bulganin, Voroshilov, Kaganovich—and that this directorate had issued a call to the nation to display "unity, solidarity, a firm spirit and vigilance." All the old clichés, Cabeza thought, adding up to the warning: *Don't try to exploit the situation or we'll have your guts!*

Rolling the shoulder . . . the repetition of pain deadening itself . . . his eyes tracing the bluish light on Gail's even features beside him.

Apart from Ludmilla, she was the only blossom in a storm-wracked landscape. Like genista, the wild Spanish broom that brings golden sunlight to the darkest day. The darkest night, too, he mused, recalling last night when she had lain with him again, her presence luminous amid the pain, a healing balm pressed to him, yet recoiling, fearful of arousing him to a repetition of the night before, arousing him nevertheless. She had been torn then between response and rejection—a caring nurse versus the phoenix, rising again from the ashes to torture her with concern for his recovery—until the truth of it had come to her: that the phoenix was the symbol of the man, that its resurrection was *his* resurrection, his recovery; that, far from taking his strength, she would be compounding it, leading him out from his darkness.

Ah, then how she had relented! How she had helped and guided and drawn him into herself and willed and, ultimately, transported him across the threshold where his senses stumbled before, and on into that rising sun that surpasses description.

The joy of it was still with them. But where in the end could it lead? he wondered. They were adrift now on a rising sea that would presently spill out to swamp every shore. Would it carry them with it, or would they drown here in the vortex? If the former, where would they end up? Where could they even hide? The Agency would scour the world for them, that was certain. For they were the possessors of a secret that could set the nations of the earth at war.

But there was the midday time signal. If their bluff had worked and Kelland had given orders for them to be speeded out of Moscow, their travel documents should at this moment be on their way to Dobryn Square.

Grechukha returned to his office at one o'clock in a frustrated mood. The interrogation had provided him with nothing fresh against Omega, and now, to cap it all, he had just heard that the traitor had been selected as a member of the interregnum government! He was gaining in strength with every hour while all he, Grechukha, was managing to do was tread water. And worse was to come.

Zapotkin had already gone to lunch, but had left a message to say that Semyon Ignatiev wanted to see him in his office at 2:00 P.M. sharp.

Arriving there on the dot, Grechukha was confronted by his superior's glowering countenance.

"I have learned by mere chance," Ignatiev began, "that you are conducting a surveillance operation on the members of the Presidium of the Supreme Soviet!"

Grechukha wondered by what "mere chance," but another cat was out and he knew he had a fight on his hands. He had somehow to rationalize his actions without revealing that he was almost sure he knew the identity of Omega. Comrade Ignatiev would learn that over his dead body!

He argued that his orders in this matter had come direct from the Leader himself, and that while the Leader still lived, it was his duty to carry them out.

"The Leader," Ignatiev reminded him, "is now Georgi Malenkov, in committee with other members of the Presidium. And you are having him and them watched! You are spying on the government, and I won't allow it, Georgi Feodor. I will not allow it!"

Two hours later Grechukha left the office, his clown's face a mask. So thwarted was he that instead of returning to work, he went down to his car and, dismissing the chauffeur, drove inexpertly, for he was an unpracticed driver, away.

The coming of darkness found him seated behind the wheel outside his summer *dacha* in Kuskovo. The thawings of the warm day were beginning to freeze again and it had started to snow, and he was by no means sure whether he had the skill to negotiate the drive home safely. But that was the least of his worries.

He had chosen to build this *dacha* at Kuskovo because of its marvelous castle and park and artificial lake, once the summer residence of the counts of Sheremetyev. The connotations were appetizingly decadent and privileged. Not that this three-bedroom frame house could be said to fall into that category. But still the overtones were ever there to remind him of the rewards available to the cool *gorodki* player.

And now those rewards were in jeopardy. He was being ordered to discard one of the two aces that could ensure his survival when the big reshuffle came. To fail to obey that order would be to kiss survival good-bye. But to obey it would, too.

Peering out at his little enclave of capitalism, he decided then to turn a deaf ear to Ignatiev's instructions and pull out all the stops to deliver both Omega and Cabeza without delay.

He headed back into the city, skidding and slithering. Finding himself within a block or two of Taganskaya Square, he turned on impulse toward the Embankment and, a few minutes later, stopped outside No. 64.

He sat there for a short time, communing with his suspicions, eyeing the darkened windows of Apartment 8, debating the quickest, surest way of bringing this Cabeza business to a head.

As he watched he saw one adult and two smaller figures approaching along the street. Could this be they now—the doctor and her brats? Yes, there was his man tailing them.

He watched them go in, watched the lights go on in the apartment. All disappointingly normal. Now she was drawing the drapes. He watched for a moment to see if any telltale male figure should appear in silhouette against them.

After a few minutes he started the engine and drove thoughtfully away.

Gail straightened up out of the roof space, reaching back to help Cabeza. He came out slowly, blinking, smiling at the children, groaning a little with pain as he stretched his cramped limbs.

Ludmilla was peeping across the street from behind the curtains. Cabeza caught the sound of a departing car.

"Qué pasa?"

She turned back, evincing relief, shaking her head, and held out an envelope to him mutely.

In it were two travel passes and two *propuski*—in the names of Nicholas and Katrina Sukachev. With these was a deck of twenty ten-ruble notes and a typed list of instructions: "6 March '53—Proceed to Kazan Station, Komsomolskaya Square—buy tickets on the Trans-Siberian express to Vladivostok, scheduled departure 7 A.M. Leave train at Khabarovsk. Wait on platform until contacted. Remainder of journey will be by car and U.S. army plane to destination South Korea."

Cabeza glanced triumphantly at Gail as she finished reading it over his shoulder. South Korea! She looked astonished.

"It worked. You did well." But his brow clouded as he turned to Ludmilla. "Not until Friday. You have us for another full day."

"Bravo!" cried the children.

Ludmilla smiled, masking the dismay she felt.

Grechukha was halfway back to his office when a sudden thought struck him. The doctor's elder child, the girl . . . It was simple arithmetic. She must be Cabeza's daughter!

Why hadn't he realized that before? That all the time he had had the perfect weapon for levering Cabeza out into the open right there in his hand!

38

THE NEXT morning's bulletin said Stalin's condition remained grave. During the past twenty-four hours there had been no substantial changes in the lungs or organs of the abdominal cavity. A blood test showed an increase of white corpuscles. Temperature high, reaching 38.6 degrees. Still serious respiratory disturbances . . . the heart enlarged to a moderate degree . . . fluctuating arrhythmia . . . Treatment consisted of the administration of oxygen and camphor preparations, caffeine, strophanthin and glucose. Leeches were used to draw blood for the second time.

He can't hang on for much longer, Grechukha thought. He arrived at his office full of determination. Today was to be the day. It *had* to be. He had scarcely removed his topcoat when he heard Zapotkin quietly answering a call from Reception.

"Who? Never heard of him. Well, tell him he can't."

"Who is it?" Grechukha called through.

"Oh, just someone without an appointment."

"I said *who?*"

Zapotkin hesitated. He mumbled, "A Mikhailovsky."

Grechukha reacted. "Tell them to send him up." He shot his aide a hard look. Mikhailovsky was the head of his surveillance team. Had Zapotkin known that and purposely been trying to get rid of him?

Avoiding his eye, Zapotkin came into the office and deposited some papers on the desk, fiddled with something and went out again. A moment later, Mikhailovsky came in—stocky, pockmarked, hands glued deep in pockets.

"I've been waiting for your directive, comrade."

"Directive?" Grechukha shut the door on Zapotkin's inquisitive face.

"What action to take. You read my last report?"

The report! Grechukha told him it never arrived.

Mikhailovsky frowned. "Well, it was signed for. By him." He jerked his head.

Grechukha took an angry step toward the door, then thought better of it.

"Have you got a copy on you?"

Mikhailovsky said he hadn't but, in short, as he knew, they had been keeping an eye on the prime suspect's day driver.

"He runs a lot of errands for his master. Several times recently he's been popping into an office on Krasny Street. We thought nothing of it at first, that the clerk there was a relative or something. Then we checked and found he wasn't. So we started following him, too. He lives out beyond the Circle. Him and his wife. She works with him in the office."

"What sort of office?"

"Burial office. I got to thinking, suppose this is it—the way our suspect passes information to the Americans? So I scrounged a radio location van and beamed in on their flat and had them run all-night frequency sweeps until they picked up something."

"And they did?"

"They did, comrade."

"Magnificent!" Grechukha leaped to his feet. "Well done! Magnificent!"

"The transmission lasted only a moment. Prerecorded and speeded up, I reckon. But we taped it. Ciphers are trying to decode it now. But," he added, lowering his voice, "for my money, we've got our man. Omega is who we thought he was!"

Grechukha was pacing like an engine. "Right. Now, listen—I don't want anyone else in on this. Just you and your team. I'll come with you."

Moments later they hurried away together, Grechukha without a word or glance at Zapotkin.

When he was sure they were clear, Zapotkin made two quick phone calls. Then he went in to Grechukha's desk and switched off the intercom set he had managed to trigger before Mikhailovsky's arrival.

The simultaneous swoops on the burial office and Omega's driver drew blanks. Both birds had suddenly and mysteriously flown. Klimenti Ivanovsky had even left his overshoes.

Grechukha stood among the coffins, holding his nose and scowling. "Is their apartment being watched?"

Mikhailovsky said that it was.

Well, that was something. But how had it happened?

Grechukha suddenly saw it all quite clearly. Zapotkin was Omega's man! It was he who had gone to Ignatiev. The ploy hadn't quite worked, because he, Grechukha, had continued his inquiries. But it had castrated him. It had left him out on his own with just Mikhailovsky and his men for backup—at war with one of the most powerful and feared men in all Russia!

Grechukha's jaw hardened. Very well. He would make it a battle to the death!

He could no longer use his own office. So be it. He would set up a field headquarters here! He told Mikhailovsky to pitch the coffins out in the alley, get in a stenographer, bring him copies of all the Omega surveillance reports, get his men to search the Ivanovskys' flat, find that radio, all the evidence he could lay his hands on, witnesses, neighbors, staff from the adjacent offices. He would do the interrogating. Together, in a few hours, they were going to build up a case against the Deputy Chairman of the Presidium of the Supreme Soviet that would expose him to the nation as an American spy!

Kelland sat in the big bulletproof Zil parked outside the Presidium building. A pass signed by the commandant had afforded him unobtrusive entry to the Kremlin. A password to the chauffeur had provided him with instant access to Omega's waiting car. The steamy windows did the rest, enabling him to sit here in the very penetralia of the USSR in absolute anonymity.

Though the driver had politely shown him the button release of the liquor cabinet, he had resisted the invitation, as he resisted now the continuing impulse to glance at his wristwatch, finger the gummy discomfort of his facial disguise, knuckle a peephole in the steam, inquire of the driver how long he thought his master would be. He held his impatience in check, until presently footsteps sounded in the snow outside. The door opened and Omega got in. Seeing Kelland, he grunted and triggered up the dividing glass before sitting back and unbuttoning his overcoat.

Kelland glanced at the charcoal-gray Savile Row suit, Sulka shirt, Italian silk tie, recognizing them as part of the flow of Western sartorial luxuries he had smuggled in to Omega over the years. His eyes lifted to the quirkish, repellent face. That he couldn't abide this man was neither here nor there. Looking at the mean, down-turned mouth, the gleaming pince-nez, he disciplined himself to see only the cobalt reaches of Lake Nahuel Huapi reflecting the Andean snows.

"Well?" cried the petulant voice. "Out with it! Have you found him—that damned Spaniard?"

"I think so."

There was a moment of almost tangible relief on the other's part. Then he said snappishly, "Not a moment too soon! The Leader's sinking fast—a matter of just a few hours now. So you're quite sure it'll be safe for me to move?"

Kelland hesitated. He wasn't sure. Nothing was ever sure with "that damned Spaniard." But he took his life, his whole future in his hands, and said "Yes."

"You do understand," Omega said, "that if you've miscalculated and I go down, I'll take you with me?"

Kelland compressed his lips and nodded. He had just discovered something in himself: that it pained him to have to eliminate a rough diamond like the General in order to ensure the survival of this son of a bitch.

He wondered what Cabeza himself would say if he knew on whose behalf he was being sacrificed, that Omega was none other than his despised enemy, ex-Minister of State Security —Lavrenti Pavlovich Beria!

* * *

Arrests were made, detainees herded in. Grechukha's interrogations went on throughout the morning. And afternoon. The radio transmitter was found under the floorboards of the Ivanovskys' flat. Evidence accumulated.

Suddenly, referring to the Ivanovsky surveillance reports, Grechukha did a mental double take. There was an entry dated yesterday—timed noon-plus—stating that the burial clerk proceeded by trolleybus to No. 18 Dobryn Square, an apartment block, entered, after two minutes came out and returned by the same means to the burial office.

Grechukha wracked his memory. Dobryn Square . . . In what context had he heard that address recently?

On the Ludmilla Patolichev surveillance reports, he remembered. It was where the children went after school.

That suggested just one thing: that there was a link between Beria and Cabeza! That Beria knew about, perhaps even planned, Stalin's assassination!

The realization sent a tremor of ecstasy through him. This intelligence was unique. Only he possessed it. It made him the key figure in a power play of such proportions that for a moment he wondered if he was equipped to handle it with his limited resources.

Then he told himself, *Live like a wolf.* Wrap it up yourself, hand Malenkov the completed package and a seat on the next Presidium will be yours!

Now he remembered yesterday's happy inspiration. He told Mikhailovsky to send four men to Dobryn Square and pick up the two children as they came back from school.

"Bring them back here, comrade?"

Grechukha said yes. Then he changed his mind. The activity and violence of the current interrogations would frighten and confuse them. Confusion was a weapon to be used to effect. He wanted them quietly on ice until he was ready to prize open their little minds. The Lubianka was out. So was his office. The only other safe place he could think of was his *dacha*.

"Take them to Kuskovo and hold them there till I'm ready for them." He added, "Tell the men to handle them gently."

* * *

Ludmilla was just finishing her afternoon rounds at the hospital when a telephone call came through from her mother-in-law reproaching her for having collected the children from school herself without having warned her.

Ludmilla hammered down the phone and rang the school. She called around the several places where the children might have gone. No one had seen them.

Cabeza and Gail stared at her in dismay when she returned with the news. The explanation was inescapable—and devastating! They knew that Tineka and Mikki could not possibly withstand interrogation, and God forbid that they should try.

Ludmilla beat at Cabeza wildly with her fists. "Oh, you fool! You fool! Wasn't it enough last time, what you did to my life? Now it's to all of us. My children—you've killed us!"

Cabeza caught her blows and held her, resistant, weeping, to him. It was true. The woman had said it in Almuñecar. The same words. The same truth. *You have killed us all!* But there was nothing to be gained by remorse; hope lay only in resolution.

"If going now would help . . ."

"Too late, too late!"

"So we must remain calm and use our heads. Who do you know?"

"Know?"

"With influence. You must do everything as an innocent woman would. First you call the police. You report the children are missing. You think perhaps they have met with an accident. You ask them please to make inquiries and call you back."

Ludmilla wailed, "What is the point?"

"When they do not call back, you become frantic. You call a friend with the most influence. You tell him you have been victimized lately by the MVD. You do not know what for. You think it is part of the Doctors' Plot. And now your children have disappeared. You can only conclude it is for the same reason. You beg your friend to intervene."

"But I don't know anyone!"

"Think. Your husband is in the navy. Who is his commanding officer?"

Ludmilla quieted a little. "We met Kuznetsov once."

"Who is he?"

"Vice admiral. He is in the Council of Ministers."

"*Bueno*. So first make your call to the police. Wait half an hour, then call Kuznetsov. Go."

He released her. Ludmilla stared at him hopelessly.

"Go!" He thrust her toward the door.

It was close on 8:00 P.M. when Vice Admiral N. G. Kuznetsov got through to Ignatiev. The State Security Minister, having received the news earlier that Stalin was failing fast, had canceled a dinner engagement to consult with his chiefs about the security measures to be taken immediately following the Leader's death. He was annoyed to be interrupted on such a trivial matter, but he told Kuznetsov that he would see it was looked into.

Indeed, he had his secretary call Grechukha's office. Zapotkin answered. He, too, said he would look into it. He hung up pensively. So Grechukha had had the children picked up. He was up to something. Working in secret now. But where?

Zapotkin had been trying all day to locate him, to keep tabs on him. These were the most crucial hours in his life. It was his job to foil any move that could prejudice Beria's accession to power. And Grechukha had discovered this; there could be no other explanation for his disappearance. And not knowing what he was doing made Zapotkin's scalp crawl.

If only Stalin would *die*, he thought. Die, you damn Georgian, *die!*

At 9:30 P.M. Stalin did just that.

His last hours had been ones of slow asphyxia. His breathing became shorter and shorter, his complexion darker, his lips blackening, his features becoming unrecognizable.

The doctors read the signs. Word was passed. Those members of the Presidium who were not already present began to arrive in their cars. They entered the room that smelled of sickness and stood awkwardly, moved profoundly by what was happening. For whether they loved or hated Stalin, he was a giant, under whose spell they had lived for a quarter of a century. A whole era was ending here in Kuntsevo. Nothing in their lives would ever be the same again.

Svetlana stood as one transfixed. Time and again Bulganin and others pressed her to sit down, but she remained rigid, staring at the distorting features of the father she both loved and hated, who had been both wonderfully gentle with her and utterly remote, who, though she had never admitted it even to herself, had murdered her mother. And ever since her death, she had blamed her mother for it! Her whole life had been a paradox, as had those of all the people in this room. And the love and hate in them would not mix. The air seemed full of electrical discharge, the rumbling of inner thunder.

Beria alone seemed impervious, aping only the emotions the others felt, leaning close to the deathbed, glasses agleam, his face dancing through a bewildering series of expressions.

If he was waiting for a sign, he was not disappointed. Stalin was choking, choking. Suddenly his eyes opened. They stared terrifyingly around at everyone in the room. Shock showed on every face but Beria's. He leaned forward, his lips parted, as if to catch his master's eye.

But Stalin's gaze swept beyond him. He lifted his left hand, pointing upward in an apocalyptic gesture of such menace that Svetlana gave an involuntary cry.

Then the hand fell and he was dead.

Slowly the face drained of its darkness, becoming pale and serene.

There was utter silence in the room. No one moved or spoke. The fire crackling in the corner was the only sound.

Suddenly Beria straightened, his face transfigured by unreadable emotion. He marched to the door and pushed his way out through the retainers and staff who were clustered there.

His voice sounded from the hall, shattering the silence of the death chamber.

"Khrustalyov—my car!"

Cabeza, Gail and Ludmilla sat in tortured silence in the apartment. It was 10:00 P.M. The MVD had never called back. Kuznetsov had been onto Ignatiev three times, with no result. There was nothing more they could do now but wait.

By eleven that night, Grechukha, heavy-eyed but exultant, had compiled a whole dossier on the Ivanovskys. Their neighbors had contributed some useful descriptions of visitors to their apartment. The most recent had been a tall, blue-eyed, sharp-featured man speaking Russian with an American accent. Grechukha was, above all else, at pains to establish the American connection. If this man was a CIA agent there was a good chance he would be on file in Records.

He bundled Mikhailovsky and the two informants into his car and drove them to Headquarters. One positive identification was all he needed, and State Security Records was in the basement, so there was little danger of running into Zapotkin or Ignatiev.

As they approached along Dzerzhinsky Street he was astonished to see that every window in the building was lit. Moreover, cars and army trucks were massed outside, parked the whole length of the thoroughfare.

On entering the lobby, Grechukha found it full of armed troops. They were milling about in their heavy overcoats, carbines slung, stamping snow everywhere, staring around at the palatial décor as if their presence here were as much a mystery to them as it was to the resident staff.

"What's going on?" Grechukha addressed an officer.

"We are not sure, comrade. We've just arrived. We're waiting for orders."

Grechukha turned to one of the staff.

"All I know is they've taken over my switchboard," the man complained.

"They?"

"Army Signals."

Grechukha frowned. They were MVD troops, a detachment of the 500,000-strong crack force allocated to the preservation of state security. They operated under direct command of the Minister himself. What was Semyon Ignatiev up to?

Grechukha thought it best to dispose of his mission first and inquire afterward. He steered Mikhailovsky and the witnesses through the crush. The corridors beyond were clear. He led them quickly toward Records.

"Georgi!" A voice echoed after him.

Glancing back, he saw the handsome figure of Boris Likachev detach itself from the confusion of the lobby.

Grechukha paused. He told Mikhailovsky to carry on and moved back toward his friend.

"Sticking your neck out a bit, aren't you?" Likachev inquired wryly.

Grechukha stiffened. "Meaning what?"

"You haven't heard?"

"What, man?"

"Stalin's dead, Georgi. The Old Man has snuffed it. Lavrenti Beria has taken over your ministry."

"You're joking," Grechukha whispered.

Likachev spread a manicured hand. "Look around you. What do you think this lot are here for—the chess finals?"

"He can't! I mean, it's not constitutional."

"Don't tell me, Georgi. With or without sanction, he's *done* it. He's ousted Ignatiev and planted his flag. And if you know what's good for you, you'll remove yourself from town for a few days till things quiet down. Now—the back way." And he grasped Grechukha's arm and began to steer him.

Grechukha resisted fiercely. "What are you saying?"

"I've just been up to your office. Zapotkin is in charge there. He's issued orders for your arrest."

Grechukha sat out in his car, wishing it were not so conspicuous, waiting for Mikhailovsky and the witnesses to rejoin him. So his suspicions had been fully justified. As State Security Minister from 1938 to 1945, Beria still had top-level connections in the MVD military. No doubt he had invoked these now as a first step to taking over the government.

Well, it still wasn't too late, he thought. In fact Malenkov and the others would be more likely to accept his findings now. *Avid* to accept them! They still commanded the huge bulk of the Soviet army. There could be a civil war. Well, so be it. He would see the country in flames before he submitted to arrest and execution at the orders of a traitor!

Ah, here were Mikhailovsky and the witnesses now. As

346

soon as they were in the car he ordered his chauffeur to drive them back to the burial office.

Mikhailovsky's expression was divided between puzzlement at the military presence in the building and satisfaction. The witnesses had made a positive identification, he announced. The Ivanovskys' visitor had been John Harman, alias Heinrich Schuster, alias David Kelland, alias . . .

Grechukha cut him short. He knew the man! *His case against Beria was complete!*

39

CABEZA, GAIL and Ludmilla waited in silence in the darkened apartment. They had turned the lights out, the better to watch the street. Though it was now 4:00 A.M., there was no thought of sleeping.

In three hours' time the Vladivostok train would pull out, but all idea of escape had now been abandoned. Cabeza refused to leave Ludmilla to face alone whatever would happen. He had told Gail that there was no sense in all three of them facing the firing squad, that she must make the attempt alone. She replied evenly that she had made her decision back in the Metropole. If he stayed, she stayed; and that was the end of it.

That end was now approaching.

Grechukha arrived at his *dacha* a few minutes after four o'clock. He came alone, driving a black Pobeda, having dismissed Mikhailovsky, his men, his chauffeur and too-conspicuous car. There were four men here with the children. They were sufficient to handle all that remained to be done. He had the dossier of compiled statements beside him. There was more evidence, of course, to come, but what he had was in itself conclusive. His mood was apprehensive, but grimly optimistic.

As he hurried up the *dacha* path, the door was opened to him.

"Where are they?"

"Sleeping, Comrade Deputy Minister," the man said, stifling a yawn. "At least the boy is. The girl—"

"You find any food for them?"

"Yes. Yes, we took the liberty of—"

"Well, find me something. Coffee will do."

Two of the men were struggling up off the easy chairs, striving to come awake, appear alert. The house was cold. They had found blankets and switched on the electric heaters, but that made little impression on the chill of the unoccupied building.

Grechukha kept on his coat and hat. This wouldn't take long. He glanced in the guest bedroom.

The children were huddled under the covers of the twin beds his wife had wangled only last month from the Kremlin supply warehouse. The girl was awake, her eyes watching him fearfully from under the quilt. The fourth MVD man lay sprawled asleep in a chair in the corner.

Grechukha kicked his feet. "Out."

He waited till the man had scrambled up and removed himself, then shut the door and turned, his mouth flexing into a grin as he snatched the covers off the two curled-up bodies, noting the girl's slim legs in their school stockings, the sturdiness of the boy. Nice-looking youngsters. The girl was a bit like his own eldest daughter.

Grechukha was sentimental about children. Like Stalin. The difference being that Stalin would have had his Security minions do what he was about to do. Even Stalin. But he, Grechukha, had learned to bypass his sentiments. He could caress a living creature, animal or human, with genuine affection, and the next moment twist its neck without any perceptible change of gear. He regarded this as a gift. A rare gift that had contributed much to his success as an extractor of confessions. It stemmed from a realpolitik awareness of the priorities.

"Now," he announced, smiling. "I'm in a hurry, so I'm not going to mess about. I want straight answers, understand?"

The girl had moved quickly to her brother and put her arms around him protectively.

"I want to know where your father is," Grechukha told her. "That's all. Nothing else. I'm not going to hurt him. I just want to talk with him. When you've told me, you can go home."

"My father?" Tineka looked taken aback. "He's at sea. He's in the Baltic."

"Your *real* father, girl. Don't get clever with me. Cabeza—Joaquín Cabeza." Seeing her totally blank expression, he huffed a sigh. "All right, don't let's quibble—the man your mother is hiding, that's clear enough, isn't it? Where is he?"

Tineka's eyes flickered. "I . . . don't know what you mean."

The flicker was enough. And he had sensed something from the boy, too.

"No?" Grechukha began to stroke Mikki's cheek, very gently, menacingly. "What do *you* say, young fellow?"

Mikki shook his head. He was very frightened.

"Been told not to tell, have you? Well, there's nothing wrong with a little loyalty." He added softly, "In the right place."

Tineka sensed the coming violence. She screamed, "Don't you dare hurt him!"

Grechukha smiled. "You're his little mother, I see. *Mamochka*. Well, there's nothing wrong with that, either. Nothing at all. You're both nice children. Very nice children." He waited. "But I am in rather a hurry."

His smile began to fix, the ripple-rings of his cheek muscles tight around his mouth, diminishing toward the soft flesh that hung over his collar.

Suddenly he hurled Tineka aside and grasped Mikki's ankles and wrenched him off the bed upside down, raising him till his head was suspended above the floor.

"Quick!" he rapped. "Where is he? Where's the man?"

Tineka stared in horror as he began to jerk Mikki up and down, preparing, it seemed, to dash his brains out.

"At our flat!" she blurted.

"Now?"

"Yes! Don't hurt Mikki, please—*please!*"

"Where in the flat?"

"In the attic. Please put him down!"

Grechukha searched her face. After a long moment he suddenly heaved Mikki up and dumped him on the bed with a guffaw, bouncing him playfully.

"See? Wasn't so bad, was it? You like a game, don't you, young fellow?" He pounded the bedsprings, jouncing him up and down.

Mikki struggled away from him, almost weeping. "You told! You told!"

Tineka tried to clasp him in her arms, but he pushed her away, shouting, "We promised!"

"Never mind," Grechukha said. "It's all over now. Get yourselves dressed. I'll take you home."

He led them back into the living room. A cup of coffee was waiting for him. He stood sipping it while the children put on their coats. A sudden thought occurred to him. He unlocked a drawer and took out his old-issue automatic, checked it and put it in his pocket.

"You're all armed, I take it?" he asked the men.

They flashed their own weapons wordlessly.

Tineka stared, horrified. "But you said you weren't going to hurt him, that you just wanted to talk!"

"He's a dangerous man, little mother."

"He's ill and weak. He had an accident."

"Did he now." Grechukha sounded relieved. "Well, that should simplify matters."

"I don't know why you're making such a fuss," Tineka cried. "He's done nothing wrong. Not very. He's just in Moscow when he shouldn't be."

Grechukha laughed grimly. "You can say that again. But we have to be careful. He may have a gun."

"He hasn't. I know he hasn't. You've got it all wrong."

"Are you sure of that?"

"Yes. Yes, I'm sure. He's a kind man. He has no gun."

Grechukha glanced at his men. "Better and better." He led the way out. "Put them in my car. Follow in yours."

They emerged into the icy shock of early-morning darkness, their breath exploding before them, Grechukha pausing to lock up, the men and children scrunching out into the lane where the cars stood frost-white under the crystalline birches.

In moments Grechukha joined the children in his car, his

351

heart beginning to pound as he saw the fat dossier on the seat. He knew he was going to win now. Coaxing the motor to life, grinding the gears, the Sheremetyev Castle out there huge in the blackness to goad him to finality . . . His old enemy Cabeza . . . ! He spun the wheels impatiently.

The lights of the city now. And sudden traffic—all moving the same way. Taillights bloodying the snow. Strings of them, like ruby necklaces. At this hour? He hammered the brakes, skidding sideways, just missing a truck. An army truck. A convoy of army trucks.

He crawled past them, echelon after echelon, all making toward the city—troop carriers, tanks, guns . . .

In the darkened apartment the snow-reflected gleam of headlights dilated to fill the room.

Cabeza sat up stiffly, the rib pain shooting through his body. Ludmilla and Gail were on their feet and at the window before the car came to a stop in the street below.

Peering out, they saw the golden splash of headlights suck back into the car as the driver killed the lights and motor, saw the bulky shape of him emerge and come around, belly thrusting, to the rear passenger door, open it and haul out the children.

Ludmilla uttered a stifled cry. She turned to rush to the apartment door, but Gail caught her and held her tight, waiting for Cabeza's instruction.

Grechukha stood staring back impatiently for signs of the following car. Where the hell had they got to? He had built up an impetus now. His energies rushed against this sudden dam, exploding in a curse. They must have got snarled up in the convoy.

He snatched a glance up at the windows of the apartment. In darkness. Good. Surprise. Use it—don't delay. He called softly toward the church. Then again along the street.

He waited, feeling the children shudder in fear and cold. Lights flashed in his eyes and then were dipped as the four men came to him from different directions. They had heard nothing of Stalin's death, Beria's takeover. They gathered around him silently, glancing at the children, puzzled, waiting for orders. It was like holding fast in the front line. The enemy close. Grechukha felt a thrill of excitement.

He murmured to two of them to stay with the children. The other two he steered into the building. He motioned one to guard the hall. The other he sent to guard the rear door.

He strode silently up the stairs alone. A sick man should give him no trouble. The element of surprise was on his side. Let it never be said he was too proud to do his own dirty work!

He reached the landing outside Apartment 8. Very cautiously he tried the door handle. Locked. No problem. These houses were made of paper.

He stood back against the rail and drew his gun, released the safety catch. He took a short run and planted a boot in the region of the handle.

The door crashed back, splintering. A moment of regaining his balance, and he was in, fumbling for the light switch. The room leaped to brilliance.

As in a flash photo he saw the man stretched out on the settee, blankets and coats drawn over him, the two women curled up in easy chairs. The women struggled to their feet, blinded, shocked.

"Don't move!"

He aimed the gun at the man's forehead—Cabeza's forehead, Cabeza's hair—no mistaking that peasant skullcap! Yes, it was the Spaniard, all right, and he did look sick— beardless, as in the Montel passport photo, but his cheeks thinner, paler than in the photo.

Grechukha stood, savoring the moment, waiting for Cabeza to recognize him. He watched the realization come slowly, the alien eyes widen—eyes that had defied and insulted him nightly in the Lubianka for almost a year.

"Yes, look well, Spaniard—it's me!" Grechukha pulled off his hat as if to prove it. Yes, the bastard knew him now. And the look on his face was a joy to see. A joy.

Cabeza felt the amazement in him sharpen to excruciating memory. It brought with it a host of images so nightmarish that it was all he could do not to abandon his pretense and hurl himself headlong into the roar of the gun and tear the Russian's eyes from their sockets then and there. He lay there trembling, watching the eyes watch him, drink in his hate, taunt him with it. Grechukha seemed to give him this moment gladly. Then he said to the women, "Get his coat. Get him up."

Neither of them moved. Ludmilla stood as though petrified. Gail seemed robbed of all volition, her arms folded oddly across her chest.

"I said, 'Get his coat'! And you women get yours. You're all under arrest. There's a wall waiting for you outside the city. Hurry!"

Ludmilla moved then, like a dreamer. She took down the coat and carried it to the settee. She leaned over Cabeza, and for a moment her body masked his.

Gail unfolded her arms. There was a hammer in her hand. She brought it down with all her strength on Grechukha's wrist.

The clatter of the gun to the floor was lost in his bark of agony. He jackknifed over his wrist, his blood vessels swelling. He made a blind move to retrieve the gun, but a woman's heel stamped on his hand.

When at last he lifted his crimson face, it was to stare into the muzzle of the silenced Luger in Cabeza's hand.

Cabeza pushed the covering off himself, the gun steady, and sat up, the gun now not so steady, beginning to quiver as his intention to use the man as a hostage came into head-on conflict with the more violent demands of his emotions.

But before he could act, the growing drone of a motor and the rupture of tires on ice sounded from the street.

Ludmilla sped to the window in time to see a car grit to a stop below and four men get out of it.

Cabeza froze, his mind struggling to regain control, to make a calm decision.

"Open the window," he told her.

As she did so, he signaled Grechukha with the gun.

"Stop them."

Grechukha stared at him, his face a clown's mask of pain. He shook his head.

Cabeza dropped the aim of the gun till it was sighted on the Russian's genitals. He began to squeeze the trigger.

Grechukha moved convulsively. He uttered a half-cry and ran to the window. He shouted out: "Wait!" He stared back at Cabeza and the gun. It was still aimed at his loins. He clasped his hands over the spot fearfully.

"Now, speak calmly or you will die a eunuch," Cabeza told him. "Say now that you have made a mistake. That Joaquín Cabeza is not here. That he never was here. Tell them the operation is canceled and they are to go home. All of them. Including the watchers."

"And to release my children!" Ludmilla added.

Grechukha stared at them, his mind staggering, groping for an out. His eyes began to zigzag. Cabeza read the signs—that he was about to shout a warning. He lashed out with his foot, sent a chair slamming across the room.

"Do it!"

The command shocked Grechukha out of his resolve. The zigzagging stopped. He licked his dry lips.

He leaned out of the window and repeated Cabeza's order to his men.

Cabeza listened to make sure he sounded convincing. Then he motioned him to shut the window and Gail to watch from the darkened bedroom to make sure that order was obeyed. Ludmilla clawed her fingers before Grechukha's face.

"If you have done anything to my children . . . !" she hissed.

After several long moments the car outside started up and drove away.

The sudden clatter of feet on the stairs told that the children were on the way up.

Now a second, more distant motor sobbed to life—the car at the intersection, Cabeza guessed. Its sound diminished and presently Gail came back into the room with a nod.

"They've all gone." She looked astounded that anything conceived in such desperation should have worked so effectively.

The children burst in. They ran to their mother, and for a moment there was an emotional outpouring of words and tears of relief. Cabeza never once removed his eyes from Grechukha's. He felt strange, drained. And this was only the beginning.

"Did he hurt you?" he asked the children quietly.

"He made me tell him," Tineka cried. "I couldn't help it. He was going to do something awful to Mikki. I just—"

355

"Did he hurt you?" Cabeza repeated.

"No. But I broke my promise to you. I'm dreadfully—"

"It does not matter, *niña.*"

"It *does* matter. I should have lied. I should have invented something, but—"

"Shh, darling." Ludmilla pressed the child's head to her breast. She held them both tightly.

"Sit over there." Cabeza motioned Grechukha with the gun. "In the chair. Open your coat. Do it slowly."

Grechukha obeyed. "You're wasting your time, peasant. You can't get away. Every street patrol, every exit point in the Soviet Union has your picture."

"As *Pravda* will have yours," Cabeza said. "Among the death notices." He told Gail to search him.

"You people never change," Grechukha said.

"Arm's length, *muchacha,*" Cabeza warned. "Not in line with the gun."

"At least once you were your own man," Grechukha went on abrasively. "Now look at you. A paid lackey of American imperialism. Hired assassin. Too stupid to know what you've done, even. You've let in Beria, that's what you've done. Your old enemy. Brilliant. The Cheka man—the old boss of the NKVD you hated so much—you've let him back in! Your interrogation—*he* ordered it, not me. And gave me hell because I couldn't break you! I owe you for that, Cabeza. And I'm going to have that pound of flesh off you. Water torture—that was child's play. You haven't had a smell of what can be done to a man yet!"

Cabeza told him to be silent. He was thinking.

Gail signified that he was carrying no other weapon, and moved away to the other side of the room.

"This was the man who . . . ?" Ludmilla stared at Cabeza.

"Yes, Doctor," Grechukha said evenly. "I could have been his friend. I told him, 'There is no point in resisting. We will destroy you anyway. You are in the wrong. Be a man, admit it. You say you adopt our philosophy, you come here as our guest, you eat our food, spend our rubles, and then do not accept our rules. Confess,' I begged him. 'Say you are wrong, serve your time in the mines and we will forgive you.'"

"What's left of you!" Ludmilla interposed harshly.

"But what does he do?" Grechukha shook his head. "He

356

resists. He inflicts torture on himself. He starves himself to a bag of bones. Makes trouble for everyone. And blames it on—who? *Me*—who wanted only to show him how to be a good citizen."

"A willing slave, you mean!" Ludmilla said, her voice full of passion. "That was all you were there for—to recruit slave labor for a system that cannot be made to work without it."

"Another traitor," Grechukha sneered. "You are burying yourself with your tongue, woman."

"I am already dead," Ludmilla retorted. "Or I would not dare to open my mouth. But now it is open, I do this—!" She strode toward him and spat full in his face. "That is for the things you did to my husband, whose only crime was that he cared for the people!"

Grechukha recoiled, but only for an instant. The next, he was out of the chair, seizing her, twisting her to face the gun, ducking to shield himself behind her body.

"Thank you, Doctor. You are as stupid as the man you avenge."

Gripping her around the waist till her feet dangled, he sidled toward the door.

Cabeza managed to remain calm. He panned the gun, waiting till Grechukha should expose just enough of himself to present a target. But Grechukha made no such mistake. He reached behind him and dragged open the splintered door and backed through it.

Cabeza heaved himself to his feet. Gail reached the door ahead of him and ran out. Cabeza followed, gasping.

He emerged onto the landing as Grechukha reached the head of the stairs. Gail rushed at him. She grasped Ludmilla's arm and tried to pull her away. Ludmilla struggled to help her, kicking back at Grechukha's shins.

For a moment there was a confusion of bodies. Then Grechukha suddenly let go and rushed away down the stairs.

Cabeza lunged to the rail, aimed the gun and fired.

Grechukha plunged sideways against the wall, pitched headlong down the last steps and lay motionless.

The three of them held their breath and listened. The shot had made only a jolting sound, but the fall of the body had been heavy.

Incredibly, though they waited a full minute, no sound came from any of the neighboring apartments.

Gail moved silently down the stairs and examined the sprawled figure.

"He's dead," she whispered.

Cabeza became aware that the children were beside him, staring, shocked, over the rail. He shepherded them back into the apartment.

"I am a fool!" Ludmilla muttered distraughtly. "Have I ruined it? What were you going to do with him?"

Cabeza said wearily, "It does not matter."

40

GAIL RETURNED to the apartment bringing Grechukha's coat and hat. The bullet hole, fortunately, was through the astrakhan of the collar and did not show. She and Ludmilla and the children helped Cabeza on with them.

"You understand what I am saying?" Cabeza demanded, looking into Ludmilla's eyes.

"That I will be safe?"

"That you will be safe, *providing* you are strong."

"I feel very *un*strong. But tell me again what I must do."

"The woman downstairs is the most important."

"The woman I can handle," Ludmilla said.

"Then you have no problem, *amada*. If she will tell anyone who asks that she saw Grechukha leave this building and drive away in his car, then you have no problem."

"Except sheer terror, my Spaniard."

Cabeza took her face in his hands and said gently, "Listen again. The MVD searched this apartment. They watched this house for days. They followed you everywhere. And still they could find no proof that I was hidden here. No one has seen me in this apartment except Grechukha. Tineka says that Grechukha contacted no one after she told him I was here,

359

that he did not even mention it to his men. So he was the *only one who knew*. And he is dead. *Claro?"*

"*Claro, amado*. If you say it, it is so." Ludmilla kissed him and clung to him.

The children watched, bewildered, frightened. When he had released her, Cabeza embraced them, too.

"Where are you going?" Mikki asked.

"Home," Cabeza said, forcing a smile, giving him a mock punch.

"Are—are you my father?" Tineka asked, then looked scared for having said it. "The man said you were."

Cabeza went very still. "What kind of question is that?" He laughed and shook his head. "I wish I were." He gave her a squeeze, then pocketed the gun and heaved himself to his feet. Gail steadied him, anxiously trying to gauge his strength. Ludmilla's hands were on him also; the children close. It reminded him suddenly of Spain and his family. His dead family.

He drew himself up and moved away from them and adjusted Grechukha's hat in the mirror, then buttoned the smart overcoat. He checked to see that he had all the right documents in the pocket. He thought, For all your astrakhan, *hombre*, you look like a tree in need of much water.

He looked at his watch. Almost five-thirty-five. The train left at seven.

"*Vámonos, muchacha.*"

"Must you really go?" The children came to them impulsively.

"Listen," Cabeza said sternly. "You will love your mother well, *entendéis?*" He added softly, with his eyes on her, "I live now only by an act of her hands and her courage."

Ludmilla embraced him wordlessly. She said, "Stay here, children. I will be back in a moment."

She accompanied Cabeza and Gail out and down the stairs. The children came to the door sadly, and that was the last view Cabeza had of them, as he supported himself down, holding the rail.

When they came to where Grechukha's body lay, the two women took it by the heels and dragged it unceremoniously and as quietly as they could down the remaining flight and along the hall and out onto the front steps.

They stopped to draw breath and look carefully up and down the street. It was the hour of utter stillness and cold. The city seemed deserted.

They dragged the body across the ice to the Pobeda. Getting the bulky form up into the trunk was no easy matter. Despite their protests, Cabeza lent a hand. When they had closed the trunk quietly and locked it, Ludmilla helped Cabeza into the passenger seat. He noticed Grechukha's dossier and opened it under the dashboard light, studying it briefly. He pushed it out into Ludmilla's hands.

"Burn it!"

She nodded and embraced him through the window. She was shivering. She stood back, hugging herself, stamping her feet. *"Vaya con Dios."*

"You will catch cold."

She made a face. "If that is all I catch, then I will know all has gone well for you."

"It is dangerous to be out without a coat, *amada*. Go back."

"I am going." She did not move.

Gail was behind the wheel now, starting the motor.

"Think of us," Ludmilla whispered.

Cabeza nodded. He could no longer trust himself to speak. Ludmilla's hand crept in onto his shoulder. He touched her cold fingers. The car was moving. The hand trailed away and was gone, and there was nothing outside but the blind houses sliding past and the echo of their tires and a gathering rush of searing air through the window. He closed it quickly. He could see, without turning, the small figure returning to the house, pausing, hugging itself, to stare after them. Stepping back into the drab hallway now, stamping the snow from her feet, her heart empty, praying they would make it.

Madre, he thought. What have you left her to anticipate? What nightmares have you left in her head?

Gail said quietly, "If we are caught, please will you shoot me?"

He glanced at her sharply, thinking, She reads my mind. And as he looked he saw a rectangle of light projected onto her face from the rearview mirror. It grew to brilliance, blinding her, and staring back, he saw a car pulling out to pass them.

It came up close, its engine roaring beside them, with three occupants, the one beside the driver etched sharply because he had lowered his window, his face bony-white, eyes two poker holes as he leveled something across the sill. Now *three* poker holes.

"Down!" Cabeza bellowed and pulled Gail toward him even as the third hole spat flame.

The stream of bullets shattered every window behind the windshield, snapping past their heads, perforating the car's interior in one long crackling burst. The Pobeda veered crazily, first one way, then toward the other car, which had to swerve wide to avoid being struck. There was a splintering crash. Chrome and glass and a sheared wheel rocketed past them. Something exploded in the roadway behind them.

Cabeza grabbed the wheel and wrestled the car back on course, staring around to see that they had missed a central island by centimeters, that the other car had hit it, was wrapped around the concrete lamp pylon, which had fractured and dropped its glass egg like a bomb.

They were entering a wide, empty square, Gail regaining control from him, ashen-faced, the car filling with cold air. The windshield only was intact. She steered blindly around the central statue, Cabeza looking back for signs of life from the wrecked vehicle. He saw a door sag open, but that was all before a building interposed itself and they were in a wide avenue that could only be Chkalovskaya Street.

"Holy Jesus, who was it? The MVD?"

Cabeza shook his head. It was inexplicable—and more was to come.

Ahead now they saw a barrier of lights and shapes, a swarming blockage of trucks, tanks and motorized infantry! They were halted across the Ulanovskaya intersection in confusion, motorcycle police circling to disentangle the snarl, shouting up to the leather-helmeted tank captains, waving, beckoning.

And beyond them, just visible, were more tanks and more infantry, guarding the approaches to the bridge that was their only route to the station.

41

It was too late to turn off or back. Cabeza motioned her on toward the column.

"You are my driver. We are on a mission. Make for that gap." He indicated a narrow space between two tanks.

He checked his watch. Five-fifty. They still had an hour in which to catch the train. But there would be lines at the station, he knew, as everywhere else in this city.

White and scared, Gail nosed the car right up to the column. As she did so, the engines of the rear tank snorted and its sprockets jerked, clawing the tracks with a screech. The gap closed.

She braked to a slithering stop within feet of the thundering giant. Its motors shuddered the car, its exhaust fumes spinning a fog around them in the freezing air, choking them. Somebody yelled. They were stopped crosswise to the traffic flow. The front of an armored truck loomed toward them from the right, stopping within inches, its headlights blinding. More vehicles tried to pass behind them. In moments they were surrounded, trapped.

A fist hammered on the shattered window. A red face bellowed in at them, then turned to try to organize a gap behind them so they could extricate themselves.

Cabeza shot Gail a wild look. He marshaled all his strength and got out.

The man, an infantry sergeant, began to shout at him. Cabeza remained calm. "Take me to your officer."

"Never mind the officer—get your car out of here! Wait till I make a space, then tell your driver to back out!"

"She is not backing out," Cabeza told him. "We are going through." And bracing himself against the pain and weakness that was in all of him, he strode away in search of authority.

Deadpan faces of men in MVD uniform stared down at him from truck after truck, turret after tank turret. The Security army. They were taking over the city, there was no doubt, though whether in a coup or to guard against one, he neither knew nor cared.

An NCO wearing the insignia of a tank regiment barred his way. "Civilians are not allowed," he shouted against the noise. "Go back to your home or you will be shot!"

"It is you who will be shot," Cabeza retorted. "Your column is a disgrace. The orders were an orderly advance. This is chaos."

The man hesitated, but his men were watching and he was not going to give way.

"Who are you?" he demanded. "What is your authority?"

"That is not for you to know. Take me to your commander."

The NCO scowled. But after a moment he pointed to a jeep parked at the corner of the intersection. Cabeza strode away toward it. He felt weak and sick, but refused to falter for one step.

The officer was sitting on the hood of his vehicle, the center of a milling group of subordinates and runners, barking clipped orders over his radio. He was a captain, square-shouldered and neat, with a hard, clean-shaven face and gray eyes.

Cabeza thrust his way forward, delving into his inner pocket.

"Stop!" A machine pistol was thrust into his belly.

Cabeza withdrew his hand slowly. In it was his OOKK card. He hung it out for the man with the gun to see, then he swung it under the captain's nose.

"You are in command of this mess?"

The officer was talking into his microphone. His gaze rested blindly on the card for a moment before its significance came through to him.

"Sign off, comrade," Cabeza told him. "You can finish that later."

The officer frowned and went on talking.

Cabeza took the microphone from his hand, killed the pressel-switch and tossed it on the seat of the car.

"This is Priority One," he said harshly. "My car is back there. You will order your vehicles to make a space for me to get through."

The officer shook his head. "You will just have to wait, comrade. We are in a tangle, as you can—"

"Listen," Cabeza rasped, spreading his feet to counteract the faintness that assailed him. "I am on an urgent mission. *Urgent,* do you understand me?"

"I understand you well, comrade. But if you will use your eyes, you will see that—"

"A tank," Cabeza cut him off hard, "can turn in its own tracks. You have but to order it. Refuse and I will have you arrested and shot."

"Corporal!" The captain slid off his rump, beckoning to an MP motorcyclist. To Cabeza: "What is your destination?"

"Komsomolskaya Square."

The officer gave rapid orders to the MP. Then to Cabeza: "He will see you through. Show him where your car is."

Cabeza turned away without another word. He walked ahead of the MP, fighting to keep his gait steady.

The captain watched him go for a moment. Then he retrieved his microphone—with a quick glance at his men, to kill dead any grins at his expense.

Reaching the Pobeda, Cabeza climbed in. He was about ready to collapse. He nodded to Gail to prepare to move.

The MP had been joined by another. They nosed their bikes alongside, wailing their sirens, signaling up to the captain of the tank that barred their way.

Within seconds they had cleared sufficient space behind the monster's stern quarter to enable it to rotate. Its engines snarled. Its tracks screeched in counteropposition. A gateway swung open in front of them.

The motorcyclists spurted on through, trailing their feet,

kicking to maintain their balance on the ice, Gail right behind them.

At the bridge it was more organized. Blocks had been set up at either end. The outriders swarmed toward the first like hornets, preordaining a passage for them. Curious military eyes watched them pass over their gunsights. The frozen reaches of the Yauza River spun below them. The second block melted before them, opening the way to a clear run along Chkalovskaya Street, which, apart from a few bewildered early workers and a woman street-clearance gang, was totally deserted.

At the Obukh intersection, however, there was another blockage. The MP's were already there, chivying with their sirens at a double wall of ammunition carriers. This time they had their work cut out. There seemed to be some distraction. A radio loudspeaker was blaring somewhere. The troops were listening to it.

Eventually a gap was cleared for them and they drove on. There was yet another snarl-up at Kirov Street. But now, instead of trying to cut across it, the MP's swung right. They squeezed them past a full column of medium tanks, then under the railway bridge at the end, and there it was in front of them already—the hugeness of Komsomolskaya Square with its three railway stations: Leningrad, the smallest; Yaroslavl, looking more like a fairy palace than a station; and Kazan, with its big central tower.

Military transports were parked around the square's perimeter, but the traffic routes, with their scribbles of tramlines and trolley cables, had been kept clear.

The MP's, their assignment complete, spun their bikes and rode back past them with a final salutatory moan of their sirens, to vanish the way they had come.

Gail drove judderingly across the tramlines toward the Kazan Station. She followed Cabeza's pointing finger to where some ramshackle buses were parked along the front. And now they could hear the intonations of the same broadcast coming from inside the station, relayed apparently through the public-address speakers.

She tucked the car between the buses and killed the lights and motor with a sigh of relief. They got out and she locked the doors and supported Cabeza into the station.

The huge marble hall was packed. Travelers tailed back from the ticket windows in lines that snaked back and forth among the columns—lines that were not even moving. Everyone was listening to the broadcast.

Cabeza eyed Gail in dismay. "There will not be time," he muttered. "We will not reach the ticket office before the train is due to go!"

"Can't you use your card to jump the line?"

"Our travel passes are in a different name." His voice faded. He had noticed the expressions on the faces around them, the tears of grief. He inclined an ear sharply to the speakers. Their reproduction was woolly. It was hard to interpret every word, but the gist was clear. All travel in and out of Moscow was forbidden, the voice was saying. The object being to avoid the chaotic influx of millions of people from outlying districts that had occurred after the death of Lenin. The government, the voice said, called upon the people to stay calm and go about their business in a normal manner. The body would lie in state in the Hall of Columns. Details of these arrangements would be broadcast later.

For the benefit of late listeners the announcer then repeated the principal news item: Josef Vissarionovich Stalin had died at 9:50 P.M. last night.

The newscast ended, to be followed by sepulchral music.

The profound emotion that surged around them found echo in Gail's eyes as she stared despairingly at Cabeza. He stood motionless, his face like stone.

The music was suddenly amputated. A railroad announcer's voice came on to say that though all trains into the city had been canceled, certain outbound trains would still run. The express to Vladivostok now standing at platform 6 would depart as scheduled.

"Thank God!" Gail leaned her head against Cabeza, utterly relieved. He held her thoughtfully. It was only half a reprieve. The problem of getting aboard still remained. The time was now six-fifteen.

Then something quite unforeseeable happened. The crowd began to break up. Group by group, the people slowly turned away and began to leave the station. It seemed that the prospect of difficulty in returning to Moscow once they had left, of missing the ceremonies of the Leader's lying in state and the funeral, had changed their plans.

In minutes the line was reduced to a mere straggle. The remaining travelers closed up around the ticket windows. Gail and Cabeza took their places among them. The MVD guard at the barrier had yet to be negotiated, but if the Ivanovskys had done their stuff, this should prove a mere formality.

Within minutes they were sitting in the train. It was so empty that they had a compartment to themselves.

Gail's gaze remained riveted to the platform. Cabeza could read her fear: that a curious patrol might have decided to investigate the solitary private vehicle parked outside the station—and found Grechukha's body. He watched the pale, anxious features fatalistically, knowing that whatever happened outside would be mirrored in her eyes.

Ten minutes remained. He wondered who had been in the car that had tried to gun them down. Grechukha's last words haunted him—*"You have let in Beria!"* The military invasion was plainly part of this coup, but was the coup itself the product of Beria's opportunism, or had it been an integral part of Sunflower from the start? He couldn't begin to guess. He didn't even care—not now. He would later, he knew—care profoundly. If there was a later. But right now, his only emotion was of deep weariness. He had used up much of his little strength to reach this point, and there was still a long, long way to go.

Somewhere a whistle shrilled. Now there was a jolt and a clank. The train was moving, rolling, the pistons punching the great wheels into motion, the steam bluffing and shushing under the high canopy above.

A couple of late passengers were running alongside. He heard them scramble in, the door slam. The station lights faltered, vanished, and they were out in the darkness of early morning, the signal pylons idling past, now commencing to stride a little. Cold, lonely lights swung by. A man came along the corridor. He passed their compartment, then came back and entered and sat down. He was breathing heavily. Obviously one of the late arrivals.

Cabeza glanced at him idly. A tall man with bushy eyebrows, a heavy, drooping moustache and an unslept look about him, conveyed by a growth of stubble and a swollen bruise on one cheek, wearing, nevertheless, an expensive coat and sealskin hat and leather boots, which were becoming a luxury. Fiftyish. No, younger—the graying moustache was deceptive, the skin around the eyes dark but unwrinkled. Blue eyes. They glanced across to meet Cabeza's casually.

Cabeza looked away. Then he looked back. It was only when he saw the gun that he realized it was Kelland.

42

THE TRAIN clattered, rocking, the city's lights wheeling by in the blackness beyond the windows. Reflected against them in the dim illumination of the compartment, the three figures swayed in unison. No one spoke.

Then a jerk of Kelland's chin ordered Gail across into the seat beside Cabeza. She was utterly stunned. As she moved to obey, Kelland relieved her deftly of her sling bag.

"Now Holz's gun, General." The blue eyes were as steely as the muzzle of the .38 that stared into Cabeza's.

Cabeza sat like a rock. At the end of the track ahead lay their only escape window. Any other man rising to plant himself in their path he would have swept violently aside before he'd had time to establish himself fully in control. But this—incredibly, and there was no time to reason out how— was Kelland. Kelland was something else—his equal, and also his exact opposite. To beat him, Cabeza knew, he would have to turn his mind around completely; for hot read cold, fast read slow. It would take all the self-control and concentration he could muster. Perhaps more than he could muster in his present state.

Bitter questions began to tumble from Gail's lips. Kelland

ignored her. She had betrayed him and he wanted no part of her.

"Don't think about it, General. Pass me the gun or I'll shoot you where you sit."

"Pull that trigger," Gail whispered, "and I'll tear your eyes out!" Then she added with growing conviction, "But you won't. You can't. Shoot us in here without a silencer, you'll blow your cover. Joaquín, he's bluffing!"

Eyes still on target, Kelland raised a hand to his disguise. "Pay her no attention, General." He peeled off first the moustache, then the eyebrows. "These are just a hangover from before the coup. I'm in the absolute clear now, believe it—with official sanction to vacuum you two up and spit you out dead. Signed by the new boss man himself, Lavrenti Beria."

So it *had* all been a part of Sunflower! Cabeza felt something in him blaze, then die to a coldness.

"Kelland," he said slowly, his mind now readjusting to form a terrible resolution, "you picked me out of a hat . . . You crawled into my head. You used me, it seems, to open the door to a monstrosity. So far, you have had it almost all your own way. But now, to end it as you plan, you will need more than a piece of metal in your hand."

Kelland's reply was to thumb back the hammer with a click.

"No!" Gail flung out her hand. "Kelland, listen—Joaquín did everything you wanted, didn't he? Everything but die. But does he have to? Think about it. He's not going to talk! My God, he'd have to be crazy to—!"

"I'll say it just once more." Kelland's voice cut her off icily. "Give—me—the—gun."

Her protestations died in a sharp intake of breath as his finger tightened visibly on the trigger. She wrenched a look around at Cabeza. He hadn't moved a muscle. Cabeza felt her horror as she read his expression: that he wasn't going to give way.

"Joaquín, he means it—give it to him."

Cabeza shook his head. "Let him shoot," he whispered. "Before I die, I will kill him. As I killed Holz."

Kelland sneered. "With a nine-millimeter hole in your head?"

Cabeza nodded, his body gathering itself. "As with Holz."

The sneer became a frown. "He shot you, before . . . ?"

"His bullet could not kill the message that was left in me."

Cabeza lowered his head like a bull, his expression taking on a terrible intensity as, watching the cold pupils minutely for their last contraction, he implanted the final command in every fiber of his being. Weakened though he was, he *knew* it could be done. And having been done . . . He said to Gail: "After we both are dead, leave the compartment quickly. When you reach America, tell the newspapers our story—*all of it.*"

He heard Gail utter a choking sound, but his gaze was on Kelland for his reaction. Nothing changed. The gun stared him in the eye. The finger rested on the final pressure point of the trigger, hair-balanced . . .

The sudden roar of a train bursting past them the other way shuddered the car. Cabeza all but hurled himself forward. Kelland did not even blink. The train thundered on past.

Then very slowly something did change. The finger eased its pressure. Kelland gave the thinnest of grudging smiles.

"Who else in your position, General, I wonder, would try to call the shots? But why the hell should I let myself be hustled? Gail . . ." He signaled her. *"You* get his gun."

"Keep away, *muchacha."* Cabeza felt the prickle of sweat all over his body, but the bastard was backing down, and when the enemy retreats, you follow, you eat up all of his space.

"Let her give it to me," Kelland said, "and you win for yourself maybe four extra hours of life."

"Qué va," Cabeza muttered. "I am dead anyway. Let it be here, where you do not want it." And he waited, bringing his body forward a little.

He saw Kelland's eyes flicker. Good. He brought his body forward more.

The train rumbled hollowly over a bridge. Kelland seemed hypnotized.

"What do I have to do," Cabeza rasped, "to make you shoot?" He almost wanted it. Anything to get his hands on the son of a whore's throat! A kind of exultation gripped him. He had done it—turned his mind around—the survivor grasping at death. Kelland was thrown completely, but it would only last a moment. Now—now was the only time—to swallow up the last of his space, overwhelm him!

Even as he started to move, Gail hurled herself at him, pinning him back. "No, Joaquín!" Her face was close. "Let me do it! Let me give it to him—*please.*" In her eyes was a message. They clung to his beseechingly.

Cabeza stared at her, his heart hammering, about to push her away. But she had destroyed his impetus. He felt it all start to ebb from him—the advantage he had gained, the strength he had mustered. Anger flared, then stilled.

Gail slowly released his arms. She began to reach inside his coat. "It's loaded?"

Cabeza nodded. "The catch is on." He wanted to stop her, but there was nausea in the back of his throat. He felt strange.

"All right, Kelland," he muttered thickly. "Four more hours. You—"

"Slowly!" Kelland sat forward, the spell now broken.

Gail slowed the movement right down, turning her face to Kelland as she pushed her hand gradually inside. Cabeza could feel her body coming to a tension against his as she prepared to make the last part of the movement very fast. He strove to reconcentrate his energies, but it was like grasping at liquid.

"It was you from the car, wasn't it?" he said bitterly.

Kelland did not reply. Instead, he jerked forward and struck Gail's hand away and plunged his own inside the coat. Cabeza reacted with all that was left in him and gripped Kelland's wrist, holding it there, clutching it to his chest. The rib pain shot through him. Somehow he hung on, but before he could kick Kelland's legs from under him, the .38 whipped across his temple. There was a flash and numbness, a sense of the world tilting. As through a swarm of fireflies he saw Kelland sit back calmly with the disputed gun in his possession, saw him open up his briefcase and cast it inside, heard the crunch of glass as it hit something, probably a liquor flask.

Kelland said something coldly to Gail and she blazed back at him, her voice almost exploding in Cabeza's ear as she hugged him to her, nursing his head, her frustration venting itself in a rush of words. Cabeza let himself go slack, pretending unconsciousness, awaiting a second chance. But Kelland's eyes never left him for a second. He had pulled it all back now, regained control.

He opened up Gail's bag beside him and fished out the weapon she had taken from Grechukha. He dropped that, too, in the briefcase and delved again, came up with the stick of plastic gelignite. From under closed lids, Cabeza watched him finger it incredulously.

"You've still got this? Shut your mouth, girl, and open up that window."

Gail was still in full verbal spate, but trying to goad him now, Cabeza sensed. To no avail.

Unruffled, gun leveled, Kelland got up and moved crabwise to the window. Now surely there would be a chance! Cabeza watched him juggle the explosive for a moment, then tuck it under the brim of his hat so he could open the latch with his free hand. The latch wouldn't budge. The window was sealed, as were all windows on Russian trains.

Frustrated, Kelland moved back to his seat, reopened his briefcase and was about to drop the explosive inside, but remembered there was spilled liquor in there. He checked himself. As a temporary solution, he tucked it back in his hat—and still the gun remained as steady on Cabeza as a compass needle on north. Kelland eased back into his seat, held his watch up level with the gun and checked the time.

He said calmly, "All right, General, you can quit foxing. Gail, sit him up."

"Can't you see he's hurt?" Gail cried. "He's still weak from the operation." She could have bitten her tongue.

Kelland digested this information with a glint of amusement. "Performed by . . . let me guess. Dr. Patolichev? Well, well. And how is your good ex-wife these days, General?" Slyly provoking: "More important, how much does she know?"

Cabeza opened his eyes slowly.

Kelland's lips twitched. "Thought that'd wake you up."

"She knows nothing."

"Not that it matters . . ."

"Nothing at all," Cabeza said, trying hard to keep the dread from his voice. "*Nada.* You have my word."

"And mine," Gail said quickly. "We kept her in the dark so as not to put her in danger."

"I'm afraid, the mere risk of her knowing . . ."

"There's *no* risk," Gail retorted. "I'm telling you—there—is—no—risk."

"The mere risk, even, of there *being* a risk . . ." Kelland said.

"Listen"—Cabeza's dismay was beginning to show—"if you are going to silence everyone who offers you risk, you will have to kill many people."

"Including your fellow conspirators!" Gail cried. "The Ivanovskys for a start!"

"The Ivanovskys," Kelland said, "are already dead."

The words fell with callous significance, to be taken up by the wheels' clatter on the tracks—*already dead—already dead—Ludmilla is as good as dead—you are all as good as dead.*

Kelland watched them digest it, nodding a little with the car's motion, feeling in his pocket, bringing out his gold cigarette case. "I have a full list. Headed by the chauffeur. Then Zapotkin . . ." He opened the case on his lap, took out a cigarette. To do so, he had to push the gun forward so it protruded slightly beyond his knee.

Through the haze of his consternation, Cabeza's eyes seized on it. They gauged the distance between it and his foot.

"Zapotkin?" Gail had seen it too.

"The man who clued me in to the possibility that it was the General and not Holz you were holed up with." Kelland did not bother even to barb his words, though it had been her defection that had almost cost him his plan. But that was all in the past now. He was talking to dead people. He lit the cigarette. "The moment I saw through your story, I got down to the Patolichev apartment, set up shop, and watched Grechukha's men watch you. And waited."

"You should have dropped in," Cabeza said. "For a glass of tea and a bullet."

"Stalin was still alive. Until he died, the MVD were working for him, not Beria. I could hardly walk in under their noses."

Already dead—already dead—already dead . . .

"So what could you have done if Grechukha had arrested us?" Cabeza slid down fractionally in his seat.

"Gunned you down from my car. As eventually I tried to do. Seeing a body being dragged out, I thought naturally it was yours. But when the car came by and I saw you in the front . . ." Kelland drew watchfully on the cigarette. "Fortunately for you, my Russians blew it."

Cabeza slid down still further. Gail tried to mask his movement with one of her own.

"Why aren't they with you?" she asked, to keep the ball rolling.

"They were smashed up. I was lucky. Got to a phone. Zapotkin sent me another car." Kelland flicked ash on the floor and aligned his watch with the gun for another look.

Cabeza had slid right down to marshal his strength for the final bid, confident that they had a long journey ahead of them. Now he was not so sure. Kelland seemed to be waiting for something.

He said experimentally, "We have a train to catch?"

"A train to get off. In about six minutes."

"He's lying." Gail looked startled. "Kazan's our first stop."

"Not anymore," Kelland told her. "I fixed it with the guard. A truck will meet us, drive us back to Moscow." He drew again on the cigarette, blew out a long plume of smoke, his eyes clouding slightly. "But before we get off, General, let me say one thing. You did me proud back there. The way you swung it was a masterstroke. Don't think I relish what I have to do. If there was any other way, believe me, I'd take it."

"When I win the lottery," Cabeza said, "I will relieve you of the pain of such work."

Kelland did not smile. "It'll be done quickly, I promise you. You'll sign a full confession, then you'll both be shot trying to escape."

The train began to brake. Kelland glanced automatically toward the window.

In desperation Cabeza began his move.

But at the same moment Kelland stood up, the gun leveled. He picked up his briefcase and Gail's bag.

"This is us. Move out nice and slow."

43

THEY STOOD on the platform of a village station. All around, the snow lay thick and blue in the early-morning darkness. There was no one there to meet them—not a soul or a footprint in sight. A solitary electric lantern above the open gate to the station yard made golden daggers of the icicles that fringed the roof of the shuttered building.

As the train labored away, Kelland snatched small glances about him. Clearly, he had expected the MVD truck to be here and waiting. He motioned them through the gate and looked briefly around the deserted yard. Muttering to himself, he herded them back onto the platform to wait.

Cabeza guessed the truck had been delayed by the military snarl-up. It was a reprieve, however short. They must make swift use of it. But the cold—*madre!* His blood could not resist it. The very act of bracing his body against it was already draining his small remaining strength.

"Here." Kelland indicated the very center of the platform, well away from the building. "Stand right here."

They stamped their feet, their breath white in the lantern light, Gail turning to Cabeza, pulling down the earflaps of his hat, tucking up his collar for him in a motherly gesture that

moved him suddenly and deeply. He put his arms around her.
She did the same to him, scrubbing at his back with her
gloves, careful to avoid the wound, trying to feed strength
into him, her small face amid the furs pale and desperate in
the reflected snow light, her eyes searching his for a lead—any
lead; she would follow him to the end.

He knew in that moment that he loved her. Holding her
smallness in the big coat hard to him, he thought of her and
the red hills of his own land in the one thought, of her and
the parched mountains, the goatherds tittering and tinkling
down through the hand-labored terraces in the blueness
after sunset, and realized that never before had a woman
shared equal place with these things of his heart.

Pressing the coldness of his cheek to hers, he surveyed the
scene around them carefully, as he had surveyed many scenes
and drawn up many plans for attack and survival—with the
difference now that her survival was paramount over his.

The time: seven-thirty or thereabouts. Dawn still an hour
or so away. A long, bare, snow-covered platform without
seats or any of the usual equipment, bounded by the double
railroad tracks, a far platform and open country on the one
side, and a picket fence on the other, separating them from
the station yard that was no more than an open turning space
surrounded by trees. An exit led between the trees toward the
village street, the far side of which was lined with houses, the
lights of their upper windows casting golden squares on
the roadway. Through these squares now was moving a man
dragging a sled piled with firewood, winking and dying like
the tip of a nervous man's cigarette. Somewhere, faintly, a
sawmill whined and clanged. Otherwise all was silence.

Cabeza's gaze lingered on what looked like a heap of
freight stacked farther along the platform, but it was snow-
covered, impossible to see what it comprised. Otherwise,
there was nothing, not so much as a shovel leaning against the
building, that could be used as a makeshift weapon.

"Cut that out," Kelland told them. "Keep apart and face
me."

"Don't you think a man needs some comfort, *hombre*,"
Cabeza growled, "after what you have had me do?" He gave
Gail a final squeeze. *"Valor, amada,"* he murmured, releas-

ing her. "Wait till the people find out," he told Kelland, "that we have exchanged one tyrant for another—the Georgian poisoner for the Cheka butcher! I will be dead, but you—with luck, they'll tear you apart!" *Goad him to a mistake, it was the only way now.*

But Kelland laughed. "First they'll have to catch me."

Cabeza stamped his feet for a moment, chattering his teeth audibly.

"Kelland, I cannot stand here. My legs are too weak. I am going to sit down."

"Stay right where you are, General."

Cabeza turned and stumbled toward the snow-covered heap.

"Hold it!" Kelland snapped.

"Shoot me," Cabeza said. He had to find out what the stack contained.

Gail, with a fearful glance at Kelland, followed him. The hair on Cabeza's neck crawled for a moment. Then he heard Kelland's footsteps come crumping after them.

Reaching the stack, he swept some snow off it. Revealed was a tarpaulin—*mierda*. He sat down on it, testing with his rump what lay beneath. Packing cases it felt like. Again *mierda*. He dug his feet in the snow, hoping to encounter a rock, a buried chunk of something—anything. But the ground beneath was hard and smooth.

Gail seated herself beside him, her shoulder touching his receptively. Kelland came to a stop in front of them, the briefcase and bag under his left arm, hands deep in pockets, the right, without a doubt, gripping the .38. He smiled thinly.

"Nothing there, General? Tough." He added evenly, "Just my good nature saved you from a bullet in the back then."

"I spit in the milk of your good nature," Cabeza said.

Kelland laughed. He inclined his ear for a moment for any sound of the truck, then he said, "Always remember, General, I read you all the way. There's nothing you can think of that I haven't already been there. Dirty tricks are my job. I've connived and outsmarted my way right around the world."

"And lied and cheated," Gail added bitterly.

"Sure. But listen who's talking. What happened to your oath to Uncle Sam?"

"What happened to yours, *double agent!*"

Kelland tilted his head back and looked down at her, arrogantly pitying. "A hackneyed phrase and you think you've covered it. If you only knew . . . If your suburban little mind could *begin* to grasp . . ." He kicked his heels for a moment, then said bitterly, "God, it's been lonely. Never being able to talk to anyone. Even you, General, in Siberia you could blow off steam to your prisoner comrades. But me . . ."

Cabeza sensed he was about to turn and saunter reminiscently. He gathered his feet under him, preparing to launch himself. But Kelland held his ground with a mocking smile.

"Relax, I'm not going to blow it at this late hour. Not after all I've been through. You two are all I need now to slot into the machine and fetch out the jackpot. My just reward for having pulled off the biggest coup in history." He added, "But I'll put your mind at rest on one score. Things *will* change here, and in the rest of the world, as a result of what you've helped me to do. There'll be a thaw in the cold war for a start. As for the Russian people tearing me apart, they'd erect a statue to me if they knew. Trade and other restrictions will be lifted, consumer goods from the West come flowing in. How can I be so sure? Because I fixed it. With Beria. It was my condition for killing Stalin for him."

Cabeza ground his teeth, barely listening. To get to this freight heap he had sacrificed their mobility. Now they were stuck here, a captive audience to Kelland's need to unburden himself.

Kelland stamped his feet. Shivering, he started to pace, but his eyes never left them.

"You see, Stalin found out the U.S. had a man in the Kremlin. He didn't know it was his buddy Beria, but he was well on the way to finding out—"

"Beria one of *our* people?" Gail cut in scornfully.

"Has been for years. I'm his go-between with Central Intelligence. So if, as you say, I'm a double agent, it's one with a difference. I operate with the *full knowledge and approval of both sides.*"

Cabeza began drumming his feet against the cold, scraping the snow together between his boots, hardening it—even an icy snowball was better than no weapon at all—at the same time searching his mind for the one move that Kelland would least expect. It would have to be more than one move, he reckoned—a succession of interlocking moves . . .

And all the while Kelland paced back and forth, the swing of his shadow at their feet, like a pendulum—the pendulum of a clock ticking away the minutes to the hour, the terminal hour. Everything was very sharp and frost-clear, Kelland's breath hanging in the air after he had passed, writhing like ectoplasm against the light from the gate lantern.

"Beria knew his only chance of survival against Stalin was to strike first," he told them. "And—if he could swing it at the same time—take over power himself. But he couldn't organize the Old Man's death from the inside because Grechukha was treading on his cuffs, so he tried to con me into getting the Agency to do it for him." He laughed shortly. "Well, Jesus, I didn't fall for *that*. An Agency assassination team—if they'd been caught, we'd have been into World War Three! So I dreamed up Sunflower for him, with you as point man, General, anti-American to your fingertips . . . Well, I don't have to spell it out." He broke off. "There's no sense in your making that missile, General. I'd kill you before you could pick it off the ground."

Cabeza froze with a scowl. "I am trying to keep warm."

"I know. It's tough. But we'll be in a warm truck soon. Meanwhile I'd like you to hear this—you being a Lubianka fan. Because that's where it all started—back in '47."

Cabeza shot Gail a baffled look. He pushed an arm out sideways and leaned on it. Then he went very still. Under the snow was what felt like a brick. Put there, presumably, to weight down the tarpaulin.

"I was in Moscow on a mission." Kelland's eyes were hard on him. "The NKVD penetrated my cover and I was clapped in the Lubianka. They put me through all the usual disorientation crap. I held out, but they had me so fogged I knew in the end I'd spill my guts and not even know I'd done it. When guess what happened?"

Cabeza very gradually got a grip on the brick and tried to shift it. It was frozen hard to the tarpaulin. He levered it gently.

"In walked the demon king himself—Beria! I was the first American they'd pulled in since the war; he wanted to look me over."

Fearful of exerting too much pressure lest it show, Cabeza was getting nowhere. The brick was frozen solid.

"To cut a long story short," Kelland continued, "he fished me out of the tank, had them clean me up, feed me, then he propositioned me. He wanted to take out some insurance, he said, with Uncle Sam. He didn't say why, but I guessed it was in case Stalin turned the knives on him. The deal he said he was offering was information—Presidium decisions, projections, troop dispositions in Western Europe—in exchange for a cast-iron fire exit to the West, plus fat—very fat—monthly payments into a Swiss bank. I was to convey this offer direct to Truman, no intermediaries."

Kelland stopped and faced them with a laugh. "Me! From the Lubianka to the White House in just one crazy jump!"

Cabeza had just felt the brick come loose. He didn't move.

Kelland peered toward him in sudden suspicion. "You're very quiet, General. Am I boring you?"

"Go on," Cabeza said. "I am listening. To what a great man you are."

"Whatever I am," Kelland said, "I owe to that one moment." Pacing again, but still watching him. "And to the fact that I had the wit to recognize the potential of that moment. That's one thing I will take credit for."

Thank God for your taking of credit, Cabeza thought, as he began to pull the brick closer to him. For your need to tell someone. Keep talking, Kelland, he willed. *Only with your head a little more that way.* He waited for him to oblige.

"Well, I told him that, so Stalin shouldn't find out, he shouldn't risk any broad-front liaison with the White House, but channel all his information through a one-point contact, with maybe just a minimum signals staff at either end. And I convinced him the one-point contact should be *me*."

Me, me. Time is running out for us, me. Turn away, me.

"Beria fell for it. I contacted Truman and the deal was set. The information started to flow, and I became indispensable. When the Agency was formed, I was jumped straight in at super-grade—fat pay checks from Uncle Sam, Swiss-franc handouts from Uncle Beria. Hell, I was getting rich! But I was riding a tiger, I knew that. I started thinking of ways to get off. But how?—that was the question.

"Then, back in January, the purge started. Beria started to panic. I knew here was my chance to clean up and clear out. I went cold on him, played hard to get. I told him killing Stalin was a pipe dream. He started throwing money at me. I pushed him up—up. In the end, my fixing Sunflower for him cost him the dollar equivalent of *two million.*"

Gail gasped.

Kelland stopped to face them. "When I get that sum—*fffft,* I'm gone. I have a pad stashed away where the bastards'll never find me—good fishing, sailing, and nothing but dull Indian eyes to watch me do it. But I don't get that money until Sunflower is fully complete. When both of you are dead." He drew his gun and thumbed back the hammer. "Which you'll be *in one second,* General, if you don't drop what you've got in your hand."

Cabeza sat motionless. He calculated his chances of slinging the brick straight at Kelland's head. And in the charged silence that followed, the sawing of an approaching motor reached them.

"That's our truck," Kelland said. "I want to see that hand empty, General. *Now.*"

Cabeza knew he hadn't a chance. He relinquished the brick slowly.

"Right," Kelland said. "On your feet. Move ahead of me and keep it steady."

They could do nothing but obey. Gail's arm crept sympathetically around Cabeza's waist; his around hers. Together, like lovers to the scaffold, they trudged toward the gate.

In quick succession, every conceivable remaining possibility flashed through Cabeza's mind: stab him with an icicle, lead him across an icy patch and cause him somehow to slip, stumble into him, then hurl him onto the spikes of the fence . . . Wild stuff, impossible. Then how about the moment the truck's headlights swung onto them? There would be a split second of blindness . . .

They were through into the yard. They could hear the *slap-slap* of chains now as the truck came along the street.

Gail's arm tightened around Cabeza, growing tighter as the vehicle appeared, slowing, then turning off the road toward them.

Cabeza knew then that there would be no blinding moment of headlights. The vehicle's lights were dull and golden, as if the battery was low. Their glow lit up the scene like a stage set, revealing for the first time a magnificent old cedar tree, the snow-laden branches of which overhung the yard. Cabeza's eyes rested on it momentarily, noting that a public seat had been fashioned around its base, that what looked like the remains of a children's swing hung, frayed, from one of the spreading boughs, and his mind gave a kick as it struggled to remember something—something vital that he had overlooked. Then the vehicle came racketing up past them, and as it pulled around in front of the station house preparatory to turning, he saw that it was a van with a square wooden back.

One glance at Kelland's disgusted face as he slipped the gun back in his pocket told Cabeza this wasn't the vehicle he had been expecting. It was backing now, its wheels spinning in the loose snow as the driver strove to bring the rear end close to the platform entrance.

Sharp pressure from Gail's arm urged Cabeza to somehow utilize the diversion, but Kelland gave them no chance, circling quickly behind to cover them.

When the driver could reverse no further, he killed the motor and lights and swung down—a huge man with a black beard, greasy cap and a leather apron around his middle that trailed almost to the ground.

He threw a gruff *"Dobrye utra!"* in their direction as he unhitched the tailgate and clambered onto it. The van was full of sides of meat. He swung a hook into one, dragged it out into the gate, then got down, preparing to heft it.

"Hey, you," Kelland called out. "You see a truck on your way here?"

The man paused, the meat half on his shoulders.

"A truck, comrade?"

"A militia truck. Which way did you come?"

"From the slaughterhouse, comrade." The driver pointed beyond the village to the north.

It was the wrong direction. Kelland huffed a sigh. "Never

mind." Then, as the man humped the meat onto his back: "Wait. I want to get into the station to make a phone call. What time does it open?"

"When old Sergei Sergeivich gets here."

"When's that?"

The man spread a hand. "Before the first local train. Eight-fifteen. Thereabouts." He carried his load off toward the platform.

Kelland made one of his wary consultations with his watch. As his focus lengthened again to his prisoners, he was alerted by their rigid postures. A quick estimation of their eyeline guided his own to the tailgate of the van.

On it lay the driver's meat hook, curved and wicked-looking.

"Don't even *think* about it," he warned. "Move away." He herded them well clear, stopping them in the center of the yard, where he began stamping his feet and cursing under his breath.

The cold is getting to him, Cabeza thought. He is becoming impatient. The very coup he organized is delaying him within sight of his goal. So the impatience is with himself. A man divided is a man halved. But I, too, am halved—half frozen! Gail, too; he could feel her shivering against him. Pretty soon, he thought, his gaze lifting again to rest on the snowy terraces of the cedar tree, even if Kelland does make a mistake we will be in no condition to use it.

Why did the sight of those branches so stir his memory? He groped for the solution, wading after it, reaching for it like a dreamer through the slowing processes of his mind. But for long moments it eluded him. Then suddenly he had it by the tail and dragged it out. And, *madre,* it was *beautiful.*

He let his knees buckle. Gail grasped his arm quickly, holding him up.

"Kelland," he gasped, his eyes rolling. "Again . . . I must sit down."

"Then sit," Kelland said, indicating the snow. "If you think I'm going to let you back near that van, forget it!"

Cabeza shook his head. He pointed to the base of the tree. "There is a seat . . ." He gripped Gail's hand, willing her to back him up.

Her response was immediate. Pulling his arm around her shoulders, she told Kelland flatly, "I'm going to take him there. You have the gun, you're the big man—what are you scared of?"

Kelland's eyes bit into hers suspiciously. He seemed about to refuse, but eventually shrugged, following behind them warily.

As they came under the tree, Cabeza appeared to stumble. Knees sagging, he hastened, arms outstretched, toward the seat, momentarily widening the gap between them and Kelland. Then shoving Gail forward, he changed direction sideways and dived toward the frayed remnants of the children's swing.

Kelland stopped in his tracks. In the split second of Cabeza's action, he computed its effect: rope—branch—snow —calculated his own position—remembered the explosive in his hat. As Cabeza hit the rope and hauled on it with all his strength, Kelland snatched the hat from his head and flung it away from him.

The rope broke. The bough above swayed. Its outer branches whipped. Snow cascaded on Kelland.

From where he had fallen, Cabeza peered back, bracing himself in anticipation of the explosion. Gail stared, mesmerized, from the region of the seat. For a moment it was like a blizzard—nothing to be seen. Then the whiteness slowly cleared—to reveal Kelland still standing, hatless, the gun held in both hands, aimed dead at Cabeza.

In the darkness it was impossible to see his expression, but his very stance proclaimed his shock and cold fury. He remained without moving or speaking—a whitened statue— seemingly paralyzed by the horrific nature of what had nearly been done to him.

Cabeza lay helplessly in his sights, striving to grasp what had gone wrong. A second later, from where the hat had landed, leaped an orange tongue of flame and a shattering explosion. Glass tinkled somewhere. More snow cascaded from above.

The shock wave seemed to bring Kelland alive. He came striding forward through the powdery curtain.

"You son of a bitch." He aimed a kick at Cabeza's head.

Cabeza rolled sideways. The boot caught him a glancing blow on the temple. Kelland aimed another kick. "You—" *kick,* "son—" *kick,* "of a bitch!" *kick.*

"Stop it—no—stop it!" Gail rushed at him, clawing at him. Kelland hurled her aside. His coldness was gone; the molten something she had glimpsed only twice before possessing him utterly as all his frustration and fury found their focus. She rushed in again. He swept her aside, planting a boot hard in Cabeza's ribs.

Agony exploded through Cabeza's body. Stunned, he tried to grab the foot. It caught him several more heavy blows before he managed to capture it. He hung on to it, his head swimming, trying to twist it, to bring Kelland to the ground. But Kelland was too strong for him, dragging him through the snow as he fought to release the foot. His strength, in rage, seemed superhuman, but Cabeza would not let go.

Kelland swiped at his head with the gun. The fur hat took most of the impact, but the second swipe dislodged it. The third cracked across his bare skull. Cabeza relinquished his hold and fell on his back, blood streaming. Kelland stood over him, the gun swung back to beat him to a pulp.

He froze there—perhaps in answer to a warning shout from his professional instincts that he was breaking every rule in his own book, that he was allowing one prisoner to occupy his whole attention when there were *two*. The sudden approaching rush of footsteps and clothing confirmed the intuition, bringing his head and gun around simultaneously.

With her lips strained back from her teeth, Gail swung the hook at him two-handed with all the strength she could muster. Kelland's finger jerked the trigger in reflex, his head straining away in the first movement of throwing himself to one side, the sound of the gun inaudible to both of them in the trauma of the moment. The steel claw buried itself deep in Kelland's throat. Gail gave a cry as she plunged forward, the fingers of one hand locked around the bone handle and the fingers of the other gripping them tightly so that the weight of her impetus upon the hook tore out Kelland's jugular.

His eyes flared horribly as the blood leaped from him in a spurting arc. He sank to the ground, his mouth working, staring down incredulously at the crimson spring that welled up out of him pulsingly with each beat of his heart, to pour thickly down his chest onto the snow, melting a dark hole in the whiteness.

Cabeza saw this as in a trance, and to his reeling senses it was his father's body sprawled beside him and for an instant he fancied he saw the soldiers standing around them in that silence that is twice silence following an explosion. The body had Kelland's face. This seemed inexplicable and his mind wrestled to make sense of it; also why it was contriving to aim the gun at him. Then he heard his mother's voice calling to him distantly from across the plain. He felt it must be late, time for him to milk the goats. But there was a strangeness in her voice; it filled him with such foreboding that he hurried and pushed and struggled his way back to the surface of consciousness.

"Joaquín . . ."

"Muchacha!" His worst inner fears were realized as he saw her huddled form, her very position filling him with the dread of waking intuition. He dragged himself to her and raised her head. Her eyes were clenched, her body fighting, as if against some hidden adversary.

The gun wavered in Kelland's hand, following him, but Cabeza was blind to it as he pulled Gail up to him and nursed her against his chest, striving to understand what had happened, feeling down her with his hand, biting off the glove, feeling again under the coney fur to encounter a horror of warm drenching.

Her eyes came open and looked into his distantly. The distance melted and she came forward till she was all there in her eyes, loving him.

"Amado." Her lips curled.

Cabeza could not speak. He moved his tongue in his dry mouth till the words came. *"Muchacha,* I will get you to a—" He fell silent, knowing that his words were an echo of hers to him in the alley in Moscow, but that in the alley she had found an alternative, and here there was no alternative. All such medical solutions were, under these circumstances, impossible. She had saved his life and yet now, when she needed his help, he could do nothing!

Holding her to him, he gathered himself in a surge of will to halt what his instincts, drawn from bitter experience, told him was inevitable. Throughout his life he had achieved what others said could not be done. Surely he could do this for her now—preserve her by sheer power within the bulwark of his shoulders, sustaining her with his blood, his breath?

As he fought the battle not even he could win, Kelland's gun held him waveringly in its eye and footsteps whispered toward them, drawn by the explosion.

Gail whispered anxiously, "The truck. It will soon be here. You must go quickly."

"And leave you to those bastards?" Cabeza rasped, holding her closer.

"What does it matter now? What can they do to me? Go, *amado. Anda.* I beg of you."

Cabeza shook his head. He had never thought that a woman could divert him from the straight road of survival, that she could turn him from the logic of preserving one out of two so that the one could continue the struggle and perhaps avenge the other who had fallen. But "one" and "other" were the language of the field. Here was another language. Where could he go without the heart she had captured from him by her loyalty and courage?

She was plucking at his sleeve. "Listen. I think I hear it—the truck."

"It is the engine of the mill, *muchacha.*" He added thickly, "But if it is the truck, let them come. They won't lay one hand on you—not while I still have breath. I'll—" He remembered the gun and looked toward Kelland. It was still pointing in his direction—rock-steady now. Kelland lay with his head back in a great darkness of snow. He was dead.

Supporting her carefully, Cabeza moved his body around till he could prize the weapon from Kelland's fingers. He thrust it in his own pocket.

"When they come, I will sell our bodies dearly. I'll—"

Her finger pressed his lips to silence. "No. You must go on." Reproach and agitation grew in her voice. "It's why I love you. Because you never give up. Don't disappoint me now."

"*Cálmate, muchacha.* One day, for everyone, there comes

an end to running. For me it is here, in this place, beside
you." He brushed the snow from her face with gentle
fingertips and tried to move her so she would be more
comfortable, but her body resisted him.

"No. Don't you see? If you stay . . ." She fought with the
pain for a moment. Then, more weakly: "What sense will it
make? What will I have died for?"

The smallness of her voice turned a knife in him. He could
find no answer. He only knew that his mind was made up and
there was compensation in the awareness that he had decided the place for himself, chosen it of his own will and not
had it forced on him in some other place, alone, without her.

When she saw she could not move him, her desperation
grew. But he only held her more tightly, his face pressed to
hers. He could feel her lips trembling for words. He willed
her not to utter them but to accept these moments peacefully.

At last she murmured, "Then . . . if I can't make you go
without me . . . I'll have to go with you."

Cabeza drew back slowly and looked at her for her
meaning.

"Help me up," she whispered.

He did not move. Even now, her one thought is to save my
life, he thought. I do not want it, but she gives it to me. He
looked around for the first time at the shadowy figures that
had gathered in the yard—peasant figures, like himself. They
feared to approach. He understood why—that for them the
dark happenings under the tree were a visitation from
elsewhere that they could in no way relate to. It is her last
wish, he told himself. How can I refuse her? He drew in a
deep breath, his jaw slowly hardening.

He reached for his hat, crammed it on his head. He got to
his knees and lifted her, stood up and lifted her again. It took
a great effort, but she was so slender, so light . . . He carried
her in his arms, staggering a little, trying hard not to jar her,
toward the van. The driver and two of the villagers started
forward now, as if to help.

"Keep back," Cabeza warned. "Keep away!"

Almost fainting with pain and exhaustion, he got her to the
vehicle and somehow lifted her into the front. As he closed
the door gently against her and came around, the burly driver

stood in his path. "We have a doctor, comrade. I will drive you."

"No you won't," Cabeza told him, brandishing the gun. "You will step aside."

He pulled himself up onto the cab and, leaning across, arranged her as comfortably as he could in the angle made by the seat and door, wincing for her pain, not his own, the sweat running down from his hat into his eyes. He could scarcely contain his concern for what would happen when he drove out onto the bumpy road. But he said gently, "See, *muchacha*? We are here in the *camión*. We are going now, you and I together, just as you wished. Can you hold yourself there? I will try to drive slowly." He started the motor. As he engaged gear he looked across at her again, deeply anxious.

Her body was slumped, her head back, eyes just glinting between their lids. Her breathing was very shallow. Her face, framed in the darkness of the furs, looked like a child's, small and translucent and beautiful.

She was smiling.

The village houses faltered and vanished behind them. The road showed golden between blue fields of snow that reached into the darkness. Cabeza struggled with the willfulness of the wheel among the icy ruts, trying to keep the van steady.

Presently a pair of headlights came rushing toward them. They did not dip or slow but came blinding past, almost driving them into the ditch.

"That was the truck, *muchacha*," Cabeza said gently, not looking toward her. "They will come after us, but, see, here is an intersection. We will take the left road of the three—are you watching? So already the odds are two to one in our favor. And at each intersection the odds will grow . . ."

He said it not believing it, simply to comfort her in her need to help him escape. In him was a deep pain that had little to do with his wounds, a weariness of the spirit. His vision kept blurring, causing him to drive even more badly than usual.

A short while later they came to another intersection, and again he took the left fork.

"We will skirt Moscow to the south," he told her. "Far to

the south. We have money for fuel and food and most of the militia will be occupied in the city today. Their lines of communication will be busy with the city, what is happening there. Perhaps too busy to bother about us." He smiled hopefully, adding, "But if they throw up a roadblock, have no fear, beloved, we will find a way around it."

He wiped something from his cheek. And presently the snowy fields and woods grew less blue as dawn began behind them. His eyes were never long from the rearview mirror, but as time passed and no truck appeared to grow in it, and the unfurling road ahead revealed no blockage of vehicles, no uniforms, he felt a slight stirring inside him.

A few moments later they passed through a village. The shops were shuttered, the local folk standing around in solemn groups. Scarcely an eye turned toward them. The stirring became a kindling.

Is it possible, Cabeza wondered, that I am right and the telephone lines are indeed choked, like the throats of the people, with news of Stalin's death and what is happening in the city? That our escape has been dwarfed by Beria's coup and the mourning of a nation? What, after all, he thought, could Kelland have told the MVD about us? Not the truth, that is certain. So we have killed an American spy and stolen a van. Neither of them crimes against the state.

"You ask where we are going?" he said, staring at the road. "To Riga on the Baltic, beloved. A long way? *De veras*. But not impossible. Once there we will find ourselves a boat . . ."

Did he believe it? Why not. He still had the OOKK pass. Coupled with a little bluff, it could be made to work miracles. He straightened a little, pressed himself back in his seat and tested the heart of the motor with his foot. The truck was old but sound and her tank had been filled not long ago. Why not a boat—a fishing boat? The sun was up now, glistening on the snow, veining it with tree shadow, igniting the little houses to a glowing redness.

"And once across the sea, what then?" He shrugged and smiled. "The Agency, the MGB will hunt us for a while, but the world is a wide place, *amada*. So long as we are together, what will it matter?" He added, "Whatever the problem, remember always, there are a thousand ways to skin a horse!"

He talked on thus to himself, with steadily growing confidence, through the long hours that followed, sometimes touching her hand, pointing at some feature of the scenery, but never, never looking at her. Though he was almost ready to face the future again, he was still unable to face that death had taken Gail from him even as they drove from the station.

AUTHOR'S POSTSCRIPT

Lavrenti Pavlovich Beria failed to exploit his Security army's occupation of Moscow. Having seized the advantage, he then delayed. The infighting with Malenkov and Khrushchev began. The initiative slipped from his grasp.

In June of that year he was arrested. It was announced on Christmas Eve that after a six-day trial by a Supreme Court committee in closed session, Beria had been executed as an "imperialist agent."

Though this was the official version at the time, Khrushchev, in his report to the Twentieth Congress in 1956, claimed that Beria was in fact machine-gunned to death by the commander in chief, Moscow District, General Kiryl Moskalenko (in collusion with Khrushchev himself, Malenkov and Bulganin) during a special Presidium meeting in the Kremlin.

Whatever the truth, Stalin's demise did result in an easing of repression in Russia and a thawing of the cold war abroad.

ABOUT THE AUTHOR

JOHN KRUSE was born in England and educated at Harrow. He served as an infantry officer in the Mideast and Italy throughout World War II, after which he returned to England to begin a career from scratch at age twenty-six. He joined London Films as a clapper boy and, during the next seven years, progressed to become cameraman, working on most of the big movies of the period, filling in with stints as truck driver, builder, photographer and artist, at the same time working nights to perfect his writing. His short stories began to appear in top magazines on both sides of the Atlantic in the early fifties; several were made into movies. Since 1954, when he switched to full-time scriptwriting, Mr. Kruse has written many hundreds of episodes for British and international TV series, plus a dozen or so movies. Between these projects and dragging his wife and son on spearfishing trips around the world, building his own house, photographing and landscape-painting, he never found time to write a novel—until now. *Red Omega* is his first, but not, he promises, his last.

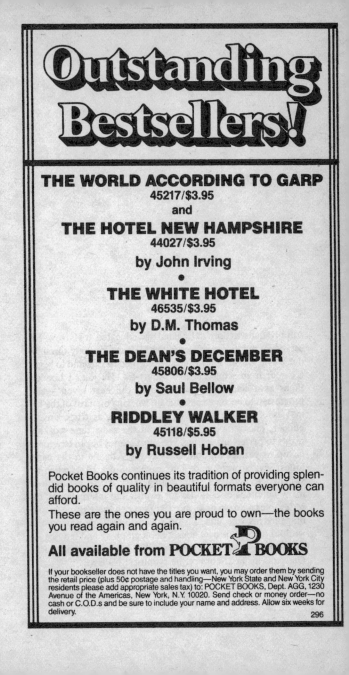